FOR THE
Love
OF PARIS

HISTORICAL FICTION
PARIS ~ 1936-1946

-SECOND EDITION-

THOMAS M. RUTTER

Final Second Edition – November 15, 2011

Web site: fortheloveofparis.com
e-mail: tomasmrutter@gmail.com

ISBN: 1-4392-6795-2
ISBN-13: 9781439267950
Library of Congress Control Number: 2010903162
CreateSpace, North Charleston, SC

For the *Love* of Paris

Dedication

This story is dedicated to Christine Becker, who, with a good-bye kiss at the end of the sixth grade, opened my heart to first love and, to my wife, Donna Marie (Lumia) Rutter. Christine and Donna are the bookends of my heart and I love both of you though I have not seen Christine since we graduated from McKinley Elementary School, Burbank, California, in 1957!

For the Love of Paris is also dedicated to men like Ed Holton and Gerry Cormier, members of the Allied fighting forces and the countries that supported them. They saved the world from the evil of the dictators of Germany, Italy and Japan and made it possible for my generation and the generations to come to live in a freer and better world.

Author's Notes

This is not a children's book. It contains sexual content. Please restrict it to adult reading, as with any materials that use explicit language and are written for mature, adult audiences. Like film director Ang Lee's in his movie *Lust, Caution,* sex is a core element of the story of Christine and Paris. *For the Love of Paris Abridged,* with little adult content, is available at sources listed on my web page, <u>fortheloveofparis.com</u>, or directly from the author at tomasmrutter@gmail.com.

I used the representative terms of the Boy, the Artist, the Professor/Husband, the German, the American, the Wife, and the Aunt instead of names to de-emphasize these characters as individuals; they could be any boy, any artist, any German, any husband.

This final second edition was written to correct factual information and typographical errors, remove repetition, respond to readers' comments, add photos and, present a drawing of mine. The book has been shortened to give a sharper presentation though a "first time" section with the German was added. The quotes on the chapter title pages are mine. I offer this quote from one of my favorite authors as a statement about life and of Christine's life in particular:

"Of the saddest words of mice and men,
are those; it might have been."
—Kurt Vonnegut

Acknowledgements

I give my special thanks to Denise Adams, who motivated me to write this book through her many words of encouragement, her editing and, her wise advice; I am grateful to Denise and her husband Gerry Cormier for sharing their amazing and true WWII Paris stories with me.

Ludmilla Temertey was of immense help in producing this book. She read and reread Christine's love story and provided excellent advice on historic context and human relationships. Her wisdom and grace led me through numerous edits and improvements.

This book was helped enormously by the editing and story enhancements provided by my wife, Donna Rutter; my brother, Paul Rutter; my sister, Kathi McBride; and friends Victoria Lavigne Fife, Gisella Petrone Cardamone, Eustace and Dudley de Saint Phalle, Jamie Lunder and Catherine Manfredini-Cohen. The second edition was enhanced by the comments and work by my daughter, Justine Rutter, Peter Robinson, Michael Simpson, "Foo" James Kennedy, Janet Brawley-Sadoff (and her Gold-Country book club) and Steve Schrey. The excellent editing by CreateSpace was essential in improving my story from the original version. Dana Kelly's proofreading was immensely helpful in correcting errors in the final version.

My deep thanks go also to Raymond, the Irish poet. He is a living example of how, through forgiveness of those who trespass against us, one can use suffering the insufferable to expand one's love and joy of life. He is a rare man among men.

The title of the book, *For the Love of Paris*, was revealed by David Bramnick. It represented the content more than any of the many other titles I considered. The author photo on the back cover was taken by Nike van der Molen of www.nikevandermolen.com. The drawing of St. Julien le Pauvre was drawn by the author and the interior photos were taken by the author except for the photos of the 1937 World's Fair in Paris (Gallica, Baranger), Synagoga and Ecclesia (Nitot), and the Opel truck (Bundesarchiv).

PROLOGUE:

Much of human pain can be overcome
Through one's will, courage and forgiveness;
Forgiveness is best

Paris is always a lover but, until now,
Paris has never been my lover

I know Paris, I know nothing about Paris
I know love, I know nothing about love

For the Love of Paris

Café Talk: Postwar

1945. **P**aris was finishing a warm summer and she was full of life. The Nazi devil was driven out of Paris twelve months before and, the Second World War had ended in all of Europe only four months earlier.

The sun wrapped Paris in a blanket of soft light which helped heal the fresh wounds of her Nazi violation. She stoically mourned her dead, missing and wounded. During the four years, two months and ten days of the Nazi Occupation, the murder of Paris hung like the blade of a guillotine over her head, but through miracles and heroic deeds, her death never came.

There were some cars on the Paris streets but now the cars were driven by French citizens. The Panzer tanks, the Blitz trucks and the Opel command cars had disappeared; they would be nothing more than scrap metal or an occasional museum piece. The precise, incessant marching of Nazi soldiers, with their songs of world conquest, was also gone.

The occupying Nazi soldiers who escaped capture or death went home to a defeated country occupied by their enemies' military forces: the Russians, the British, the French and the Americans. The victors divided Germany into four military "Sectors" to involuntarily assure that this time Germany would take its peaceful place in the world's society of nations and would not again rise up to terrorize her neighbors. This was not the weak-kneed World War One peace plan of 1919, which trusted Germany to control itself; this was the full military occupation Germany deserved after her imperialistic bullying and killing of the best of Europe.

The Nazi swastika flags, the sober symbol of the hell Parisians endured, were torn down from the buildings, spit upon, burnt or taken as souvenirs. Instead of the swastika, the French flag proudly flew on seemingly every Parisian building. The drapeau tricolore was striped with blue for the bourgeois class, white for the clergy and red for the nobility. Often, the drapeau tricolore, with the Cross of Lorraine in its center, hung in honor of the Free French Forces who liberated her.

Parisians strolled up and down the streets and parks of Paris, walking in haste, walking to think, walking to see and walking to cross bridges, leaving their lives on one bank in exchange for new adventures on the other.

The river flowed and flowed, caressing the left and the right of Paris' river bottom, giving her an everlasting replenishment of life. A few long barges, loaded with coal and supplies, plowed their way up and down the Seine in an increasing rebirth of the lifeline of commerce.

Lovers sat on the riverbanks kissing and holding each other tightly, just as before, during, and after the war; for Paris is love and love in Paris never stops. For those blessed with such love, there is Paris and then there is everywhere else.

Parisian women outnumbered their missing and dead men by the hundreds of thousands and many wore black armbands of mourning. They were again shopping to the daily aroma of baking bread, the allure of the patisserie, and the frenzy of the open market, core elements of life in Paris absent during Occupation. French mothers of half-German babies strolled alone with shaved heads only partially grown back and "sins" still unforgiven.

Now the military presence in Paris was solely French and American. The rubble from the six days of street fighting and a last-ditch, rogue Luftwaffe bombing in August '44 was removed. The barricades erected by the Résistance were torn down. Only the scars on the buildings' facades and in the people's hearts remained as evidence of the darkest hours in the two-thousand-year history of the City of Light, the Nazi Occupation.

Prologue

In a café on the Boulevard Saint Germain, an elderly priest slowly stood up and excused himself from the man and woman who remained at the café table. Cloaked in a white robe covered with a black cape, Father Jean, a Greek Catholic Melkite priest, entered the sunlit sidewalk on Boulevard Saint Germain wearing a slight smile of satisfaction. He began the ten-block walk back to his church, Saint Julien le Pauvre. As he proceeded step-by-step on his journey, he was pleased with the café connection he made between the Old World and the New.

Father Jean instinctively walked toward the Seine and, at the river's bank, he turned right toward the church, to his place of worship and preaching. He walked slowly; his back bent from so long in prayer, the curvature of his spine was eternally altered. Parisians moved out of his way in respect, but his downcast eyes saw only the ground as he lifted one foot after the other in pain and prayer. As they watched him, some wondered if his prayers were answered, but after the mass destruction and the incredible death and suffering in places like Warsaw, Dresden, Malta, Auschwitz, Leningrad, and London, most thought not.

During the Occupation, Father Jean was warned. His acts of converting Jewish children to Christians to save their lives did not please the Nazi occupiers. He continued to convert others to Christ for some time but, to avoid a one-way ticket to a concentration camp, he was eventually evacuated. Father Jean spent the last year of the Paris Occupation exiled in California. He only recently returned to his home in the City of Light.

Remaining in the café were a Parisian woman named Christine and an American author whom Father Jean had introduced. They were planning to write a journal of the last ten years of Christine's life: a war-filled odyssey of lust, betrayal, intrigue, forgiveness and bravery, with revelations of truths yet to be told.

Christine was one of Father Jean's favorite parishioners and he knew her from birth. He was the priest for her family, who were longtime members of St. Julien. She shared many of her life experiences with him and often sought his counsel. Father Jean was one of a handful of people who knew how closely intertwined were the survival of Paris and the will of Christine.

The American's mother was also of the Melkite faith, and it was his parents who gave Father Jean refuge in their California home when he escaped the Nazi threat. While living in California, Father Jean frequently visited the American, his Wife and boys, for he lived nearby with the American's parents. It was an important connection for both the American and his Wife.

Father Jean and the American had many deep discussions about the spiritual world, life, the war and love. The American and the priest had become close friends, and Father Jean invited him to visit Paris after the war ended. It was a highly attractive invitation, and when Father Jean returned to Paris, the American followed. As a playwright, he sought to write a play about the Existentialists, and Paris was the perfect place to do so. He also came to Paris to "run away from home" and to get away from himself or, more accurately said, to find his lost self.

Father Jean knew Christine and the American could each give what the other needed, so he brought them together to embark on their journey of mutual discovery. Christine was searching in vain for the right someone to write her Journal, and Father Jean highly recommended the American as the perfect candidate.

As they sat in the café, Christine's face radiated with a wounded beauty which partially transcended the consequences of the four years of Occupation. Looking closely, one might notice the trappings of the life of comfort she once lived in the quality of a bracelet, a blouse, or a piece of jewelry. Looking deeper, one could also see a life which bore the burden of physical beauty, something only a woman of such magnificence could know.

The American was older than she, but not so much to be from a different generation; they shared the challenges of the Great Depression, immediately followed by the horror of World War II. Next to him was his always-present, thoroughly worn suede case for his glasses and pen. He was a writer, and as such, he always needed his spectacles and his pen nearby; he never knew when he would need to record an observance or a thought. Though seemingly an inconspicuous object, anyone who knew the American recognized his glasses case. It was a gift from a mysterious Venetian girl he met on a post-college trip to Italy midway between the great wars of Europe. It was unlike the kind of case an American would typically have. He misplaced but never lost this reminder of his youthful adventures of European discovery and romance as he lived through a variety of life's challenges and created new realities through the movements of his pen.

Near where they sat, two buses lined up back-to-back to let their passengers off and pick up new ones. As the buses drove away, there was a considerable discharge of diesel smoke. The smell of diesel engines was a pre-war memory, one of the many sights, smells, and sounds absent during the Occupation but were slowly returning to Paris. As much as the exhaust smell was not pleasant, it was a comforting reminder that the long nightmare was over. Though wounded, Paris was alive again!

Christine focused intently and looked openly into the American's eyes as they spoke. Her close attention brought him pleasure. Was he being manipulated? Was her attention phony? He didn't believe so. Christine gave her full self and made him feel at his best as a man and a person. She was completely sincere, and the longer he would know her, the more confident he would become of that fact.

Christine laughed gently to herself over the clothes worn by the American. He wore Levi pants. At that time in Paris, only visiting farmers wore canvas pants or overalls. He wore a white T-shirt with a collared neck clearly visible under his open shirt. Only Americans wore T-shirts with collars. French and other European men wore spaghetti-string undershirts which were not visible under their shirts. His shoes were a strange kind of American tennis shoe. They looked comfortable but a little silly off the court. He was clearly an American; no one would have taken him for a Parisian. Christine was more amused than critical.

Christine and the American talked about life, love and fate; they spoke openly as if they had known each other their entire lives. The American touched on various highlights of his life: growing up in California, his trip to Europe as a young man, past girlfriends, marriage and children, and how he loved to write and must write because his soul demanded it.

Christine asked the American to briefly describe his personality. "I can do that," he said. "I care immensely, I love completely and I feel intensely. Therefore, what you say and what you don't say matters deeply. I am a man who will stay awake late to watch the moon set and wake up early to watch the sun rise. I am a writer for whom words and written expressions are the joy of life."

It was upon his expressions and Father Jean's unconditional recommendation of the American that their relationship began. Christine knew the American was the person to write her story. She said to him, "Write my Journal. Write about the loves I have had, about the lives I have lived and, the adventures I have experienced.

"However, you must agree to this: if you are to write my Journal, you must write the whole truth. I am going to tell you everything, even things people often don't admit to themselves with full candor. I want to transcend the mental filters that prevent us from telling the truth to one another or cause us to change real life into socially acceptable half-truths.

"Some aspects of my life may shock you. Some may offend you. Some may hurt you. However, you must agree to stand aside from yourself and function on a higher plane. In order to write my Journal, you cannot be lost in petty thoughts of jealousy, embarrassment, or preconceived notions of what is or what is not discussed openly.

"There are aspects of my story that will not be initially believed. I was involved in the actions which protected Paris from Hitler's obsession to destroy her, events of betrayal that the French government has lied about, for reasons you will understand later. I want you to know that writing the truth about these top secret events may cause some risk but, your American citizenship should shield you. This is one reason why I didn't want the author of my journal to be French, so the author could reveal my truth and not be punished.

"Without full disclosure and total openness, my journal of liberation may as well not be written. I am dying and I do not want my final act, my 'swan song,' to be another lie lost in social denial. It is like Nietzsche said when he spoke of the 'courage for the forbidden.' He was speaking of the level of truth I expect from us. The Journal will be my rebirth, my rebirth posthumously.

"You must become the seeker of my reality: correcting me when I deviate from the truth, pushing me to go deeper into my mind in search of what really happened and why. I want you to push me to give everything to my Journal.

"You, my new American friend, must be prepared to write what others would not write, say what others would not say, present my life in ways others would not do. Telling you my story in the most frank, open, and honest manner possible will be an act of immense relief for me. Writing the truth, my truth, will be an act of courage for you; you will be the one to face the criticisms and doubts of others. You can give my Journal nothing less than

your total commitment—it must be an act of love given without
the returns one might commonly expect from such giving.

"I will share with you the most intimate details of my
relationships with the men in my life. Sex is as much a part of my
story as fate, forgiveness and choice, and I will not suppress my
experiences for anyone's sake. I am free from childhood silliness
or embarrassment about sex. I will openly disclose how my sexual
self impacted on my life and the lives of others, because, unlike
most, I can reveal it.

"Can you do this? Can you be this great of a man? Can you
give this much? Can you be the vessel upon which I unequivocally
cross the bridge from life to death, only to be resurrected through
your words? Can you be strong enough, man enough, to help me
die honestly? Can you put your American-male self aside? I will
literally give you the rest of my life; it is all I have left to give.
Please, I need you now; I have precious little time left."

The American listened carefully and watched intently. He
had not met a woman like Christine, so radiant and tragic all at
once. He watched her mind travel in a direct, linear trajectory,
commanding and unintentionally seducing him with each move
she made, with each word she spoke. He found her manner and
grace shockingly attractive. Her story was compelling from these
first hints of mystery, sexuality, tragedy and intrigue.

A familiar feeling began to rise in him. He unexpectedly
began to plunge again so easily, falling anew while simultaneously
running from the domestic burdens of his failing marriage and
other entanglements. He knew he would descend into love's
embrace again, even after everything that had happened and even
after the love-sting he had recently felt. Was he a fool to fall so
quickly, when there was no hope of consummating this love and,
so many burdens remained on his shoulders?

He looked unwaveringly into Christine's tragically beautiful
face and she looked directly back at him. Then his thoughts

turned to his Wife. My Wife no longer gives me this kind of attention, he cried out silently.

He agreed to write Christine's Journal—a story called Le Journal Parisien de Christine. Like many of the most important journeys, especially those that originate in Paris, the American was diverted from his initial path to do something greater; his experience in Paris would not be limited to the expectations he brought with him. Instead, he would have new adventures, travel to shores about which he knew nothing, and fall in love with Paris forever. He would venture intensely into the life of Christine and deeply into her experiences before, during and after the war. His choice to write Christine's Journal would also permanently change the American and much of his life.

Two tables away, a young French couple sat together. The husband looked extremely nervous and the wife incredibly pregnant. They carried a small valise with them. She held onto her husband with one hand and her stomach with the other. She appeared to be in considerable pain. An ambulance approached and the traffic and pedestrians parted to let it through. The medics assisted the pregnant woman into the ambulance carefully and then left with a shriek of sirens. A new human was about to be born on this special day.

Christine exclaimed, "Can you imagine the life ahead for a child born today? With the war behind them, they will have incredible opportunities living in a peaceful world. But think of the impact of the last nine months on the mothers and the babies who were conceived and carried in their wombs during an unprecedented time of hate and killing."

Another bus stopped, dropped off its passengers and took on new ones. As it departed, a cloud of diesel smoke again filled the air. The bus turned left and drove to a bridge leading over the

Seine. It made one of its many Paris crossings of the day, which changed people's lives on the hour. Christine commented, "How ordinary, how perfectly normal. For the love of Paris, let's get started!"

A Pre-Story: Boy Sees Girl

A small vignette unfolded a few hours before the time and place where Christine would begin her story. A Boy was sitting at a window table in the restaurant Camille pondering the tactics for the championship soccer game he was about to play in. He was distracted by an amazing girl sitting at the table across from him. Her glorious face and porcelain skin were framed by her thick, coal-black, wavy hair. She was the most beautiful girl he had ever seen.

She sat facing him as she conversed intensely with two younger boys whose backs were all he could see. At first she appeared to be timid, as if too much attention might scare her away. While she was listening to the boys speak, she rested her chin ever so lightly between her thumb and forefinger. When she wanted to make a point, her hand would wave to some unknown place, blissfully reducing all else to nothing. A considerable amount of her nonverbal communication was done with her lips. Sometimes it was a two-part move: lips pouted out and a turn of her head slightly up and away.

For a few moments, her eyes followed her friends' every word. She would temporarily lock her eyes on one boy as if he were speaking of the most important ideas a person could express. Then she shifted her focus to the next boy without skipping a beat, giving him the same volume of femininity and momentarily erasing all his insecurities. In doing so, she demonstrated that she already knew how to give one of the best compliments a woman could give a man: her undivided attention and respect for his every word and thought.

Next, in a fraction of a second, she gave a coquettish little glance down and to the side and a mysterious look came over her face, a look that could melt the hearts of the hardiest of men. For no apparent reason, she would suddenly lift her head and focus on something outside, pulling the pleasure of her eyes away, leaving her friends in a valley of confused self-doubt. Her mind would go to a place where they were not invited; her catlike pose seemed to say to them, "And who are you, anyway?"

Any man watching would have seen that the young boys didn't understand how close she was to becoming a woman and how far from them she would quickly travel. They couldn't see how she was evolving into someone they could not yet understand, about to become someone who would leave them for bigger-and-better with hardly a backward glance. Soon, with a flick of her hair, she would be gone.

The Boy looked carefully. She floated there: pure, untouched beauty with long, dainty fingers, without a piece of jewelry but for the slight risk she took with her dangling earrings. No makeup was needed or wanted on her face; her natural beauty would make men lust to paint and yearn to love her. He noticed her clothes. She was dressed as if she were going to play sports, maybe even soccer.

The Boy was amazed and dazzled. His mind screamed out as he carefully watched her: *Who was this She-Angel? Did she know her beauty? Did she know her power?*

In a moment of confusion, the Boy received his bill and briefly exchanged comments with the waitress. When he turned his attention back to the girl, she and her friends were heading out the door. He gasped at his lost chance to make contact. Before she passed through the portal, she unexpectedly and quickly glanced back at him, a demure look down and back up; she was all eyes and charm. What did it mean? He thought he was invisible to her. Was she showing off to him all along?

The girl rushed out into the world giggling and exuberant as the Boy sat back to pause. He had just encountered the most incredible girl of his life, one he would love to meet. But he returned to his original focus: an important soccer game. It was time to go to the field to play. In his boyish priorities, he could not let himself be distracted any longer; he had to let her go.

Café Talk: Christine Begins

1945. Christine was ready to tell her story. "I have kept notes at various times so they are almost a diary. They will help us capture the details of the events of my life. I hid these notes along the way, using a technique I developed at home when I wanted to hide things from my parents; I carefully took the stitching out of one side of the bottom of a chair, inserted my notes, and stitched the material back together. While sometimes it was difficult to recover my notes, I was always able to do so. I kept notes because I always thought I would write a Journal about the adventures in my life, even before I experienced them.

"I will begin by telling you of the first love of my life, a love without a past."

The American reached for his glasses and pen, setting his old suede glasses case aside while indulging in only the briefest thoughts of the memories it evoked. Christine coyly began her life story.

"He was just a boy and I was just a girl and we were about to meet. I was sort of a 'tomboy' as you Americans like to say…."

CHAPTER ONE
THE BOY

*Boys and girls love to play at love
but playing at love is not love
it is love; not yet*

*Even a beautiful boy has not learned to be a
man for he is a man; not yet*

*But a beautiful girl is more than
just a woman; not yet.
A girl may already know how to want, to get and
that her power can be limitless*

Christine's Story

November 15, 1936. I was twenty-one years old and in the last year of my baccalaureate studies at La Sorbonne University. I studied journalism and art history and took a minor in German. My parents lived in a suburb of Paris, which was too far from the university, and it was too dangerous to travel back and forth alone, so I stayed in an apartment with other girls. Therefore, I had an unusual amount of freedom for a young woman in Paris during the late Thirties.

My family's willingness to accept my living alone in Paris was prompted by other things as well. Beginning at the age of thirteen, an intense woman-to-daughter conflict with my mother made it impossible to live in the same house with her for extended periods. As a result, I lived away from home a great deal of the time. I went to my Aunt's home each summer from the time I was thirteen until I went to college. I became highly independent at an early age.

My mother was my constant critic. She detested my boyish ways of playing rough sports and fighting with my brothers. Nothing I did was good enough for her. Her criticisms ranged from direct insults to more subtle comments, such as her understated response to my school projects, into which I had poured my entire self.

Other mothers just seemed to be like *home-machines*, performing their motherly activities without a word of resentment or resistance. That simply was not an option for her. She achieved control by grinding down my father and us children with verbal techniques one could only describe as emotional abuse.

My mother was also an established Parisian art critic and knew most of the artists in Paris. She let very few things interfere with her work. In our home, paintings were exceedingly important; more important than current events, than sports, than everything. Art was her strength, her *raison de vivre*.

My mother spoke critically about artists, including comments about their personal lives. She dragged me to art shows before I was old enough to have the verbal skills to pronounce "Picasso." I met strange men and strange women with whom she had a close association. They acted as if they were best friends while together, but the moment they were gone, her comments would often turn biting. There was an exception; she always said complimentary things about Picasso. Once my mother became a loyal fan of an artist, she would stay faithful as long as he or she remained true to their art. If they pandered to their commercial interests or lost their creative gift, she would publicly say so without hesitation.

My mother studied at the prestigious Ecole des Beaux Arts. Interpreting art in unique ways was where she excelled. She did comprehend artists and one time I remember her saying, "Creativity is a sixth sense: it is the ability to see more than with your eyes, hear more than with your ears, smell more than with your nose, touch more than with your skin and taste more than with your tongue."

She understood how the "new" artists, the Impressionists, were not an assault on the quality of painting but an adventure into expressions of beauty in new and creative ways; they were the next step in the artistic continuum. She was controversial in her opinions and often drew criticism which did not influence her at all. Her courage was limitless, her opinions unflappable, and her perspective undeniably unique and defensible.

Picasso and my mother engaged in a personal/public art duel over the value of the Impressionist painting. Picasso stated that Impressionist painters represented a loss of discipline and, instead of focusing on their subject, were indulging themselves. He viewed their work as the end of art as we knew it, but even his strong criticism failed to influence her.

Painting became an integral part of my life through my mother. She taught me the value of artistic creativity. Her intellect was equal to or greater than any man's, and it was coupled with the unbridled spirit of a wild mare.

My father was a passive man at home. He met my mother's independence and criticisms silently. They didn't argue. He just withdrew and pursued his profession as a craftsman. He was committed to our family without expressing his affection openly or frequently. He rarely had physical contact with us.

The only time I recall him picking me up was upon our return from a family trip when I was about eight. I was asleep in the car and continued to sleep as we arrived home. He picked me up and carried me into the house. It was cold outside but as I awoke in his arms, I felt warm and happy. I didn't let on I was awake for fear he would put me down and make me walk by myself. He carried me to my bed and gently placed me on my pillow and tucked the covers in all around me. I smiled privately. I can remember my eyes becoming wet and a tear falling from my cheek in happiness as he whispered good-night to me.

My father did not put us in the center of his life. We were the children and he was the father. Our family roles were well-defined and seldom broken. When my brothers and I had problems, he didn't solve them for us. He would listen, offer support and comment. In the end, he made it clear that our problems were ours to solve. We learned to take responsibility for our solutions and to live with the consequences. The one exception to our father's emotional distance was spending Sunday afternoons together. He took us on walking tours of Paris as he admired the architecture from the various ages and taught us about the inspiring structures that dotted the city. "His

Paris" came alive in flying buttresses, magnificent gargoyles and cathedral ceilings.

We were given a great deal of freedom as we grew up. We would roam the streets of Paris, watching people and sitting on the banks of the Seine eating crepes and nuts purchased from street vendors. Those were days of innocent childhood, explosive discovery, wandering about without an agenda engaging in thoughtful conversations; a young *flaneur* on the Paris streets. These are some of my fondest memories of my early life.

As my mother was different from the other mothers, I too was not the same as the other girls. I learned more about art and life than my peers. My family didn't worry about me. They knew my stubbornness, willpower and willingness to fight would keep me safe. It was as if the boys and my father were afraid of me, like they walked on eggshells to avoid my reactions. They didn't want to have to deal with two strong, agitated females in one house; they had enough with just my mother.

However, they misinterpreted my independence and strength; they thought I didn't need their affection, but I did. There were times when my aloneness turned to loneliness, but none of them recognized it.

In my youth, I prayed a lot. I spent time asking God for favors and solutions. After some time, I realized it wasn't working. I didn't lose my spiritual beliefs; I just concluded that one cannot beseech the Lord with prayer to get things and solve problems. I came to see that God was not responsible for fulfilling my worldly desires. While valid theologically, this awareness detracted from my devotion to prayer and moved God onto a different plane, further away from my daily life.

As a young girl, I didn't feel pretty or beautiful, but the public's mirror reflected back that I was physically attractive. While adoration gave me a certain confidence and pleasure, it was initially embarrassing and a bit confusing. I didn't understand the power of a woman's beauty and sexual attractiveness. I wasn't just the "me" I knew inside of myself; I was also the person others wanted me to be and the person they thought I was, based on my appearance.

My Aunt helped me survive the critical teenage years and overcome my family issues. She was German and remained a citizen of that country her entire life. She was from the Alsace region, where language, culture and genes were a mixture of German and French. She was married to my uncle for only two years before he was killed by Prussians when France successfully defended Paris during World War One and Paris was saved by "The Second Miracle."

She was born into a wealthy and highly educated German family, but there were also Frenchmen and Englishmen in her family tree. Her upbringing was proper and sophisticated, in the way of an old, traditional German family. She and my uncle did not have the opportunity to have children before he was killed, so I became her special niece and the child she didn't have. I was one of the reasons she didn't return to Germany immediately after my uncle died. She wanted to stay close to me. In his correspondence from the battlefront, my uncle pointed out that I would need another grown woman in my life for balance and support; he knew his sister well.

My Aunt maintained an immaculate home and kept up her education through extensive reading, which she did in multiple languages. She spoke two languages fluently: German as her native tongue and French as her second language. She also learned to read and speak Italian and English as a hobby.

She was a professional art critic like my mother, though she did not publish nearly as often. She was only twelve years older than me, having married my uncle, fourteen years her senior.

She was quite attractive, in a classy way. Her beauty and social status were clearly evident though, she didn't treat anyone with disrespect.

My Aunt provided my true education. Our summers were spent speaking German and English. I was the only person in Paris with whom she spoke her native tongue. I learned to speak Hochdeutsch, the language of the barons and the baronesses and poets and authors, and proper English. We read the German classics, poetry and German news items together. Her intellect was superb and her ability to point out the meaning of the written word was incredible. She loved politics and we would have endless discussions about world events and people in the news.

She tutored me in the finer things of life, such as manners, posture, speech and femininity. Unlike the negative reaction I received when I showed my independence to my mother, my Aunt embraced and encouraged my strength and uniqueness. She pushed me to do what I wanted to do and helped me to be who I wanted to be. My Aunt emphasized the meaninglessness of others' criticisms, and how to push on despite their discouraging words. These lessons gave me strength as my life progressed and kept me centered when I desperately needed my vigor later on.

We often strolled up and down the streets of Paris together, arm in arm, watching everything and everyone. She was a wealth of information about famous and infamous Parisians. We took tea; she didn't drink spirits or smoke. Her posture was like a tree, straight and correct, even when she was sitting on her own sofa in her own home. That was just who she was; it was not an act.

There was evidence my Aunt had men friends. Sometimes it was a call or a gift or a floral arrangement. I didn't meet anyone special, though many men greeted her as we sat in the Paris cafés. She wasn't a prude about men and sex, she was discreet.

We talked about everything, including sex and woman things. I was living with her when I became a woman, when I started my menstrual cycle. She prepared me before, so I knew what to expect. She had a matter-of-fact attitude about all things that were part of nature and part of the human body. Nothing fazed her, not even my sexual experimentation with boys.

I dated quite often in my late teens. I played with sex with two boys but I remained a virgin. The boys were somewhat aggressive but I would only let them touch and kiss me.

The second boy was a bit older and we spent time in the bed of a small hotel room he rented for us. We progressed quite far in our sexual exploration, including spending time naked with each other and pleasing each other with our touch. I can still remember the thrill of those innocent, sexual discoveries. Despite my desires, I held back. I knew I was not ready for intercourse, either because I was too young or he was not the right boy. I waited to have a particular feeling for someone before I gave away the last vestiges of my sexual innocence. I was also looking for a boy who was more like a man, someone with strength and beauty. I was looking for my match and one day I found him.

I loved to play soccer when I was young. My brothers played on the neighborhood soccer team and one day they were short a player. At first, they reluctantly let me play on their team but, after a few games, they saw how good I was at ball control and defending the goal, so they included me as a starting member of the team. I was the only girl player in the league. Later, when a new and highly skilled player joined the team, one of my brothers was replaced but I remained on the team. He didn't forgive me for that!

One day, we were playing a championship soccer game. The captain of the other team, a slim, muscular, deer-like runner, came sweeping down the field like the warm wind blowing in from Africa. We were in the last seconds of the game and my team led by a one-goal margin. He masterfully dribbled the ball as he confidently charged toward our goal, expecting to tie the game with his mighty kick.

I came on hard from his left and slide-tackled him at full speed. We rolled as a pretzel of boy and girl chaos spread across the playing field, ending in a puddle of mud. He was livid with passion and vigor. We started wrestling and rolling in the grass. He cupped my breast with his strong hand and kissed me violently. It was an act of lust laced with anger and covered in sweat. It was astonishing! The other players were stunned at our frolicking, but they broke into spontaneous applause as he rolled on top of me. How quickly it happened, how strongly we felt the instant passion of the moment. My team won the championship game and I found my first real boyfriend!

When I stood up, I looked at him directly and shook my hair to clear out debris. He realized he had seen me before...yes! I was the one he had watched in the café just a few hours earlier. It was love at first sight, and second sight, too.

After the game, we were sitting with our teammates, who were laughing, talking and teasing each other mercilessly. In the middle of the crowd, the Boy and I were alone in a separate world. The power of our sexual connection hushed aside the mundane drone of the others' voices. We had played soccer against each other, wrestled on the field, touched and kissed. Now we wanted to talk.

He gave me a sign, a backward tilt of his head and a slant of his eyes toward the playing field, which said, "Let's get away from this." First playfully, then shyly, we rose from the group and walked together to a small clump of trees. It was a place where we could be alone. As we walked across the field, I could smell the torn grass, the dirt, the sweat and the fresh air of life rising from the soccer field and from our bodies. I brushed mud from my jersey; we were used to playing in the mud, for it often rains in Paris.

An old stone bridge sat across from the playing field. We focused on the bridge, looking ahead as we crossed from strangers to lovers over the flowing river of our lives. My heart was pounding loudly. My youthful breasts were heaving with excitement. My taut nipples were thrust upward as an invitation to his touch.

First Time: The Boy

During our first night together, the Boy was passionate, fast but loving. We quickly progressed through the stages of sex that I had previously experienced and, I was ready for the final act. My first feeling was one of detachment. I felt dizzy, like I was losing my balance, but I also felt a sense of accomplishment. He smelled like an animal, the special smell of sex that I would learn to embrace as I became more experienced in the art of lovemaking.

I was surprised how quickly it happened, how I traveled from virgin to non-virgin without the earth moving, without a tremendous feeling of anything. Maintaining my virginity was always made into such a big deal by my mother. Now it was over and it didn't seem like such a giant leap from the foreplay with the other boys. I became aroused but I didn't come close to reaching my peak feelings, not close to the pleasure I was able to reach on my own. I didn't think it was particularly sensual; I remember thinking the act was somewhat mechanical, more physical than emotional. But I was interested in learning more about this Boy, finding out how to make love without holding back and, how to find greater sexual pleasure with him.

I am not ashamed to say we had gorgeous bodies. We were like young gods. We touched each others' bodies over and over again, worshipping the sensual feelings and the freedom brought on by our intimacy and our nakedness.

We were together every night for a week after that first time. We learned sex from each other's bodies. We didn't miss one aspect of experiencing first love, including our inability to see our differences. Our physical pleasure made us certain of *"us,"* sure that our feelings were sincere and secure. We acted as if we invented sex, like no one else had done it before. During that week we became the next, unwritten act of *Romeo and Juliet*: lovers who lived beyond their first and only night together.

Our first outing wasn't really a date; we went to lunch with his brother. The three of us ate in a little restaurant, Camille, on Rue des Francs-Bourgeois at the edge of Le Marais. As the menu of the day, they served an excellent potato soup and an entrée of roasted duck. I drank a glass of dry Rhone white wine and the boys drank red. The three of us, and virtually every other patron in the restaurant, smoked incessantly during our meal. This gave the air a ghastly smell, but it was Paris. We accepted the fact that smoke would be the foremost taste on our palates by the end of the meal, overpowering the flavors of our excellent food and wine.

During the lunch, the Boy revealed his expectations of a girlfriend. It would be the first time a male made me feel uncomfortable and disrespected, though it would not be the last.

The Boy and his brother's continuous conversation lasted from the time we sat down to order to the time we completed our meal and left the restaurant. I was barely included. I guess I was supposed to sit there as their audience, hanging on every word they said and laughing at their feeble attempts at humor.

When I tried to interject an idea, they would talk over me as if I hadn't said anything. When I tried to participate, I was like a third thumb, reduced to a giggle here and a smile there. I even noticed my laughs became too loud and too long as I awkwardly tried to fit in. To this, the Boy would give me a patronizing smile as if to say, "Isn't she cute." I felt so awkward I would put a piece of bread in my mouth and chew slowly, using each bite to help me cope with the elongated seconds of discomfort and rising anger.

Their rudeness took me by surprise; I wasn't prepared for it. What I did determine was that this would not happen again. I was beginning to learn what I did not want from a lover. Next time, I would be part of the conversation or I would walk out.

A week later, we went to a party at the home of a friend of mine. The Boy had known me *biblically* but not socially. Other than the disastrous lunch with his brother, we hadn't gone out in a group since we'd met at the soccer game. He knew no one else at the party and nobody made an effort to know him.

My girlfriends and I loved to talk. He didn't pay attention to our words, but I could see him studying me carefully from across the room as the girls and I chatted incessantly. It felt good to turn things around, leaving him to his discomfort as he had left me to mine. However, he did not see his insensitivity when the situation was reversed. He just became resistant to spending time with my friends.

The next week, we went out with his friends to watch a soccer game. They screamed, shouted and drank too much. They weren't even drinking wine, they were drinking beer. I didn't know anyone who drank beer! I only knew men who drank red wine and women who drank white wine or champagne. Beer was for the lower classes. I couldn't imagine my mother being involved with such a group.

The boys became rowdy and loud, with a great deal of shoving, shouting and hitting. While I loved to play soccer, their public drunkenness during the game was not my idea of fun. When we returned to his house, we didn't make love, didn't caress each other, and didn't even kiss. I sat up in bed trying to understand what was going on. He fell asleep and didn't wake until the next day.

He liked nothing more than watching professional soccer at the stadium, followed by nonstop discussions about one player or another's accomplishments or failures. He knew every player's name, the numbers on their jersey and the number of goals they had scored. Reciting player statistics was the challenge in every conversation with his friends. He became more of a soccer voyeur than a soccer player, but soccer was *his* obsession, not mine. He was revealing his one-dimensional interest in life.

The Boy's highest goal in life was to play professional soccer. It was the only vision that could take him from his status as a factory worker to an imagined future of fame and fortune.

He wanted me to join his life, almost as if I were one of the boys. "What is wrong with that?" he asked me when I complained. My first thought was to shout at him, "I don't even drink beer!" I held my tongue and let my mind take me to another place where there were no shouting boys chasing their balls and worshipping their toys.

I loved to play sports, but I felt that sitting and watching them on a spring day was a complete waste of precious time. It was someone else's glory, someone else's game. I wanted to live my own life to the fullest, not pay homage to a bunch of men I didn't know. I didn't care who they were, what they did in one game or another, or how many points they scored or blocked. What a bore!

A broad variety of activities and life interested me: art, music, politics, history, literature, philosophy. Many things excited my curiosity.

When I went out, it was usually with groups from the university. We would engage in extensive conversations on a variety of subjects, including relationships, politics and the world situation. Going out in Paris was my world. The social street scene was my domain. To the Boy, I seemed to know everyone. To me, I had just begun.

On our strolls along the stylish cafés on the Champs Elysées, I would tell him about the people we would see—"She is so and so who does such and such and lives with whomever"—an ongoing commentary on the people of Paris. I read the social magazines, knew the faces and the stories, and remembered the comments my Aunt made about the people of Paris.

At first, the Boy liked our strolls along the Paris streets in the look-meet-and-greet dance, but soon he started to feel left out. Then he refused to go out with me on my Paris strolls altogether. He simply wasn't interested in the people we would meet or the topics of our discussions.

The Boy didn't really like Paris. He constantly complained that it was a boring playground for the rich and famous. Everything I loved about Paris he found unpleasant. I looked at him during one of his tirades against Paris as if he were another species. His criticisms hit me like a wasp's sting on hot skin.

It was apparent that my friends didn't like the Boy and his friends didn't particularly like me. There was a growing gap between us. We were brought up in different worlds. Our differences would become a breach that I would deny until I could no longer do so.

Our different relationships with Paris and sports sowed the seeds of discontent. Maybe I was moving too fast and it made him uncomfortable. After a couple of months of dating, I began to admit to myself something was seriously wrong in our relationship.

I wondered, would Romeo and Juliet's differences have become so pronounced if Shakespeare had allowed his famous lovers to live beyond the first stage of love, if they were given a chance to know one another in a day-to-day, ongoing relationship beyond a one-night stand?

The Boy did not attend the university. He held a union job at the Renault factory where his father worked. He earned fair wages, so he lived well for someone his age, though it would peak early and offer little opportunity for growth later on. He was one of the few young men I knew with their own apartment in Paris, albeit a small one.

He intentionally did not dress well, which evoked an image of commonality. He was happy to accept his place in life, while I was looking for greater adventures. Style and appearance were important to me; to him these things were phony and a waste of money.

In those days, I wore my hair short and cropped, a style the Americans call "bobbed." I was playing a lot of soccer and didn't want to emphasize my femininity in an all-male world. During one of our disagreements, the Boy took the option of criticizing my hair: "You don't look good with short hair," he said. "It makes you look too much like a boy."

I retorted, "You like to treat me like one of the boys, so what's the difference?"

He tried to cover his tracks by adding, "I love your hair. I just want you to grow it longer so there is more of it."

Despite my short hair, my appearance and personality brought me into a widening social circle of interesting friends and acquaintances. The separations in our perfect love expanded. As each pillar of our relationship failed, our last common ground was our nakedness in bed. Only then was our connection not distracted by differences in lifestyles, class or self-image.

As time passed, he began to doubt me—was I going to grow away from him? Of course, I would and I did. I moved away from our lustful love like a ship slowly leaving the dock, heading out to the endless sea. We completed the interrupted Shakespearian tale of "boy meets girl and they fall in love," but instead of physical death, we met the reality of people becoming more themselves, and a lust-love slowly dying.

The Boy and I were involved in one issue that was bigger than our relationship, a soccer game, his work building Renaults, our friends or my education. This was the only time we experienced a meeting of minds about something of a worldly nature, something meaningful and historical: the bombing of Guernica, Spain by the Nazis and Italian fascists.

April 27, 1937. The war planes of the Nazi Luftwaffe and the Italian Legions used their dive bombers to kill the citizens of the Spanish/Basque city of Guernica in support of

Generalissimo Franco's military coup. Over a thousand civilians were killed and many more wounded, as tons of explosives rained down on them from the flying-machines-from-hell circling above.

As survivors of the bombing fled the inferno, the Axis planes strafed the terrified families clogging the roads and they became easy targets for the machine guns of the Nazi and Italian fighter planes killing without mercy.

The news coverage of the carnage in Guernica was extensive. Recordings of wounded and grieving victims screaming in agony and photos of the injured and dead resulting from these bombings were lead stories in every media outlet. At this same time, Paris was in the midst of hosting the World's Fair and the world was also focused on our city.

1937 World's Fair – Paris
The Nazi German and Soviet Russian Pavilions

May Day, 1937. Over a million people marched in the streets of Paris in opposition to the savagery of the Nazi and Italian attacks on Guernica. It was the largest protest march in Parisian history.

The Boy and I joined the massive demonstration. Even in our self-indulgent youth, we could not ignore this blatant disregard for human life and the indiscriminate use of airborne bombing to kill civilians. We marched, shouted and screamed against the evil fascists.

We marched past the Nazi monolith the Germans had built as a monument to themselves for the World's Fair. It was an ugly, intimidating mass of cold concrete with a giant eagle and swastika perched on top. As we passed the Nazi monument, the Boy spit on the monument three times and disparagingly shouted, "Fascists!" at our Nazi guests.

This was the only time we were truly connected beyond soccer and the acts of sex we regularly performed with each other. For a moment, he rose above life's trivia to feel strongly about something bigger than himself, and to vehemently care about the unjust suffering of strangers in a distant place. I felt hope that we could continue to meet on this grander emotional and psychological plane. Unfortunately, our empathetic connection with the outside world was short- lived.

A painting by my mother's friend, Spanish artist Pablo Picasso, would inadvertently but significantly enter our lives. This painting would further demonstrate the vast differences between the world as I saw it and the world of the Boy.

Amazingly, in only three weeks after the Germans and Italians bombed the people of Guernica, Pablo Picasso released one of the most significant works of political art ever painted. It was simply called *Guernica*.

In *Guernica*, Picasso demonstrates how the wretched agony of torture and death and the violent impact of unresolved conflict can be presented symbolically in paint.

Picasso was a Spaniard living in exile in Paris, so the events occurring in Spain were especially personal to him. The 1937 World's Fair in Paris provided the perfect setting for his painting; he displayed *Guernica* in the Spanish Pavilion, not far from the German/Nazi monolith the Boy had defiled. Because of our marching and his concerns, it was not too difficult to convince the Boy to visit the Spanish Pavilion to see *Guernica* depicting this horror.

The massive size of the painting—eleven feet tall and twenty-three feet wide—and the complexity and clarity of the images of dying and suffering people and animals was overwhelming. With *Guernica,* Picasso set a new standard of artistic communication so high and so unique it may never be matched.

The moment I saw *Guernica,* I was captivated. I wanted to stop my life and spend hours and hours trying to understand this painting and the meaning of each image. I saw anguish, shock, desperation, horror, disgust, conflict and mystery. I felt for the tortured women, the dread of the mother holding her dead child, the violence of combat, and the horror of humans in their final death throes. The prominent position of suffering animals reminded me that victims of war included innocent animals. It was impossible to grasp the entire painting without walking from side to side, looking up and down, and returning again and again to find Picasso's many dire, symbolic messages.

Guernica forewarned the world of the growing evil that was to expand beyond the imagination. It was a dramatic signal flare, a warning shot into the hearts and minds of those who saw it. It exposed the negative effects of the celebrated new airplane technology gone awry; no gallantry, no heroes in mortal combat, no commanding figures leading courageous troops, no flags proudly carried to a flute's whistle and a drum's roll; only the rain of death and devastation dropped from random killing machines destroying whatever or whomever lay in their path.

I expected everyone to have the same reaction when they saw Picasso's masterpiece. However, the Boy saw something entirely different. He saw the work of a madman. He saw a level of chaos that offended him beyond his perceptions of the possible. To him, there was something wrong with the artist, something wrong with anyone who would paint the primitive, childlike, and offensive images he saw in *Guernica*.

The Boy's rejection of the painting was distasteful and uninspiring. He wanted to leave Picasso and his art behind and return to his own world across the river. "It is uncomfortable, unnatural, unfamiliar, and ugly," he said as I examined the bull's head. "I want to go home and leave this…confusing mess!" I turned my attention to the image of the glaring sun to the right of the bull, and the horse kneeling below. I was trying to ignore the Boy and keep my attention focused on *Guernica,* but it was no use; my connection to Picasso's genius was broken. We left the Pavilion, crossed the river and went to his apartment.

I would not see *Guernica* again. I saw reproductions here and there in art magazines, but they did it no justice. It was too complex for reproduction. My once-in-a-lifetime exposure to the genius of *Guernica* was cut short by the Boy being a boy. I should have stayed alone; I should have let him return to his world while I stayed in mine. As I had at the lunch with his brother, I learned something that day. I increasingly saw the need for independence, for a separation from the Boy. I began to follow my own instincts.

My mother spent a day with Picasso's *Guernica* and, of course, she loved it. She raved about the symbolism and the deeply human messages contained within. She saw things in the painting—secret, mysterious things others missed. Maybe there was a harlequin, a jester, a hidden skull, the body of a horse gored by a bull, and a diamond-shaped tear hidden in the images. Maybe Picasso was thumbing his nose in Christ-like defiance at death itself to show his disappointment in God for allowing such suffering to occur. I was amazed at my mother's insight or, at least, her active imagination.

One week after our visit to the Spanish Pavilion, the Boy and I quarreled. I wanted to go to an art show in the Palais de Luxembourg and he wanted to attend another game of soccer, some play-off or another. His boyish limits were becoming increasingly irritating. What was cute had become unattractive.

Neither the Boy's soccer game nor my art show was truly important to either of us. The importance of these events grew because of our individual desires to do what each wanted to do and not let the other dominate. The soccer game and the art show were battlegrounds, metaphors. There would be no compromise, only a digging deeper into the trenches of our childish wills.

As the Boy once again tried to convince me to go to the game, I turned my head away from him and gazed longingly toward the stone bridge ahead that led over the Seine, away from him to another world. This was a "Y" in the road of our lives and we made our choices; I would cross and go to the art show and he would go in the other direction to the soccer game.

As I walked away, I glanced back toward him. He wasn't watching me; he was kicking the ball around in the street, dreaming of making an imaginary goal in a fantasy game and hearing the cheers of a nonexistent crowd. I kept going. I learned not to let him limit me to his world or keep me from mine.

I knew I was also opening myself to new love and, when it came, I would fully welcome it like the blazing sun engulfing a summer morning. Next time it would be a *man*, a worldly man, someone who could take me to the places I yearned to go.

At lightning speed, I crossed the short bridge, which took a girl from one shore and rushed her over to the almost-woman on the other side. The not-yet-a-man Boy could not come over that bridge, not yet and not with me.

A Posthumous Good-bye

May 10, 1940. The Boy was drafted into the French Army as the Nazis crashed through the Allied defenses. As a slightly trained soldier, he was sent with a million other boys to stop the Nazis who were destroying the forts of Holland and Belgium, crossing the French border, and starting toward Paris.

His group was sent to meet the Nazi army face to face, bayonet to bayonet, and tank to tank to protect France from the assault. We relied on the Boy and the other French soldiers to keep the Nazi Blitzkrieg from overrunning the borderlines of France and taking Paris. There were no reserves behind them.

On the second day of fighting for French soil, my brother died. He was shot through his heart and his head by a Nazi machine gun as he and other boys charged up a hill. He was stacked with the bodies of thousands of his youthful comrades who didn't know anything about the whys: why they were there, why they failed, why they died, why they were charging head-on toward flaming barrels of hate and death. In a letter delivered by his mother, the Boy said if he died, it would be with a "last kiss" for me on his lips—a kiss as important to him as our first kiss, but a kiss we would not ever have. In his tent the night before his last battle, he wrote a poem to me.

LOVE IS FOR ALWAYS—FOR CHRISTINE

We were only grown-up children
Knowing how to take
And little how to give
Only grown-up children
Always on the make
Just learning how to live

We once shared our heartbeats
Pounding so tightly
Our separation
Ceased to be
But, I didn't know yet
How to do it
How to love you
More than me

Come again
Some sunny tomorrow
I'm sure
You could be
Much more than me

Now I see us there
in that 'morrow
Sailing in the shining sea
Me loving you so very hard,
Loving you for eternity

Good night, Christine, wherever you are.
Good night, my almost-love
God's night is not so far,
We share the same stars above
A twinkling testimony to our love

They made me an instant man
on this hill;
I had to do it
I had to learn to kill

I love you now
Even more than before-
I understand Guernica
May you never know its horror

I know now
What you were trying to show
How you needed a man
To lead you over the next bridge
To be more than I think I can

Where have you gone
Now I am ready to love you
From now until forevermore,
From this day on,
Till the last morning,
Through the final door

The Boy created an innocent love poem for me. It took the loss of love, the terror of war, and the fear of imminent death to awaken him. Dug into his foxhole, with death and suffering only inches away, his creative self was wrenched out of his heart. Crouching in the mud, he found the intensity of life and the importance of love beyond a soccer game. In battle, the Boy grew into a man, strong enough to feel, strong enough to write, strong enough to kill.

From this awakening, he might have come to understand much more—art, music, literature, poetry—the giant creative forces of life into which men can soar. Was it too late, coming the night before his death, or *is the opening of one's creative self, like repentance and God's forgiveness, glorious even if it only comes at the last second before the end?*

If the Boy had stayed at his job at the Renault factory and married an accepting wife like his mother, I don't think he would have touched his feelings and emotions. The reflective need to express himself would not have developed. He would have remained a boy...but then he would have lived.

I cried and cried. I grieved for my dead ex-lover. I hurt deeply for lost love and what could not be. I felt the loss for his family. I couldn't understand the futility of war's waste of youth. The tenuousness of life was no longer an abstract philosophical discussion; it was my first lover's blood splattered on my soul.

Knowing he was thinking of me at the end drove the pain deeper. It wasn't guilt from ending our affair. I knew it was the right thing to do at the time. We had to cross our own, separate bridges to become whole, but I did not consider the possibility of such a tragedy. All I wished for him was to become a man--to experience an awareness of life on a grander scale, to develop an awareness of the many dimensions of life—not to befall the fate of a soldier and die in the mud of an unknown battlefield.

Images of us together swirled through my mind. I saw him playing soccer. I remembered his beautiful body and the first times we were together. I dreamt of his face helplessly floating in a pool of water, his eyes closed and his head split open.

Dead—so young. Dead—forever and ever more. Dead—for nothing...he and the other French soldiers didn't even slow the Nazis down.

I visited his family, but they included me in their grieving only on a superficial level. They knew the other major hurt the Boy suffered came from me leaving him.

I didn't deny the trauma of his death; I gave him a loving position in my heart. I didn't turn my back on our memories; I tucked them away in an honorable place.

I wondered what might have been—what if he had lived, what he would have become. I realized our relationship was doomed from the start, not only because he was a boy, but also because I was just a girl, incapable of having a fully intimate connection with another incomplete person. I could not bring much more to a relationship than my body and my youth. I would learn the grander lessons of love, but they would be taught by others, not by a Boy too focused on himself, one who still knew too little of life.

The death of the Boy was an alarm, a notice that it was time to move forward, to become who I was to become without delay, for life is unpredictable and short. I stopped crying, wiped off my face, stood up, and went out to the streets of Paris. A gust of cold wind came at me like a slap in my face. I pushed forward as I leaned into the weight of the gushing air and pressed onward to the complex life that lay ahead. I had found worldliness but there was much more to come, much more.

Café Talk: Warm Day, Hot Coffee

1945. *The American was impressed with Christine's ability to articulate her feelings so clearly, openly and honestly. Her passion for Picasso's painting Guernica showed her special awareness of life and art. Her tender yet strong story about the Boy gave him insight into the woman she would become. He only needed to choose the right words and Christine would come alive on paper. As he ordered a second coffee for the morning and reached for the sugar, he gave thanks to Father Jean for making the Christine connection. The American realized he had met the most interesting person of his life.*

The American asked if she resented giving herself for the first time to someone with whom she had little in common. "Was it a mistake? Do you think you should have waited to cross over the bridge of first love until you found a different kind of person and you were in a different kind of relationship, maybe with a man instead of a boy? Don't you think the way you lost your virginity was more mechanical and not so much a sensual experience? It seemed like you crashed into each other in soccer, in sex, and as individuals. The two of you didn't appear to have a deep emotional connection until he wrote his poem and died. I am hoping I don't sound too much like an American prude, but I idealize first love and a woman's loss of virginity."

Christine responded, "It was not a mistake. I was already twenty-one and I didn't want to wait any longer to have sex the first time. Besides, he was almost beautiful for a male. I wanted to make the leap through virginity without too many emotional connections. It is true, the Boy was young, emotionally immature and mostly wanted to satisfy himself, but that is how boys are.

"The Boy was a bridge to where I wanted to go; we are French, so this is how we behaved. Beyond his battlefield revelations at the end, it was impossible to think it could have been much more. However, his moment of awareness at the end reminds me of a Confucius quote I once

read, "If a man hears the Tao in the morning and dies in the evening, his life has not been wasted." I believe the Boy's life was not wasted."

The two parted with a kiss on each cheek and good-byes in mixed French and English. The American watched Christine walk away. He was pleased. Fate had brought him to this exact point in life, to this precise street corner, at this specific moment in time, and into this incredible woman's life. "Au revoir," he said, but the traffic drowned out his words. Before she turned the corner, Christine looked back with a wave, a slight smile and she was gone.

That night he reviewed his notes and, for a moment thought his questions might have been too direct. He truly did not want to be judgmental or appear to be too American. She warned him that she was going to be honest and open. She had responded in a curt, French-like manner to his questions about losing her virginity, but he decided he was correct to query her; after all, he was not a secretary simply recording her words. He was a writer, and he would continue to ask questions when he saw openings in her logic, or if he didn't fully understand her actions or feelings. That would be the only way he could know her well enough to write her Journal.

It was time to go on with the next chapter, the intense story of Christine's relationship with a man, the Italian Artist.

CHAPTER TWO
THE ITALIAN ARTIST

If you can see magnificence in the ordinary,
Then, for you, everything will be magnificent

You create what you are,
You are what you create

On not so rare an occasion,
The art is greater than the man

Walking Through Paris, Walking Toward the Future

My metamorphosis into womanhood began when I left the Boy playing an imaginary soccer game and crossed the bridge to the art exhibit. I felt a new level of exhilaration and excitement. I walked straighter and taller, in anticipation of something special. My stroll was effortless; I was almost dancing. I followed the curving shore of the Seine as riverboats chugged along past me; it seemed as if life's movements were all in order. At one point I giggled for no apparent reason. I asked myself, "What is going on? Why am I feeling so alive? Is this feeling coming from letting go of my past or the anticipation of my future?"

I aimed my walk at the Luxembourg Gardens but not in the most direct route. Instead, I walked up Rue Bonaparte, through Place St. Sulpice. I stayed outside on Rue Guyemer so I could enter from my favorite side: through the gates on Rue Auguste Compte. This way, I could enjoy the longest walk possible through the exquisite gardens. It was the proper way to approach the palace, the route of respect for such grace and beauty. I savored every moment of my uplifted feelings. I was in no hurry to arrive; I enjoyed the journey too much.

I passed through the tall, gated entrance onto the long paths which crisscrossed massive, tree-filled gardens framed by well-trimmed hedges. They flowed around ponds to the grand entrance to the palace. As Parisians leisurely strolled along with me, we were escorted by various species of birds flying straight up and down in a dazzling pattern of aerodynamic celebrations of life. The acrobatic birds enhanced the garden canvas with their spectacular movements of joy.

The artistic patterns of pansies entertained me. I was also curious about the unusual plants organized in geometric patterns next to large lawns, but I passed them by without stopping or looking too carefully.

I was fascinated by the gulls' splash landings on the central ponds as they steered clear of the little boats and negotiated the perilous waters of a massive fountain. I was amazed how the ducks navigated the ponds in catlike arrogance, indifferent to everything and everyone. I enjoyed the children squealing in delight as their aquatic drama unfolded. Their lives were full of discovery and pleasure, as everything lay ahead of them in their unknown future.

I stood before the palace in its magnificent splendor, but I felt no loneliness. The sun shone down like a beacon, warming me and lighting the outside palace walls in a Tuscan-like, mustard-colored sunlight. It was a strolling day in Paris and everyone was out.

Luxembourg Palace

It was impossible to go directly to the palace without veering off to a special place, the Medici Fountains. The fountains spewed forth foaming water while the bees buzzed about doing their pollinating business. Ducks happily dove and disappeared into the dark, mossy water, only to reappear again nearby, quacking in delight.

I walked around the fountain and stared at the Greek mythological figures holding their stone embrace of innocent love under the violent threat of the jealous Cyclops. Pigeons flapped their way from woman to man to Cyclops and back, as if they were trying to warn the lounging lovers of the looming threat. The sky overhead was heated blue, an unusually dark hue for midday, and lovely. This was one of my father's favorite places in Paris, and one of mine. I would return here again and again through every stage of my life.

Medici Fountains

The Luxembourg Palace was rebuilt by Marie de Medici, Queen of France, in the seventeenth century, after she married King Henry IV. Marie became one of the most powerful queens in French and European history. She rebuilt the old Palais de Luxembourg in the incomparable Italian style of the Medici family's Florentine home, the Palazzo Pitti. Marie wanted to live in Paris in the familiar surroundings of Italian grandeur and she accomplished her goal with perfection.

As a magnificent complement to her palace, Queen Marie created the equally magnificent Italian-accented gardens outside the Jardin de Luxembourg, through which I strolled. The garden, a living tapestry of trees, bushes, lawns, ponds and fountains, was once simply a preamble to her palace's front door and a playground for the royal families. Since the seventeenth century, dignitaries from around the world were wooed and entertained in this great structure and its gardens. They visited the French royalty, attended lavish parties and formed international alliances in this hallowed place. Sadly, Marie was betrayed by her son, King Louis XII, and died in exile without living in her palace.

After the French Revolution in 1799, the Palais de Luxembourg was used as a prison. Later, the palace and gardens became community property and were opened for the public's enjoyment. Marie's palace stood proudly in its massive and historic glory; on this day, it was enhanced by boldly colored canvases for the entire world to enjoy.

I picked this exhibition to visit based on a curious article written by my Aunt about the Artist. She reported that the Artist was Italian, spoke fluent French and charmed the Parisian art critics—not an easy thing to do, no matter who you were.

My Aunt said the Artist lived deeply in his Italian heritage, which they discussed even before reviewing his art. He noted early on in their conversations how the Romans created the first true city on these grounds almost two thousand years ago, long before there was a country called France or a city called Paris. He spoke about marriages of Italian and French royal families of the eighteenth century which linked Italy and France together. Tongue in cheek, he referred to Paris as *Lutetia* during their interview, the original name of the Roman city upon which Paris sits today. He described how he often visited the city's Roman ruins to find inspiration to paint and as a comfortable place to think about his family, his heritage and the Italian homeland he missed.

In her interview, my Aunt inquired why the Italian moved to Paris. He replied, "The Mussolini Fascists drove me out of Italy, out of my beloved home. I came to Paris to escape persecution for publicly opposing Italy's alliance with Nazi Germany, and to establish myself as an international painter in the City of Light."

My Aunt gave her impression of the Artist's looks as "extremely intense, not particularly handsome, with deep-blue eyes as the exception to the rest of his face." Accented by his dark Italian hair and his olive skin, his haunting eyes reflected his northern Italian heritage. Nothing escaped his eyes. "They are his windows into life. It is from his eyes, through his vision, that he sees in unique ways. His eyes guide his hands in the creation of his special art." Speaking more as a woman than a critic, she wrote, "Looking into his eyes elicited a most unusual response. To look him directly in the eyes causes all but the most secure to turn away in self-conscious embarrassment. No doubt his penetrating eyes would cause many women to swoon in his presence. He seemed to know his power and magnetism. He freely used his Italian charm on each person who stopped by during the interview, particularly the women.

"The Artist explained why the Medici (Luxembourg) Palace was such an ideal location for exhibiting his art. Paintings were hung along wide corridors of limestone, worn in the center by hundreds of years and hundreds of thousands of footsteps. The multitude of separate rooms, tall ceilings and excellent light created perfect spaces to display his paintings. As he and I walked through his exhibit, diffused sunlight streamed through the palace's deep, stone-framed windows, and golden rays anointed the Artist's creations as *near-holy.* The dignity of the palace, laced with the power of his paintings, brought a hush of respect from its visitors."

During the interview, my Aunt described how the Artist basked in the warmth of the day's sun and the positive reception the Parisian press gave his paintings. She wrote of him as an Italian competitor to the Spaniard Pablo Picasso, who was showing his works across town, and to other great artists like the departed Dutch master Vincent Van Gogh, who was once scorned by the French and later anointed as *their* artistic genius.

The Artist painted day and night for six months to prepare for the show and was pleased with his work and with himself. This was his first show in Paris and he was anxious for a huge success.

I thought my Aunt had swooned over him too much in the words she wrote. I wondered if she had gone beyond her role as an objective critic, and if she knew the Artist more on a personal level than what might be considered professional. It was a compelling piece, and I could not miss the show after reading the first half of her article.

I stopped reading after my Aunt finished writing about the Artist and the palace. I didn't want to read my Aunt's descriptions of the paintings. I wanted to encounter them fresh, without her preconceptions influencing my thoughts. I was deeply curious to see his art and I hoped for a glimpse of the Artist, too.

As I approached the palace, I saw sun shining through the large windows onto the paintings inside. Though it was a bright day, the palace's fancy chandeliers sparkled like stars in heaven as I peered through the arched windows. The clock struck noon— twelve chimes marked the moment.

I looked back toward the gardens and the fountains. It was the last time I looked back for quite awhile. After the bells stopped tolling their midday notice, there was too much in front of me to think of the past.

Entering the grand palace, I saw several dramatic paintings and was immediately daunted by their power and intensity. The information brochure said the paintings were grouped by style and by floor. My Aunt wrote, "It was as if there were two artists, two completely different men; one the *downstairs* painter and one the *upstairs* painter." I anxiously went forward to meet them both.

The downstairs paintings reflected an aggressive, strong, masculine style. There were animals and humans painted in ferocious colors with broad strokes. They depicted strong action scenes with animals painted with contorted, strange features, as though someone twisted them and pulled the different parts of their bodies in unnatural directions. The underlying tone was of a madman gone amok with a paint brush.

Intense emotions stirred deep inside me as I looked into these paintings, and as I began to fantasize about the man who could paint such works. My intrigue increased as I sought to comprehend the meaning of each painting, taking long drinks of the amazing images with my eyes. The horizontal sunlight poured warmly through the windows, and my entire body was becoming hot.

I was attracted to a painting hung over the garden entrance doors named *Buio Contro Luce* or *Darkness Over Light*. Most of the canvas was dominated by two animals: a unicorn (*unicorno*) with glowing alabaster eyes and a scraggly goatee, and a black panther (*pantera*) with deep, cold, endlessly black eyes which were too dark to penetrate. To me, the mystical unicorn depicted earthy enlightenment and spiritual actualization, while the secular panther symbolized physical domination, brute strength and cunning violence.

The animals were engaged in mortal, airborne combat. The panther's teeth were sunk deeply into the flesh on the back of the unicorn, and his left claw ripped the side of its neck in long gashes of gory, torn skin. Blood ran down the unicorn's side as he futilely kicked his heels high in the air, widely missing the targeted attacker. The unicorn's fully opened mouth, pinned-back gums and protruding teeth shrieked in pain and agony. Despite his pain, his horn continued to point straight up in defiance. The scene reeked of the unicorn's predictable death and the panther's vicious victory.

Four unicorns, two grown and two yearlings, grazed peacefully in the distance. They stood in a background of lovely trees and a meandering, moss-banked stream piercing a wide meadow. The four were ambivalent to the suffering of their dying brother as they enjoyed their meal of tall, abundant grass. This pleasant background scene highlighted the indifference to the pain and suffering of others, and reminded me of my own lack of concern for the tragedies of people I knew, and some I didn't.

I pondered the image and the meaning of the painting: why does ferocious physical strength so often defeat the gentle spirit and idealistic mind? How can intellectuals, artists, philosophers and prophets and other peaceful people protect themselves from the violence and domination of the barbarians at the gate?

I looked and let my mind and heart wander deep into the scenes of *Darkness Over Light* and I saw the deaths of gentle souls at the mercy of those physically stronger. I contemplated how *one must be strong and able to protect oneself even in an enlightened state, for the forces of evil are truculent and dominating and can appear anywhere and at any time.*

The second painting that hit me hard was a violent, passionate embrace between a guiltless, virginal-looking, pubescent girl and a satyr. The Artist's title for this debauchery was *Violazione Brutale Negata, A Brutal Violation Denied.*

The satyr's features were painted in extraordinarily clear detail. The minute hairs in his beard, his deep, black, bulging eyes and his enormous penis were painted with more precision and clarity than one would wish to see. His massive testicles belonged more to a full-grown bull than a faun. The monster grimaced in passion and ecstasy as he mounted the virgin girl and gorged himself on her innocence.

On the ground near them lay her dainty parasol, turned upside down, torn on one side and soiled in the mud. Nearby, her small purse had fallen open and silver coins were spread out on the dirt. A comb was lying nearby. Her ruffled silk corset was also on the ground. It had been violently ripped in the back in a desecration of the neat, feminine pattern of ruffles on the properly flowered silk undergarment.

Her face was ashen white, her wide eyes bluer than the sky, her hair orderly and proper but for one strand undone. She was looking far away in detachment and denial. Implausibly, her face appeared unaware, in denial of the deviant reprobate violating her young, precious, beautiful body.

The muscular man-goat held her with a tight grip, leaving her no choice but to succumb, but her placid face confused me— was her survival dependent upon denial? *Violazione Brutale Negata* made me feel dirty. It made me turn away. It made me wonder what perversions were in the Artist's mind when he painted this scene of revulsion.

I overcame my fear of being violently conquered and looked again. I was amazed at the strength of the painting and the sharp emotions it evoked. Rapid-fire questions kept coming about the innocent girl. How could she stay in deep denial during such a brutal act? How did she let herself be pursued and caught by this half-animal, half-man savage? Where were her protectors? Why did life include such profanities as an innocent girl's desecration by a foul being?

Ageless and timeless questions came to me: why does such evil exist? If there is a God, why would He allow the evil violation of this young girl? Why are the dearest of the dear so frequently abused by the lowest of the low? Isn't it God's role to protect the innocent and to destroy evil? My head was spinning.

I speculated about the Artist's purpose for painting this image. Did he use his brush to stimulate these questions in the viewer's mind? If so, he succeeded brilliantly.

As I was leaving this frightening and provocative painting, a middle-aged mother and her young daughter entered the room. I wanted to warn them, "Madam, don't bring your daughter to see this—don't expose her to this harsh reality, not yet. It was too much for me, an almost-grown woman, to bear, so keep your girl outside!" Instead, I fled toward the stairs; I didn't have the strength to save others from the art of this mad genius.

I left the first floor feeling as though I had been bitten by the panther and sexually sullied by the satyr. I had a bad taste in my mouth. I hoped such evil existed only in the world of the Artist's imagination and nowhere near me. I felt like I had done something to myself, some sin for which my parents or a nun would have scolded me. To be honest, I also felt a strange sense of pleasure. It was like the feelings one has after performing forbidden acts that lie mostly unspoken in the human experience; acts we keep to ourselves or share only with partners in sin. The palms of my hands were wet. I had to move on.

My ascension to the second floor was initially difficult; my legs were heavy and resisted the pushing and pulling needed to climb each stair. Was I exhausted from the first-floor experience or anxious about the mystery of the second? I plodded upward, looking to the top of the stairs as a portal through which I would escape the fires of hell below. I could not predict what I would see upstairs, but I hoped it would be less disturbing than the images below.

As I emerged onto the second floor, a pleasant coolness came over me. The last few stairs were easier; my anticipation turned positive as I reached the top. Was it really cooler or was something else changing my mood and temperature? I immediately felt safer. I took a deep breath and proceeded forward.

Before me was a garden of an entirely different type of painting than the bestiality below. Here was gentleness, calmness and passion like a cool drink of water taken by a man long lost in the desert; a comfortable oasis full of welcomed relief.

I looked through the garden of beautiful images and focused on a spectacular painting placed alone in the center of a small, circular room, obviously a position of honor. It was much cooler, more Impressionistic than the blatant, blazing realism lurking below.

At first glance, the subject in the center of the painting appeared to be a woman, but it wasn't entirely clear. On the ground below was a young man on both knees, desperately reaching out to the figure rising before him. The title explained part of it: *Dolore Terreno e Gioia Divina*, or *Earthly Pain and Heavenly Joy*.

The kneeling man was a son reaching out to his dying mother as she ascended into heaven. Her swirling, cloudy mass was no longer a fully human shape as she left the physical plane of life and moved into the spiritual, massless cloud of death.

While the son was painted in the deep desperation of dark, foreboding colors, the ascending mother was presented in light, positive pastel blues, greens and roses, giving an uplifting feeling to her image. Above the rising clouds of her spirit, her softened face looked upward in peace and gentleness. Far above but clearly in the trajectory of her ascension was a strong light, the waiting beacon of God in heaven. His images told the story—the grieving, living son in the depths of suffering on earth while his dying mother knowingly moved heavenward toward her final peace and calm.

I thought about life and death. I contemplated the human dichotomy—*people hold onto life tightly to avoid death, in direct contrast to the promise of eternal harmony and peace in the afterlife in Heaven. Was our doubt in the joy of afterlife because humans really don't believe God's promise?*

I was in a thoughtful but pleasant mood when I moved on. The next painting was named *Le Finestre Desolate e Sconsacrate,* or *Windows of Desolation and Sacrilege.* It was a painting of an ancient stone church, set in the middle of a large wheat field, on a night filled with a million bright stars. Dark, tawny paths led into and around the church. Harvested bales of golden hay were formed into large, round spools which symmetrically dotted the surrounding landscape. The naturalness of the farm contrasted pleasantly with the opaque gray walls and projecting tripod steeple of the church. There was a small travertine bridge to the right.

Le Finestre would have been simply a good painting but for the stars, the unique color of the sky and the vacant windows of the church, which made it extraordinary.

The stars were littered across the top of the canvas and glistened like live sparklers celebrating the existence of the earth. They followed me as I changed viewpoints, as if they were the watching eyes of heaven. The word "exquisite" involuntarily came out of my mouth.

The sky was an unusual color of inky purple with a touch of ebony blue. It gave me a sense of warmth and comfort. The vibrancy of the purple sky helped project the bright stars out of the painting, shooting them toward me.

I was so captivated by the sky and the stars, I didn't initially focus on the glassless, godless windows framed by immense, somber stones. I did not search inside to see the dead "Temenos," the now-empty, once-sacred space of worship.

The deep rose color coming from the windows was, like the purple in the sky, supernatural in its vibrancy. I continued to search for something inside, but there was nothing in the windows and nothing to be seen through the windows; there was nothing or no one in the church at all. After the deep warmth of the sky, the comfort of the farm and the attractiveness of the stone walls, I expected to see—a welcoming human touch, an icon, a pew, a person, something religious. What was creating the rose-colored light emitting from the church windows? Why was the church empty, with no altar, no candles, no Bibles, no cross hung on the wall, no statue of the Virgin Mary, and no worshippers. What was making me love this painting so? The response came only in the answerless, rose-colored light.

This painting took my breath away. I didn't want to leave it. I wondered about the human exodus—if they chose to die or if they were taken away by God's wrath.

Had the imperfect religion of man violated the Holy Spirit of the unblemished God? I thought of Jesus' anger in the temple when the merchants misused the holy place for impure purposes. *This painting was an aftermath; it represented the existence of nothing where something significant had once been. I felt as if no other person existed, I was utterly alone, the last human being left alive on earth...as if God Himself abandoned the world and forgot me for eternity.*

The unexpected absence of life touched fears lurking deep inside me: the painting provoked thoughts I did not share with others and often concealed from myself. My own loneliness began to burst out in the middle of the crowd. I started to sob. I turned and walked toward one of the large windows of the palace, where I could look out without revealing my agony. This painting projected the extremes of human desperation similar to the abject loneliness described by the Existentialists. It was as if their written words were translated into paint and brushed onto canvas.

A deeply felt tear rolled down my cheek; I quickly wiped it away. In the raw, emotional honesty of those rose-colored windows, I knew my relationship with the Boy was over. I knew it as well as I knew anything in my life. I had walked away from him early that morning to follow my own calling, and I wasn't going back. Our relationship became as empty as those vacant church portals with nothing left inside. I needed more than he could give; I yearned for someone with a deeper soul and greater awareness. The Boy needed someone who wanted less. My search for my sacred self could not be accomplished with the Boy, for he created loneliness and despair instead of abating it.

I didn't know what my next romantic adventure would be, though I knew it would be much more than simply playing soccer and losing my virginity. I didn't know what was waiting as I crossed over my next life-bridge, but in the Medici Palace that sunny afternoon I would soon find out.

I stood back from the paintings. I was enthralled by what I saw and astounded by the intense emotions I felt. I saw the powerful influence of Van Gogh. The paintings were full of effervescent, feminine colors; wheat-field yellows, powdery soft, summer sky blues and stunning purples. The colors must have come from the most vivid dreams, a palette of colors absent from our conscious minds.

The paintings drew me in; each depicted intense light and color in a vast array of creative expressions. How could the purples be so purple and the violets so violet? How could the barrenness of our souls be revealed through the empty, rose-colored windows of a church? How could stark human loneliness be exposed so vividly in a place where man searched for God but instead found abandonment?

At first, I thought the Artist was all male downstairs and all female upstairs, and his complexity was simply a clash between the man and woman inside of him. However, as I thought it through, I saw no femininity at all; the emotions and expressions were unquestionably those of a man—albeit a man with an incredible breadth of emotions, a unique amalgamation of human perceptions, and an extraordinary insight into life itself. I was enthralled with this man, this man I hadn't met.

I surmised that only an Italian man could simultaneously be so strong, emotionally open, and comfortable with a public display of his emotions; other men were divided into weak or strong, submissive or dominant.

Café Talk: A Break and a Breath

1945. The American's conversation with Christine's about the Artist proceeded furiously. After two cappuccinos, the American needed a break and a few minutes to assimilate the first part of the chapter on her Italian Artist. Christine was patient. She told him she had a quick errand to run on Boulevard San Michel and she would return in half an hour.

The American reread Christine's detailed descriptions of the paintings. Her questions became his questions. Why do the innocent have to pay? The American had had an extremely difficult experience when an innocent child paid dearly and he still did not understand why. He felt God's abandonment in a highly personal way. He knew the man on his knees grieving for his dead mother; the loss of his own mother left him with a great deal of emptiness. He loved Christine's analysis of the paintings, but he noted that her interpretations said as much about her as they did about the paintings and the Artist.

Christine returned from her errand carrying a bouquet of twelve pure white tulips. She gave them to the American and said, "When you go home, put these in a vase on a table near the window. They will help you spend time alone. French tulips are my favorites. Flowers are special gifts from God, I am just the messenger. Their beauty will bring you happiness before you go to sleep at night and lighten your new day when they greet you in the morning."

Though the American had many lovers before, none gave him flowers, especially not a beautiful, charming French woman. No lover, and certainly not his Wife, did these small, caring things for him, the things women say they want from their men but seldom get. He was thrilled and touched. He laughed at himself and the American male protocol that produced embarrassment at such an open expression of affection from a woman. The American thought, I have only seen a spark of this woman, a tiny hint of what must have been a roaring fire.

Christine paused and looked deeply into the American's eyes as she crossed the space separating them to build a bridge of human trust. She emotionally gave herself and he opened to receive her. The walls protecting their hearts were being dismantled brick by brick as light was winning over darkness. Christine smiled softly. Writing her Journal was becoming a journey in and of itself. The American was becoming another story, another chapter in her Journal.

Christine prepared the American for the next events in her life. "Don't be shocked. I must tell my story my way, and you are going to hear exactly what happened, uncensored."

Christine looked away from the American and her mind leapt outside, crossing time-bridges away from him and the present. Christine went to her alone-place with her memories, as today's café windows became portals to her yesterdays.

Christine Meets the Artist

As I walked farther along the hallway of the canvas-enhanced Palais de Luxembourg, I saw a group of schoolchildren around twelve years of age sitting on the floor with their teacher. They had come from the nearby school to visit the exhibition. The children were listening to a man whom I immediately recognized as the Artist. He was describing his creations in musical, Italianized French. I stepped back and leaned on the wall for support. I watched him in awe and listened carefully to every word he spoke. I stared intently. There he was, the Artist who created this conflicted array of beauty and truth. He matched my Aunt's description exactly, his eyes flashing with light and passion as he spoke with the children.

He stood between two of his signature paintings, one selected from each of his painting styles. The painting to his left was a strange animal strung up in the sky. Its contorted body parts were not located in normal places and not shaped in the ways one would expect. The animal's teeth stuck out of the canvas in a frighteningly real image. The children appeared to be perplexed by this unusual form. It was unlike any animal they knew.

The painting to his right was a clearer image, a long look at the Seine wandering through the heart of Paris. What was uncommon was the brightness of the colors, the beauty of the sky, the welcoming of life on the river, and the trees of blue. As I watched the exchange between the Artist and the children, I moved closer to hear him. "But of course the trees in Paris are blue. Haven't you seen the blue trees along the Seine?" he said in answer to a wide-eyed boy's question. "At least, this is how they look to me."

Standing there, between the animal he distorted and the river Seine he beautified, he questioned the children about their visions and what they saw. He explored their answers gently, lovingly, almost like he was singing them a lullaby. He spoke of his thoughts when he painted these paintings. He held the children's complete attention; there was no squirming or giggling. Every child's eyes and mind were focused on the Artist and his paintings, each fascinated by this grown man who, through his art and words, brought the children deeper into a fantasy world they were eager to know.

After the children gave their impressions of his paintings, he revealed more of what his art meant to him and the visions he saw. The children dreamily traveled into his creations. I remember him explaining a dichotomy: "As a creator, you are never alone—you can always create. But as a creator, you are always alone—creations come from the *creative you* inside yourself, a different place and a different person no one else can fully know." I wondered if those children understood how profound his words truly were.

A girl shyly asked him if he felt angry when he painted the strange animals and happy when he painted the beautiful river. He looked at her for a moment, drinking in her virtuousness, her waning childhood, and answered simply, "No, not angry or happy. The different paintings just came out of me, out of different parts of me—maybe like your different stomachs—one for regular food and the special other one only for dessert."

I think she was feeling a not-to-be-forgotten, girl-man crush on the Artist as she looked down to her lap and her face flushed with glee. She wasn't even supposed to like boys yet.

I saw all of this. I watched him give his God-given, creative self to those children freely and lovingly. Not only was he a profound artist, he was a performer and an excellent teacher. How could any woman resist this man? Impossible!

As he spoke to the children of his art and his visions, he glanced my way only once. His eyes darted into me like lightning bolts piercing my core, His power left me naked; my body, heart and spirit were instantly available to him.

I stood immobilized while children and visitors milled around me. Exposed to his heat and the rising fervor in my soul, my skin flushed in excitement and anticipation. I half-heartedly tried to control myself, but all my efforts were overridden by the force of his glance.

It was the first time a mature man looked at me in the special way a grown man looks at a woman when he wants her. He saw me not as a girl to wrestle with in the dirt, but as a woman to be loved passionately by a man, with all of her womanly complexities. He acknowledged my growing womanhood and the many possibilities of a man-woman union with his eyes. I was flattered and excited but unsure of what to do. I let fate unfold without interference. I waited to see what would happen next.

When he was finished speaking with the children, he motioned me to come to him. I gingerly approached as the magic of lustful love began to grow in me again.

He spoke directly. *"For now, I don't want to know you by your words or by your story: I don't want you to speak or tell me who you are or where you have been—I want to paint you as purely as I see you right now, without your words to interfere with what I see. Please, come to my studio now and say nothing."*

I was a woman without choice; I gave my free will to him. He captured me with his glance and the cogent energy of his creations. Nothing came before him and nothing else existed in that moment except this man and his art. As we walked to his nearby studio, I focused on him entirely; here was the man of the world I had been searching for.

I sat on a stool in his studio and he approached me like an animal approaching his prey: carefully, slowly, indirectly—he was like a cannibal and I was soon to be served for lunch!

He pulled off my sweater, directing me in a strong voice: "Take everything off! I want you naked; I want to see all of you—there is no hiding from me!"

His painting was a frenzy of motion and tension. Smoke filled the air as he burnt through cigarette after cigarette. On occasion, he gulped whiskey from a short water glass. As he had commanded, I didn't speak. My body ached from posing for so long and my initial embarrassment from sitting naked was overcome by fatigue.

No one had ever looked so closely at my body, not even the Boy in our naked, frequent lovemaking. The Artist was examining every hair, every part of me: my face, my eyes, my hands, my nipples, my sexual crevice, everything.

He came to me, moved my leg and touched the curves of my body, slowly, like a blind man seeing through the touch of his fingers. His hands were dirty with paint and rough on my skin, but each touch energized me. Each time he repositioned or stroked me, I awoke from my weariness and gushed with heat.

I wore my hair in a tossed, carefree look. I let it grow down to my shoulders and it usually looked like I had just awakened. My effort to straighten my natural curls was only partly successful. Instead of the straight hair I sought, I produced small curls. He playfully lifted my hair and let it fall back down like it was a toy. I guess the Artist liked it, because that was how he painted me.

I smelled cigarettes and whiskey on his body and his breath when he came close to me. He was not merely a man but part beast too, stalking me in a sexual, threatening way and leaving me in doubt of what would happen next.

First Time: The Artist

He didn't stop painting until he finished putting his vision of me onto the canvas. He wouldn't show me the painting. There was more to come. He gently but surely guided me off the stool to the large oak dining table and laid me down on my naked back.

After slow, long caresses, he casually took off the paint-stained shirt he had worn all day, then unbuttoned and dropped his American Levis, showing he wore no underwear. His body was thin and muscular in a wiry way.

He climbed on top of me, touching me. As he moved himself toward and over me, he paused and said in a direct manner, "No matter what happens, don't close your eyes; keep them open and look directly into mine. I want to see into your intimate, passionate self. I want to see the totality of you. Don't close them!"

As he commanded, I did. I flowed with each move; when he pushed; I pulled, when he thrust, I squeezed. Deeper and deeper I fell into his haunting, beautiful blue eyes. I had never seen into the being of another human the way I saw into his soul during our eyes-wide-open lovemaking. I saw everything in him and he saw everything in me. *He looked so deeply into my heart, he saw tears I was yet to cry and breaks in my heart I was yet to feel.*

I didn't feel the hardness of the table on my back; I felt only his hardness as I stared into the captivating pools of his eyes. We exploded into simultaneous ecstasy. It was ultimate sex because it went beyond physical sexuality into the shared intimacy of our deepest selves. I was moonstruck.

We hadn't spoken beyond his instructions. It was clear he was not a man who needed months of conversation to determine who or what he wanted. He knew the second his eyes traveled into mine, the second he ventured into my deep, unprotected self. He knew he wanted me, knew he could have me, and he did.

When he collapsed with his passion spent, he rolled off the table onto the floor, lit a cigarette and went over to look at his painting of me. I watched him stare at me in oil: did he like it? Who was I to him? Could I speak now, after he had me in two different ways?

I was lying on the wooden table when the Artist brought a soft blanket to cover me and a pillow to hold my head. I closed my eyes and relaxed, trying to grasp what had just happened; I crossed a long, new bridge to a different shore. Did I leap too fast? I wondered silently to myself, but then quickly dismissed my doubt. I was doing exactly what I wanted to do, running full-speed-ahead to a place I wanted to go.

Standing naked, the Artist used his brushes to make a few changes to me in paint. Maybe he saw something else in me as we made love, something he wanted to add or change to the painting. He didn't say.

He motioned to come see my painting. I wrapped myself in the blanket as if I had something left to hide. There I saw myself as the Artist saw me—an image frozen on canvas before we had spoken or made love. I appeared more beautiful and stronger than I really was. There was an added mystery. The difference was particularly evident in the eyes, which seemed deeper than mine, deeper than they could possibly be. What did he see? Did he know me so well he saw more of me than I knew of myself, or did he paint his own eyes into mine as a sort of feminized self-portrait?

After a few minutes of viewing, he took my hand in his and led me toward the bathroom. We showered together. He washed me; he soaped every part of my body from back to front. Then I washed his beautiful body with both of my hands. The warm water, the soft, slippery, soapy bubbles, and our sensuous touching aroused us again.

He turned me away from him, bent my head down under the hot water and took me from behind. His was much more aggressive than when we were locked into each other's loving eyes on the dinner table. I knew I was being taken by the Downstairs Artist, the lustful, dominant animal-man.

He became a stranger again, an unknown man. Hot water flowed over my body. I closed my eyes. He reached around and tightly held my right breast with one soapy hand and gripped my left shoulder with the other, pinning me to him.

He took me a long time before he finished. I did not climax. Facing away from him wasn't the intimate, eye-to-eye connection we enjoyed on his table and didn't bring out the same level of sensuality or sexuality. On the table, we were deeply connected and shared the passion of becoming one. In his shower, I didn't fully give my mind and body to him; I couldn't even see his face. However, in a way that is difficult to explain, I enjoyed his animal strength and his physical control. The violation and deep, sexual connection brought me a strange sense of pleasure, a feeling similar to how I felt after looking at the painting, *Violazione Brutale Negata*. The Artist clearly enjoyed making love this way, as he let out a deeply passionate scream in Italian at the end.

Exceedingly clean from our long shower and spent from making love twice, we finally sat down to dinner and conversation. I wore his bathrobe and he was shirtless and shoeless. He cooked pasta and we drank strong red Italian wine out of water glasses. The garlic and anchovy aromas overwhelmed the studio's dominant smell of oil paint and cleaning solvents. Finally, he asked my name. When I told him, his only comment was to say, "Hmm, Christine, like Christ, the She-Christ." Only then did I start to become a person instead of a detached object for painting and prey for his sexual desires.

He told me about his life and his world travel experiences. As I listened, I yearned to cross from girl to woman with his guidance and love. I wanted to learn more about creating paintings than simply looking at them, more than a detached analyst like my mother, the art critic; I wanted to know the heart, soul and body of the creator. I said to him, "Show me everything you know, teach me all you have learned."

We awoke late in the morning to a sky streaked with hues of red, rose and yellow. The air was still. Curled clouds marched across the horizon as if an army of interior decorators designed the sky just for this day and just for us. I did not fully understand the implications of connecting with this man, but I knew he would permanently change me.

We drank strong espressos together but it was his time to paint and it was my time to go. I gathered my things, dressed and slipped out the door. He was at his easel, shirtless, shoeless, wearing the same Levis from the night before. Heading to the door, I was proud of myself; I'd had a Boy and now I had a man!

He didn't look up or say good-bye; he had reentered his creative domain and wasn't to be disturbed. After writing a note with my phone number and my full name, I opened the door, took a deep breath and headed outside to face a new world and reorganize my life. I knew I was coming back.

My mind was racing as I walked down the street. I made love with two Artists; one who was charming, confident and captivating, and another living in the same body who was driven, dominant, aggressive, strong and potent. He touched my innate feminine needs for both men, the gentleman painting my portrait and caressing me emotionally on the table and the uber-man gripping and pounding me blindly in the shower.

Was this man wise enough in the ways of women to know we need a man who supports and passionately loves us *and* a man strong enough to care for and protect us? His duality created a strong reaction in me; an aphrodisiac.

I left the studio wanting more of the man whose art expressed deep emotions, the lonely, tortured, vulnerable one hidden far back in the tunnel of his deep blue eyes. I smiled as I walked the Paris streets and she smiled back at me. My mind was full of thoughts and questions. Was he the man of my dreams, a creator and a real man? Was he my connection to the worldly, multidimensional life I dreamt of? Or was it me, hoping in my womanly fantasies for a man who didn't exist and never would?

I concluded he was the One. I found the answer to my persistent questions about finding the right man and it was a resounding yes! I longed for a man who could play the strings of my heart in a way they had yet to be strummed, and I wanted him to assist me in discovering my own talents as I grew into womanhood.

The Artist became busy with his show and his junior-celebrity status. We didn't see each other for the week after our first and only tryst so far.

I returned to clean up the mess with the Boy; I gathered the things I left at his house and moved back in with my university friends. The Boy and I had crossed all the bridges we could cross together; he and his juvenile ways were behind me.

The Boy didn't understand why I was leaving and I didn't try to help him figure it out. It was about who he was in total, it was his full boyhood presence that drove me away. There wasn't one thing or just a few things he could change to make our relationship work. He thought and acted like a boy because he was a boy. I wanted a much larger world than a bunch of soccer-crazed, beer-drinking, shouting, youthful boys could give. I wanted a man, something the Boy could not yet be.

I couldn't explain it to him, so I didn't. I crossed over the bridge to the other side, to the opposite shore toward a new life. He stood motionless and remained silent. This time, he wasn't kicking the ball or imagining himself making the winning goal in a championship game that didn't exist. This time, he watched carefully and thoughtfully as I walked away for the rest of our lives. Maybe he started to grow up as he felt the enormity of our parting. I wanted to believe he did.

Though I momentarily glanced back as I crossed over the bridge, I was already gone—living on the other side without him. As I walked along the river, it began to rain. I opened my umbrella, pulled my coat tighter to my breasts and picked up my pace. I knew I was heading toward grand, new adventures; I had a rendezvous with a new life and I was anxious to discover what my future would bring.

Seven days after our first meeting and our sensuous night together, the Artist invited me to his studio for dinner. I expected it to be an evening of dining, drinking, talking and lovemaking and I was not to be disappointed on any count.

I felt privileged to be there, a place where beauty was created, where blank canvases sprang alive with magnificent color, and meaningful images came from the Artist's mind and soul. Unlike the dead space in the windows of my favorite painting of the desolated church, his studio was a *living Temenos*—a "holy" place of creation full of life and vibrant images.

I thought about my first visit the week before. We had made love twice but not in his bed; instead, he chose the dining table and the shower for our lovemaking. I laughed at my memories when I entered the studio for the second time: how unusual it seemed, but how thrilling it had been.

I carefully looked about to preserve a better picture in my mind. The studio was one large room; his painting area was isolated to the right, with canvases lying about in semi-orderly chaos, and paintbrushes stuck in coffee cans like large, multi-colored candles. The kitchen, bed and bathroom were on the left. There was plenty of room for working and living. Wide windows along the top of one wall let in the natural light needed to paint. There was the wooden artist's table, obviously used for multiple purposes, marked with paint from past creations, stained from food and wine and holding memories of sexual passion. There was the bathroom with the infamous shower. The painting of me with exaggerated eyes posed on its easel. There was the stool upon which I nakedly sat for so long. It was electrifying to return and to see him again on this hallowed ground.

On the dining table was an open bottle of Italian red wine, two large, colorful ceramic plates, large, silver knives, forks and spoons, and decorative cloth napkins splashed with bold flowers. Two candles were burning. It was a table for another special occasion and it was set like a painting.

Pasta was cooking in a large pot, while another smaller pot simmered with chunky tomato sauce. There was something magnificent cooking in the oven; it smelled delicious. I looked in; it was a rabbit roasting in rosemary, olive oil and aged balsamic vinegar surrounded by vegetables, all cooking in one pan. Also in the oven was a terracotta dish filled with potatoes cut into squares, covered in olive oil and sprinkled with crushed rosemary and, as he explained to me, sea salt from Sicily. There were antipasti of tomatoes, mozzarella cheese and basil covered in green olive oil and sprinkled with coarse salt and pepper on an ornate platter in the center of the table.

Was this what it was like to date an Italian man? He appeared to be more adept in the kitchen than I. There was no doubt who was to be the chef and who was in charge for the night.

When he invited me to dinner, he hadn't asked me to bring anything. This was his game with his rules and it would be played in his exacting, Italian way. He said in a strong, clear voice that he only ate Italian food and only drank Italian wine. He couldn't stand the sauces the French used to cover the taste of their food. He couldn't drink French wines because they tasted strange to him, as if an unnatural ingredient were added.

As he prepared our dinner, there was nothing for me to do but to watch him, nibble on the antipasti, drink the excellent wine and peruse his studio. He talked incessantly, whether I came close to him to observe his cooking or if I walked away to view his paintings. He talked about the show, his paintings, himself, who he met, the comments about his work, and about the various critics' reviews of his paintings.

He spoke about his mother teaching him how to cook, the importance of selecting the tastiest, freshest ingredients, and how to choose a proper Italian wine. She had died some years before, which I thought was his motivation for painting *Human Pain and Heavenly Joy*. Until her death, the Artist lived at home with his mother, which amazed me for he was quite old by then. They were very close, as Italian mothers and their sons can be.

"I could not eat or be satisfied eating anywhere else but at home with my mother, eating her incredible cooking," he openly declared. "I didn't have to take care of myself when I was home. My mother loved to make a fuss over me." He went on unapologetically, explaining how his mother would "say things about my lack of discipline and the mess I left behind, but then she would jump in and take care of my life's logistics, even paying my bills and making my bed every day."

He didn't reveal his inner thoughts about his paintings like he did with the children; he spoke of his art in a commercial sense and what pieces he sold and how much he was paid. When I asked him directly what he meant by a painting and how he felt during the time he was painting it, he avoided the question and took the conversation in a different direction.

There was no doubt he loved art and loved being an artist, but I saw something else that night, an intense need for the approval of others, for public recognition, and a hunger for financial success. I contrasted his commercial focus with Van Gogh, whose passion for creating art produced some of the most admired paintings of the nineteenth century. Van Gogh painted the world as he saw it—full of torment and beauty—and he was panned and criticized for his iconoclastic style. Van Gogh sold only one painting during his lifetime and it was bought by his brother, Theo. He did not experience approval, adoration or financial success, but he achieved one rare and immeasurably valuable thing in life: immortality granted for true artistic genius. I thought the Artist wanted to be more like the star Picasso, who achieved public recognition and financial rewards in this lifetime.

The Artist continued to talk as we ate our way through the wonderful antipasti, the pasta, the rabbit and the special dessert made with Italian liquor. The first bottle of wine went quickly so he went to the back of the studio for another. He explained how this second bottle was particularly special. He carried it with him from Italy, and it was a gift from a collector of his paintings. The wine was made from a special grape called *Brunello*, a varietal of Sangiovese. The wine was called Brunello di Montalcino. This wine was only produced in one tiny area and only by the Biondi-Santi family in their winery named Il Greppo in the hills of Montalcino near Siena. We were drinking their 1925 vintage and it was the best wine I ever tasted. The Artist was teaching me about Italian wines and food. I loved the lessons.

We drank Italian espresso after dinner and, without breaking stride in his talk, he cleaned the entire dinner mess himself: pots, pans, dishes and all. It was fascinating; I hadn't seen anything like this. In my family, the women cooked. The men did nothing to help with the meals or clean up. What a difference it was to be with an Italian man who loved to cook and didn't mind cleaning up either!

Café Talk: Gabriele D'Annunzio
"Me ne frego"

1945. *Christine focused on the American sitting across the table. She spoke for quite a while, speaking in her other voice, the one from long ago. She gave the American a smile in recognition of her return to the present. The American was busy writing, but when she paused he looked up to see what was on her mind. The explicit man-woman sexual encounters were more graphic than expected. They fascinated him in an unusually erotic way. He was ashamed of his boyish feelings and did his best to conceal them, but she saw all.*

"It is OK," she commented. "I know I am being explicit about things you are not used to discussing openly with a woman. I warned you, I am not embarrassed by my sexuality or by these experiences. They are an important part of me and I want them presented honestly.

"Why don't we take a walk and sit in the park for the next part of my story? You look like you could use some air."

The American placed his glasses and pen in the old glasses case and put it in his coat pocket. As he put them away, no memories of past encounters came to mind. He was captured by Christine and was living fully in the present.

After a short stroll to the park and finding a comfortable place to sit, Christine asked, "By the way, have you heard of Gabriele D'Annunzio, the Italian pre-Second War poet, columnist, novelist, soldier and man about town?"

The American shook his head and asked, "No, who is this Gabriele D'Annunzio?"

Christine smiled again. This time it was the kind of European smile of understanding she gave when she saw the American in his tennis shoes and canvas pants the first time. "D'Annunzio," she said, "was the most important and the most controversial Italian author of the past hundred years or more. He wrote in a style new to Italy, and of subjects not previously presented in the ways he created them. His work is famous throughout Europe. His life is legendary. You will learn about D'Annunzio as my journey continues. Someday you may wish to learn more about this man who has evoked so many strong emotions in Europeans, and whose quintessence dominated my life with the Artist."

Christine and the American returned to her past. They sat in the park with the full expanse of the land upon which to gaze and to remember. Again, she didn't miss a word or an event as she began exactly where she left off. The events of her life were palpably seared on the permanent memory of her brain.

Hero Worship, Creativity and A Dose of Reality

After we finished our meal, the Artist drank grappa. He spoke of the man he most admired, Gabriele D'Annunzio. D'Annunzio had died the day before, March 1, 1938. He collapsed at his desk, quill pen in hand; a 74 year-old man blind in one eye, toothless and bald. As he spoke, smoked and drank, I noticed I was not offered grappa. He assumed, correctly, that it was too strong for me and for most people. Italian men primarily drank it as a *digestivo,* but it tasted like pure alcohol to me.

The Artist went on to exclaim the exploits of D'Annunzio beyond his writing: a World War One pilot and hero, a minor dictator, a *bon vivant,* a politician and a lover to many of the most beautiful and important women of his time.

"Think of his name," the Artist said enthusiastically, *"Gabriele D'Annunzio—Gabriel of the Annunciation."* His first name was that of the archangel Gabriel, God's divine messenger. Gabriel, the angel, was so important to the Jews, Christians and Muslims, that each believed Gabriel was sent personally by God to reveal His truth to them. And his last name, D'Annunzio, was a variation on the Annunciation, the announcement to the Virgin Mary by the angel Gabriel of the incarnation of Christ. What a name!

The Artist shared D'Annunzio's philosophy that life and art were a single entity: a flow of seamless energy, without separation. In a belief system the Artist called *Artistic Elitism,* society was divided into two groups. The first group was the *Creators,* those who actively create things that have not existed before, like paintings, literature, music or poetry. The second group was the *Creations,* the rest of us who hadn't created anything new and were, therefore, simply placed as passive creations.

In the philosophy of Artistic Elitism, we Creations were put on the earth to support the Creators so they could create without being concerned about the difficulties and practicalities of life, like supporting themselves or cleaning up their messes. It was not a matter of one group simply using the other, as one might assume. To them, it was our purpose, our *raison pour laquelle nous existe*. Their "philosophy" reminded me of hives of bees or ants, full of workers who live only to support their queens.

"Because I am an accomplished artist," he said without a sign of modesty, "I, like Gabriele D'Annunzio, Dante Alighieri, Michelangelo di Lodovico Buonarroti Simoni, Filippo Brunelleschi and Leonardo da Vinci, have risen to a separate, higher plane of human existence, one not shared by those who have not created masterpieces of art, literature, or music in their own lives." He threw out these names like they were his intimate friends, like they all grew up on the same block in some small, holy town filled only with Creators, where we Creations stayed out of sight as they created masterpieces in a rarefied world of creative geniuses.

The Artist further claimed, "I am a living representative in the historic *'Continuum of Italian Artistic Geniuses'* who have been honored throughout history for their contributions to the civilization of mankind, and for the beauty they have brought to the earth. I have inherited the spirits of demi-gods such as Michelangelo, Leonardo, Dante and D'Annunzio. They are how and why I stand here today, in Paris, creating works of art in their honor for the world to see. It is from these masters that I have inherited my resolute strength to paint, to live and to love! Their blood runs in my blood; their creative juices flow with my creative juices. I know them intimately in my heart and my mind every day and every night—I see life through their eyes as I paint a painting and, when I make love to a woman.

66

"Sex with an unknown woman is the only way, other than painting, when I temporarily touch my godlike essence. Sexual conquest and passion with a stranger complements creating works of art. This is why I wanted to paint you and make love with you before I knew you—I wanted the addicting boost of self-gratification from uncluttered sex that men have sought throughout the world and for all of history.

"The drudgery of ongoing relationships destroys these intense feelings of excitement, discovery and pleasure. Long-term relationships produce the exact opposite: sex without passion, boredom and the loss of the godlike elation from having sex with a new woman. It is like creating a painting: when it is done, it is done and it is time to start a new one."

The Artist then declared how difficult it was for a Creator to have normal or equal relationships with others, especially with those who are not Creators. "The disparity is too great. How can a mere mortal compete with creating like gods? Creating trumps common human love; the acts of creation have no equal in human relationships, not in love, not in family and not in friends. Human relationships are flawed and temporal, limited in depth and duration; creations are pure, immortal and monumental.

"Even sex, clearly the most pleasurable activity in the man-woman connection, only lasts a short while. It is often impure because it is attached to greed or manipulation. Do you understand what I am talking about?" he asked at his first pause for some time.

There were many warning signs that this man was going to be trouble. But in my youthful blindness, I chose to ignore them. I was strong, young and beautiful and I truly believed, as many women do with their men, that I could change him. I would charge forward into my relationship with him, but first I would challenge the philosophy of the Artist and his mentor, Gabriele D'Annunzio.

I knew about D'Annunzio. I had read his works in French and we studied him in school. I remembered he wrote a successful play named *La citta' morta, The Dead City,* for the actress, his lover, Sarah Bernhardt. I knew D'Annunzio had led the black-shirted Fascist militia and was called IL Duse by some.

D'Annunzio was a philanderer with a history of having many lovers and engaging in multiple love affairs at the same time; writing glowing love letters to one woman while he was having passionate liaisons with others. His affairs with the actresses in his plays, including a tragic public affair with Eleonora Duse, a celebrated, bisexual Italian actress of the silent film era, were infamous. His relationships frequently exploded into violent conflicts, including duels with angry husbands and public conflicts between his jealous lovers. On more than one occasion, he fled his dramas in Rome back to the safety of his homeland in Abruzzo to avoid unpaid debts and arrests for adultery. He would hide at his friend Raffaele Pizzica's beach home in Francavilla al Mare until the pressure subsided, or he made enough money to pay off his creditors or to buy his way out of a jail sentence.

For the fifteen years before his death, D'Annunzio retreated to the Italian north in self-imposed exile. On the shore of Lake Garda, he built an impressive, multi-acre monument to himself. He filled it with his personal memorabilia: his uniforms, his MAS 96 "motor boat-anti-submarine," his airplane, and the greater part of a still-commissioned warship. It is called *Vittoriale degli Italiani* and was built as a glorification of D'Annunzio's full and complex life, and to the glory of Italy.

The newspapers wrote of D'Annunzio's friendship with Mussolini during Mussolini's rise to become the dictator of Italy. D'Annunzio provided Mussolini with the philosophical and political premises for Italian Fascism, much of which D'Annunzio took from Nietzsche. It was upon these ideas that Mussolini built his Italian Fascist political party, which eventually brought a disaster of horrendous proportions to the Italian people.

However, D'Annunzio adamantly opposed Mussolini's Italian alliance with Nazi Germany. This conflict led to D'Annunzio's exile and his permanent withdrawal from Italian politics.

According to the newspaper accounts, D'Annunzio died near his ever-present German whore, Emy Heufler, who was paid to worship, provide drugs and have sex with him. Commentators questioned if she was a Nazi agent, sent to keep him in a drugged state of mind and to assure that he stayed out of the politics of the German/Italian unification pact. This suspicion was supported by the fact that she fled to Berlin after D'Annunzio's death to work for Joachim von Ribbentrop, Nazi Germany's controversial foreign minister.

After his little speech to me about D'Annunzio and his pride about the impersonal sex we shared, I was angry. I asked him pointed questions: "Did you make love with me last week or did you simply use my body as a form of lazy masturbation? Were you actually having sex with yourself? Was I a real person to you or is that why you didn't want me to speak—so you wouldn't be making love with a genuine woman? If that is what you want, why don't you find a whore like D'Annunzio did and get it over with?

"In the D'Annunzio model for society, am I simply here to serve you, to be your audience when you want to speak and your sex toy when you want sex? Is that it?"

"How did D'Annunzio's life ultimately turn out when he tried to live a real life? Do you think sex with whores and taking drugs for fifteen years sounds like a great way to end one's life? Is the final curtain of this self-love, I-am-god philosophy an act of drowning yourself in drugs and tainted sex to cope with the lonely life you have created?

"You say you can't have an adequate relationship with mere, creative-less mortals. Then why don't you find a Creator-goddess, so you and she can fornicate directly as 'god to goddess' and forget using us servants as vessels for your semen? You know why you can't? Because two overgrown egos can't fit in one relationship, that's why. Because you and some soprano singer would each require control of center-stage where there is only room for one star at a time.

"You search for mere mortals who, because we worship your gift of creativity, can be used by you and discarded at will. You want us to remain inferior because of your endless quest to fill the emptiness in your heart. Man searches for someone to look down to; you and D'Annunzio say artists are superior to everyone else. It is the same hierarchy northern Italians have been claiming with Sicilians for centuries!

"I want to tell you about your idol, Signor Gabriele D'Annunzio. Gabriele and D'Annunzio are not his real names. He was not named at birth for the Archangel Gabriel, the Messenger of God; Gabriele was a nickname he was given for his angelic looks. His father's family name was not originally D'Annunzio, as in the annunciation of Christ to Mary, as he wanted the public to believe. D'Annunzio is the name of his great uncle who adopted his father. His birth name was *Gaetano Rapagnetta*; such a common name for a Creator-god! Of course, he wanted to change his name; he was always full of big plans for himself. Gaetano Rapagnetta created Gabriele D'Annunzio. Once, he even faked his own death to gain sympathy and attention. Gaetano Rapagnetta is an actor and an impostor. There is no Gabriele D'Annunzio!"

The Artist was shocked. He had no idea I was such a fighter. He was unaware that I had grown up with two older brothers, and keeping them in line took guts and a willingness to fight for equality. He hadn't watched me outplay boys in soccer. He was confused. He thought my attraction to him and my respect for his paintings would make me afraid and passive. I was neither. He didn't know me yet.

He was speechless. He leaned back, took a long breath and reached for the grappa. He looked away from me and lit a cigarette. He exhaled the smoke and it wandered up to the ceiling in a twirling, dissipating white cloud. He drained his glass of grappa in a gulp.

"No one, especially someone who is almost a stranger, has ever directly challenged my Creator-centric philosophy. No woman has stood up to me in the way you have just done. Other women have easily accepted my superior artist position, especially when I validated my artist-deity status with the philosophy of D'Annunzio.

"You amaze me," he said, locking his stare deeply into my eyes for the first time since we'd made love on the table a week before. "You say things I have not heard from a lover before. You remind me of my mother! She would have said the same things; criticizing my talk of superior and inferior people and making gods out of men because of their creations. She would have declared such ideas silly and blasphemous. She didn't let up on me. She criticized me often but, like you, she didn't say "no" to me either. Your strength and courage are stimulating. Is it true about D'Annunzio's real name? I didn't know that.

"You are amazingly beautiful. I am more attracted to you than ever. You have ignored my defenses and my diversions. You have leapt over walls protecting my heart and found the raw me. If you make love with me now, I promise I will answer everything you want to know about me afterward. I promise!"

My trust in him was low but my lust was extraordinarily high. I wanted to make love with him, too. My expressiveness in standing up to him, the aphrodisiac of the art and the artist, were exciting me into a sexual frenzy. I wanted to tear his clothes off even as he made his irritating claims of artistic superiority. Maybe I also wanted simple sexual gratification without the complexities of a relationship—at least I did for the moment.

Regardless, I was going to make him work for it. I wanted to see him spent and exhausted from sex, to cry out loud with my legs wrapped around him, to temporarily die in my arms. I was willing to let his self-revelations wait.

The comfortable food and dark red wine were heating me everywhere. I took off my sweater. I could feel my desire rising as we headed to his bed for our third sexual encounter—I was ready for whatever it was going to be—making love, sex for fun, or a little of both.

Our lovemaking was extremely sensual but it did not rise to the intensity of the first time when he captured my eyes in passion. I loved making love with a famous artist in his studio full of canvases, dirty brushes, paint and stacks of half-completed paintings, though I was already full of doubts about the man behind the image.

As we drank espressos the next morning, the Artist said he thought my D'Annunzio comments were too critical and emphasized only his negatives. He asked me to sit at the infamous table. He reached behind him and pulled out D'Annunzio's novel, IL trionfo della morte, *The Triumph of Death*. "Listen," he said, "I want to read a few pages of his book to you. I want you to understand D'Annunzio's command of language, action and thought."

I sat back and listened. He turned a few pages of the book to find a conversation between Giorgio and his lover, Ippolita:

"She began by asking Giorgio the question, 'So, you think I do not love you, Giorgio?'

"Well—no—I think you do love me,' he replied; 'but can you give me any proof that tomorrow—in a month—a year—you will be equally content to belong to me? Can you even prove to me that today—at this moment—you are mine, wholly? How much of you can I call my own?'

"All.'

"Nothing—or next to nothing. I do not possess that which I want— you are practically an unknown person to me. Like every other human being, you carry a whole world in you, into which I cannot enter and no amount of passion will open the gates for me. Of your feelings, your sentiments, your thoughts, I know only a small part. Words are an imperfect vehicle of expression. The soul is incommunicable—you cannot give me your soul. Even in our supremest raptures we are and remain apart—solitary. I kiss you on the brow and behind that brow there lies a thought which possibly is not for me. I speak to you and who knows but what some chance phase of mine may not awaken in you a memory of some other hour in which my love had not place or part. A man passes and looks at you—that stirs in your heart a something which I may not catch. And I can never know when some recollection of your past may not illumine the present moment. Oh, that past life of yours!—it fills me with absolute terror. I may be beside you, I feel my whole being permeated with the rapture which comes to me at certain moments from your mere presence, I caress you, I talk to you, listen to you, abandon myself utterly to your charm. Suddenly a thought will strike me cold: what if I, all unwittingly, should have evoked in her memory the ghost or some sensation felt once before, some pale phantom of the days long past? Never could I describe to you what I suffer. The glow which gave me an illusory feeling of community of soul between us is suddenly extinguished. You become remote, inaccessible; I am left alone in horrible solitude. Ten, twenty months of intimacy are as if they had never been—you are as much of a stranger as in the days before you loved me."

The Artist then read Ippolita's linked words in response to Giorgio's attempt to repair the wounds of their relationship: *"Dissection presupposes a corpse."*

He looked like he had just swallowed the last bite of a gluttonous meal as he waited for my reaction. I agreed D'Annunzio's writing was clever and descriptive. However, Giorgio's need to possess Ippolita to the point of controlling her every thought was harmful. The ending of the book verified that Giorgio's possessive "love" for Ippolita was very unhealthy indeed, as they "locked in that fierce embrace."

The Artist rose up, straightened his posture and said enthusiastically, "These words, these ideas are from a genius! He has lived these things and he knows the pieces of the man-woman puzzle like no one else. His hyperactive imagination has transformed the ordinary into the epic. I love D'Annunzio!"

I thought D'Annunzio was writing about himself or, more likely, his fanaticized self. It revealed his insecurity about love, his fear of giving himself deeply to a woman and his inability to focus on the lover he was with. I finally made a comment about D'Annunzio: *"A man who has continuous feelings and thoughts of others while making love has loved too many and can no longer truly love at all".*

Our relationship changed significantly during the following months. I was not the stranger with whom he merely wanted to have impersonal sex. I regularly confronted his self-centered philosophy. I asked for his open heart and he gave as much as he could, for as long as he was able to do so within the limitations of his philosophy of life.

He occasionally let me into his vulnerable self and treated me humanely. He shared his thoughts about things like the vastness of human loneliness inherent in our gigantic, cold universe and various ways he could capture these concepts in paint.

One night, we were sitting on the rooftop of his studio absorbing the beauty of the clear night. He mused how the night sky became a lonely place when the Greek gods stopped racing their chariots of living stars. Did the streetlights chase them away? His mind produced a continuous stream of unique thoughts about whatever part of life stood before him.

Another night, we discussed sex, cleanliness and the tastes of each other's bodies. He was Italian; he could talk to a woman. The Artist explained how cleanliness and sexiness are closely connected. A woman or a man who clean themselves frequently can bring their partner to arousal quicker and longer. Smells and sex were partners. "Use the bidet, wash all of you, then use perfume, scented soaps and powders. After you make love, take a shower and use perfume. Then go back to bed fresh and you may be surprised at the renewed energy of your lover. Many French girls are good at this part of the sexual dance. If you smell good and taste good, your lover will always notice and will seek the most intimate and pleasurable sex with you. It is important to remember what I have told you."

There were occasions when he cried in my arms. He was exceedingly homesick for Italy, his family and the joys of Italian life. He would put his arms around me, lowering his head and cuddling with me like a little boy. He deeply missed his mother. He felt guilt from not loving her enough when she gave him so much. He realized he had lost the chance to show his love and it hurt him terribly. Giving himself to others, even those he loved, was not his strongest quality.

During these moments, I believed I had all of him: his body, his heart and his soul. His verbosity and chaotic masculinity were tamed as he tenderly opened himself and melted into me. The scent of his body and the odor of the paint became the smell of the Artist. We would fall into peaceful sleep, quietly holding each other in a lover's embrace. My heart sang; and when he was vulnerable, I thought of him as a boy and me as his mother.

However, after sharing intimacies and openness and making me feel loved, he would confuse me by becoming cold, distant and aggressive. Too much intimacy created a need in him to emotionally withdraw. His vulnerability could not be left exposed for very long; soon he took it away by closing his heart. Sometimes I wondered if he used our temporary intimacy and openness as a ritual to put him into a mood for painting in his sensitive style.

Our days were spent making love and having interesting discussions, hyphenated with periods of emotional and physical separation. He produced a significant volume of paintings and I finished my baccalaureate courses at the Sorbonne and prepared for post-baccalaureate study.

It was hard to compare our first days of lovemaking with our ongoing love affair thereafter. In some respects, I agreed that romance with a new person was like a drug, an overwhelming experience which often made other sexual and romantic experiences pale in comparison. I could see his wide-open blue eyes as he took me on the table. I could feel the heat of water, smell the scent of the soap and the clutch of his grip on my breast in the hot shower. Those passionate moments would remain as a part of leaving my innocence behind. They were indelibly etched into my heart and mind.

As a man, the Artist was neither the panther nor the unicorn. He struggled like everyone. He wasn't bigger, happier or stronger than the rest of us. He didn't roar like a lion but, more often than our neighbors liked, I could make him scream in Italian ecstasy. We didn't make love on the table and we didn't lock our open eyes during lovemaking again; the eye connection was for sex with strangers, not for a woman he knew. Our relationship did grow in other ways. We learned to appreciate each other's strengths and to support each other but, I also began to see through his facade to a lesser man hidden behind.

We constantly jousted about Italy versus France. It could be about football, politics, wine, food, women, Paris versus Rome—anything. For him, Italy was the center of life and the source of everything in the world he cared about. He lived in Paris but he made love, ate, drank and thought as an Italian. He hadn't come for the French food or wine. He came to Paris for freedom, for safety and to paint. He came to escape the barbarism and repression of the Mussolini and Nazi fascists but he remained Italian to the core.

Paris was everything to me. There couldn't be a better place. In the mid-twentieth century, Paris was the world leader in philosophy, food and high society. Parisian *haute couture* defined fashion. The Artist and my debates comparing Paris to Italy were amicable and fun. One day he admitted, *"I would agree Paris is the best city in the world, if only it were in Italy!"*

While I wasn't obsessed with the creator-as-little-god philosophy to the degree Gabriele D'Annunzio and the Artist were, I was fascinated by the ways artists were able to capture so much truth, beauty, emotion and imagination in their paintings. I loved how artists conceptualized life through images and colors. It was why I let him take and control me from his first glance into my eyes to the lovemaking on the table and in the shower. I wanted to connect with his creative force. I was there to *touch* the special place that sets the Creator apart from the rest of us. I loved the world about him. It was full of prestigious galas and time with other Creators. I moved from the Boy and his friends drinking beer at soccer games to the Artist and the Parisian art world of dazzle and light. I was only twenty-three years old and I felt like I had arrived! As a young, confident woman, I again pushed forward toward lust, love and danger, ignoring all warning signs, unlike a wise woman would have done.

I often thought of my mother's propensity to worship artists, though she seemed to have the wisdom to keep them at a safe distance, at least in her older years. However, one night, I awoke to a memory of a conversation with my Aunt when I was quite young. She said strange things about my mother, things about a long-past relationship with an artist from another country, a man who possessed the fire of a Latin and became very famous. I thought of her secret life as I looked at my Artist breathing in the bed next to me. Who was her Latin painter? Who was my mother's artist-lover? Was I reliving my mother's life?

I spent most nights and many days with the Artist. While he was painting I carefully respected his creativity by sticking to quiet activities like studying or writing. I waited for him to break off his creative spell to have a coffee, eat lunch, go for a walk or make love. I often watched him in his trance: painting, creating, building layer upon layer of paint without losing his pace or concentration. He could stand there for endless hours, brush in hand, touching the canvas with his visions. I loved these times. I relished my cat's-eye position and honored the outpouring of his genius. He usually dressed the same way when he painted: American Levis, no shirt and feet bare or, during the winter, with old paint-stained sandals and a sweater for the cold. I loved his strong, muscular back. I watched distinct muscles flex as brush strokes filled the canvases. He smoked when he worked. They were American cigarettes, which were expensive and hard to find, but the Artist's American friends were willing to supply his vice. He said smoking centered him, kept his focus and helped him push himself to paint more and create larger works of art.

There I was—watching the live, God-given, creative force D'Annunzio said separated artists, Creators, from common men. I was impressed. I was searching for the source of creativity and why some had it and some did not. How were Creators able to touch the force of creation when it was time to paint or write? Could their gift be lost? Did everyone have a creative gift somewhere deep inside, just waiting to come out?

I wanted to explore the creative gift deeper than simply as an observer or one of the unwashed Creations sent to earth to support the Creator-gods. About six months into our relationship, when things were going well between us and I felt our relationship was stable, I posed a question to him one evening after dinner. It threw the Artist off-center, like when I had challenged D'Annunzio's creator-as-god theory during our second night together.

"Knowing I am not a Creator, could you teach *it* to me? Could you teach me to tap into the creative force within myself so I can paint like you and become a Creator in my own right?"

The Artist was floored by my question and it made him exceptionally nervous. He reached for the grappa and lit a cigarette, as he always did when he was confused or frustrated. His face became distorted as he uncomfortably contemplated the possibility of an artist transferring his precious gift of creation to another person, to a non-Creator, to me. He downed the grappa and poured another.

"No, no, it can't be done. As Cezanne said, 'Painting is something you do with your balls!' You have no balls! You are either born with the creative gift or you are not. I started painting as a child; I learned to paint when I learned to speak, walk and run. How could you possibly begin to acquire these skills as a twenty-three year-old woman? It is impossible. You can't travel through the stages of mental and emotional development necessary to become a Creator and you can't jump in and expect to instantly become something you are not."

He resisted and resisted the question. He was incensed; he was outraged. It was as if a Catholic worshipper asked the priest to teach him to pray directly to God without having to go through the Pope and his emissaries. The Artist was the gifted one, he was different, special, and he was the High Priest of Creation, the Lord of Paintings. I was to honor him, not try to take his glory for mine.

"First of all," he said, "to be an artist, you must be able to 'see' differently than non-Creators see. When you were walking up to my studio today, did you notice the flower box on the left of the building? Did you see the flowers, the dirt, the newly sprouting weeds and the worn wood sides of the box that are cracked in two places? Did you see the rusted trowel in the left corner with a peeling red handle and the caked mud on the blade? No, you didn't 'see' them—you walked right by as you headed to my door, missing the opportunity to observe a special object of art. If I asked you to describe the flower box, you couldn't do it, could you? You probably didn't see it at all.

"When I walk up to the door, I see that flower box. When I am sleeping, I see that flower box. When I want to paint, the image of that flower box and hundreds of other images are in my mind, ready to be sketched and painted whenever I choose. I can 'see' the flower box right now, can you? No, your vision is not the same as mine. How could I possibly teach you to *see*?

"In fact," he went on, "I don't even see in the same colors or shapes as you. Why are my Parisian trees blue? Why are my animals and people configured in ways you cannot imagine? I truly see them that way. I paint what I see and how I see. You think I am creating, while I am actually duplicating the 'real' visions in my brain. I see ex-lovers flying apart in pieces. I saw and felt the pain of the unicorn before I painted him. I saw my mother ascending into heaven and knew the desperation of begging God for her life on my knees and the disappointment of my unanswered prayers. I virtually felt God's abandonment of the people and the world when I painted those sacrosanct windows emitting the lonely, rose- colored light. How could I teach you to see images as an artist sees them, to bring life and your imagination to the brush? How could you learn to bring life into your mind's eye and then brush it onto canvas through your own style? How can you paint images you don't see in your mind or feel in your heart? Impossible!

"You are interfering in a special area of my life where you have no business," he shouted after his second glass of grappa. "You are crazy, *tu sei pazzo*! It is disrespectful; you want to take my power for your own."

I knew to temporarily back off as he became agitated. When there was a sensitive issue I wanted him to deal with seriously, I knew to wait and let his thoughts work their way back naturally.

Two days later he returned to the possibility of one giving the creative gift to another. He was still resisting the idea but he was curious. How could it be done? It could take years—a master-pupil training program—but he knew I wasn't proposing years or a painting school. I wanted to learn how to create quickly and I wanted him to give the secret to me now, as a gift.

I explained how it would be similar to the molding of the classless Cockney woman, Eliza Doolittle, in *Pygmalion,* or the ivory Galatea in Ovid's *Metamorphoses*, bringing my dead, creative self to life through his loving attention. "You could teach me, like Professor Higgins!"

A week passed. The Artist decided it might be fun to give it a try. I had watched him paint, so I understood his style but none of his thoughts during his "holy" time. He created alone even when I was standing right behind him. *The piece of the puzzle I didn't understand was where the creative magic was hidden and how to bring it out.*

He was working on a complex image with many colors and a difficult structure. On a second easel there was a nearly blank canvas but for some penciled sketches which were unclear from where I sat. When the Artist finished applying the last color to his work, he turned and said, "Come here."

Then and there we began the experiment, his attempt to gift to me the ability to create inspired art. I was a little nervous but ready to proceed. He came behind me and firmly held my two wrists. He rocked me back and forth a few times like we were dancing a waltz.

He put the paintbrush in my right hand. The familiar smells of the paint and the cleaning fluids were strongest there, in the core of his creating area. He spoke in a gentle manner: "Relax, open up, let your mind go where it will go, give up control, you cannot make this happen—creating has to flow out of you, it must come naturally. What do you see? Look, really look. See with your mind and soul!"

Boats of the Luxembourg Gardens

To the right of the easel there was a photo of a cart full of the little boats children sail in the Paris ponds of the Luxembourg

Gardens and the Tuileries. Their bright sails were patched and the wooden hulls were scraped and worn. The guide sticks were stacked in neat order on the wagon used to bring them in and out of the park each day. Behind the wagon full of boats and sticks, there was a shimmering, round pond with ducks floating peacefully. He had drawn a preliminary pencil sketch on the canvas to make it easier to paint. It was a typical Parisian scene; I had watched these boats all my life and played with them as a young girl. What a perfect subject for learning to paint, a subject I knew so well.

As he guided my hand holding the brush from the color palate to the canvas, he spoke of form, color and light. "Look! *See* the colors. Absorb the exquisite patterns of light and form; invest your inner self. Watch how the water reflects and changes the pure images into art. God is an Impressionist! Monet only documented the beauty you see reflected in every pond, and he is considered a master. There is the creative genius you seek. It is right there in front of you."

He gave me more insight: "Notice the duck's neck; it is bent behind and resting on his back—he is asleep. Look at the vivid colors of the sails and the varied colors of the patches. During sail mending, there was no effort to coordinate the colors or patterns of the original sails and the patches. The randomness has created a more interesting image than if the patches were matched. Touch the rough, distinct stitching and the random symmetry with your eyes. It is lovely. It is perfect within its imperfections. It is like life because it is life. There is a master painting locked inside these little boats; just find it and let it out!"

He encouraged me with his tender voice. "Let it happen. Stay focused on the task. Creating will be automatic when you put yourself into the special mental and emotional place where it occurs. Come, we can do it together."

We painted and painted; it could have gone on all night. However, no magical feeling of creativity rose in me. I enjoyed having his body touching mine. I loved his attention as he tried to teach me to paint but I didn't find the holy grail of creation. I agreed with the Artist's first impression, it was hopeless; "it" could not be gifted from a Creator to a Creation. I didn't have it and never would. It was like an illiterate trying to read. We finished about half of the painting before I cried, *"Basta, basta—enough!"*

The Artist and I followed our normal routine of eating, drinking, lovemaking and sleeping. However, I awoke in the early morning darkness and silently climbed out of bed into the night. I could get up without the Artist waking; he slept like a bear in hibernation.

Using a small light, I spent hours completing the painting of the little boats in the pond. It was a warm night, so I wore only French panties. My breasts were free from bra or shirt and paint spattered on them as I worked.

As the sun rose, I finished. I didn't have the Artist's arms around me, his guiding hands, or his encouraging words, but I painted the rest of it—all by myself. I went to bed with the paint stains still on me. The corner where I worked was a mess but I felt satisfied and slept soundly for a couple of hours before we woke.

The Artist made cappuccinos. He spent time looking at my painting, nodding in approval and amusement. He even said it was good. He was kind enough to avoid saying it wasn't great, but I already knew.

While I thoroughly enjoyed myself, I didn't become a Creator-artist-god. That night became a milestone in our discussions about gifting creativity. We laughed at ourselves, a healthy sign that this issue ceased to be a negative. My little painting sat near the window, out of the way of his masterpieces. My experiment ended my girlish dream of becoming a famous artist.

I continued to enjoy watching the Artist paint, but I was more interested in watching him and his body than the methods he used to produce paintings. I decided to seek my own way, to pursue my own creative gifts, and leave painting to the Artist.

I noticed something of importance from our attempt at giving the creation gift: as much as he sincerely tried, the Artist was not capable of giving that gift. He could not be like Aphrodite; he could not breathe the creative gift into the dead, ivory statue of my creativity. He proved that he was not *truly* godlike, that he was a man, not even a demi-god. Only God could give the gift of creation, and God had not chosen to give this particular gift to me. I also concluded that *creating is an active verb; many "see" yet few have the will, the talent or the commitment to act, to create their unique visions in paint or word.*

One of my favorite days with the Artist was a picnic on the exquisite grounds of the Palais Royal. The Artist did the food preparation, as he did for all of our meals. We ate prosciutto and mozzarella cheese sandwiches on foccacia bread, fresh tomatoes with basil and garlic. We drank a bottle of Chianti and another of sparkling water: a simple Italian lunch. He brought real wine glasses and a red-and-white checkered table cloth, which we spread on two chairs to create a table for our feast.

Everything about the setting was superb. The crisp air smelled of deep fall. Leaves gently fell from the perfectly pruned trees and lightly landed in the still water of the ponds, causing small ripples in the water's surface. Rose bushes guarded us with their thorny branches and richly scented flowers. The Artist pointed to two sparrows—splashing, kissing and full of joy—and we watched them dance in silence. Our décor was rows of proud trees. The warm sun gave us light, and the cascading water and cooing pigeons provided a symphony. The splashing love birds contributed to the pleasant ambiance. The sparrows served as companions and provided a special show for our exceptionally private lunch.

The Artist was in a particularly good mood. He was attentive and full of plans and ideas. As he spoke, he would touch my hair, pushing a lock out of my face, and hold my hand. Once he softly wiped a crumb of bread from my mouth with the back of his hand. A considerable amount of our conversation was about my life and my plans. His sincere interest in me was encouraging and flattering; he seemed to care and treated me as a person rather than as a mute sounding board for his proclamations of self-aggrandizement.

Nothing spectacular happened; it was just a day when we took the time for each other and didn't rush anything. It was a moment when two people sat, ate, drank and loved in a Paris afternoon.

At the end of the meal, he held my face with both hands and kissed me for a long time. I kissed him back. When we stopped kissing, he hugged me tightly and then kissed me again. We were curled up with our hearts together. These circumstances brought out the best in him; he blossomed when life was simple and clear and there were no critics or fans to interrupt his focus.

The clock struck four and we slowly, reluctantly packed up the remains of our lunch and took a last drink of wine. We walked home silently, contently, arm in arm, passing over cobblestoned streets, crossing over bridges, and musing at passersby as they were amused by us. The Artist drew more attention than I. People wondered--who was this longhaired Italian man wearing an open black shirt; a movie star, a famous writer, or an artist? But none recognized him, though many seemed to want to.

Café Talk: The End of the Day

1945. The *day cooled and Christine and the American grew tired. Christine stopped speaking for a moment as she changed from one time period to another. She shifted to the Luxembourg Gardens at a later time when she again visited the fountains.*

"Two months after Occupation, I went to the Medici Fountains alone one evening. My memories were kinder there than in most of Paris, softened by forgiveness, time, the gently flowing water and joyful birds. After I ate and finished a demi-liter of white wine from Orvieto, the Artist's favorite white wine, I drifted away, down into the shimmering, dark water—into a dream of emptiness and peace, as if the war hadn't happened. Even the boxing pigeons, the passing clouds and the cool air couldn't keep me in the present. I slipped into a trance as I disconnected from my physical being. When I awoke, it was to almost total darkness. I had been sitting for a long time.

"I could only vaguely see the stone lovers, Galatea and Acis, in the darkness, held forever in their sensuous marble pose. Galatea's body leaned back into the lap of Acis, the Sicilian Sheppard; her bare breasts and smooth stomach shining milk-white in the dimming light. They held a pose of peacefulness flowing from their lovemaking. What beauty. What perfection of a woman and a man. What art. What love!

"Reluctantly, I looked up to the dark shadow of the brute Cyclops Polyphemus directly over them. He was even more threatening in the dark. Before jealousy took over this brutal, primitive monster, Polyphemus fell deeply in love with Galatea and believed she loved him too. His obsession with writing love poems to her displaced his duties. Love transformed him into a musician, singing love songs and playing his pipe with a hundred reeds. He bragged to Galatea that his father was Poseidon, the King of the Sea.

"But Galatea didn't love Polyphemus; she loved Acis. Had she deceived Polyphemus and encouraged his love by flirting with him, while

giving her true love to a man? Did her deceit infuriate Polyphemus and drive him to kill? When Polyphemus discovered them together, he was turned into a murderous beast by jealous envy. It was the eternal triangle, perfectly set for disaster.

"The three sculptured figures in the Medici Fountain were captured at the last minute before Polyphemus killed Acis in a jealous rage. I knew, from my studies of Greek Mythology and Homer, that Polyphemus would have his one eye poked out by Odysseus in an act of trickery. What drama the Greek gods lived! Their mythological stories were full of love, revenge, murder, ego, boasting and force.

"I thought back to my many visits to this fountain with my father, the Boy, the Artist, my Husband, the German, or alone. I always came back here. It was always a place to think and a place to share. I was tired but happy. I felt the process of recovery and forgiveness working on my soul."

The American broke the spell of the Medici Fountain by asking a random question floating in his mind: *"Do you think your mother's lover was Picasso?"* Christine shrugged her shoulders, tilted her head, puckered her lips, raised her eyebrows and opened her hands and arms in a maybe-yes, maybe-no manner.

The American and Christine walked a while together and then parted for the day. With each new story, with each page of the American's notes, they became closer and more intellectually connected. Each time that she gave him her honest self, he stepped deeper into complete amazement and awe of her. The more she opened herself to him, the more Christine became aware she was experiencing a new form of intimacy; a previously unknown dimension of love. In the continuum of love, they skipped the physical stages and landed in a wonderful connection of the mind, heart and soul.

The next time they met, it was a windy day. Leaves and debris were flying around the streets and Parisians were leaning into the wind to stay on their feet as they moved from place to place. Christine was in a pensive mood when she continued her *story.* "*Our relationship changed when we started into our 'second-year relationship' and our individual personalities, strengths and weaknesses began to bring conflict into our lives.*"

Foolishness and Appropriation

My relationship problems with the Artist escalated after we spent the four seasons together. We knew each other well, maybe too well. We loved without really loving. There were problems; his negative philosophy of superiority resurfaced. My criticisms were increasingly directed toward his need to present himself as someone he was not, and his paintings were looking quite similar to the copies of Van Gogh and Picasso paintings hanging in his studio.

I tried to understand him, but he put continuous limitations and restrictions on our relationship. I had a place and he expected me to keep it; I was to honor his creativity by not interfering in this core part of his life. I was to support him in practical matters and do most of the housework other than cooking. His earlier words rang true; it seemed to be impossible for him to love a real person, to love me. His worldview separated him from others and he retreated into his creative hermitage, leaving me outside. He loved himself first, other Creators second, and a real woman like me last. My resentment was building up.

He painted his past lovers in a repeated sequence. In the early stages of their relationships, the women appeared soft and feminine, with flowing curves and gentle, appealing colors. As these relationships unraveled, their images were twisted, tortured and dismembered. Feminine curves became sharp angles of twisted breasts, asymmetrical hips and inflated lips. Former girlfriends were drawn-and-quartered like traitors to the king, their exaggerated and mutilated body parts flying everywhere in total disarray across the canvas, or were attached to places where they did not belong. The bold colors of their clothes and missing buttons depicted anger and disappointment.

The Artist's self-absorbed perception of life and volatile character made him behave erratically and unpredictably. I

90

complained. I told him it was too difficult to *not know* who he was going to be on any given day; would I wake up with Picasso or Van Gogh? His inconsistent personality was driving me crazy!

I pushed further. I dared to comment about his new style of painting. I thought he was deviating too far from the style that had made him successful. His new style was not well-received by his fans or critics, and some of his paintings looked like those of other artists. He responded strongly, directly and negatively.

"Sometimes I do awake as Picasso, sometimes Van Gogh, and sometimes someone else. Sometimes I see with my eyes and sometimes I see with my feelings; sometimes with my heart and sometimes with my soul. I am not a single-dimensional man. I am not your Boy who lived on one boring level and didn't want to see the life happening around him. I change often to become who I am, when I am, where I am in the moment or the day. I live and paint what I see and I am not changing. Don't put me somewhere I don't want to be or try to make me someone I am not. Don't try to hold me to patterns or techniques you think should be my style. My creations come from a place I obviously cannot share with you. They come from inside me and from the artists who have preceded me. Don't use your narrow vision to try to understand who I am and what I create. It won't work—you can't 'see.' Stop judging me and my art!"

The Artist walked to the other side of the room and shuffled through some papers. He pulled out a sheet with a poignant, self-describing poem by Charles Baudelaire, a Bohemian writer from the century before. The Artist tossed it at me and said, "Read this, maybe you will understand."

> *I am the wound and the knife!*
> *I am the blow and the cheek!*
> *I am the limbs and the rack,*
> *Both the victim and the torturer!*

I ignored his tantrum, but I liked the poem. I was emotionally involved and tried to hold on too hard. I wanted him to love me as I needed to be loved. *In the dance of love, his pulling back drove me to pursue him more intensely.*

So, one day I told him I loved him; I loved him as an Artist and as a man. I knew I was giving him what I wanted in return, but I couldn't stop myself. He glared at me and responded quickly, "Why did you say this to me? Why do you want to spoil everything?"

I said, "Picasso and Van Gogh each live in only one dimension. Picasso doesn't paint with Van Gogh's deep sensitivity and humanness; Picasso has become all bravado with his animal-like male aggression; the bullfighter. Van Gogh was not the kind of man Picasso is; his work doesn't reveal the courage or the complex insights into mankind as those reflected in Picasso's *Guernica,* but he understood beauty and truth. You have the power of both sensitivity and masculinity. No one else is a complete man, and that is why I love you!"

He was so thrown off by my "I love you" that he didn't hear the compliments I gave him. He furled his forehead and squinted in frustration. He was not ready to hear those words, and certainly he was not going to say them back to me.

I was learning that love wasn't what he wanted; he wanted something else. Maybe he was already beginning to separate from me when I hit him with those three words, I don't know, but it was a mistake. It was part of my leftover little-girl syndrome; following the hope of love even when it conflicted with reality. I wanted something not there, something I hoped I could create over time. I was still becoming a woman, but this error and my insecurities proved I hadn't fully arrived.

My words of love triggered a male signal, a warning telling him to quickly rebuild his emotional walls and put space between us. He ran and ran fast. I don't know if he felt trapped, afraid or, since he had conquered me as a woman and taken what he wanted, I was a now burden to him.

His reaction directly conflicted with the female signals I felt. After one year, I wanted to become closer, more emotionally involved, and move our relationship forward. I wanted a commitment of fidelity and love and was having unfounded dreams of marriage.

The three little words opened a giant schism between us. He was afraid in a male way I couldn't understand. I was frustrated and confused; I needed help.

Café Talk: Help from Father Jean

1945. *The wind died down and it became very still. The waiter brought tap water to the table and asked if they needed anything else. Christine gave him the first answer the French typically give to any question: "no." The American quickly handed him money and thanked him. Then Christine changed her mind. She called the waiter back and asked for water with gas.*

Christine asked the American for his opinion regarding the mechanisms of love, to give his view the connections between a man's and a woman's body, mind, heart and soul. To Christine, these four components were one continuous flow of energy between the emotional and physical workings of love. When she gave her body, she also gave her heart, her mind and her soul; it was a complete package. She asked the American if, as a man, he felt the same way, or were the dimensions of love compartmentalized and disconnected from one another?

This was difficult for the American. He read and wrote about all-encompassing love which joined two people together as one but he had never experienced such love. He had often compartmentalized love by only giving his body. Sometimes he gave his heart, rarer still he shared his mind, but he never gave his soul to another. The thought of such complete intimacy made him nervous. A feeling of suffocating came over him as he related to the Artist's reaction to her words of "I love you".

Christine pressed further. "If a man knows me intimately, our bodies having joined deeply—his love is flowing in me—why wouldn't he want our connection to go beyond sexual pleasure to reach this all-encompassing level of intimacy? Why would you want to hold back on love and experience only a part of love?"

The American had nothing to say. Christine opened questions for which he did not have answers. Their conversation turned to other things.

Christine and the American spoke of Father Jean frequently since he had introduced them, but she had a new story to tell. "You know

Father Jean is a spiritual and intellectual giant who can and will speak on any subject imaginable. His knowledge of current and historic events and world leaders is only exceeded by his spiritual consciousness, through which his thoughts flow. Father Jean's knowledge and deep understanding of right and wrong allow him to see life differently than most. He knows my life from many sides. He often says he loves me like a daughter.

"When I have been confused, concerned or feeling guilty, I have gone to Father Jean for guidance, wise counsel, and to make my version of a confession. My visits usually followed my leap into behavior not traditionally acceptable to the Church, usually something the Church considered immoral. Regardless of what I had done, Father Jean's patience, understanding and love always permeated the words he spoke and the advice he gave. He didn't waver in his loving support. However, without criticizing me, he was also careful not to condone behavior outside the scope of his moral values.

"I decided to seek Father Jean's loving help about my relationship with the Artist. I had discussed the Boy with Father Jean and he was nonjudgmental; he had learned the lessons of Jesus well.

"When we met, I told him everything. I particularly wanted his opinions of the D'Annunzio/Artist's creator-as-god philosophy, and if it was possible to have a successful romantic relationship with someone who believed such things.

"Father Jean knew I was involved in something significant because he hadn't seen me for some time. My absence from church was a signal I was wandering off on a path of my own, determining my own moral standards, making my own life choices, and not looking to God for guidance. He was right; it seemed he was always right. I thought I was smart enough and old enough to make decisions based on my own desires and opinions, but that proved to be untrue, and I was in deep emotional trouble as a result."

The Moment of Truth

Father Jean listened to my story and my frustrations. He asked if the Artist and I would visit him together. I told him yes, we would come. The Artist learned respect for priests from his mother, and he knew how important Father Jean was in my life.

On what began as a sunny afternoon, the Artist and I walked to Saint Julien to meet with Father Jean. We waited in the old church basement. It was cool and smelled of old stones set there for a thousand years.

Icon in St. Julien le Pauvre

96

Christian icons adorned the walls as they did in the church above. As a child, this basement was my Sunday morning home while my parents attended Mass. We were supposed to learn about God, Jesus and the church, but we mostly learned about mischief and pranks. It was a wonderful time of life. I loved this basement.

The Artist spoke of how Saint Julien le Pauvre was built upon Roman stones, earth and ruins. He felt comfortable there, like he owned the place. He leaned back in his chair thinking this meeting was going to be easy and relaxed; a walk in the park.

While the Artist was speaking of Italy, my eyes turned upward to the small ventilation window at the top of the basement wall. I watched a group of tiny brown and red sparrows flitting about, singing and dancing to the joy of life's music. My gaze and focus wandered off, through the little window, as it did when the Boy first watched me long ago, before I started on my journey of discovery, romance and lust.

The meeting with Father Jean was one of the most interesting human interactions I have witnessed. Unlike most people in the Artist's life, Father Jean was not intimidated or self-conscious while looking directly into the Artist's seductive blue eyes. On the contrary, it was the Artist who quickly fell off his mark as Father Jean focused on him. Though he was a short, roundish, older man, Father Jean's power clearly exceeded that of the young Artist as he took immediate charge of the conversation and didn't let go.

Because Father Jean lived in Rome during an assignment to the Vatican, he spoke fluent Italian and could switch back and forth between French and Italian at will. When he wanted to dangle thoughts for the Artist to contemplate, he spoke in French. Whenever he pressed a point, he spoke in Italian.

Beginning in French, Father Jean acknowledged the magnificence of human creativity and the enlightened genius of some artists. He granted that, at its finest, the act of creating gives humans insight into the Kingdom of Heaven to a greater degree than most other human actions. The ability to create new beauty and truth was one of the greatest blessings God gave to mankind.

"Think of it, it is a miracle. Humans can read books written hundreds or thousands of years ago and, in doing so, share knowledge across time and across the lands from stranger to stranger. Books have been translated into the different tongues of millions of people around the world. Look at the Holy Bible. It has been printed more than any book and has been read by humans all around the world for thousands of years.

"Authors build upon the knowledge of their ancestors. We know the past through their stories. We have history because authors wrote it down and painters painted it. Have you thought about this incredible phenomenon? Can you imagine the human condition without the knowledge and art we inherited from our ancestors? Can you imagine the world without the Bible, without the Sistine Chapel?" asked Father Jean, who was not looking for an answer.

"Some special humans are destined to create beauty and truth which has not existed before: a painting, a novel, a song. They leave us their creations, vast amounts of knowledge and joy. It is like this old church built upon one church and then another and another. It is a magnificent evolution. I have the greatest respect for the ability of humans who create.

"In comparison, the fate of other living creatures is mostly predetermined; birds instinctively migrate to the same place every year, fish swim up the same stream to spawn, plants reach to the sun for light and dig in the earth for water. Dogs know nothing of their ancestors, and neither do cats, whales or birds. They are able to leave offspring but they cannot create or pass to the future knowledge of art, music, writing, history or anything for future generations of dogs, birds and cats. With the death of each animal, most of its learned knowledge, experience and behavior are lost. Human creativity separates us from the plants, the stones and the animals. *Only humans paint, and we have been painting for a long time; only humans write music, and we have been singing for a long time; only humans create stories to pass from generation to generation, and we have been telling stories for a long time.*

"I like to think about our ability to create from this perspective; in the entire world--and as far as we know in the entire universe--only humans on Earth have been given the gift of creating. The gift of creating is the way in which we were created in God's image.

"You are among the very blessed. Through your eyes and the talent of your brush, you create beautiful art. Few people have even one round of applause for what they have created. You have continuous applause and recognition and, on top of this recognition, the beautiful and precious Christine cares for you deeply. You are a very lucky man."

The Artist began to relax. I could see by the way he was sitting that he believed Father Jean was going to support D'Annunzio's philosophy of artistic superiority. I knew he was thinking: Yes, *I have it, I have the creative gift and few others can share it with me!* He was smiling like a cat, agreeing, basking in the perfect sense of it, and letting his guard drop further and further. I knew he thought of himself as the victor, as if Paris was Lutetia and the Romans were back in control.

He missed the Trojan horse Father Jean ingeniously hid in the conversation, a force of logic about to trounce the core of the Artist's beliefs of self-importance, superiority and the self-anointing of Creators as deities.

Father Jean's crooked spine seemed to straighten and he became taller as he switched languages and began speaking in Italian. He touched the fingertips of his right hand together and rocked his hand toward the Artist as he spoke. It was a movement every Italian grandmother used to drive her point home.

Father Jean quickly debunked D'Annunzio's assertion that man became God simply by creating things. "Man cannot become God," Father Jean said. "Never!" He was strong, to the point and left no room for debate. The Artist retreated from his air of overconfidence as Father Jean began to decimate the artist-as-god philosophy as blasphemy.

"Because you think you have done everything for yourself, you have excluded God. Self-love is the Devil's trick. It is the tool he uses to find your weaknesses; it is the probe he uses to find your price. He wants your soul and he will briefly make you a 'demi-god' to get it. Be careful, my son, you are in dangerous territory! You are hanging on the precipice of hell!"

The Artist looked as if he was going to say something in protest, but Father Jean held up his hand and said, "You don't have to say anything, I know you.

"When schoolchildren and the starstruck Christine applaud your art, you think you have ascended into D'Annunzio's creator-deity status, but God is laughing at you! I have studied your Gabriele D'Annunzio and Nietzsche before him. You all miss the point when you proclaim the greatness of your achievements and say in your heart, 'Look at me, I am great. I am God!' Your creative gifts have only been lent to you by God; you don't own them.

"No matter what you create or how much you think you know, you will not become God. Can you create a leaf or a bug? Can you create a rabbit or a lion? How about a rising moon or a setting sun? Can you create a star? How about water? No, you can only create *images*; you can only try to copy God. No man can create as He does, not a single living thing, not even a flea or an ant.

"Your duty is to worship and honor God with your creative works, not to become Him. Your "Creationism" is not a new, self-centered religion where God is replaced by self-appointed Creators, it is not an excuse for self-worship, and it is not a justification for minimizing the importance of other people by driving another false "we/them" wedge between us. Your creative gift is not a license to live an immoral life. Instead, your artistic gift is the best reason to spend your life worshipping God in never-ending thanks.

"You are a man. Be humble in your abilities, not arrogant. Proclaim your creativity as God's gift. God mysteriously created life from clay, water and fire, as you create from oils and solvents. Thank God, obey God, worship God, but don't try to become God. Don't try to gain God's knowledge beyond what He wants you to know and what has been determined to be in our dominion.

"Man is a tool God uses to produce creations on earth. When man creates beauty in humble worship of God, he becomes closer to Him and creates the finest beauty and the wisest words imaginable. It is amazing! Celebrate it!

"Do you know love? You are Italian, a people who know love as well as anyone. But do you know the true definition of love? *Love is what you do to bring another person closer to God.*"

At the height of his admonishment, Father Jean was shaking his finger back and forth at the Artist. Later, the Artist told me that movement was exactly what his mother used to do when he met her disapproval. Father Jean knew the Italian language and he knew how to "speak" in Italian hands.

Father Jean paused and looked directly at the Artist, pushing back against those blue eyes that intimidated others. "Are you really from Florence? True? *Vero?*" he asked. "I know the tones and accents of the Italian language quite well. Many holy men and mentors of the Church are from Florence, and I have known several of them as close friends and associates for years. There is something else in your Italian, a mountain clip I think. Where are you from, exactly?"

The Artist stiffened and didn't respond immediately. "Well, I am from the Florence area; I lived close to Florence. I was born in a hospital in Florence because my mother was older and there was some fear of problems with my birth. So I have a right to say I am from Florence."

Father Jean knew the Artist was speaking less than the truth. "Where was your home? Where would you have been born if you were born at home like everyone else?"

There was no escape. The Artist glanced at me sheepishly. He had to reveal the false impression he gave to me, my Aunt, the press, and to everyone else with whom he had spoken of his Italian heritage. "I am from mountains near Fiesole," he answered softly in a declaration of self-condemnation as if he were from Sicily. "My family farms the hills. We are country people, but I was able to escape the milking, the picking and the planting through my art." It was the end of the Artist's contribution to the meeting with Father Jean.

I was shocked. I did not know the Artist was like D'Annunzio in this attribute as well, someone who could easily lie and would do anything to promote himself and his art, even change his hometown. *He isn't even Florentine.* His grand claims to be the next link in the continuum of great Italian masters of art were severely compromised by this lie.

I felt a chill run down my back. I didn't really know this man from the hills outside of Fiesole. He was not the man from a distinguished Florentine family at all. He was a fraud and a farmer. A feeling of disappointment clouded over me.

Father Jean firmly said to the Artist, "While you are able to 'see' many things in life, I am afraid you are also blind in many ways. We may miss what you see as an artist, the patterns, the colors and the light, but each person has gifts and each has blind spots. You are missing precious sources of life and love laying unseen right in front of you. Now go. Drop down on your knees and thank God for the gifts you have been given. Find a better way to live your life than the shallow, immoral path you are walking. Ask God for forgiveness. And honor Christine!"

The humbled Artist and I left the church together, but outside the door he said he had to go. There was a slight rain and a chill in the air; a significant change in the weather since we'd gone down into the basement. He turned right and I left. We walked separately toward our own lives, not on a single path leading toward one life together.

We returned to the studio at separate times later in the night, though he arrived first. Except for a nod and a hello when I walked in the door, he didn't speak and neither did I. We didn't reflect back on Father Jean's words and didn't discuss the philosophy of D'Annunzio or the existence of God. We didn't make love. He didn't paint. We slept in the same bed but we faced opposite directions; walls were growing between us, separating our hearts. He was fighting with his demons. Later I heard him crying, but I left him alone. I didn't hold him. I pretended I was asleep and stayed where I was, turned away from him. I knew he wanted his mother but she was gone, and at that moment, so was I.

It was midafternoon before we discussed the conversation in the church basement the day before. The Artist was contemplative. I was expecting him to begin with hostility, but he gave resignation. I prepared for attack but found him in retreat. I thought he would be fuming but he was quiet. His lack of hostility encouraged me to leap forward as I tended to do.

I asked him if we could bring the real God into our lives and our relationship. I thought God could fill the void between us and bring us to a holy place. I wanted a spiritual center to our relationship, not as we were and not centered on self-interest, servitude or ego.

It was another mistake to ask him to seek God's help. It was like telling him I loved him. Father Jean and Gabriele D'Annunzio were battling in his mind. My question prompted a quick resolution to the conflict and gave D'Annunzio the victory. He stopped his pensiveness and snapped back into his aggressive self.

"Your Father Jean is a sanctimonious man! He wouldn't even let me speak. He assumed he figured me out and didn't let me say a word. It is not right; it isn't what a priest is supposed to do. It is hypocrisy!

"God doesn't care about me, about us or about the world. I don't believe in God. I only believe in myself, my ability to make my life whatever I want through my work, intelligence and dedication. I make my successes and determine how to reach my goals. I do it myself. There is no separate God who is managing my affairs. There is no caring God to beg for favors or forgiveness. There is nothing more than what we have right here and now. There is no heaven in the skies above or hell below. God is a grown-up fantasy; a forest fairy for weak, childlike adults who never grew up. The sooner you understand that there is no God to help you and you have to do it yourself, the better off you will be.

"God doesn't care about our relationship either. What you call a relationship is nothing but lust. Relationships are nature's way of tricking us into reproducing, like salmon swimming upstream to spawn and die. We differ little from animals except in one respect: humans have four seasons to mate and we are always in heat. Where is God? Is God my lust? Is God your lust? Show me God!

"Look at *Le Finestre Desolate e Sconsacrate*. The empty solitude of the deconsecrated church is real; they are spiritually empty even when they are full of people. You know the loneliness I painted. Is it from God? God as you and Father Jean want him to exist would not give us hate, evil, suffering, pain and death, but they are everywhere in his universe. Who needs such a God? I have lost faith in God because God abandoned man from the start. I am my own Messiah, my own Christ!"

I argued back. "I told Father Jean about you and your beliefs. What he knows about you is how I described you. Father Jean was annoyed because he thinks you are disrespectful to me. That is why he denied you an opportunity to argue. You need to listen to what he told you. He was speaking the truth. It was not a debate.

"God isn't a fantasy for the weak; God is the purpose of life! Think of your Catholic upbringing, your family history, your mother. What about love? What about beauty? What about loyalty? What about faithfulness? What about a newborn child, a flower, music? The beautiful things you worship in your *Church of Creativity* are proof of God's gifts, not proof of man's isolation. What about death? Are we simply finished when our bodies fail?"

There was no metamorphosis, no rebirth of the Artist into a believer. Father Jean's words may have temporarily hit their mark, but the Artist deflected them within twenty-four hours by retreating into D'Annunzio denial. It was another stalemate in our relationship. He reached for the grappa and a cigarette. He looked away. There was none of the passion of the lovemaking on the table or in the shower. There wasn't anything much at all. He was steadfastly committed to his beliefs and I was equally strong in mine.

The Artist abandoned God and replaced him with the god in the mirror. He turned his back on his Catholic upbringing when he looked to his reflection instead of the cross for salvation. His final comment was revealing: "Even my mother couldn't convince me God exists, so don't be surprised that you and your priest have failed."

The Artist would never become a great artist. His art was initially good but not as great as the children who sat at his feet, some early critics and I originally thought. Few reach the highest levels of artistic achievement, and the Artist would not be one of them.

He was full of excuses. He blamed others. He hated the critics for saying his work did not keep up with the promise they once saw. He blamed the other shit in his life, the day-to-day things he needed to manage now that his mother was gone. He blamed me. I was thwarting his creativity by smothering him with God and childish love.

The Paris art critics commented how his new paintings were uninspired and didn't live up to his original work. They didn't like his new style. One critic accused the Artist of appropriating the work of other painters, particularly Picasso and Van Gogh. In one scathing article, a critic printed side-by-side comparisons showing the new works of the Artist with corresponding paintings by Picasso and Van Gogh. The similarities were striking and convincing.

When the Artist exhausted his own creativity, he appropriated Picasso and Van Gogh's styles and subject matter in an attempt to achieve recognition and make quick money. It was easy for him to steal, as his only moral compass was himself and the desire to fulfill his own needs. Until the article came out, there were copies of those same Picasso and Van Gogh paintings hanging in his studio. They were gone the day the critic's side-by-side comparison was published.

The Artist protested against these accusations. He feigned outrage. He accused Picasso of routinely stealing other painters' work. "Picasso stole from Gauguin, Goya, Rembrandt and Manet. He admitted using El Greco in his Blue Period. He took their art, twisted it, turned it inside out and reorganized it. When he was finished, he called it his own. Picasso is the greatest art thief of all time. How can I steal from a thief?"

No one listened. The once-friendly critics turned against him. Only my Aunt remained loyal. His fans and the press turned their backs on him. He was finished in Paris. The lights went out in the Palais de Luxembourg and his show was over. New problems were to arise for the Artist and me, troubles that would lead us to different shores of complexity and misfortune.

We quarreled. I asked him if he saw any validity to the critics' accusations. I told him I saw similarities between his new works and the other artists'; I thought it was more like parallel creating, not copying. My eyes looked downward and I said nothing more. He could tell I was no longer convinced he was the sole creator of his art. He lashed out at the critics and then lashed out at me even harder.

He began drinking heavily—more wine and more grappa. He added an American whiskey, Jack Daniels, to his drinking routine, even though he couldn't afford it. He was becoming mean. His pattern of sleeping deeply was broken. He would pace the room at night, smoking, drinking, throwing brushes and tools and cursing everyone. I began spending more time at the university. I stopped watching him paint. He produced nothing of value and destroyed most of his new work in fits of anger. I stayed in cafes late into the night to avoid coming home to his tantrums and abuse.

Our relationship rose out of my love for his creations and the lust of our bodies and fell on both counts. Sexually, he seldom satisfied me; he cared too much about reaching his own satisfaction than to wait for me; my pleasure wasn't his main concern. I tried to explain I needed satisfaction too, that I also wanted the full sexual experience, but he turned away in exasperation. His best response was to say no one else complained. I retorted, none of his girlfriends stayed around very long either and I knew why!

This was not the end of our problems. As I lost faith in him, he sought attention from others to reinforce his tattered self-image. He had sex with at least two women while we were still living together and didn't bother to hide it. One of these women was an old girlfriend leftover from the time when he first moved to Paris. They ran into each other "accidentally" at a café and spent the rest of the day in bed. The next woman was a visitor to his exhibit, a person he hadn't met. She became the next object of his sex-with-strangers obsession and the next subject of a painting. He came home after this encounter with the smells of her perfume and their sex still on his body. He didn't even take a shower before he returned home to me.

When I commented on how his behavior made me sick, he flew into a rage, screamed and picked up my portrait and broke it over the back of the chair where I hid my notes. He screamed at me, "You think like an American prude, not a Frenchwoman. I will tell you what I want, and what every healthy man wants. I want to have sex with every woman I want, whenever I want it."

I was ashamed and humiliated. The Artist created a deep emptiness in me. I experienced the most profound type of loneliness; *the debilitating feeling of being utterly alone while living with someone I once loved and with a person who I hoped once loved me.*

After his new painting style was rejected and he was publicly accused of appropriation, he shut down emotionally. He became more the aggressive and temperamental artist and less of a gentleman. One critic claimed him to be "the worst painter in the world."

The Artist despised reality. His fantasies were breaking down. He began to loathe me for reminding him he was real and not behaving like a man. His destructive behavior further depleted his creative gift and drove me away.

The Artist was too much of a taker and too little of a giver. The logistics of life were impossible for him; he didn't pay his bills and didn't take care of himself. The Artist played at being a man but was not really a man. When life became difficult, he was like a boy who lived at home too long with his hovering mother, which he was.

I also knew myself. Half of my head and half of my heart still belonged to a girl. I still fought with the "demons" of my childhood, like the rejection by my overbearing mother, the lack of physical and emotional affection by my father, and the love I didn't receive from my family. I brought insecurities and weaknesses into the relationship with my irrational behavior, such as blurting out that I loved him when he was clearly not ready for such a proclamation.

I wanted our relationship to be something it could never be, and I continued to live within my fantasies long after the limitations were evident. I should have kept him at a distance and protected myself by holding back a part of my heart. Instead I took the leap with unrestrained enthusiasm. I should not have let him take complete control of me. I crossed only half of the bridge from girlhood to womanhood, still not far enough to have learned how to bring the man out of the boy, and incapable of nurturing another half-mature human into adulthood.

On my last day with him and after reading a particularly blistering review challenging the authenticity of his paintings, the Artist sat at his table crying. "I am finished; no one appreciates my artistic genius." He passed from sorrow to anger to blame, which he heaped on the French critics and their nationalism. "Don't you remember? They completely rejected Van Gogh when he was alive, and they don't understand him to this day. They treated him and his work with contempt. Their rejection led to Van Gogh's suicide. They could not see him and they cannot see me. I am sick of the French!"

In his conflicts and struggles, I hoped he would begin to understand what Father Jean said about God, the gift of creation, and me. But if those thoughts came back to him, he did not reveal them. My momentary reliance on hope reminded me of something my father loved to say: "Hope is not a method."

He looked up, tears on his face, and said, "Please don't think less of me for this." However, in my mind, my bags were packed and I was already out the door. I would not love his body, his creations or his mind again. I knew then, like I knew with the Boy, it was time to go. I was leaving the Artist, crossing to another shore. Late at night when he was finally asleep, I took my notes out of the cushion of the chair and hid them in my suitcase. In the morning, I packed and moved out of the studio. A quote from the Artist's own Gabriele D'Annunzio in *The Triumph of Death* came into my mind: *"All human love must end."*

I focused on my studies and spent more time with my university friends and professors. I started writing for the *Paris Match* magazine, a position I was able to secure through the editor, a good friend of my mother's. My works were well-received. It was time to be without a man determining how I should live my life and what I should think.

The Artist left me with one material gift that I would always love and cherish, no matter what problems were associated with it. He gave me *Le Finestre Desolate e Sconsacrate*, my favorite painting of the church with the godless windows. The buyer for this special painting was a wealthy patron who backed out of the sale after the public accusations of the Artist's appropriation. As I was leaving on our last morning, he handed it to me and said, "Take it. It is worth nothing!"

Café Talk: The Death of Icarus

1945. *Christine looked at the American for a moment or two without speaking, as she paused to crystallize her thoughts. She consulted her private notes.*

The American noted how Christine's feelings for the Artist were erratic; she vacillated from certainty of love to doubt, from blame to acceptance. As a girl-woman, she was enthralled with the idea of love and the glamour of sleeping with a Creator, a "thief of fire" who stole creativity from the gods. She hoped he would make her a Creator too. Their failed relationship reminded him of a Picasso quote: "There is no such thing as love, only proof of love".

"I am afraid I contributed to the Artist's downfall. I upset his philosophy and his D'Annunzio cult of extreme self-aggrandizement. I no longer believed in him or his fantasies, and I eroded his false confidence. In the end, I was his Achilles' heel because I saw through him and I wouldn't live in his delusional world any longer.

"I learned a great deal from the Artist, including the lesson not to fall so easily for the superficial aspects of the worldly life; they are as fleeting as the clouds passing in the sky. I found what was important to me in love and what was not. He helped me become more of a woman, not someone who would need glitz and glamour and accept the unacceptable from a man to get it. I learned I wanted someone with substance and depth in a relationship. I also learned that giving complete control to another person was a characteristic of immaturity, another way to avoid taking responsibility for one's self."

Christine put her head down. The American touched her arm and she gave a little jerk, like being awakened from a dream. "This is not, by far, the most difficult or complex of my stories. There is much more to come, much more." Before she went on with her next story, she wanted to close the circle with the Artist, as she had done with the Boy. They ordered coffee and she went on to describe how the Artist finished.

The Artist: Postscript

My Aunt did a well-researched follow-up article on the Artist's life after he left Paris. As the only critic who defended him, my Aunt remained his friend. She and the Artist exchanged letters when he was living in Los Angeles. The article chronicled the events as he moved away from Italy, from Paris, and from our lives together. My Aunt revealed how far his tragic life fell from the days of near- D'Annunzio-like fame. I read the story with sorrow and understanding.

When the Nazis entered France on their way to Paris, the Artist fled south to avoid the fate of their enemies. He caught the last American ocean liner out of Bordeaux, the S.S. *Manhattan*. Like many before, he fled Europe for America to find freedom and opportunity and rid himself of his past. He desperately wanted to meet people who would appreciate him and pay for his works. He believed they were in the New World. Like the Bohemians, the Artist was always looking for financial support from someone, and Americans were his next target.

On board, the Artist met international wine expert Alexis Lichine, a White Russian and an entrepreneur, who also fled France ahead of the advancing Nazis. Alexis brought his personal wine collection and they shared many bottles of excellent wine during the passage. After becoming good drinking friends, Mr. Lichine offered to help the Artist establish himself in New York. The Artist politely declined, as he was determined to go to Hollywood to meet "movie people."

In California, the Artist ended up painting portraits of bored, rich Los Angeles housewives, with whom he would often have sex. He was taken in by the Southern California culture of the forties: fast women, fast cars and fast living. In the sun and sand, he lost whatever remnants of his soul he had brought across the Atlantic and across the American continent to Hollywood.

The Los Angeles life was eventually too hard on him. The alcohol and deciduous relationships could not desensitize him to the truth: he was not a creative god and not Gabriele D'Annunzio. He became "niente," nothing.

The Artist committed suicide one lonely night on a California beach after taking sleeping pills and guzzling Jack Daniels whiskey. He died smoking a Lucky Strike cigarette; there were burns between his fingers. His was buried in Forrest Lawn Cemetery near Hollywood with other *nearly* famous people who had died in Southern California but were really from someplace else.

Café Talk: A Passage

1945. *"That was the Artist's tragic story—an Italian man who began his life full of creative forces and chose to end it when he failed. It was another sad ending, another lost soul dying alone in Los Angeles."*

The American asked himself if "hoped-for" love was just another way of loving. He made a note to himself: Does it really matter anyway? Then he answered his own question: yes, it probably does.

Christine rose to leave. "I will see you next Wednesday, here at our same café, and I will tell you of my marriage and of my Husband. He was a prince."

The American kissed her on each cheek. He could feel her soft skin as they touched. This slight physical contact with her face became a memory to hold after she departed and a pleasure to anticipate before her return. He lingered on her cheek a split second longer than was customary, holding on to an instant of her nearness before she was gone.

The American returned to the table in the café and scanned through his notes. Her life was already a large story; she grew from girl to woman, entered the highest levels of the world of Parisian art, loved and suffered through her bad choices. Before he placed his glasses and pen in their leather case, he wrote: Christine rose above it all; she stood up again and moved on. It was her only choice, she could have not accepted less, for she was Christine and her purpose on earth was not yet fulfilled.

CHAPTER THREE
THE PROFESSOR/HUSBAND

Can one fully love without knowing pain?

Can one fully feel pain without knowing love?

Café Talk: True Love

1945. *It was a long week for the American. He had no friends in Paris other than Christine and Father Jean. Father Jean was in Rome on an extended assignment, a special Vatican-based initiative to bridge the theological divisions and misunderstandings between Jewish and Christian worshippers. "Christianity is the next step in the historic continuum of worshipping the one God. Christ flows from David and Moses. I am a Completed Jew," Father Jean would say.*

The American's superficial contacts with shopkeepers and restaurant owners whose establishments they frequented was not enough to draw him back to these businesses when he and Christine were apart. After all, the center of attention was always Christine, not the American. To go alone to their places would be too empty, it would only highlight his loneliness and he would miss Christine even more. The only exception to this pattern was the restaurant Camille, where Christine's past and the American's present lives were intertwined.

As a tourist during postwar recovery Paris in 1945, the American stood out on the city streets. He was not young and brash like the American soldiers. He was not as sophisticated or as assimilated as the expatriates who continued to live in Paris during Occupation or those who had recently returned after the Nazis were driven out. He was a bit of an anomaly.

He spent the week mostly isolated in his room, working on Christine's Journal day and night. His portable Smith-Corona typewriter hammered out so many words about Christine's life that mechanical troubles began. He wore the red and black ribbon to a frazzle.

The American made himself a promise: when he couldn't sleep he would take it as a gift from God and use this peaceful, quiet time to think and to write. This week he slept little but wrote a lot. He wrote of a girl and a boy, of a girl becoming a woman and of a man not yet a man. He wrote of love found, love lost and different kinds of love. He did not write about his growing feelings for Christine; he was simply a vessel for capturing Christine's life, a means to keep her alive if only on paper.

He and Christine met again. They double-cheek kissed and then sat down. Life moved about and around them but when they connected, the rest didn't matter. He was a bit excited, like a schoolboy, while she was calm and focused. He had time, she didn't.

The American looked directly into her eyes. Her wrinkles had deepened and her color had faded from porcelain to ashen in just their short time apart. After the arrival of coffees and croissants, Christine spoke about her Husband.

The Professor

I met the Professor as an undergraduate student studying journalism at the Sorbonne University. He was my favorite professor and I hoped I was one of his favorite students.

His courses on European history were the highlights of my undergraduate university education. He was young for a full professor but his knowledge was extraordinary. He was already well-recognized by his peers for his unique interpretations of the forces of history and how historical events impacted our daily lives. His passion was French history and he gave his students the gift of learning like no teacher I knew.

He asked more of his students than any other professor. Each day, he made French history come alive, as though we were living the dramatic events right then, right there in his classroom. He integrated other academic disciplines into the march of history with references to religion, biology, medicine and geology. He showed how religious beliefs, the terrain where people lived and disease affected societies, life and histories. He taught us how to think broadly and deeply, even when many of us were more focused on the distractions of youth.

With his impeccable academic credentials, his extensive publishing and the respect he commanded in the university setting, he was given the option to teach only graduate students who had risen above their broad-based education. Instead of shunning undergraduate students as many senior professors would do, he eagerly volunteered to bring his vast amount of information to us, and we loved it.

With his enthusiasm and teaching skills, he challenged the lazy minds of educationally unwashed undergraduate students to enter his world of ongoing European battles and human struggles. Through him, we experienced the historic building up and destruction of leaders and societies. He presented a volatile world which unfolded from his mind and entered into ours.

The Professor was such a popular teacher he received a standing ovation when he began class and another when he concluded. Among my professors, only he garnished this kind of spontaneous energy and support. Our enthusiasm was created by the extraordinary high level of learning and respect he gave to us. We loved him; it was standing room only for every session he taught. His excellent reputation as a professor brought in many guests, including students who were enrolled at other universities, visitors to campus and professors who wanted to learn from him.

When he taught, his enthusiasm was so great that he would literally spit out the descriptions of the forces that shaped world history. He loved to speak of the ironies of history, of small events with a tremendous impact and how human will and fate interacted to contribute to the unfolding of history.

The Professor was also an extremely handsome man, tall, with large hands and feet. He loved to play sports. He particularly enjoyed rugby and was a physical and courageous player.

Every day he dressed for class in a similar manner: a brown corduroy coat with elbow patches, usually a deep blue shirt, with a yellow sweater tied around his neck. He wore a small mustache and carried a soft, brown leather briefcase. Though intellectually and academically a nonconformist, his clothing was the standard professor uniform at the Sorbonne. To complete his college professor image, he often rode his bike to work, carrying his briefcase in a basket in front.

The students were vaguely aware that the Professor was Jewish but, to be honest, he didn't physically fit any "typical" Jewish profile and we didn't think much about it. One of the students who apparently knew quite a bit about him indicated that he was not an Orthodox Jew, so he didn't follow many of the ancient traditions of his faith. This distinction between Orthodox and unorthodox Jew was unclear to me. Not wanting to appear ignorant or insensitive, I asked questions only to myself. What was the difference? Was it something like the differences between Catholics and Protestants in the Christian faiths?

One lesson captured the full attention of every student in the room. It was about Abelard the professor and his tutored student, Heloise, in 1117 A.D. He spoke of Abelard overcoming severe tragedies and heartbreak before he went on to make great contributions to France's university system.

When Abelard was a growing scholar, he was hired to tutor young Heloise in the Classics. After a short time, thirty-eight year-old Abelard fell madly in love with the seventeen year-old beauty and she fell in love with him. Heloise became pregnant and was sent off in shame to have their baby. Heloise's uncle felt dishonored and, in an act of brutal revenge, he had Abelard castrated.

Heloise gave up their baby and entered a convent, but Abelard and Heloise continued to love each other faithfully. Abelard was not defeated by the vicious act of the unforgiving uncle. He didn't stop his important work as a professor and he eventually founded the University of Paris, one of France's greatest universities.

Six hundred years after their deaths, Josephine Bonaparte honored Abelard and Heloise with another act of love. She sponsored their reburial in a single coffin at the Pere-Lachaise Cemetery where they lay together for eternity.

The Professor learned a great deal from studying Abelard's teaching techniques, which encouraged students to argue and interact with him in class over lessons and opinions. This Socratic Method conflicted sharply with the traditional French teaching model where professors lectured while students listened passively. What captured the class's attention were the highlights of the love affair between Abelard and Heloise and the serious consequences they paid for their romantic liaison.

Abelard and Heloise were lying dead but they were still in love, even if it was only in the minds of admirers who came to honor them. The Professor opened our thinking to the possibility of keeping infinite love alive in the midst of profound tragedy, a theme which winds through many historic events.

The Professor wasn't particularly flirtatious when I was an undergraduate student, though he knew I adored him. We went out for coffee twice and both times our discussions were about European history. As we sat in the Café *les Deux Magots* (*the two wooden statues*) sipping espressos, he didn't ask me about my life or how I felt. He seemed to have little passion but for the historic past, for the glorious history of Europe and France. I thought he lived in his mind more than his heart. The Professor's intellectual focus on history was a sharp contrast with that of my Artist lover, a man who wore his emotions on his sleeve, lived in the operatic drama of each moment and found zeal in every dimension of life and love. However, the Artist and the Professor were the same in two important ways: they lived life with an incredible amount of energy and they were intensely committed to their life's passions.

I finished my undergraduate courses and entered graduate study. My graduate studies were focused on international journalism. I was finished with the broad curriculum of undergraduate work and was no longer enrolled in classes studying European history and French civilization. I was no longer a student of the Professor. I was also working as an intern for the magazine *Paris Match,* which took a great deal of time and energy.

Because my Aunt preferred to speak German with me, I grew up speaking Hitler's language fluently. At the university, I took a minor in German, which increased my expertise in reading and writing the language. I practiced my higher language skills by reading German newspapers and novels in the university's German Department, where I became a regular visitor during my undergraduate and graduate courses of study.

I was growing as a professional woman by writing articles for publication. Through them I was achieving recognition and encouragement. My focus was on those current European political events which were of significant importance to Paris and France. In 1939, there was a great deal to write about.

As Nazi Germany continued to rearm itself and break out of the restrictions of the World War One Treaty of Versailles, I took special interest in Hitler's aggression and the passive reaction world leaders took toward Nazi Germany's expansionism. Like my boldness as a girl soccer player on the boys' team, the frank articles I wrote about Germany and the Nazis were highly unusual for a female in prewar Paris. My opinions created a certain amount of notoriety. I used quotes from the German newspapers to verify my points. I loved the reactions of the public and friends to the articles I wrote and the controversies they provoked.

My mother thought my articles were exceedingly controversial and too much like what a man would have written. I thought she was just criticizing my accomplishments again. She would have preferred me to write about art, music, cooking or design; world politics and attacking sitting dictators did not fit into her hopes for her daughter, but I didn't alter my behavior at all. Instead, I was spurred on to write more aggressively.

Brasserie Balzac near the Sorbonne was a place where many students gulped shots of caffeine when their natural energy faded or ate a late-night meal to fill their ravenous appetites. One evening I was in Brasserie Balzac having coffee and working. I was deep into editing two articles criticizing the Allies' weak policies toward Nazi Germany. The first was about Neville Chamberlain, the prime minister of England. I was writing about the impact of appeasement, which allowed Germany's unchecked rearmament and their annexation of Austria and the Sudetenland sections of Czechoslovakia. I wrote a scathing criticism of Chamberlain's recent return to England as a hero, where he prematurely proclaimed "peace in our time" even in the face of growing Nazi imperialism. The other article criticized the Americans for implementing the Neutrality Act of 1939, which gave America's de facto approval of the Nazis' actions to expand their empire through military aggression and war. I had a proclivity for writing articles sure to create a stir.

I finished two espressos and my heart was pumping like a marathon runner on his final push to the finish. I thought of *Guernica* and the terror perpetuated by the Nazis and Italian fascists and it struck a raw nerve in me. I was feeling angry at the naiveté of the world leaders as they abdicated their duties to enforce restrictions on Nazi Germany's military expansion.

I focused on my work with an intensity that blocked out everything other than the immediate thoughts of my mind, much like the Artist when he was painting and the Professor when he was teaching. Suddenly, I became aware of a person near my side. He was too close for comfort, so, with some irritation, I swung around to tell the bugger to back off. To my utter surprise and shock, it was the Professor. He was politely trying to capture my attention to say hello but I had ignored his subtle approach. I startled him with my quick movement and he dropped his cup of tea to the floor with a crash, shattering the cup and spilling his tea on the floor.

A long and eventful night began with that crash. Our apologies crossed in midair as we each tried to clear the awkwardness of this small accident. Then we began to laugh. We were crying with laughter stimulated by massive amounts of caffeine. It was a wonder I didn't become sick as I held my stomach in pain. Our howls ended in a tight embrace. It was the first time he had touched me in any way more than a handshake or a peck on my cheeks in the normal French greeting. It felt wonderful; his hug turned my longtime Professor fantasies into something warm and real.

After we gained control of our laughter, I told him about the article I was writing. We intensely discussed the political situation in Germany and Europe. He disagreed with my criticisms of Chamberlain and was sure France was more secure than I concluded. He pointed out the massive preparations the French had made since the last war: the Maginot Line, the tanks, the planes and the trained soldiers.

Because of his training and knowledge of European history, he could see the historical perspective. He believed Germany was not capable of defeating the French and other Allied militaries just twenty-one years after they were defeated in WWI. He also gave me some unsolicited but sage advice: "Be careful about criticizing the Nazis in public. Even though I don't think they are an immediate threat to France, they are a crazy lot, violent and full of paranoia and fear."

Of course, I ignored this advice. Time would show how wrong he was about the war but how right he was that I should have kept my opinions to myself. We set our political opinions aside and connected as a man and a woman. As we spoke, the warmth of our friendship blossomed. We often touched each other to make our point, a seemingly innocent touch on the arm, the hand, a shoulder and even the knee. I loved his touch, though I tried to hide the strong feelings he was evoking in me.

Later that night, he walked me home and we stood at my front door and talked some more. He opened himself up as a man and revealed he was a much more complex person than the history professor I enjoyed in the classroom. We discussed his family, his boyhood and his religion. Like me, he loved twice before but was no longer involved. His intelligence was evident; his thoughts were cohesive, well thought-out and linear. I loved talking with him and listening to his stories while the might of human love came into our lives through the depth of our conversations and our physical attraction.

The night ended with a gentle, prolonged kiss as he held my head in his strong hands. He kissed with tenderness and warmth as he gently and slowly loved me with his lips on mine.

It was my Professor, the man of my dreams. He was really kissing me and it was incredible! I cautiously pushed my eager breasts against him in a signal of my willingness and desire for more. He pulled me closer, deeper into the kiss and the embrace. Minutes lasted for hours as we drank of each other's love. It felt like it would never end.

For the first time in my life, I was kissing someone who kissed like me: we were a matched set. He began by kissing only with his lips, nibbling, sliding back and forth, pressing and teasing. He took little playful bites of my lower lip and warm feelings rose throughout my body. It was some time before he began to gently use his tongue, darting, following the form of my lips and probing my mouth. I was shocked by the sexual passion his kissing evoked. He kissed in rhythm, like a song, back and forth, in and out, rocking me from side to side, repeating his kisses over and over. It was like the wonderful repetitive musical patterns in a Beethoven symphony. His hands were in my hair and pulling me strongly but gently toward his mouth. *My God, if this is how he kisses, how incredible it will be when we make love!*

I knew he wanted me; it wasn't hard to feel his desire growing and his passion rising. We held each other tightly but eventually he pulled back. "Not tonight. I want to know you better before we cross the other dimensions of intimacy. I have watched you and thought of you for years. I want to savor every mouthful of you, from the appetizer to the *plat sucre*.

"Tonight we will leave each other in suspended passion. I want to see you tomorrow for dinner. I want to walk together slowly down these paths of life and lead you gently to an amazing place, to the world of our love."

We finally said good night. I went upstairs and climbed into bed alone. We entered the special place where only new lovers can go; a place where, if you are among the very fortunate, you are given a momentary ticket to heaven.

After a wonderful dinner the next night, he spent half the time kissing my mouth and half loving my neck. My mother called this *necking* and my Professor was an expert at it. He knew how to combine gentleness with pressure and his touch.

We spent many evenings loving without making love. My yearning rose from the ecstasy of his kisses and from pressing our bodies together where we connected with our greatest passion. I found things different with him; his support and love created a confidence free of inhibitions. His loving words made me feel precious; I could not have asked for anything more. I trusted him with all of me: my heart, my body and my soul.

We met every night and during the days when we could. On the fourteenth night, he gave me an envelope with something special inside and asked me to take it home and read it just before I went to sleep. He wrote about me instead of concluding his research on the tattered history and shifting political control of the 5,607 square miles of the Alsace Lorraine, an area which once belonged to Germany but had been allocated to France in the 1919 Treaty of Versailles.

I returned home, climbed the stairs to my bedroom and placed the envelope on my pillow. I undressed and crawled into bed before I opened it. Inside I found a love letter with the most beautiful words ever written for me. His letter sits foremost in my heart today as it has ever since that night in 1939.

My Dear Christine,

When I look into your face, floods of emotion and energy rise in me. I can hardly sit still. When we look into each other's eyes and speak of life and love, I think, quelle beautée, what beauty! I want to kiss you even when we are speaking of the most non-sensual subjects such as politics, our jobs or the weather.

I want to look at your face; it is all I want to do. I want to keep looking at you and never let go.

Your expressions are full of delight, there is magic in your eyes and love radiating from your smile. It is your magnificence I will pursue the rest of my life. You are beyond common beauty, a moonbeam in the sky, the sparkling stars in the heavens; your face is an epic, a classic told by gods.

Love-light pours out of your sensuous, white skin; your glow is nectar to my once-lonely heart.

I have seen a thousand—no, many more, a thousand times a hundred faces, but I rejoice in yours the most.

In your face I am all of me with all of you.

Your look guarantees my heart's love for you!

I want to know you in joy and even in pain. I want to watch you sleep; seeing you is to witness the image of a living angel.

I have found the source of life, the eternal flame of the universe—you light my way.

From your cheeks I will lick your tears and the rain. From your mouth I will love you totally. From your eyes I will see the meaning of my life as I fall into the channel of your soul. In your hair I will dance the dance of life. From your voice I will hear the trumpeted, ageless melody of the gods. From your neck I will gorge the Last Supper, the feast of feasts.

Face to face we pause in our detached love-bubble; the world instantly drops out of focus; we alone see one another—your face to mine and no other.

The look of love you wear is a welcoming place for me to rest. Your presence pulls me inward and downward. Into you I fall, wanting you, needing you, loving you, yearning for you.

Turn out the lights for a moment; I want to deny my eyes your beauty. I want to see you with my fingertips. I want to caress you like a blind man, touching you as if caressing a Rodin sculpture in the night.

Turn the lights on and I see "Opus Christine," an eternal composition I want to read until the last dawn.

I fear nothing but you turning away from me, that your face could be not only for me. I want nothing more than for you to stay and stay and stay. I only confess to wanting you, only for me, for eternity.

I could not hurt you, I could not harm you with criticism, a harsh word, or a discouraging thought—an impossibility.

What a face you have, your face of love.

It is not that the moon is no longer beautiful but it is only so if I can't see you; even moonlight cannot compete with your glow.

There are beams of light coming from your eyes.

I see your life has been only good; you live on the mature side of purity, your beauty enhanced by the joys of life. May it always be so.

I beg God to bless me with the greatest gift of life; to see your face before my eyes close for the last time; that is how I want to die, that is how I want to live!

Forever in love with you,

Your Professor

He touched me deeply with his sensitivity, his ability to express his emotions and his growing love. I tried to sleep but I kept thinking of our fondling and kissing, which kept the flames of my passion burning inside. I would imagine him touching me and kissing me in the most intimate places. I did everything I could to relieve my unfulfilled desire but I wanted the real thing; I wanted him.

First Time: My Professor

Finally, on our three-week anniversary, he told me to bring my things; we were going to have dinner at his house and spend the night together.

When he, the man, ultimately joined me, the woman, my passion exploded. He waited; I climaxed not once but again and again. Ultimately, he let go and gave me his loving flow of passion. We were completely spent from lovemaking.

I fell asleep wrapped in his arms and legs. We didn't stir the entire night and we woke in the morning, with him still inside of me. A peace came over us from caring deeply for one another. I knew I loved him like I had not loved before. I knew he was the *One* and that someday he would be my husband. When I opened my eyes, I was surrounded by his library of books covering European history from Christ to the present, and I wondered how I was going to fit into the immense history living in this man's mind.

Our love grew as spring blossomed in Paris. The rains became warmer. Couples were in the parks and seemingly on every street corner and park bench. The *Paris street-lovers* publicly loved like only Paris' exhibitionists can do.

When we were apart and busy with our work and studies, we were like love-angels, sitting on each other's shoulders, watching over the other until we were back together again at the end of each day.

He would "complain" how it was difficult to work when the only thing he could do was think of me. He would joke about his inability to do his research. In the midst of a military battle for the rule of France between the Catholic king and his Protestant brother, he would drift into thoughts about our passionate times together. His would leave the battle in Le Beaux, Provence, with catapults sending flaming bales of hay flying into the fortress, to fantasize about joining me under the heavy quilt in a fit of passionate lovemaking where he took me over and over again until we could not bear to make love any longer.

My Professor was ecstatic about my sexual techniques. He especially loved me taking him through his full climax by swallowing his love and then gently, slowly kissing him as he died the death of pleasure. Nothing brought a man to his knees like that.

I loved doing everything I could think of to give him pleasure. But I told him there was another side to me; I was more than my sexuality and more than a journalist. "I want you to know I have a deep and important spiritual side. My belief in God is a vital part of my life, though I don't always conform to church doctrine like waiting for marriage to make love."

He understood this dichotomy perfectly. His long religious history and strong spiritual beliefs were also modified by a willingness to bend the rules for love.

My Professor was an entirely different man than the others. My father was reserved, almost secretive when he spoke of architecture and buildings. My brothers were kids, running in circles, full of energy but not much to say. My relationship with the Boy was a playground for exploring the loss of innocence. The hoped-for love I felt for the Artist was a living canvas of worldliness and creativity but was primarily centered on him. In a final triumph over youthful sensuality and artistic worldliness, the supremacy of my Professor's intellect firmly prevailed over all others.

Eglise St.-Julia-le-Pauvre
"THE OLD WALL"

TMR

I took my Professor to St. Julien and introduced him to Father Jean. While they shook hands and made small talk, I watched and beamed. They showed each other a great deal of respect. What beautiful men they were. I was so lucky to have these truly good men in my life, for there seemed to be so few to go around.

My Professor asked me how St. Julien le Pauvre became our family church, and to explain the history of the Greek Catholic Melkites. I explained that my family had immigrated to Paris from Greece three generations earlier and my great grandparents joined St. Julien shortly after it was turned over to the Melkites in 1889. We have been members of St. Julien ever since.

"The Melkites had a long Middle Eastern history in Syria and Lebanon. They were originally under the Patriarch of Constantinople, who served as the head of the Eastern Church. However, the Melkites split with their Greek Orthodox brothers in 1724 over the recognition of the authority of the Roman Pope as the head of the Western Church. Melkites are Greek Catholics who accept the Pope's leadership and authority but maintain considerable independence, uniqueness and their own patriarch in the complex world of international church power and politics."

My Professor was surprised Melkites were not part of the Greek Orthodox Church. This distinction took some explanation to anyone unfamiliar with this small part of the rich and complex history of the Latin and Eastern branches of the Christian Church. My Professor loved learning and listening to me explain this history. He sat quietly like a schoolboy as I spoke. This time I was his professor.

He had lived in Paris his entire life but, not surprisingly, he didn't know St. Julien any more than I knew his family's synagogue located less than a mile away in Le Marais.

As we walked around the church, I spoke of the various facts about my church: "St. Julien le Pauvre is the oldest church in Paris. The building of the church was begun in 1170 and completed in 1240, ninety years before Notre Dame. However, religious structures existed on this spiritual site long before; fourteen hundred years ago, in the sixth century, there was a church located on the same sacred land and the stones from that old church were used to build St. Julien. Evidence showed there were probably even older religious structures on this site.

"St. Julien is located on an important historic site of the Roman city of Lutetia. It is located on present-day Rue St. Jacques, which was one of the main Roman roads leading in and out of Lutetia. To the north, this ancient road led to the Seine at the Petit Pont and over the river to Île de la Cité. To the south,

Rue St. Jacques took travelers in the direction of Spain and the vast Roman Empire."

In the gardens outside the church, I showed him a large paving stone remaining from the old Roman road. He touched it with both hands to feel Parisian history. He mentally chronicled the Romans' industrious past and their imperialistic accomplishments as they spread their legions and culture throughout the Western World and beyond. Later, I realized we had forgotten to touch the Lucky Tree of Paris, the city's oldest living tree, which was planted in the church garden in 1602.

St. Julien was the site of my baptism and my First Holy Communion. It was here I had met with the Artist and Father Jean during our relationship turmoil. He laughed at the drama and showed no concerns about my past relationships. They were history but not the kind he was interested in.

My Professor followed up on the information I gave him on St. Julien through research on the ancient buildings of Paris in the university library. His research skills led him to a startling and important discovery. In ancient Paris, in the times of the Romans and before Romans were Christians, the area where St. Julien is located was a Jewish settlement. On the land next to St. Julien, an ancient synagogue had stood. The gap between Jews and Christians continued to close. This information was to become remarkably important in our near future.

In the sixth month of our love fest, we took a walk along the rain-soaked bank of the Seine. A warm breeze followed the river right into our hearts. As we walked, I fit to him like a glove fits the hand, as if I were physically designed to complement the curves of his body with those of mine. We completed a puzzle, two pieces of a whole with nothing between us, bonded together by our unquestioning desire to be together as one.

We paused at the midpoint of Pont Neuf and looked to the river below and to the heavens above. A half-moon lingered in the pale blue sky. The lights of Paris were coming on as the sun and moon traded places; the setting sun celebrated one day ending and the rising moon opened the possibilities of a new day beginning.

Two elegant, snow-white doves flew low over our heads as a matched pair, knowing their direction and flying wing-on-wing through life as one. I watched as they soared through the evening sky then down to the flowing water, skimming the surface like White Angels of Glory.

I turned and asked him about our future; did he have a plan for flying our life paths together? As I paused for an answer, he dropped to his knee and pulled a small silver package out of his vest pocket. "Yes, Christine, I have been waiting for *this* exact minute. I have known for some time how deeply I love you and that I always want you by my side. You are truly the One for me. This is the moment in time to ask you to join me, for better or worse, as husband and wife for the rest of our lives.

"Before you answer, think about the enormity of what I am asking. I want to marry all of you—your body, your emotions, your mind and your soul. I want you for today, tomorrow and for eternity. I want to be buried in the same coffin with you in the Pere-Lachaise Cemetery like Abelard and Heloise. I want to spend eternity with you, joined as one, supporting each other no matter what life tries to do to us. I want to be the last love-bridge you cross, the last man you love.

"If I die first, I want to stay with you as a constant memory as I wait for you in the beyond. If you die first, my commitment to you shall not wane as I anxiously wait for my death to bring us back together again; even death will not do us part. Come with me, Christine; come with me for now and forever."

He handed me the box. Inside was a silver ring with a large star sapphire surrounded by small diamonds. Also in the box was a red, heart-shaped note. On the back he wrote, *Come with me, Christine; come join our hearts in one love forever.* He was prepared for this moment; his timing matched mine as perfectly as those two white doves soaring and diving together in the evening air.

Without hesitation, I accepted his offer. There was no doubt in my mind we would always be in love and he would strongly hold and protect me through life's traumas. On a fantastic day of love and commitment, there was not a wisp of the difficult future rising on the horizon; nothing indicated the struggles we would have to endure. The only signs we saw were of eternal love and joy.

After I accepted his proposal, he said, "Now, you will never be alone. I will be here for you. This is complete love and nothing can change it." And so we were to be married.

Café Talk: Love and Loneliness

1945. *The American was unaware that Christine had found the one man for whom she became a woman. The American felt a substantial pinch of jealousy, for he had not found love in its perfect form and he longed for someone like Christine, a woman who could love so deeply and so completely. He exclaimed, "What a fantastic story. Please go on!"*

"When the Nazis were approaching Paris, I hid his love letter with my notes in the seat cushion of our most valuable armchair. I have read and reread his loving words often since I was freed. I carry them in my purse to remind me of the total happiness we achieved. His tender words remind me of the man I used to know, the man I will always love." She pulled out the worn and wrinkled love letter and held it as if to prove by its existence that true and never-ending love was indeed possible. She opened it to show the American hard proof; yes, the fairy tale of love came true—albeit for just a moment in time.

Christine was ready for a coffee, so they returned to the café to begin to work on the Journal. Before she returned to her own journey, she asked the American about being alone and lonely in Paris. "Wasn't the reason you came here to learn through suffering? Haven't I interrupted your growth by giving you a companion, by taking you away from your loneliness? Haven't I quenched the fire you needed to grow?"

There was no need for an answer. The American knew this was not about him, so he picked up his pen and prepared to write.

Our Interfaith Marriage

May, 1939. We wanted an interfaith, Jewish/Christian wedding. We knew this would be difficult because of the differences and difficulties in each of our rule-based religions, but we were committed to having our ceremony.

We began by meeting with the Professor's family's rabbi, Rabbi Kaplan. He was a gentle old soul and received us warmly. However, he clearly communicated that there were two large obstacles to overcome: my faith and my church. He explained how Judaism, like Catholicism, functioned under specific rules and laws about marriage. We would have to comply with them or he would be unable to marry us. He also noted, for my benefit, that an interfaith marriage would be impossible if my Professor were an Orthodox Jew; an Orthodox Jew cannot marry a non-Jew, it is prohibited by Jewish law. Fortunately the student's observation was correct, my Professor and his rabbi were not Orthodox Jews. Therefore, a small window remained open for the interfaith marriage ceremony we sought.

Over the next month, we spent considerable time with Rabbi Kaplan and Father Jean discussing the various rules and our beliefs. Father Jean loved the concept of an interfaith marriage ceremony but he was not sure how to overcome the obstacles. In our favor, Rabbi Kaplan and Father Jean were dear friends and participated in interdenominational counsels together, each representing their own faiths while committed to understanding the faiths of others.

On one special occasion, Rabbi Kaplan, Father Jean, my Professor and I met for four hours. We discussed the fact that our two faiths worshipped the same God. They were brilliant men with a tremendous understanding of both religions. We explained we wanted our marriage to be a celebration of the common elements of spiritualism, belief systems and moral definitions found in Judaism and Christianity. At the end of the meeting, my Professor simply asked, "Why not? Judaism and Christianity are really one religion with two paths. We are in love. We are believers who want to live good lives. Why can't we be married in a joint service with Jewish and Christian traditions?" The priest and the rabbi looked at each other and took the question into their hearts and minds but said nothing.

Rabbi Kaplan met privately. He wanted to inquire deeper about my beliefs. He asked me to review the Seven Noahide Laws given to Noah after the flood to determine if I could follow those pillars of the Jewish faith. I found them to be similar to the Ten Commandments and unequivocally answered, "Yes, I will follow the Laws of Noah." My morals and upbringing closely followed the values expressed in the Noahide Laws so I freely committed to following them in our marriage and in the upbringing of our children if we were so blessed.

Rabbi Kaplan informally declared me a "Ger toshav" or "Jewish Gentile" on a path toward righteousness and therefore acceptable for marriage to a Jew. I left my discussions with Rabbi Kaplan feeling optimistic that our interfaith wedding and our lives would work out perfectly. We had overcome the first obstacle, my faith.

In our discussions with Father Jean, we examined our values, our relationship and our future. We delved into subjects such as our beliefs in the spiritual domain and the existence of God. It brought joy to learn that our answers about our faith and worship were similar.

Father Jean and my Professor became fast friends. Sometimes they became so engrossed in discussions of religion and politics that I would sit aside dreaming my own dreams. Unlike the feelings of exclusion I had felt with the Boy and his brother, I enjoyed listening to the exchange between Father Jean and my Professor. They would often politely ask my opinion. What special men they were.

My church remained an obstacle until my Professor mentioned the ancient Jewish settlement and synagogue that once existed on the site of St. Julien. Father Jean lit up with excitement. "We will hold the Jewish ceremony on the land outside the church, on top of Jewish soil. Jews don't relinquish land, even if it is occupied by others for two thousand years. Rabbi Kaplan will love it; it will be his victory! Let me talk to him." The second obstacle was about to be overcome.

Organizing an interfaith wedding sounded easy but it was not. My Professor/fiancé decided his role in the wedding planning and preparation would be limited to supporting me. I thought he was right; supporting me but staying away from the chaos of the wedding preparation was a wise decision. He agreed to whatever I wanted our ceremony to be; any combination of Christian and Jewish traditions would be fine with him. He only asked that I create the wedding of my dreams.

Balancing the traditions of two faiths involved many details and challenges absent in a single-faith wedding. My first step was to study the traditional Jewish wedding ceremony. The more I learned the more respect I gained for the marriage traditions of the Jewish faith.

I wanted to avoid anything offensive to members of either faith and I asked Rabbi Kaplan to give me pointers. For Jews there was no kneeling, so we should avoid asking people to kneel. Jewish tradition does not include the question and directive, "Does anyone object to this marriage? If so speak up now or forever hold your peace." Jews also do not include the question, "Who gives away this bride?" These were easy ones; I decided to remove these rituals from our ceremony. These particular traditions were not important to me.

Rabbi Kaplan and I discussed Communion. He thought Communion might be possible if everyone, Jew and Christian alike, would be welcomed to participate and it was a broad celebration of God and life. I knew Catholic Communion included a commitment to support the Catholic Church's hierarchy, so I wasn't sure if Father Jean could welcome the participation of non-Catholics. This requirement always seemed inconsistent with Jesus' inclusiveness, but the church had many rules I did not support. I still considered myself a good Catholic. I wanted to have Communion but, in the end, I decided to marry without it. I thought it would be too much of a surprise for the Jewish guests to be asked to participate in the consumption of the blood and body of the Christ, even if He was a Jew.

The central issue of an interfaith marriage was Jesus himself: how do we bring Jesus into our interfaith wedding? How do we bring Jesus into His own place of worship? Why was it so difficult to worship this unblemished Rabbi, this Son of Mother Mary and the Jewish God?

I was uncomfortable when Rabbi Kaplan said there would also be sensitivity to words like Savior, Messiah and Christ. For our ceremony to be truly interfaith, Jesus must be fully present and not dishonored or minimized. I decided to leave Jesus with the wise Father Jean, since he would best know how to handle the Son.

I planned our wedding without interference, except for my wedding dress. On this topic, my mother and my future mother-in-law formed a solid block in opposition to my desires. They wanted *The Virgin Dress*: white, conservative and a cover-up of my body, as they wore in their weddings. Even more difficult, my mother desperately wanted me to wear her wedding dress.

We were in the middle of Escapism and Existentialism and everything about style, sex, art, drugs, music, literature and philosophy was changing. Life in modern Paris was breaking out of the conservatism of the *Lying Generation* of woman who pretended they didn't enjoy sex. We were living in the end of the 1930s and they were trying to take me back to the Victorian-era. I wanted to wear something spectacular, something that showed off my beauty and would make every man jealous of my husband. They wanted me to hide myself in a white envelope.

I argued, objected and debated with my mother. "Should I also prick my finger, stain my virgin dress with blood and hang it out the window to pretend I haven't had sex? I have been through the childhood stages of love and romance. I am a woman and I want to marry as an honest woman, not as a hypocrite. I know what I want and I don't want to pretend I am someone I am not, especially at my own wedding."

"It isn't right, it isn't proper," my mother said out of frustration with me. I felt like I was twelve years old again, bucking her control and authority.

I asked if she'd heard of Edith Piaf, Henry Miller, Josephine Baker, Dali, Sartre, or Simone de Beauvoir? What about Picasso and his writer and artist friends? I threw this out knowing my mother's undefined connection with Picasso and, as part of the Parisian art world, she knew the non-traditional lifestyles of the avant-garde iconoclasts of mid-nineteenth-century Paris. Life was different now, I pleaded to no avail.

It was a mother-daughter control issue and my mother wanted me to wear her wedding dress, period. She had kept it in perfect condition, waiting for her only daughter to be married. When it came to her daughter's wedding, she reverted to the world of her mother and to the mothers who came before her. It was a long white dress; the front and back rose all the way to my neck, and it was accented with crystal lace. The sleeves covered my arms. I would be covered in white like a sacrificial lamb.

I showed her the design I wanted, an off-the-shoulders gown revealing considerable cleavage. My mother proclaimed I would look like a whore in such a dress and everyone would be offended. She dug deep into the guilt and manipulation tyranny of our mother-daughter relationship. She brought up my "incessant" nonconformist ways and how difficult it was to be my mother. She threw everything at me: my soccer playing, my relationships with the Boy and the Artist. She claimed to have suffered great embarrassment from my unwillingness to conform to her expectations of a girl and a woman. She hammered me on the content of the articles I wrote and said I sounded like a Communist.

In the end, I conceded to their wishes and agreed to wear my mother's wedding gown. I didn't want my mother and new mother-in-law to be ashamed of me in front of their friends and families. My mother-in-law was too sweet to hurt with my maverick ways. I overruled my wild side, but then I came up with an idea which made me laugh out loud.

My plan was a two-dress option. Before my father knew my mother was adamant that I wear her dress, he offered to pay for a new wedding dress and I held him to it. If I wore my mother's dress during the ceremony, it wouldn't cost anything but for a little tailoring. Meanwhile, I would have another, secret dress made to wear after the religious ceremony and formal meal were concluded. My two conspirators would be my father and my Aunt, with whom I happily re-established my close relationship after the Artist fled France. She was like an old friend coming back after being lost, and I welcomed her. Despite my father's passivity, which I blamed on my mother's aggressiveness, my father was another wonderful man in my life and he was happy to go along with my plan.

It worked out perfectly. I attended the tailoring of my mother's dress in the morning, excused myself after lunch and spent my afternoon with my Aunt designing a new dress created just for me.

My surprise dress was created exactly the way I wanted. It was traditional ivory in color but provocatively swept up my body in a two glorious sashes which flowed down my sides to my hips. A man from India once told me the most beautiful part of a woman's body was her lower back and I was determined to show it all. The back dropped as low as it could go, revealing everything I could expose without showing too much. In the front, my dress hugged my breasts and exposed considerable cleavage, then crisscrossed below. The sleeves were buttoned with satin-covered buttons from my wrists to my shoulders. I knew my husband would love to see me wearing this fabulous dress and knew he would love taking it off on our wedding night even more. I met my mother and mother-in-law's wishes but only to a point; I had to be me and do what I wanted to do. I could hardly wait!

I discussed including Orthodox Jewish wedding traditions in our unorthodox wedding with Rabbi Kaplan. Each time I approached him with my nontraditional ideas, he would try as hard as he could to accommodate us. His first reaction was always to scrunch up his forehead and squint his eyes.

Finally, he gave in. "My dear Christine, you challenge Jewish tradition without giving it a thought. For you, everything is possible. You learn our traditions and our beliefs in a matter of days and you are ready to act. We wish to be accommodating but our faiths are rooted in deep history. I ask myself every day, how can I help you? How can I bring you into our traditions without violating laws which have taken thousands of years to develop? Your enthusiasm is wonderful. I smile to myself every time I think of you and what you are trying to achieve. I honor the love you have for your future husband and his love for you.

Father Jean and I will find a way to support you and conduct a ceremony to celebrate your marriage in the way you desire. While respecting our traditions, you will be able to make use of many of the Jewish and Christian traditions. We can do no less for you."

The first Jewish tradition preceded the wedding by a week. The bride and the groom are separated for seven days prior to the marriage ceremony. The separation is intended to increase the excitement of the ceremony, but I wondered how time apart could help sanctify our marriage? We hadn't been separated for more than a day since he bumped into me and spilled his tea on the café floor. Did I want to give up seven days with him?

I recalled the difficulties my friends had had with their fiancés in the days leading up to their marriage ceremonies—busy days fraught with stress and conflict. The premarital tension gave their marriages a bad start, so I decided to include the tradition of seven days of separation. However, it was more difficult to remain apart than I imagined; I loved him so much! I missed him every hour we were apart.

June 2, 1939. After a great deal of planning and coordination, our wedding day finally arrived. In order to comply with the rules of each faith, there were two separate ceremonies, one Christian and one Jewish. Each was modified to honor the sensitivities of the interdenominational guests.

We began our wedding with the Christian ceremony which followed the Greek Catholic/Christian traditions. It was held inside St. Julien. My father walked me down the aisle to my waiting almost-husband. The organ played Pachelbel's "Canon in D" followed by Johann Sebastian Bach's "Jesu, Joy of Man's Desire." The guests and family rose to honor me. I saw the beaming faces of the people I knew best as they looked on with adoring eyes. I walked slowly, taking each step carefully, walking purposefully toward our sacred union. The notes of the lovely music perfectly matched my steps and my heartbeat. The light gently flowed through the windows, giving a blessed aura to the inside of the church. The ceremony seemed to proceed in slow motion as I paraded toward marriage, toward my husband-to-be.

The icons on the walls carried ancient meanings. I focused on the *Fete de la Visitation* with the image of St. Julien le Pauvre. I wondered if the icons offended the Jewish guests, but then I let go of the thought—there was so much else to think about.

My husband was waiting at the altar. He was dressed in an elegant tuxedo: tall, strong, dark and handsome. His face beamed with love. I had greatly missed him during the long, premarital week and my heart leapt to him. Finally, his strong hand reached out to stabilize me as I left my past and my father's arm and moved toward life with my new husband.

Father Jean welcomed guests of all faiths and embraced the special opportunity of our wedding to speak to believers in Christianity and Judaism. He spoke of simple and deeply important truths. His voice lovingly boomed off the old stones of the worn floor, off the Greek icons hung on the thick walls, down from the ceiling of planks and tile and into the hearts and minds of the guests sitting in their chairs.

Father Jean began our interfaith marriage by stating, "There is one and only one God; He is the God of Abraham, the God of the Jews and Christians. He is the God of the Bible, the same God in the Jewish and Christian Holy Books. Through our God, Abraham was the progenitor of the Jewish and Christian faiths. We have the same Father in Heaven and the same Father on earth. We share the one and only true God in common; there are *not* two different gods. This Truth is indisputable."

After a pause to let his One God statement sink in, he spoke directly of the Jewish/Christian continuum. He emphasized the historic facts that too many easily forget: "Jesus was a Jewish Rabbi. Mother Mary, Father Joseph, myrrh-bearer Mary

Magdalene and Jesus' twelve Disciples were all Jews. While Jesus lived on this Earth, most of his followers were Jews. The Christian New Testament is precisely built upon the Jewish Old Testament. The original followers of the living Jesus were not called Christians; the Rabbi Jesus and his followers remained Jews until their deaths.

"Christians believe Jesus fulfilled God's prophesies when he came to earth as God's Son, but some may have forgotten they were *Jewish* prophesies, not doctrine from a separate religion called "Christian," a term that came into existence after Jesus and his Disciples had died. Jesus was the Son of the *Jewish* God to whom He ascended after the Resurrection. Jews are spiritual big brothers of Christians in faith and worship; we are of one family, each with differences but mostly the same. Christians would not exist but for the Jews and the Jewish religion," he proclaimed.

Father Jean's last revelation surprised me, for I had not heard it before. "Remember, Christ was not Jesus' last name. The term Christ is from the Greek word *Christos*, which is from the Hebrew word for *Messiah* meaning 'one who is anointed.' In Jesus' time, Jews did not have last names. People were called by their first name with a connection to one's birthplace, one's father or the family's occupation; hence, Jesus *of Nazareth*. Today Jesus may have been called *Joshua Josephson*. However, after Resurrection, Jesus became Jesus Christ or Christ Jesus to acknowledge his status as the Messiah." Father Jean found a way to bring Jesus into our interfaith marriage; he resurrected Jesus as a Jew!

His words helped close the false gaps separating Jews and Christians. The guests gained a feeling of belonging to each other and a sense of family, of one single inclusive faith instead of one divided into two conflicting groups.

Father Jean next spoke of marriage, the union which unites a man and a woman through love. "Today we are integrating two lives as the bride and groom become one.

We join them in valuing their similarities while recognizing their uniqueness. We bless their union and their love. Their openness is an example for the rest of us; their love flourishes beyond the doctrines and traditions of each religion. They are a model for the love that mends our wounds and joins our hearts."

He spoke about love, the passion of marriage and how important it is to choose forgiveness through God as the centerpiece of married life. He looked directly at us. "Forgiveness will bring strength to your union and allow you to achieve and maintain happiness and holiness as you become one.

"The answers to life's questions have already been given to us by God. Seek His guidance and you will find truth. God loves us when we love each other, when we commit to one another and when we honor our fellow human beings with love and respect. God is angry with us when we choose hatred, when we fail to forgive and when we are unfaithful to our commitments." He concluded by addressing the rules that divide our faiths: "The rules are not the faith. Over time, we must modify the rules in order to strengthen the spirit." It was a powerful sermon: short, moving and perfect.

As the Christian ceremony blended into the Jewish ceremony, my Husband put on his *kittel*, the traditional Jewish white robe, and a white satin Yarmulke upon his head. My Jewish groom was my *chatan* and I was the *kallah*, his bride. I committed to use the Jewish names and, though they were unfamiliar words to me, to learn to pronounce them correctly.

Our procession moved from inside the church to the outside courtyard, to the ancient land of the pre-Christian Jewish settlement. My Husband's best friend led the procession and we followed. Next came both sets of parents and then the guests. We emerged into a glorious, sunny day with scarcely a hint of a breeze rustling the leaves in the surrounding trees. Holding my handsome Husband's strong arm gave me a magnificent feeling of love and security.

We began the Jewish ceremony by sitting in our *chuppah*—a four-posted canopy tent under which our Jewish wedding ceremony was conducted; the *chuppah* symbolizes the future home of the husband and wife in the tradition of the tent home of Sarah and Abraham. It was freestanding and set up outside in order to view the stars in the heavens. The four posts represented the pillars upon which marriage was built: honesty, comfort, love and family heritage. The roof of our *chuppah* was made up of traditional materials brought from the family's ancestral home. My mother-in-law made the canopy from drapes her parents had brought from Russia eighty years before. The drapes had been saved just for this purpose. We decided we would continue to follow Jewish tradition and make the canopy into a bedspread for our marital bed.

My Husband sat under the *chuppah* as I circled him seven times—as the world was created in seven days—to show my commitment to build our new home and our life together. I walked around the *chuppah* to bind myself to my Husband and him to me. At each pass, he looked at me with loving eyes and joy. After the seventh circling, I sat down on his right side. Rabbi Kaplan said a sanctification prayer to join us as one and to make our marriage holy. We shared a single glass of wine, each of us holding the cup for the other as we drank to our unification. When I drank the wine on an empty stomach, my head began to spin, but I managed to keep control by holding onto my Husband.

It is tradition to symbolically treat the *chatan*/groom and the *kallah*/bride as king and queen during the ceremony and for each to have a separate reception; the *Kabbalat Panim*. I watched as my Husband was surrounded by friends and family who toasted, sang and congratulated him. He looked happy and fulfilled as he shook hands and warmly thanked each guest.

I sat on my throne feeling the level of respect bestowed upon a queen, an honor never experienced before. I received my family and friends, glowing in my joyful transformation from single woman to wife.

Our wedding Yom Kippur was an important part of our Jewish ceremony. I knew the Jewish holy day of Yom Kippur was a time for atonement and forgiveness. What was new to me was that each Jewish couple has their own Yom Kippur, in which the *chatan* and the *kallah* are forgiven for past mistakes and merged into one, complete, new soul absent of prior sin. I thought of the Christian message of forgiveness I'd heard so often from Father Jean. Christians and Jews are truly one spiritual family seeking God and goodness; our will to forgive is our common theme.

The veiling is called the *Badeken*. My *chatan*, his family and friends brought the veil to where I was sitting. My Husband placed the veil over my head to symbolize his commitment to clothe and protect me. I closed my eyes and basked in the strength of his love. I held profound honor for him in my heart. When I opened my eyes, everyone was looking directly at me. I gave a slight bow with my head and a gentle smile in appreciation of their blessings. This was the only point during the wedding when I almost began to cry, but I held back my tears as we went on with the ceremony.

In a traditional Jewish wedding, the exact words "according to the law of Moses and Israel" are used to give legality to the ceremony. I had learned it would not be possible to use these words, since interfaith marriages were prohibited under traditional Jewish law. However, my Husband said the beginning of the traditional verse, "Behold, you are betrothed unto me with this ring," leaving off the reference to the old law. With these little adjustments, we followed Jewish traditions without blatantly violating Jewish Law or offending the faithful.

I wore no jewelry during the ceremony in the *chuppah*. In a symbolic message to emphasize the simple, nonmaterial values of life such as love and family unity, we followed the Jewish tradition for my wedding ring. It was a simple gold band without adornment, to symbolize the pure joy of love. Once he placed the wedding ring on my finger, we were officially husband and wife. Happily, the custom of simple jewelry did not apply to my engagement ring, which sparkled with love and precious beauty and was held by my mother until after the Jewish ceremony was completed.

The breaking of the traditional glass sealed the nuptials at the end of the ceremony. It was one of my favorite Jewish wedding traditions, a dramatic reminder of the destruction of the Temple in Jerusalem over two thousand years ago. The glass was placed on the floor before my Husband. He stomped on it and it shattered to pieces as the guests roared in applause.

We finished the Jewish ceremony and my Husband and I were escorted by our parents to a private *Yichud room*. We followed another tradition as we stepped over a sterling silver spoon at the entrance. We were left alone for a short period of time with food and wine. In the tradition of the ceremony, I said to him, "May you merit to have a long life, and may you unite with me in love from now until eternity. May I merit to dwell with you forever." These few moments gave us a chance to comprehend the totality of marriage and the commitments we had made before returning to the activities of the wedding celebrations. It was the first time we had eaten all day.

When we were alone, I kissed him and ate, kissed him, drank a little wine and ate again. "What have you been doing for seven days?" I asked as though I were already his wife, which I was. He smiled at me, took a sip of his wine and told me he loved me.

He complimented me on my beauty and thanked me for the joy of our marriage ceremony, which he had thoroughly enjoyed. He was amazed at the sensitive way in which our two worlds had come together in love and celebration.

"What a genius you are," he added without answering my question about the last seven days. He was already acting like my Husband, which of course he was. I was elated that our wedding was enriched with the precious Jewish traditions and faith. It was a seamless match with the beauty and wisdom of the Greek-Catholic ceremony.

My *chatan* helped me grow as a woman by being such a wonderful man and by bringing the Jewish traditions of his family and faith into my life. They were wedding presents given without wrappings, gifts that last for a lifetime.

During the reception, there were many Greek and Jewish toasts of joy and happiness. The shouts of "Mazel Tov!" were given with such joyous energy that I believed these congratulations would surely surround us for the rest of our lives.

The celebration included food and entertainment from both cultures. The guests' energy kept increasing as one group tried to outdo the other on the dance floor. Greek and Jewish dancers competed for the unofficial prize of who was the best and most enthusiastic. There were no clear winners but each side claimed the prize for themselves with exuberant claims of victory.

I waited until the guests finished their dinner and consumed a couple of glasses of wine before I discreetly excused myself. Not even my Husband knew what I was up to, as I simply said I was going to refresh myself and would return shortly.

It took me only fifteen minutes to change. I let my hair down and it tumbled onto my bare back. I slid into my gorgeous creation. I wore my finest jewelry and placed my engagement ring back on my left hand. I felt pampered and beautiful.

My father met me outside to escort me back into the reception. He looked at me approvingly, his eyes wide as he looked at his daughter, a grown-up, sensuous woman dressed in Paris' finest and a married lady. Though I was sure of what I was doing, I was happy to have my father's strong arm to steady me and to give respectability to my entrance; I could not have done it alone.

The music was playing loudly and men and women were swirling and stepping their way around the dance floor. When my father and I entered through the front door, everything froze; the musicians, the dancers, the drinking, the talking and the eating all stopped. There was complete silence but for a collective gasp by the guests from the shock of seeing my transition. Gone was the 1914 bygone era of my mother. In my new dress I leapt 25 years into 1939, to an era of passionate living.

Everything moved in slow motion as I walked across the floor. My father again walked me to my Husband, who recovered enough to give me the smile of support I needed. Then everyone in the room started clapping. It was a spontaneous roar. I knew I had made the right decision. They loved the dress!

My Husband looked at the musicians and gave them a commanding wave of his left hand and took mine in his with his right. The band started to play. The song was our new favorite, *Sur les quais du vieux Paris (On the Riverbanks of Old Paris)*. As we walked onto the dance floor, our guests quickly moved aside. It was our turn to dance and our turn to shine on center stage. We didn't simply dance; we floated, we transcended the ordinary into the extraordinary as they sang, *"On the banks of old Paris, along the Seine, we retrace the sweet and simple steps of our very first dates…I let my heart, overcome with happiness, beat next to yours…"* It was a storybook moment as we glided effortlessly across the room.

Neither my mother nor my mother-in-law said anything directly about the dress, but I did catch a little smile on my mother's face as we floated by. They had their tradition and I had my grand entrance. I was particularly proud of my plotting and the success of my secret plan. My Aunt was beaming. I think I fulfilled some of her hopes and fantasies, or maybe it brought back pleasant memories of her own wedding.

I couldn't think of anything else I desired from life. A welcoming world spread out before us. Our future was there for the taking and it would be brilliant. I was sure. We believed nothing could bother us; our love would conquer all of life's obstacles. We were ready for our wedding night, so we bid the party adieu.

A horse-drawn carriage picked us up after the reception. We went straight to the hotel to consummate our marriage in a night of passionate lovemaking. When we closed the door of our room, my Husband was so eager for sex I thought our wedding night might end quickly. I didn't know if it was the seven days apart or the dress, but his passion was overwhelming. His eagerness was humorous but I didn't laugh, because I didn't want to dampen his enthusiasm. Maybe seven days apart wasn't such a good idea after all or, maybe it was.

My Husband was normally a "you-first lover," focusing his attention on me so I would reach my climax before he reached his. But this night, his arousal was too intense to hold back. I knew he wasn't going to be able to wait.

He pulled me close for passionate kisses and reached inside my dress to caress my breasts. He was sexually more aggressive than ever.

I spoke lovingly and asked him to slow down so we could have more time and more pleasure. "Let this night unfold as a graceful dance. Let me show you how our wedding night can be an unforgettable night of sexual pleasure. I love you and promise when it is over, you will have missed nothing. You will have felt every pleasure a woman in love can give her man, so please be patient!

"First, I want to take a bath. Undress me, unbutton me and take off my clothes. I want to bathe in the luxury of French perfumed soap in our large tub so I will be clean for you. I have picked a special scented bar from the perfume company *Silence* and you will love how it makes me smell. Pour us a glass of champagne and come into the bathroom. You can watch; better yet, you can help."

In his anticipation, he fumbled a bit with the buttons but he soon achieved success. My clothes were in a pile on the floor but I stopped to hang up my wedding dress. I still wore my French stockings, which stopped mid-thigh. On the top of each was a small pink ribbon tied in a bow. I slowly removed them one by one before heading to the bath. My Husband stripped to his undershorts. I think he was trying to hold himself back by keeping his shorts on, but his bulge was so large I had to laugh. I lit four candles and placed them at the corners of the tub. The light around the tub was low and perfect. He brought in the champagne; it was from the House of Veuve Clicquot, a 1932 vintage. Exquisite.

"Wash me. Wash every part of my body. Leave nothing unclean!" This new Husband of mine obeyed perfectly and it felt wonderful. He soaped each of my extremities, using both hands in his quest for total cleanliness. "This is going to be a magnificent night," I softly whispered.

I pulled him into the tub as he desperately tried to pace himself. I peeled off his shorts, soaped up my hands and returned the favor of cleansing his most intimate parts. My touch drove him crazy. He was aching with passion and needed a release, so I made him a deal. I would please him in the tub and then give him a half an hour to rest. When the time was up, he was going to make this a memorable wedding night for both of us.

He pleaded with me, "Yes, yes, yes—please do that!" I think he would have done anything for the pleasure he knew was coming.

The hot water and soap made everything more sensuous. I continued to softly soap him, slowly ending at the tip of his manliness. He was in heaven as he slid way down into the hot water, moaning in pleasure, wanting for nothing.

As I stepped out of the tub, I reminded him he could rest for only a half-hour. "I will be back," I promised. He said nothing, his eyes were closed and he smiled in pure joy and satisfaction.

My pacing was perfect, though I gave him a little extra time. He climbed out of the bath and dried off on the rich hotel towel. After a couple of sips of champagne, he looked at me and said, "OK, now it is your turn, you naughty girl!" As much as I aroused and satisfied him, he paid me back three times more. He didn't stop until I rose to his caresses, arching my back and climaxing even before he entered me and consummated our marriage. I was in love! I had found my man! We slept like children without a care in the world...indifferent to the pending events that would permanently disfigure our future 1,939 years after the birth of the Christ, the Jew.

My Husband wanted to honeymoon on the island of Malta, located in the heart of the Mediterranean between Sicily and Africa. He painted a picture of a small, peaceful Mediterranean island surrounded by the vast blue sea, filled with friendly native people. He convinced me this would be a wonderful place for our honeymoon.

We looked at the map and my Husband said, "Look, Malta is dead center in the Mediterranean, it is the same distance from Malta to Cyprus and Gibraltar; it is sixty miles from Sicily to the north and two hundred miles from Tripoli to the south. It is only seventeen miles long and nine miles across. Her population is only a quarter of a million people. You will love Malta's history."

Malta also floated on the edge of my Husband's studies as it marked the end of Europe, beyond it the great continent of Africa. He wanted to learn more about this apex of the Mediterranean. Malta, he explained, was a small bastion of stubborn people who, together with the Knights of St. John, faced down the world's most powerful military in the Siege of 1565. The Maltese and the Knights were relentlessly attacked by the forces of the Turkish Empire ruled by the Turkish Sultan Suleyman The Magnificent and his powerful slave wife Roxolana. There were more than seventy thousand cannonballs shot at the forts of Malta and only one fort, St. Elmo, fell to the attackers. The sultan wanted to use Malta as a base to attack Sicily and southern Europe, and he wanted retribution for the attacks on his ships by the Knights of St. John. Despite their massive attacks, Malta emerged victorious.

My Husband quoted Queen Elizabeth I, who spoke in typical British understatement when she said in the sixteenth century, "If the Turks should prevail against the Isle of Malta, it is uncertain what further peril might follow the rest of Christendom." After attacking with two hundred ships and forty thousand men, the Turks withdrew from their siege on September 8, 1565. They were severely bloodied, and they would not attack her again. They learned an important lesson: the Maltese don't give up.

The Maltese victory in 1565 was an emblematic item of interest for my Husband—an event where, but for a surprised turn of fate and human will power, history would have been changed dramatically. He called these historic occurrences "Y Intersection" or "Kingpin" events, where the outcome could have easily gone the other way. These events not only greatly impacted the world at any given time; they continued to influence it for generations to come. At the intersection of the "Y," two potential futures are posed, each waiting for fate and human will to determine which direction history would record.

My Husband wanted to meet these people, see their defensive facilities and stand on their shores imagining the siege of thousands of warships and attacking armies. He added another fact: Malta's ancient history preceded Egypt's. Malta's temples are more than seven thousand years old.

When we arrived at Malta by boat, we found things a bit different than we expected. The huge British Mediterranean Fleet was docked in the harbor. It was a grand site to see: battleships, cruisers, aircraft carriers and hundreds of supporting vessels waiting for the rising tides of war. Malta was the point of control for the central Mediterranean Sea. Whoever controlled Malta controlled the supply lines from Europe to North Africa and the back-and-forth trade from the Mediterranean to the Atlantic. The reason for the strong British military presence was to protect Malta and control the Mediterranean.

The harbors were surrounded by giant stone forts standing alert for the next siege. The "beaches" and hills were rock. Rocks were piled up for fences and littered the landscape. The island was one huge rock fort. Malta did not appear to be the peaceful little island for romance and relaxation that I had expected, but it was the perfect place for a historian to take a honeymoon! I loved him so much it was easy to adjust my honeymoon expectations. I loved him on Malta just as much as I would have loved him anywhere in the world.

We stayed at the Grand Hotel in Valletta, a city named after the Grand Master of the Knights of St. John who led the defense of Malta in 1565. It was wonderful and perfectly located for our strolls through the ancient town and along the fortified walls of the Grand Harbor. The days brought a warm, temperamental wind from Africa called the Sirocco. The hot weather matched the temperature my Husband had promised, but the beaches were not the long, sandy stretches I sought. It was an island of limestone and more limestone.

We took full advantage of our lack of responsibilities and other distractions to spend an inordinate amount of time in bed pleasing one another. The excellent British breakfasts offered by the hotel were consumed in bed. We ate, showered off the vestiges of the previous night's lovemaking and returned to bed for more affectionate time together. I used different soaps and perfumes to entice him and seduce him. He always rose to the occasion. What a wonderful man I had found. We were perfectly matched. He taught me about history and life but, in bed, I was often the teacher and he the enthusiastic student.

My Husband remained intensely interested in Maltese history throughout our honeymoon and purchased numerous books to take home to his library. He traced the incredible march of Maltese culture through the Neolithic and Copper Age to the Phoenicians, Carthaginians, Greeks, Romans, Byzantines, Arabs, Normans, Spanish, the Knights of St. John, Napoleonic France and finally Britain. Each of these societies had invaded and occupied Malta at one time or another.

I also learned from my Husband how St. Paul was shipwrecked on Malta in 60 AD and founded the Maltese Christian church which has continued to exist for almost two thousand years. Regardless of who tried or succeeded in conquering Malta, the Maltese peoples' strength came from their uninterrupted faith in Christianity. The intense history lessons made my head spin. I was married to a professor, a man of the mind whose appetite for historic knowledge was limitless.

We innocently returned to a cool Paris as the world's war became hot. We left Malta before Hitler violated his token agreements of containment and attacked Poland, before Mussolini foolishly tried to bomb Malta into submission and before the world formally declared total war on itself.

Café Talk: History Impacts Marriage

1945. *Christine gazed back to the lavishness of her wedding ceremony and said, "Food was so plentiful. During the Occupation and afterward, I thought back to our fabulous wedding meal and imagined how we could have lived half a week on each couple's dinner portions."*

The ship Christine and her husband took from France to Gibraltar and on to Malta followed the same route that the Santa Maria Convoy, including the USS Ohio, would follow three years later—a convoy that brought the last lifeline to Malta and provided the supplies she needed to barely survive, fight and live to save the day for the second time.

Things became much more difficult in Paris. Christine and her Husband were dead center in the complex and dangerous changes taking place in Europe. "As you will see, the events of the world directly impacted our lives. We experienced things no one should have to experience. Life came crashing down just one short year after we were married." She was through with the preliminary talk and said, "Let's begin".

Our Marriage

The year before the Nazi Occupation, my Husband and I lived the bourgeois lives of two educated Parisian professionals. We socialized with friends from the university and took the full month of August for vacation, a privilege enjoyed by most middle-class and affluent Parisians. We foresaw a long future together and expected to continue at the same, gentle way of life until our lives ended naturally. We stubbornly believed nothing would change our world. The Boy and the Artist were long behind me. I had found my place; I had my man and I was happy.

My Husband was tender, considerate and caring. He loved my hair. It grew longer during our marriage, so I wore it in a loose ponytail, pulled back without bangs. My Husband liked to help loosen it at the end of the day. He would remove the elastic bands to release it from the restraints. He would run his fingers through my loose hair, making me purr like a kitten. He wore a gentle smile of appreciation during these precious moments. His tenderness often led to increasingly sensual touching. We were in love.

Existentialism and various manifestations of it were the most popular philosophies in Paris. New ideas from the philosophers and writers of Paris were exploding during the late 1930s like Impressionist painting had 50 years before.

Sartre, Camus and de Beauvoir were creating and expanding the basic premises of the Existential philosophy in their books and plays, while they were also exploring nontraditional personal lifestyles. Their works followed in the philosophical footsteps of Kierkegaard, Nietzsche, Freud and Marx in a parade of learning from the past into a surge of creating in the present.

One of the activities my Husband and I enjoyed most was our participation in discussion groups and book clubs. We examined the philosophical premises of Existentialism and other philosophies. Half of the group were professors and the rest were intellectually curious non-academics like me.

When Sartre wrote *Nausea*, we were thrilled with the depth of his thinking and the direction his work was taking. *Nausea* would serve as a prime example of Existential thinking for years to come and it placed Sartre in the heart of the Existential movement.

The university professors were well connected to the Paris literary society and they used their connections to invite various writers to speak to our group. A year after *Nausea* was published, Sartre visited us. He shocked us by declaring that the beginnings of Existentialism and the beginnings of Christianity were very much the same, but he left without expanding on this idea. His comment sat disturbingly in our minds as our group spent considerable time trying to figure out what he meant. In what ways did Existentialism and Christianity have similar beginnings? We agreed each was an iconoclastic philosophy in its own time but could not find other similarities between the two beliefs.

On another occasion, Camus gave us a mini-lecture on how he differed from Sartre and Existentialism. He expounded upon his unique thinking about the absurdity of man's search for the meaning of life. To him, life was an empty void, which therefore, by definition, could not have meaning. He explained why he had joined the Communist Party, which he also criticized, as part of his opposition to the fascist Spanish politics of the time. I thought of *Guernica* and how those days of mass horror marked the beginning of enormous changes in the world. Even Picasso became a Communist, something I could never understand about him. He was always such a strong individualist. His conversion only made sense in the context of the Franco Fascists taking over Spain and the Communists as the only force opposing their dominance.

Our group discussions were complex and interesting, though I questioned the motivations of the Existentialists. I had read Nietzsche and Kierkegaard in school and observed a philosophical continuum from their philosophies to the Existentialists of my generation. The old masters were better philosophers than the modern writers who reinvented them. The old masters thought deeper than their counterparts of the Thirties. However, the new Parisian Existentialists appeared to be more sensual and artistic in their prose and the images they created. Could it be the old masters were more masculine and those of the Thirties were more feminine?

As much as Sartre and Camus intrigued me, I thought both of their philosophies were attempts to avoid life's sting and difficulties. I told Sartre as much and said I thought his philosophical destruction of traditional standards and social morals were techniques he used to overcome female resistance to his sexual conquests, of which there were many! Not surprisingly, he was not particularly receptive to my comments, but he didn't deny them either.

May 10, 1940. The Nazi Blitzkrieg left Germany to attack Belgium, Holland and France. Each day, an anxious world held its breath as the war news unfolded. The map of Europe was rewritten on an hourly basis as the Nazi military stunned the world with the unbelievable speed of their conquests.

The Nazis launched a combined force of machine guns, cannon, air bombing and tank assaults against waves of Dutch, Belgian, French and English soldiers. Our soldiers were repeatedly sent against the German killing machine in deadly frontal charges. Other Allied soldiers waited in their concrete bunkers, only to be pulverized by the juggernaut. An immense number of human lives were extinguished as metal and concrete imploded from attack after attack. The Nazis left decimated fields of battle filled with the stench of death and defeat behind and moved ahead with the clarity of victory.

Sitting comfortably in our stylish flat, Number 1, Quai d'Anjou, on the Île St. Louis, my Husband and I enjoyed the river view from the fourteen-foot, floor-to-ceiling curved windows overlooking the Seine. We read censored and manipulated newspapers and listened to government-controlled radio broadcasts. Time and again, the victories of the Allies and the bravery and success of the French soldiers were conveyed dishonestly to the anxious public. "The French defenses are holding, the Germans will again be defeated," the censored news media lied and lied again.

Meanwhile, three-and-a-half million Parisians continued to live as they'd always lived. They continued to smoke their Gauloises, sip their espressos, drink their wine and dine on delicious French food in the café life of indulgence and pleasure. We were living as if the war were on another continent, in a parallel universe of denial as it came exploding toward our front yards. The opera opened with a full house every night until the Nazi war machine was literally parked on the edge of town, ready to pounce on Paris like a lion on her precious, defenseless prey. It was the virgin and the satyr all over again as Paris remained in innocent denial until the last possible moment of her violation.

Many Parisians hoped for a repeat of France's lucky military victory against the Kaiser's forces in World War One, when the Germans gave us their flank and we drove them away. Others prayed to St. Genevieve to provide another miracle like the one she performed in 1870, which sent the Germans around Paris without hurting the city. In 1940, we waited for a third strike against the Germans, a knockout punch to send the Huns back to their lair. We hoped against hope that the Nazis would bypass Paris in pursuit of the British Expeditionary Forces and the remnants of the French army.

As the Nazi monster approached Paris, the French government begged England for more air strikes, to use their England-based bomber fleet to protect the continent. The British planes were not launched; England was protecting her own nation with the small number of planes she still possessed after losing hundreds of aircraft and pilots in failed continental battles. England, which had cheered Chamberlain for his phony peace compact with Hitler, was now in great fear. The screaming Nazi Blitzkrieg that attacked France stunned them into hushed inaction. In this new kind of warfare, the Nazis were only a matter of so many air minutes away. England knew their turn at the Huns' abuse was coming. It was just a matter of time and time was running out. Britain didn't help the French with more planes; many British didn't even like the French.

As the Nazis attacked, the shocked Allied commanders relied on World War I defenses and tactics to oppose the most advanced, highly motivated military machine in the world. The low morale of many of the French troops who didn't want to fight and the poor leadership by many officers made the French no match for the disciplined, well-armed and well-led Nazi army which advanced on them effectively and unmercifully. Soon the Allied fortresses in Holland, Belgium and France lay in ruins and rubble, their flattened cities destroyed and their troops massed in bloody piles of the deceased or rounded up and sent to prison camps where the suffering was often greater than death itself.

The great French army quickly became but a distant memory, a lost hope. With their vastly more mobile forces, the Germans simply drove around and flew over France's highly touted but immobile Maginot Line. The millions of French francs spent on building these huge defensive forts barely created a pause in the Nazi attack as French defenders and weapons were quickly destroyed or captured.

The equivalent of a large city's male population was taken from France after only twenty-three bloody and destructive days of battle. Hundreds of thousands of Dutch, Belgian, British and French fighting men lay dead. Over a million Frenchmen were captured and crammed inhumanely into Nazi prison camps to suffer, perform forced labor and often die of murder, disease or starvation.

My brother died on the first day the Germans crossed the French border, though we didn't know of his death for months. He was the brother who didn't make the cut on the soccer team when I stayed on. When I thought of him over the years, that event always came to mind. I'm not sure I remembered it because it hurt him so much or because I was so proud of myself at the time. His death began painful etching on my parents' faces, deepening scars that became more and more pronounced as the war continued.

After the Nazi Blitzkrieg plowed into France, there was no one left to defend the most beautiful city in the world. Hitler turned the sites of his massive killing machine toward the big prize, the City of Lights, the capital of France, and aimed them directly at my Paris.

The mighty Nazi army stood on the doorsteps of Paris, poised to take her by force or by willing submission. The wishes for a third reprieve from Nazi Occupation would not be realized. The Nazis were coming and coming fast.

June 2, 1940. My Husband and I innocently celebrated our first wedding anniversary by dining at our favorite local restaurant, Chez Julien, located just over the Pont Louis-Philippe from our island on the Right Bank on Rue Hotel de Ville. It was located at the entrance of the Marais, not far from the Jewish ghetto and my Husband's synagogue.

As a first course, we snacked on delicious hors d'oeuvres. They were complimented perfectly by a 1936 Rhone Blanc.

A 1932 Grand Cru accompanied our *canard sauvage à l'orange*, wild duck in orange sauce, followed by a magnificent *crème brûlée* for dessert. During dinner, we spoke little of the Germans and the war. Our conversation focused on the pleasures of fine dining in Paris and the celebration of our marriage. The restaurant owner, Luigi, an old friend of ours, frequently stopped by our table to discuss internal Parisian politics and the superior nature of French food and wine. Though he was born in Italy, he lived most of his adult life in Paris; he thought, ate and drank like a Frenchman.

Luigi naturally wouldn't consider wine from any other country other than France as proper to serve with a good meal. I silently thought of the Brunello di Montalcino, the best wine I had ever tasted, but I said nothing. The restaurant was full and we greeted friends and family members who, like us, were doing what Parisians do best: living the good life.

"Paris is safe," my Husband assured me with an *I-know-better-than-you* pat on my leg. "The French defenses will hold." It was foggy when we walked home. Though it wasn't cold, I felt a deep chill as we crossed over the Pont Louis-Philippe to the comfort of our familiar island. The gigantic thirteen-ton bells of Notre Dame chimed their assuring rings as they did every night and every day at the appointed hours.

Arriving home, we sipped a small snifter of 1919 Courvoisier cognac to finish off the night. Unknown to us, this would be the last time we would enjoy a quiet, restful night, so innocent, carefree and confident.

While my Husband was an excellent historian, he had been lulled into the illusion of safety like millions of people around the world. We slept serenely one last night because the free world underestimated the immense power of evil birthed by the Third Reich and their leader, Adolf Hitler.

A few hours away, unseen Nazi tanks revved their engines, loaded giant shells full of deadly explosives into the gun breeches and their drive toward us began. Paris was anything but safe. While we slept in each other's arms, the Nazi's weapons hung over Paris like a knife in the hands of the Angel of Death.

The Nazi military covered more territory in a shorter period of time than any army had achieved in the history of warfare. It was inconceivable that the Nazis could knock out the defenses of the Allies in a matter of days and would be sitting on the threshold of Paris. But it was just what they did.

June 3, 1940. We were awakened from the bliss of the first morning in the second year of our marriage by the sounds of Nazi cannon fire outside of Paris. Time began a slow motion roll into a new history. Bombing and heavy artillery hit the thin outer defenses of the city. The naïve confidence in the French defenses and the safety of Paris vanished. Civilian and military refugees streamed into the city, desperately camping on the riverbanks, the parks and anywhere they could find space. The looming Nazi siege of Paris was a dragon's sword poised to kill, a monster ready to plunge our lives into a full-time nightmare.

Mussolini, encouraged by the Nazi advances, declared war on England and France. The next day, his forces bombed Malta for the first time in what would be a three-year-long siege. We were sickened by the reports of the intense bombing of the Grand Harbor and the city of Valetta, places we had enjoyed on our honeymoon and an island which held special memories for us. Great Britain, aware of the potential threat from Fascist bases in Sicily, withdrew her Mediterranean fleet to Alexandria, leaving Malta with limited defenses against the Italian attack. The French government wanted to surrender Malta to the Italians as an act of appeasement but, thankfully for the free world, the new wartime Premier of Great Britain, Winston Churchill, said no.

June 10, 1940. **E**ight days after we dined at the Chez
Julien, the French government cowardly fled to the south, leaving
Paris politically naked. Millions of Parisians grabbed whatever
belongings they could and quickly left Paris. Desperate families,
fearful of rape, torture and murder by the Nazi hordes, walked,
drove and rode out of town. Their faces were locked in masks of
refugee anguish as they pushed forward, hushing their frightened
children, down heavily clogged roads. The evacuation of Paris
was in full swing. Many fell and died on the road. The ally of the
Nazis, Fascist Italy, added to the dreadfulness of evacuation by
sending waves of their airplanes to shoot and kill fleeing Parisians,
just as they had done when the Spanish citizens fled Guernica
three years before.

Evil had made a home in the hearts of the fascists and soon
it would be walking in the streets of Paris. My Husband and I
decided to remain in Paris and live out the Occupation in the
home we created together. He was adamant; we would not let
the Nazis drive us out of our home, out of our city and out of
our country. We would stay and survive. "This is France, not
Germany! They cannot kill every French person!" he shouted
unconvincingly and with less credibility than before France
fell.

This life-changing, life-threatening, irreversible decision led
us down paths of horror no one could have imagined on that
sunny day in June. We missed our chance to escape and we
would suffer the consequences. Day by day, the magnitude of our
error would be slowly and then violently revealed to us.

June 14, 1940. **O**nly twelve days after our first anniversary
and only thirty-four days after the Germans began their assault
on Western Europe, killing the Boy and my brother, Paris was
declared an open city by the mayor and was handed over to the
Nazis without a fight. Paris succumbed easily and quickly to the

thrusts of Nazi infantry and tanks as she quietly lay down to accept her Nazi domination.

The clatter of steel Panzer tank tracks and roaring engines drowned out the other sounds of the city as these enormous machines rumbled down the cobblestone streets and over the bridges into Paris. Behind them, tens of thousands of Nazi soldiers marched into the heart of Paris and sang the dreaded Nazi song of conquest, "Deutschland, Deutschland, Uber Alles." On that damned day, the day of Paris' surrender and for the days, months and years to come, it did seem as though Germany was winning overall—over all.

We were shuttered in our home. The world was stunned: Paris fell without a fight. Optimism turned to fear and fear turned into terror.

The Nazis took control of what was left of the Parisian and French governments and agencies. Surprisingly, the initial impact of the Nazi Occupation of Paris was not as negative as expected. Nazi soldiers were under strict orders to treat Parisians with courtesy, to become friendly occupiers and to demonstrate to the world how "civilized" the Nazis could be.

Putting on their pleasant face of pseudo-respectfulness, the Nazis began to win over Parisians. Some Parisians let down their guard and started to cooperate with them. The cafés reopened, as did the restaurants and the opera. In some quarters of Paris, Nazis and Parisians ate and drank side by side in the cafés and restaurants. Parisian café life quickly reasserted itself on the Paris streets.

The French collaborated with the Nazis to create the Vichy French government to institutionalize Nazi control over most of France; Frenchmen of Vichy France were appointed to government offices to rubber stamp and enforce Nazi decisions.

My Husband held these fellow Frenchmen in the lowest regard. They were known as *Collabos* or Collaborators. To him, these Frenchmen were handing France over to the Nazis "on a silver platter." I commented that for some, it might not be so simple—their lives and the lives of their families might have been threatened. They might not have had an option. I pointed out that no one knew what choices they would make until they were faced with similar circumstances. He scoffed at my empathy for these traitors and exclaimed, "We will not forgive them, ever!"

Over the strong objections of many French citizens including, Charles De Gaulle in exile, the governments of America, the USSR, Britain, Canada and Australia recognized the Nazi-supported Vichy as France's official government. I screamed, "Don't they know France is occupied by the Nazi military and we lost hundreds of thousands of men and thousands of citizens trying to stop these fascists from occupying our country?" In my journalistic mind, I wondered if Nazi agents were controlling these governments. If I were still working as a journalist, I would have blasted these small-minded, short-visioned fools in every media outlet that would accept my writings. I was aghast at the repeated stupidity of their concessions to evil.

The Nazis approved all appointments of mayors and police captains throughout Paris and the occupied French territories. They made the basic services of water, electricity, telephones and sewage work with a blended Nazi/French administration.

My Husband and I knew Nazi occupation would be horrible. We argued vehemently with neighbors and friends about the impact of the Occupation on Parisian life. They argued that Paris was better off with the rebellious Communists under control and the Bohemians removed from the streets. They reminded us of the death and destruction of the Commune and how such wanton ruin would not take place under the Nazis. They spoke of the ineffectiveness of the Parisian and national governments of pre-occupied France. They believed life in Paris would be better under Nazi Occupation than when we were free. They did not convince us. Replacing one evil force with a worse one was not the solution. We were horrified by the compromises in France's national sovereignty. I said to my Husband, "My God, our world is collapsing. Hold me, protect me, save me. I only want to love you and live!"

January 16–19, 1941. In their continuing siege on Malta, the combined forces of the German and Italian air forces launched a three-day, intense bombing attack on the island. Many civilians were killed and a great deal of property was destroyed. My Husband and I were further saddened by the on-going bad news from Malta. We visualized the small, rugged, determined people of Malta hiding in their limestone bomb shelters until the raids ceased and emerging to rebuild their cities and their defenses again and again. Maltese had endured sieges before but nothing like the modern weapons of the twentieth century, including dive bombers and high-altitude airplanes dropping one-thousand-pound bombs on their cities and their people.

In Paris, the Nazis continued to hide their true intentions under a disarming veneer of politeness and efficiency until they began to unfold their sinister plans. Their first step was to issue an edict requiring every Jew in Paris to register with the police and a mandate that all Jews wear a Star of David patched on their clothing. Wearing the Star psychologically and symbolically separated Jews from the rest of the French population. The Star of David badge would become a passport to the hell of the Nazi concentration camps and death. However, refusing to wear the Star could be an even quicker and surer way to meet the same fate. The Jewish population's fear grew and grew each day.

By appealing to the latent hatred of the Jews by many French people, the Nazis divided Parisians on the *Jewish Issue*. In doing so, they minimized French resistance to their plans to forcibly remove all the Jews from Paris.

Many Jews followed the tradition of living in a "ghetto" in the Marais across the Seine and up the Rue du Temple. This preexisting self-segregation made it easy for the Paris police and the Nazis to treat Jews as if they were a different form of human being than the rest of the Parisians. The Jews' physical isolation also made it easier for the non-Jewish Parisians to bury their heads in the sand; what they didn't see didn't bother them.

Many Parisians turned their backs on the Jews. They ignored the arrests, imprisonments, deportations and murders of Jews as the "cleansing" proceeded in their own backyards, while some Frenchmen supported it.

The Nazis said the Jews were being taken to Germany to work and many Parisians willingly accepted this lie as truth. At first, few knew of the inhuman acts taking place when the Jews arrived in the Nazi concentration camps. Later, everyone knew the truth but still very few acted to save the Jews of Paris.

The French police and the Gestapo used Parisian Collaborators to identify the Jews living in their neighborhoods and throughout Paris. The Nazis and some Parisians were rewarded for capturing Jews through rewards from the systematic stealing of Jewish property and transporting valuable art, jewelry, gold and precious stones to Germany. Some Parisians kept the stolen loot for themselves.

The Nazis announced they were going to open everyone's safety deposit boxes in Paris. This motivated many Parisians to return to the city to claim their valuables and cash. Only the contents belonging to Jews would be confiscated by the Nazis, the property of non-Jews would be given to the actual owners.

My Husband refused to follow the law requiring him to wear the Star of David. He would not register with the police. He would not assist the Jew-haters by identifying himself in such a humiliating manner. No matter how much I explained the clear risks of imprisonment, I could not convince him to comply with these rules. I told him this would bring trouble, but he refused to follow the Nazi-French laws. Secretly, I was proud of him; to degrade Jewish citizens in such a manner was subhuman, but I was very afraid.

Because of the swiftness with which Paris fell, the government's abdication of leadership and the initial positive interactions, there was little confrontation with the Nazis. Swastika flags unfurled throughout Paris as the Nazi officers moved into the city's best hotels and residences. Based on positive reports from Paris on the civility of the occupiers, many Parisian refugees returned and Paris filled with people again.

It would take more than a year and a surprise war with Russia before the organized Résistance disrupted the artificial tranquility and superficial peace. Hitler's economic and nonaggression pact with the Soviet Union in August 1939 encouraged the Communist-dominated French labor unions to give tacit support to the Nazis during the first year.

The Parisian Communists aggressively withdrew support when the Nazis invaded Russia. Many union members became part of the Résistance as their beloved Russia was ground down by Nazi butchers. The fake coexistence between the occupied and the occupiers in Paris ended as violence begat violence. The Nazis performed relentless, day-after-day searches to track down members of the Résistance and imprison, deport or shoot them on the spot. Regardless of their losses, the Résistance didn't stop fighting, bleeding or killing Nazis until Paris was liberated from the grip of the Nazi fist.

My Husband and I didn't have much contact with the Résistance, since most of them were members of the Communist Party who we feared as much as the Nazis. The Parisian Communists were closely linked with the other, highly imperialistic nation of Europe, the Soviet Union, which also coveted dominance of Europe. The Communists were too violent, too casual with human life for us.

Only a third alternative to the Nazis and Communists would work for France, and it was the Gaullists. One of General de Gaulle's supporters was my Husband's family banker, Alexandre Saint-Phalle. My Husband's family had relied on Alexandre for many years and he served as the family's Trustee. Before the Nazis stole their wealth, my Husband's family had considerable assets managed by Monsieur Saint-Phalle. Alexandre led a double life, managing the money of the wealthiest Parisians, including Collaborators, in his private bank during the day and working with the Résistance behind the scenes at night. He reappeared later in the Occupation of Paris when he was sent on a strange and important mission.

My Husband worked briefly with members of the Gaullist element within the Résistance, but mostly he kept his distance from them in fear of reprisals. He was an intellectual, a historian and a professor. He didn't want to fight in the streets; he wanted to continue his life as a professor and as my Husband.

One Parisian, a well-known poet named Robert Brasillach, was particularly harmful because he helped the Nazi efforts to exterminate Jews. Even before the war, Brasillach was a Jew-hater. He explicitly hated marriage between Jewish men and non-Jewish women. I had the unfortunate experience of encountering Brasillach on three separate occasions in my life.

Our first encounter was just weeks before the Occupation began. It occurred in the Casino de Paris during a cast party held for actors Josephine Baker and Maurice Chevalier for their new revue *Bonjour Paris*. Most guests were in a good mood as Parisians ignored the growing Nazi military machine and the Nazi invasions of Austria, Czechoslovakia and Poland over the past two years.

There were four high-ranking Nazi officers in attendance. They were in Paris to convince French government officials the Nazis came in peace with no intentions of starting a war with France. Unwillingly, my Husband I met two of them. Brasillach was moving them around the room and he brought them to us. He introduced me with false charm and barely said my Husband's name, as if it were an unpleasant duty he hated to perform. The Nazi generals projected confidence and pride as they spoke of a peaceful Europe. I noticed one of them was particularly good looking. His presence was commanding and his face looked like a German poster of the Nazi uber-man. Many French women were charmed by him. Despite my aversion to Nazis, I had to admit he was a handsome devil but, nonetheless, the devil in human form. My Husband half-laughed at my impressions of him. He quickly replied, "He is a wolf in sheep's clothing and behind his toothy smile and those blue eyes is a heart of hard, dead stone."

Brasillach was clinging to the Nazi officers, who finally shunned his sloppy looks and behavior. When I saw Brasillach later, he was in a foul mood from drinking too much champagne and eating too much caviar. He taunted me as I walked to the ladies' room, "Why would such a beautiful Parisian woman like you marry a Jew?" He was close enough to smell his awful body odor. His bloodshot eyes bulged out of their sockets and his shirt partially hung outside the top of his pants in a wrinkled mess. I stared hard at this unkempt pig of a man and, after slightly raising my chin, I tossed the remainder of my champagne into his face. As I turned with a twist and walked away, he was cursing me, "You fucking Jew-lover!"

When Paris was occupied by the Nazis, Brasillach and the Nazis were "having an affair of the heart." He was one of the many Parisians who were delighted the Nazis were occupying Paris.

With the blessing of the Gestapo, Brasillach became the editor of a newspaper called *Je Suis Partout*. Soon, he was publishing the names and addresses of the Jews in Paris under the newspaper's banner "I am everywhere!" He often included other bits of hateful and damning information on these Jews as well.

A year and two months into the Nazi Occupation, the Nazis began to implement the second and third steps in their evil plans to purge the Jews. On authority of the Nazi occupiers, the French police began to capture and imprison large numbers of Jews and turn them over to the Nazi Gestapo. The third step was to deport them to Nazi concentration camps. In the initial wave of deportations, 1,148 Jews were sent to Auschwitz.

Brasillach didn't forget my Husband and me. He exposed us in his newspaper. He made sure we would be included in the swelling hatred of Jews the Nazis were drumming up throughout Paris, France and the rest of Europe.

In his newspaper, Brasillach wrote a hostile description proclaiming that my Husband and I were living extremely well and continued to eat abundant good food while most of Paris starved. His implications were clear: my Husband and I had money and were illegally living a lavish lifestyle deserving punishment. He correctly stated that my Husband refused to wear the Jewish star on his coat. An unusual item was mentioned in the article. Brasillach included a biased recap of my articles warning against appeasing Hitler and the threat of Nazi imperialism, which was particularly odd and threatening. Why would my writings be part of his hate journalism, which was typically directed only toward Jews?

Information such as this article was the only pretext the French police needed to raid a home, take a person off to jail and turn them over to the Nazis for shipment to their concentration camps. We took the precaution of hiding valuables and papers.

I carefully placed the pages of my notes into the cushion of two chairs and sewed them up neatly. The stitching perfectly matched the others; only I knew where my diary was hidden. The chairs were antiques and I calculated that they would be recognized as valuable and would not be ripped open if we were searched.

On the same day Brasillach's newspaper identified us, the Nazi-controlled French police interrogated our Nazi sympathizer neighbors. These neighbors told the police everything they knew and everything they could dream up to condemn my Husband and me.

The neighbors reinforced Brasillach's account by stating that we had eaten many gourmet meals and had dinner parties during the Occupation, something impossible on the meager food allocated by food rationing cards. They recalled the smells of cooking from our apartment when they had nothing to eat. On occasion, they heard laughter and the clinking of wine glasses. Some had eaten from our garbage. Our neighbors readily told the Nazis and the French police Collaborators we must be buying food on the black market. They confessed for my Husband: "Yes, he is a Jew. No, he doesn't wear the Star of David."

Some Parisians sunk to this level of despicable behavior which was called *Epuration legale* where Judas-like Parisians turned their neighbors over to the police and to the Nazi occupiers. Their hearts were full of jealousy, wrapped in the stink of hate and fear. With their words, lies and revelations, they condemned us to hell.

Four French police and two Nazi SS troopers burst into our home at 5:30 a.m. the next morning. They pulled us out of bed. I gasped for breath. I screamed for them to leave us alone, to leave our home. They didn't care what I said. I slapped the Nazi soldier and, in return, he hit me hard on the right side of my mouth with his pistol. The blow knocked my head back and opened a large gash from the corner of my mouth to the middle of my cheek. Blood gushed out of my face as he violently threw me on the floor.

My Husband urinated in his pants as fear took over his bodily functions. He swore at the police and tried to call out to me. They said, "We are here under the direct orders of the Prefet de Police and the SS. You are under arrest for violations of the standing orders for Parisians, which requires the purchase of goods and food through the provisions of rationing. In addition, you have violated the laws requiring every Jew to register with the local police authorities and wear the Star of David at all times."

Three neighbors watched approvingly as we were dragged toward the waiting police truck. The others peered out of their window shades, hoping to remain unseen, saying and doing nothing that might incriminate them.

There were twelve Nazi SS soldiers standing outside our door. The soldiers were lined up like a cattle shoot, six on each side. They were prodding us forward as if driving animals to slaughter. At the same time, French policemen pushed us from behind and we fell to our knees. The soldiers on each side kicked us and laughed. After we stood up, the policemen roughly pushed us into a truck. When I vomited, they cheered as if they had just scored a goal in a soccer match. A trail of my blood followed us out of our home into the police truck. The truck door was slammed with a loud bang, a signal that our normal lives were over.

Café Talk: Two Cups of Coffee

1945. *Christine looked down into her empty espresso cup as a reader of leaves might look into her tea. The American's coffee remained untouched. His papers were full of writings and notes. He had no time and no inclination to do anything other than give Christine his undivided attention; other things simply did not matter. The story of the violent violation of her beautiful face, the slash to her tender skin, was almost too much to bear. Her ever-present scar testified to these brutal events and gave them a real, right-now presence, even though five years had passed. The American held back his instinct to protect and heal. He yearned to gently kiss her scar, to take away what it represented in her painful life. He knew such an act would be highly inappropriate and unwelcome; their relationship was not at that level of personal intimacy, not yet.*

"My Husband and I celebrated our first anniversary dinner at the restaurant St. Julian in a free Paris. Barely more than a week later, Paris was occupied by the Nazi army. A year and a new world after, we were captives of the Nazi SS. Life changed rapidly. We were taken away from everything we knew and forced into degradation, torment, fear and pain. We would grow no further as a married couple; our relationship was abruptly halted by terror and hate. We would not love each other into old age. We would not know the pleasures and challenges of a long-term marriage. We would not have children, grandchildren or great grandchildren together, as we had deeply desired. For my Husband, there would be no heirs, no ongoing lineage. Life would become even more conflicting and confusing as the Nazis, in their attempt to conquer the world, permanently changed our lives and took away our futures."

Before they concluded for the day, Christine closed this chapter and summarized what was to come next: the passing from life with her Husband over the bridge into the world of the Nazi general on the other side.

Café Talk: Snow in March

1945. *The American and Christine pulled themselves out of the snow flurries swirling around the Paris streets and quickly entered their favorite café. It was unusual for it to snow in March, but not unheard of. Inside the cafe they were welcomed by pleasant smells of roasting morning coffee and freshly baked pastries, which mingled with the odors of cigarette smoke and yesterday's spilt alcohol. The customary greetings from the waiters were friendly as always and the service was excellent.*

An espresso sat near Christine as she spoke incessantly. The crumbs of her morning croissant lay on the table, giving evidence of her daily routine. A casual observer might have thought they were lovers. His attention to her was so utterly complete, so encompassing, that his adoration was clear. However, a detached observer might be confused by his note-taking, which he occasionally interrupted to ask her a brief question or make a fleeting comment.

If the observer were to stay a while longer, he might see this one-sided lecture evolve into a two-sided, intense discussion. Their morning drama ran almost daily, Christine talking, the American taking notes, and then discussions. To the people-watchers of Paris, Christine and the American were among the stars on the city's grand stage of the Paris Promenade.

"I wrote many notes while I was alone in the suite of the Hotel Meurice. I wrote when the German was away on 'business' and I was free to record every detail in tiny letters on the hotel stationery. When the German was 'home,' I wrote in the bathroom, the only place out of his sight. Unlike most toilets in France where old magazines were used for this purpose, the bathroom in the Hotel Meurice was furnished with ample, real toilet paper and I found it perfect for writing. My consumption of toilet paper was not questioned. Using the same trick I had used since childhood, I hid my notes carefully in the cushions of two beautiful chairs in the German's suite. I kept one area of the seat cushions

loosely tied so I could open them, insert my notes and close them quickly without revealing my deposit."

The time of Christine's captivity was her most prolific period of note-taking. She was fully aware of the significance of the events unfolding around her. Her unique circumstances and training as a journalist helped her to record events as a professional, capturing the important elements of each unfolding story of living history. Christine's notes would contribute greatly to her ability to describe what happened during Occupation in great detail. Possibly the most important benefit of her note-taking was to connect Christine to a life she had lived before and a life she hoped would return; writing was her link to hope, a method to keep her sane.

The American could tell by her seriousness and her furrowed brow that Christine was beginning on a difficult path, more multifarious than her descriptions of her relationships with the Boy, the Artist or her Husband.

"It is fresh in my mind, as if it were yesterday. It was a period when light turned to darkness, hearts beat without joy and each day brought us further into the pain of our distraught future. It was also a time when I discovered my personal destiny and completed my mission on earth."

Entering Hell: Crossing from Husband to German

September, 1941. On one side of the bridge my Husband was held by three French policemen. On the other side stood a German Nazi general; his Mercedes command car idled nearby.

My Husband and the German both stretched their arms out to me, each beckoning me to come to them. While I was holding my face to keep the blood from flowing, I was forced by gunpoint to move away from my Husband and toward the waiting German general.

I glanced back to see my Husband in blind panic and fear as he attempted to run toward me. Immediately, he was knocked to his knees and surrounded by uniformed police. He looked at me and I, letting the blood flow as it would, responded by opening both of my arms toward him to show my love. This was my last vision of my Husband as a complete man: fighting back as they beat him and dragged him into a truck filled with other Jewish prisoners.

Ahead of me, the German stood tall and arrogant. He commanded me to come to him. For the first time in my life, I felt small and completely undone. As I diffidently crossed the bridge, two Nazi SS storm troopers pointed their weapons at my face and another pushed me toward the German.

When I reached him, the German gave me his handkerchief to hold to my face to avoid spilling blood on his car. I looked at him carefully. In shock, I realized he was the German we had met at the opening of the Casino de Paris, the night Brasillach and I had confronted each other. *He was the same Nazi officer my Husband had called the handsome wolf, the man who lied when he said the Nazis came in peace.*

We entered his Mercedes, the doors slammed and we drove off in a roar. The German and I rode through the streets of Paris without speaking. There were two Nazi flags waving in the wind on the front fenders of the speeding Mercedes. I fought back the tears as I thought of my Husband and the danger he was in. I feared deeply for my own life and wondered what awful fate I was about to meet: something horribly real, a multitude of experiences beyond my worst nightmares.

We arrived at the Hotel Meurice across from the Jardin des Tuileries. We passed through the elegant hotel lobby and rode the elevator to the top floor. He led me to a waiting room in his private quarters in the Belle Etoile Suite and left me alone for some time. An army medic came in and put a bandage on the gash in my face without fully cleaning the wound. The Nazi guards were very near, I could smell the smoke of their cigarettes and hear them shuffle their feet. Everything else was quiet. A full panorama of Paris could be seen through the large windows of the room. I shivered, though it was not the least bit cold.

The German emerged from a side door and stood uncomfortably close. He looked straight into my eyes and spoke in an even, controlled monotone. I could hear a clip in his German, something indicating an educated but not noble upbringing. My Aunt could have pinpointed it precisely. After five or six sentences, she could tell a great deal about the background of any German-speaking person.

As he delivered the details of my damnation into Nazi hell, the German's eyes didn't blink. Behind him hung a large, twelfth-century painting depicting the Christ child held by his pure, Virgin Mother. It was the *Pieta*; the ultimate empathy between one human being and another, the holy connection between Madonna and Christ Jesus. To his left was another painting of Jesus, bloodied and hanging from the cross in pain, betrayal and death.

The German explained that he was the second-highest ranking Nazi general in Paris. He was in charge of the hated

SS and Gestapo troops for all of Paris. My arrest wasn't simply a matter of putting me in jail on trumped-up charges. His plan was much more grandiose. "You were carefully selected," he said. "You will frequently appear with me in public to show the world French people are happy to accept the Nazi Occupation of France. We will demonstrate through our public presence that the new high society of Paris remains alive and well, with Nazis but without Jews. You will serve the Third Reich in a special way because you are a beautiful, intelligent, young Frenchwoman who speaks fluent German."

My immediate reaction was an emphatic *no!* I would not support the Nazis in public. I would never collaborate with them! But he went on to describe the harshly persuasive methods he would use to change my mind.

In addition to using me for Nazi propaganda purposes, he insisted on my full cooperation as his sex partner. I was to be used as an object for his amusement. He made it clear he would stop at nothing to get everything he wanted. He would take whatever actions necessary to take control of my life or he would end it.

The German's threat was unambiguous, "Your Husband and your family can be executed on a moment's notice with one brief phone call. Either you fully cooperate as my sex partner and publicly support the Nazi Occupation of Paris or you and your family will die immediately. If you cooperate, I will assure your Husband's basic survival needs and allow your family to live, though I guarantee nothing more."

The German continued to speak in a direct tone and manner. "Through your relationship with me, you will show Paris that Nazis are decent people by openly living with me as my mistress. This is your life-or-death decision to make—for you and for your family. If you choose life, you will be choosing a life I control in the most intimate ways. If you refuse me, you choose death. I will turn you over to my soldiers before midday has passed. You will be gang-raped for days until they tire of you. When my generals are finished with you, they will pass you down through the Nazi SS command, first to the officers and then to the privates. Eventually, the soldiers will kill you because they know they can, because you have no power, no control and no way out.

"You belong to us as do the pigs in the farmer's pens— waiting for slaughter to satisfy our gluttony while your people starve to death in their pathetic lives. You belong to us like the paintings we take from your museums and send back to the Fatherland. You are nothing more than chattel to us.

"Your Husband still has his breath and holds onto the last light of life. His survival dangles upon the choice you are about to make and the words about to leave your beautiful French lips.

"As a Collaborator with the Nazis, your photo will often appear in the newspaper: attending the races, buying beautiful gowns and socializing with important Nazis and Collaborators in Paris. As a 'special friend' of the Nazis, you will eat the finest food, wear the fanciest *haute couture* clothes and live in the luxury of my opulent and warm suite on the top of the Hotel Meurice. The French people will see you dining at the Ritz as they starve, freeze to death, are captured, tortured and driven to the lowest depths of human depravation.

"You will be sharing your bed with a Nazi general. The fact that you were forced to become a Nazi whore to keep your family alive will not be mentioned or known. I am sure many men have lusted after you as a beautiful woman in Paris. Now many more will hate you and go to bed plotting your murder instead. This attention, your future fame, is courtesy of the Third Reich."

The pleasures he promised meant nothing. I wanted to live as the wife of my Professor, work as a journalist and enjoy the social life with our intellectually stimulating friends. I didn't want his caviar and champagne. I certainly did not want a sexual relationship with him; faithfulness to my Husband was an honored vow. I wanted my life back—but it was not to be, so I sat silently as he went on describing my hell.

He made it clear it didn't matter much if I accepted his contract or not. There were many beautiful women in Paris who wanted to live in luxury at the Hotel Meurice and who wanted their families to live. If I refused his offer, he would find another Parisian woman to happily be his mistress before the day was over. "Living with me is voluntary; the choice is up to you," he added with a sinister smile.

"One more thing," he said leaning closer. "Running away or suicide won't work. If you run away or kill yourself, your Husband and your family will be tortured and killed in a similar manner to that I described for you. If you try to escape, we will find you and that will be the end of all of you.

"This is only a one-hour option. This choice will not come again. We Nazis are not leaving Paris; we will stay here for a thousand years. We will take everything Paris has to offer or we will kill her. The same goes for you. If you choose life, dress in your finest outfit. Your clothes were brought here from your home; they are hanging in the large closet. We are going to lunch at the Ritz. If you choose death, you won't have to worry about your clothes or anything else and you will not see me again. I will only hear of you when my officers are bragging about their sexual conquests of you and the final report of your death. Then you will cease to exist.

"Oh yes," he said casually, "the Ritz has obtained some lovely, fresh white asparagus and an excellent Rhone wine. I hope you like white asparagus; they prepare it perfectly at the Ritz."

The air hung heavily in the waiting room of the luxurious hotel suite. I felt as if I were Marie Antoinette being led to the guillotine. I broke out in a sweat. It dripped down the sides of my armpits, soiling my blouse in a rain of horror. Moisture gathered between my breasts and beads of sweat fell down my stomach. My hands clammed up with moisture and fear. There was no exit, I was trapped.

The German left the room and I stared out the window, toward the Tuileries, the Eiffel Tower and the Arc de Triomphe. I was falling into my own Dante's Inferno. I feared mental and physical torture. I cursed God, the Nazis, the French and humanity. I cursed my fear, my pain and my fate. I cursed the choice I was forced to make.

How did life change so fast? How did I, a free and educated Parisian woman who had found true love, suddenly become a sex slave to a Nazi Gestapo general? My Husband and I were living such a normal life; reading the newspaper, having our coffee, eating delicious food and drinking fantastic French wines. We thought nothing was going to change and our comfortable way of life would last and last. It didn't. My heart sank. I gasped for breath. I forced myself to see the situation clearly.

I made the only choice I could: I chose to live. I knew, even if I survived, nothing would undo the horror I was about to undergo. I wondered if I chose life because of fear of my own death or because of the death sentence for everyone I loved. Either way, there was nothing I could do but follow his orders.

I made the decision to continue to keep writing my secret diary. Recording the events of captivity would help me survive mentally and provide a record of events I could use later. I spotted two chairs, special ones with overstuffed cushions. The Meurice bathroom contained a sewing kit which was perfect for the camouflage job.

We dined at the Ritz. The food and wine he ordered were excellent choices, but I could hardly taste a thing as I mechanically chewed and swallowed my food. The asparagus was steamed, covered with butter and presented with serving handles made of decorative china. As we dined, there was the daily parade of the Nazi soldiers marching down the Champs Elysées singing their haunting songs and beating their incessant drums. The Nazi-controlled press took photos of us and the German said something about the glory of the Nazi and French cooperation. As he introduced me to the reporters, he carefully gave them my full, real name, publicly damning me as a Nazi Collaborator. Our pictures and an article about the cooperation and friendliness of Germany and France were front-page news for all of Paris and the world to see. The German tried to limit the photos to my uninjured side; to keep the Nazi abuse from my public face. However, as the pictures were being taken, I turned my head and exposed my scar. I received a disapproving look from the German but felt pride in my little act of rebellion.

Café Talk: The Victors

1945. "*It was the lunch of dread. The German spoke about the world and the future as he saw it unfolding. He spoke with an arrogance and assurance I had not experienced from another person. I felt the full weight of the Nazi presence as I sat in the luxury of the Ritz. We were slaves in our own country. I want to tell you every detail of the German's perceptions. It exemplifies the frightening Nazi vision that nearly became the reality for the entire world. I want you to understand how the Nazis thought and how we were in no position to stop them.*

The German's sexual demands would violate my deepest commitment, to honor and be faithful to my Husband. How could I have sex with a Nazi monster when I loved and cherished my Husband?"

Christine and the American shifted in their chairs and sipped their coffees. She prepared for speaking and he for recording. A critical period in history had passed; the Nazis had easily conquered the most powerful nations in continental Europe and looked forward to consuming the rest. With the help of her notes, Christine began the detailed description of her lunch with the German.

The Nazi's Thousand-Year Vision

"Let me give you a glimpse of the future of France," the German said as the waiter brought a bottle of French champagne to our table. "Paris and France will become a permanent Nazi territory. What you call the Nazi Occupation will be called Nazi Liberation. French schoolchildren will be taught in the German tongue, which will become the official language of France. Textbooks will reflect the glorious victories of the Nazis over the rubble of the French and Allied armies. We will define history our way because we are the victors.

"As a colony of Nazi Germany, France will feed us raw materials and human labor. We will clean up your country for you; Jews, gypsies, Bohemians, homosexuals, vagrants, Communists and other dissidents will be rounded up and exterminated. We will take the best of France—your wine, your art and your women—as our reward for our victories. Your children will grow up in a France you and your elders won't recognize. Your youth will belong to our Nazi Youth Corps and live under our swastika flag. They will become soldiers in the Nazi war machine and workers in our military factories as we conquer the rest of Europe and the world beyond.

"Why can we do this? Because you were betrayed by your own people, you were betrayed by your allies, you were betrayed by the weak French military, you were betrayed by your politicians and you were betrayed by the divisiveness created by the French labor unions and the Communists. You were betrayed by the weak-willed, fearful French people; you were betrayed by yourselves!

"France refused to wake up to the reality of the Nazi army coming in full force toward Paris. By the time the French came out of hiding it was too late and nothing could prevent us from conquering you. Even after your armies were decimated, you pretended you were safe until we arrived on the outskirts of Paris. How naïve you were.

"I participated in the planning to conquer France, so I know you have not been safe for years. We have been preparing to take Europe ever since Germany was forced into the unacceptable conditions of the World War One treaty at Versailles. We have taken Poland, the Netherlands, Belgium and France, as well as Austria, and the Sudetenland of Czechoslovakia we annexed. We own you. It is sweet revenge!

"Please have some champagne and caviar, my dear," he said before continuing. Eating fancy food was the last thing on my mind. All I wanted to do was escape, to run, to find my Husband and live in a safe place away from these monsters.

"The Allies failed to contain the Nazi military machine as it grew, they failed to act when Germany violated the peace treaties of World War One and they failed to contain the Nazis when we began invading our neighboring countries. How did we accomplish this right under your noses? The Allies were weak and wallowing in impotent denial. Your leaders believed they could talk with the Führer and through their gutless, pacifist words, they could change Hitler's mind about his imperialist goals. They could not. Hitler used their words to weaken their resistance; their spineless words actually encouraged Hitler to attack because they demonstrated their weakness. Hitler talked to gain time for his military build-up in preparation for world domination. It was obvious, but your leaders hid their heads in the sand and refused to see it. They didn't want to know the truth because they didn't want to take responsibility through action. They didn't have the courage or the will to stop the Nazis when we were weak. Now, my dear Christine, you and your countrymen will pay dearly for their cowardliness and stupidity.

"During the military build-up in Germany, we called our twenty-ton tanks armed with .77 millimeter guns 'tractors' so we could avoid the appearance of violating the restrictions of the 'Treaty' of Versailles. You sat in cafes and restaurants, drinking, eating and frolicking like fools as we methodically built our military machine. Your leaders led you in prayer to St. Genevieve begging for another miracle to save you as we marched and loaded our weapons. Prayers could not stop us; they were just more empty words. We were coming to take Paris and we did. In the end, there was no fight; there was no French army, no British Empire, no American armies—nothing to stop us and no one to protect you. You gave up Paris without a fight. Everything you took from us after World War One has been returned to us. Most of France is conquered and we aren't leaving; you belong to us. France is ours!

"I want to tell you an irony of this war and our victories. When France's newly appointed undersecretary of defense, Charles de Gaulle, was a young officer, he published an excellent book on military tactics. It was titled, *The Army of Failure*, published in 1934. He designed a method for using modern military equipment in a coordinated assault on an enemy. Tanks, planes, cannon, mortars and soldiers would simultaneously hit the enemy's defenses from multiple directions in a devastating attack. The firing of weapons would be timed so the shells and bombs would coalesce on the target at the same time. This integrated firepower would cause a synergy of destruction which far exceeded the impact of firing these weapons individually.

"De Gaulle also strongly criticized the French government's dependence on static defenses like your ineffective Maginot Line. He was brilliant but too low in the military hierarchy to make a difference.

"For the old leaders in charge of the French military, the Maginot Line was the answer: build a fixed wall of armaments to

contain the Germans. It cost an incredible amount of money and
drained the French military budget, but it failed completely.

"Your military leaders rejected de Gaulle's premises and
his methods and punished him for his contrarian ideas by
taking him off the promotion list. The old French generals were
committed to a defensive war, vested in immobile concrete
bunkers where they could hide like cowards. They were still
fighting World War One, but everything about warfare has
changed. They did not prepare for a war of highly coordinated
air attacks working together with soldiers and huge tanks on
the ground to move the battle rapidly from one place to another,
outflanking and then destroying fixed, defensive emplacements.
The Maginot Line was only effective if attacked from the front:
once we were able to get behind it, we easily destroyed it.

"One reason why de Gaulle stood out among the short-sighted
French military officers may be because of his Germanic roots.
Did you know Charles de Gaulle is the descendent of German
aristocracy, from the ennobled Knighthood of Frankish and
northern Germanic families? De Gaulle's maternal great-great-
grandfather was born in Germany. He thinks like a German and
fights like a German because he is a German.

"There is a man who read Charles de Gaulle's book carefully
and learned de Gaulle's new concepts of war well. His name
is Adolf Hitler. He embraced de Gaulle's tactics and directed
the Nazi military to use them as attack strategies. We named
them the *blitzkrieg* or lightning war. We used de Gaulle's
battlefield tactics to conquer Holland, Belgium and France. Each
fell easily to this new kind of warfare. De Gaulle's ingenious
military strategy brought me to Paris over your dead soldiers
and destroyed forts. Now we control you, your city and most of
France. *Merci*, General Charles de Gaulle!

"By the way, where is your de Gaulle now? He lives in the
comfort of London as Parisian children starve to death. He won't

be back. France betrayed him by ignoring his brilliance and by putting the wrong people in charge of your military, and he knows it. We have killed, wounded or imprisoned over two million Frenchmen. The captured Frenchmen work for the Nazis, just like you. They are like the sixteenth-century captive slaves who built the sultan's ships and provided the manpower to row them into battle against their own people. French prisoners are the engine of our military machine. The French army, air force and navy are finished. They will not rise again.

"The British military has also fallen apart; they ran from us at Dunkirk and now stand on their own shores with pitchforks, shovels and pistols without ammunition, silently waiting for our invasion. Each day, our Luftwaffe rains bombs on British cities. The bombing will be followed by another Nazi Blitzkrieg, which will roll over their weak military into their cities like we did in France and Paris. England will be conquered. The British have no defense other than a short twelve miles of water and a few airplanes. We will cross the channel and take England as easily as we flew over and drove around your Maginot Line. England hangs like a ripe piece of fruit ready to drop into Nazi hands, ready to be eaten like a *plat de fruit*! England is the next stop on the Nazi military's agenda of world conquest. Soon London will be flying the Nazi swastika flag just as Paris does today!

"In July 1940, in the Attack on Mers-el-Kébir, French Algeria, the British bombed and sank the French fleet. They were fearful Germany would capture and use your navy against them. They killed 1,297 of your beloved French sailors in what can only be called an act of war. Britain won't save you. Many Frenchmen detest the Brits even more than they despise us. There is much the same feeling for the French across the channel; the English don't think much of you French either. Fortunately, we don't need your navy; we have our own and it is immensely powerful.

"As we enjoy our lunch at the Ritz, where is the French government, the government that repeatedly promised to protect you from the Nazis? Where are they? They fled to the south of France and left you alone. They aren't starving; they aren't dying. They failed, they lied and they fled. They won't be back. They have given us Paris and you. They are the greatest cowards of all!"

He focused on lunch again. "How do you like the white asparagus? Lovely, isn't it? Have some more Rhone wine; it is refreshing with the salad."

Café Talk: Words versus Evil

1945. *Christine grimaced as she spoke of the German's arrogance and self-assuredness. She thought back to her articles criticizing appeasement before the war and made two observations:* "Words cannot stop evil. The ability to accommodate evil and good at the same time is not a blessing; it is a curse.

"*I asked myself, where could enough good exist to overcome this evil of the Third Reich? What force on earth could possibly defeat these Nazis when nothing was able to slow them down? I couldn't see an answer. I could only see Nazi domination and the end of life as we knew it. I took mental notes to be recorded later and saved in my secret place.*"

With the exception of writing with his pen and the occasional shift of his glasses case, the American didn't move. Christine was taking him deeper into occupied Paris and further into Christine's memories. "*I hated asparagus, I hated the Nazis and I hated the German. I feared for my Husband, my family and myself. My instincts told me to agree with everything the German said. I knew it was time to keep my thoughts to myself and do everything I was told to do, anything to survive. I ate the asparagus and drank the wine. I ignored the pain of the gash on my face and I silenced the hatred in my heart.*

Christine looked down and stared at nothing. She added a twist to the story. "*At the point of our capture, we believed it was because my Husband was a Jew who did not follow the rules, and that Brasillach's publication brought us to the attention of the police and the Nazis. Later, I found there was much more behind our capture. Brasillach was just a pawn and my Husband's Jewish religion was just a pretext.*"

Succumb or Die

The German continued on with a fractured smile. "Nazi Germany is the strongest country in human history; nothing can prevent us from taking whatever we want, from whomever we want, whenever we want. This is the era of Nazi domination; it is our destiny to conquer Europe and the world beyond. Whatever or whomever we have to destroy in our path of conquest, we will destroy.

"Our enemies have a choice just like you: succumb or die. The new leaders of Vichy France serve as our puppets. They do exactly what we tell them to do or they are exterminated. As one might expect, their cooperation has been magnificent!

"What about Parisian intellectuals and entertainers? Your artists continue to paint, write and sing under the Nazi flag. Even Picasso has stayed in Paris during our occupation despite his painting misrepresenting our victories in Guernica. Edith Piaf sings her heart out and Maurice Chevalier charms us with his acts and songs. Sartre publishes prolifically and freely roams around Paris, carousing with Simone de Beauvoir as if it were the Belle Époque of Paris of the nineteenth century. They and their brethren seem happy to have the Nazis in control of Paris. I haven't heard any of them complain, have you?

"You might ask if the Americans can be counted on to help you, since they were the last-minute force that tipped the balance of power in your favor at the end of World War One and led to our temporary defeat. Let me answer that question for you. The Americans have been like allies to Germany this time around.

"We greatly respect the American mass production know-how; they are so productive. Many Nazi tanks, trucks, cars and planes were built by American-owned factories in Germany. This massive production of military equipment helped the Nazi war machine rapidly conquer Europe. Three American companies have been particularly helpful to the Nazi military: General Motors, Ford and IBM.

Bundesarchiv, Bild 101I-303-0554-24
Foto: Funke | 1944

The Blitz truck built by Opel, General Motors

"General Motors owns Opel, which builds cars and trucks for us. The Opel truck built by GM is named the 'Blitz,' for God's sake! It is the most common truck in the Nazi army, the Wehrmacht, and it was the workhorse of the Blitzkrieg that brought me to Paris and to you. In 1938, Hitler awarded American James D. Mooney, the president of General Motors Overseas Corporation, Germany's highest civilian medal, the Nazi Eagle, for his service to the Third Reich. You may be surprised to know, the largest producer of vehicles for the Nazi Army was not Mercedes-Benz or BMW—it was the American-owned GM Opel production facilities.

"Another company that helped the Nazi war effort immensely is Henry Ford's Ford-Werkes. Hitler's admiration for Henry Ford is so high he keeps a full-length picture of him on his desk. I have seen it personally.

"In addition to their unwavering support of Nazi Germany, Mr. Mooney and Mr. Ford hate Jews as much as we do. They have said as much publicly.

"Do you know IBM built an updated Hollerith punch-card system to identify Jews, keep track of the Nazi prisoners and the loot we take from France? Your Husband's name and the information we need about him is on one of those punch cards somewhere in an American-owned IBM sorting machine.

"At the same time we invaded Poland, and as a result France and England declared war on us, American-owned factories were working overtime to produce immense amounts of Nazi military equipment. They continued to do so even as we invaded Holland, Belgium and France. It was largely because of American-built equipment that we were able to reach Paris so quickly, barely giving Parisians time to close the doors of the opera house before we marched in.

"The American companies in Germany are generating huge profits for their American owners, so they aren't leaving any time soon. On the contrary, the presidents of these companies are lobbying President Roosevelt and the U.S. Congress on our behalf. They are doing everything they can to keep America out of a war with Germany.

"As we sit in Occupied Paris in September 1941, these American companies are producing tanks, trucks and planes for the Nazi military. As we sit having this lovely lunch at the Ritz, important American industrialists are doing business in Nazi Germany on a grand scale. They are true friends of the Third Reich.

"Think of the irony: the Nazis, using French General Charles de Gaulle's military tactics and riding on American-built equipment, destroyed Allied military resistance and rode into Paris as conquerors without a fight.

"Politically, Americans don't want to become involved in another world war. They want nothing to do with a second European conflict in this century, where American soldiers would again die in a European 'family fight.' Americans view Europe as outside their domain of responsibility. They are unwilling to die again for the glory of France or the pride of Britain. The cost of becoming involved in our war would be overwhelming and, from an American perspective, nothing would be accomplished anyway.

"In passing the *American Neutrality Act of 1939*, the American government made it federal law that the United States could not provide aid to any country involved in the war. They didn't differentiate between those of us who were invading and those of you who were being invaded. This law reflects America's strong isolationist fervor. This Act pulled America out of the 'game' of international politics and allowed us to annex and invade our neighboring countries with little resistance. Our friends and operatives, including Henry Ford, Mr. Mooney and Charles Lindbergh, were intimately involved in passing the Neutrality Act. We want America to continue to help Germany produce equipment for our war machine and stay neutral. We will conquer all of Europe before the Americans wake up to a Europe where Germany is 'Uber Allis,' where we are *over all*!

"Many Americans, like the great American pilot Charles Lindbergh, believe the order and stability brought by Nazi domination of Europe is an improvement over Europe's history of constant bickering and perpetual war. Mr. Lindbergh is connected to Germany on many levels. He was Gerneralfeldmarschall Hermann Goring's personal guest at the 1936 Olympics and was awarded the Silver Cross of the German Eagle by order of the Führer himself. He has spoken publicly and privately blaming America's problems on the Jews. Lindbergh is a leader in the *America First* movement, which strongly opposes American involvement in the European war. Because of his historic flight across the Atlantic to Paris, Lindbergh became one of France's most important American heroes. Now, through his efforts to keep America out of the war, he is helping Nazi Germany occupy France. It is all quite ironic, isn't it?

"We have a great deal of information about America today; we have many spies there. Americans are not building new war machines to counter the highly developed military equipment of the Nazis and our partners, the Italians and the Japanese. While we keep improving the potency and number of our weapons, the Americans are manufacturing consumer goods to meet the insatiable demand of the common man. American refrigerators will not stop Nazi Panzer tanks. America will continue in her self-indulgent path and keep her head in the sand until all of Europe, from Russia to Greece, from Portugal to Norway, and including the British Empire, is flying the Nazi swastika flag. Europe will soon be controlled by one man, Adolf Hitler, and his Third Reich. It is an amazing world we live in, don't you agree?

"We have other plans for the Americans—plans that will incapacitate their military before they have a chance to save Europe again. You will see. We will keep the Americans blindly hoping we are not seeking world domination.

We will keep talking to the Americans; they love to talk. The American companies will continue to make money off the German economy; they love to make money. Germany will continue to share our harmless technology with Americans; they love technology. We will keep promoting the image that Germany is the only European country capable of bringing order to the perpetual political chaos of Europe; they love order. We will continue to claim Germany is the only force capable of containing the Communist insurgents; the Americans fear and hate Communists even more than Nazis.

"We will engage in cultural and technological exchanges to keep them thinking we are their partners, not their enemy. Don't forget, over 1.2 million Americans are German-born and America was created in places like Germantown, Pennsylvania. German immigrants played a large part in America's foundation and her success. German influence was strong in early America and continues today. But for one vote, German would have become the official language of early America instead of English. America is a hardworking, disciplined country similar to Germany. They fought for their independence from England 160 years ago and again just 130 years ago. Don't hold out hope of America saving France or Europe this time around.

"Please, have some more of this excellent duck," he said as he stuffed a forkful into his mouth. "What a lovely day!" the German exclaimed.

As he went on enthusiastically about the Americans' friendship with Nazi Germany, a little piece of duck flew out of his mouth and landed on the centerpiece of the table. I pretended not to notice. I ate and drank as little as possible, but he kept pushing me to eat more. I did not enjoy the food, the wine or lunch. Each bite hurt my wound and I wondered if I would start bleeding again, but I didn't.

"My dear Christine, Germany is the future of France, the future of Europe, the future of the World and the future of you. Nothing can be done about it. We won.

"There is one more irony to surprise you. You and your Husband were captured because we wanted your support for our conquest of France, not because your Husband is Jewish, he didn't wear his star or you enjoyed an extra meal now and then. You were chosen for this special role to represent the 'marriage' between Germans and Parisians because of the penetrating articles you wrote criticizing the Allies' appeasement of Hitler. Those articles drew the attention of the Nazi propaganda machine, which assigned agents to investigate and follow you. I read the extensive dossier on you long before you were captured. Nazi High Command and I decided it would be advantageous to use a beautiful, perceptive young journalist who wrote about Germany's rearming as the perfect Nazi propaganda tool. We studied you carefully. We considered killing you as a dissident once we controlled Paris but decided to give you the opportunity to switch sides and publicly endorse the Nazi Occupation and live.

"Our meeting was not accidental. When Brasillach introduced us at the Casino de Paris, he was following orders as part of our plan to use you or destroy you. After we met, I thought you were so amazingly beautiful that I added your role as my 'mistress' to the plan and sold the idea to the High Command. They loved it. I admit that part of the plan was for me, not for Germany. You must admire our tactics and cleverness even if you don't agree with our ends."

Café Talk: The Nazi Vision

1945. **W**hile the German was bragging about the successes of the Nazis, each methodically presented detail caused Christine to sink further into mental depression and physical illness. "I excused myself and went to the bathroom, followed by a female Nazi officer. I vomited my lunch and more. My stomach could not tolerate the fear and elimination of hope I had involuntarily swallowed for two hours."

"The crackling fires of hell reverberated in the German's possessed voice as he spoke of Nazi conquests and how my fate would be defined by his tormented mind. I could see the repugnant Nazi future for my beloved France and my adored Paris in his unflinching, steel-blue eyes. I saw the helplessness of my life and the lives of the citizens of France.

In my defeated self and in my defeated country, I unfortunately agreed with his analysis. It was as I had predicted. My articles on appeasement had come back to haunt me as unwanted truth. But why was the United States cooperating with the Nazis, supplying their military, ignoring Nazi imperialism and refusing to stop this evil? Why had the Americans turned their backs on the civilized world, recognized the Nazi puppet Vichy French and allowed Hitler to gain so much territory? Was it simple greed, political manipulation or both?

Christine needed to regain her strength before moving on to the more difficult events to come. She took a short break and went to the counter to speak with the waiters and have a glass of water. When she returned, it was clear, despite her efforts to conceal it, that she had been crying. Her eyes were puffy and there were lines down her face where tears had fallen. Nevertheless, she returned to the table and the conversation with the American.

The snow stopped. Outside the steam-fogged windows, everything was white and pure, another sign of hope and life returning to the world's most exotic city. A second espresso, accompanied by a brioche, arrived at our table. Christine divided the pastry into two pieces by pulling it apart with her fingers, exposing the white cream inside. The American eagerly ate his half while her piece sat torn open but uneaten.

"My Husband warned me about writing those articles, but I was too stubborn and too self-assured to listen. I was a marked woman, an enemy of the Fatherland, long before the Nazis occupied Paris. I had created the hell we were living in and the hell that was to come with my brash overconfidence.

"After lunch, the German and I returned to the Hotel Meurice. He left me in his suite by myself for the afternoon. He went out to perform his duties as an occupier and oppressor of Paris. My time alone gave me the chance to write the notes of my captivity. I carefully documented the lunch conversation of the Nazi's perspective as world war overshadowed Europe and the entire globe. His disturbing words and demented visions were written on toilet paper secretly stored under the seat cushion I had spotted earlier."

Christine added sugar to her espresso and took a sip. "The next part of my story will be difficult to relive. I will say it once and not again. I am destroying my notes after today. The only thing that will survive is what you write." Christine unconsciously touched her scar and continued. "What I didn't know was that my life would soon become worse, considerably worse."

A Nazi Message

When the sun set and evening began to blanket the day's light with darkness, four Gestapo troopers came in and escorted me to their vehicle. They drove me up the Champs-Elysées in their GM Opel truck into the dark basement of the Gestapo headquarters at 84 Foch Street for interrogation, intimidation and torture.

A Gestapo officer showed me photos of my family members, accompanied by a list of their names and addresses. He wanted me to know they possessed full records on everyone I loved, including my brother, my father and my mother. They were marked as victims for rape, torture and murder should I resist the German, run away or kill myself.

Two Gestapo soldiers suddenly came in the room, grabbed me and threw me on the floor. One held me and the other ripped off my clothes and threw them aside. Then the Gestapo captain, the one who had threatened my family, violently raped me. His assistants watched and took pictures as he committed his dehumanizing act.

I was raped to degrade me; I was raped to break me; I was raped to torture me; I was raped to control me. I was raped because these men knew no other act gave such terror to a woman or left her with such permanent emotional scars as rape. It worked only too well.

For me, sex had been for pleasure, a natural joy in life. I distantly feared rape as women do, but I didn't believe I would ever be violently forced to have intercourse with a stranger. Rape was not sex; rape was abuse, rape was terror and rape was pain. Nothing I can imagine could violate my being, my core as a human and my essence as a woman more than that Nazi pig tearing me open with his penis. Until that moment, I had not felt complete, abject, all-encompassing hate for another human being.

I utterly reviled that Nazi with every bit of my heart and soul. Killing him would have brought me only pleasure.

After he finished with me, he slapped my face with his right hand and then back-slapped me with the same hand the other way. The impact of the two-stage blows reopened my wound and I began to bleed. As he pulled up his pants and departed, he said in ugly German, "I read your articles criticizing Germany. Now you have paid the price for writing them!" He threw my torn clothes at me and walked out.

I whimpered on the floor in the corner of the room in excruciating mental and physical pain. As I lay there, I remember sucking my thumb and sobbing; I could see myself crying and sucking and I tried everything to stop it but I couldn't. I was reduced to infancy and my thumb was the only security I retained on that cold floor. I heard laughter as the Nazi soldiers passed by and lasciviously leered at me. *I had reached the lowest point of my life, the very bottom.*

I was returned to the German's suite at the Hotel Meurice. I received their message loud and clear. There was no possibility of missing the overwhelming evil lurking in the hearts and minds of these Nazis bastards, no possibility at all.

That evening, I was left alone and allowed to take a long hot bath and sleep by myself. After my bath, I looked into the mirror at my naked body and I hated myself. The medic returned and replaced the bandage on my face. My mind kept focusing on those pictures of my family members and the Nazi's cold eyes staring at me. A message screamed in my brain—*"They own me!"* I couldn't fathom how I could live very long with these evil people who were controlling every part of my life.

Café Talk: The Choice to Live

1945. Christine spoke slowly as she described the aftermath of her rape. "For a long time after the Gestapo officer assaulted me, I experienced on-going, late night horrors. While the activities during the day distracted me, at night I would have excruciating flashbacks to the rape and the helplessness that it made me feel. Thoughts of the pain and horror would awaken me in a cold sweat. I could see his face, feel his abuse and remember my loss of control. I would go to the bathroom, close the door and cry uncontrollably. I had acute anxiety attacks that led to nausea. I fantasized finding and killing him over and over again; sometimes it was with a knife and sometimes with my bare hands as I scratched him bloody with my fingernails. When I involuntarily visualized his body on and in mine, it felt like snakes crawling on my nakedness. A shudder would pass through me; an internal tremor at the core of my being. These sessions of lost rationality inevitably ended with a long hot shower, a futile effort to cleanse and purify my body and my mind."

Christine was unable to continue meeting with the American this day. She was vomiting up memories and tasting the Nazi bile and soured morsels of her life that had been forced down her throat for too long. It was impossible for her to speak more until the vile taste of regurgitated hate and the rancid smells of abuse had been washed from her nostrils, her mouth and her throat.

The American bid her good-bye as their boots crunched the snow and nearby church bells rang the hour. She said little, turned left and walked toward the Île St. Louis, leaving her burdened footprints in the gentleness of fresh snow. He looked back at her; she seemed heavier than she really was, laden with the weight of her memories, leaning forward with her head down as she went. The American turned right, slowly walking toward his hotel, trying to understand her frail strength and grasping his privileged entrance into the amazing and intimate world of Christine.

German Instructions: A "Gentleman"

The next day, the German and I sat down for another eye-to-eye conversation over a Bavarian-style breakfast of meats and cheese. The hotel served us breakfast on their best china with ornate silverware. The service was precise, though the French waiter avoided eye contact with me. I sat looking at the man responsible for the attack on my Husband and me, the man who had ordered my Husband to be taken to a concentration camp, the man who held me prisoner and the man who commanded his staff to rape me to make sure I knew how far they would go to control me. The German was the uber-male persona grown into its evil extreme. He and Hitler were the living embodiment of the devil. He ignored my glare of hatred and anger as he spoke rather lightheartedly.

"I will not rape you. I will not force myself on you physically or sexually. I am not a rapist. I am a gentleman, but I have an insatiable appetite for sex. I need an active and innovative sex partner and a French woman who looks good in public. I have chosen you for those roles. It is up to you to fulfill them or not.

"Understand this carefully and completely, our sexual pleasure-giving will be initiated by you. You will be the originator of all of our sexual activities. This is one area of my life where I don't like to lead or be in control. It is your job to create an exciting sexual relationship for us. You will please me or you will die; you will 'enjoy' sex with me or you will die. I will not discuss this matter again. If you are allowed to live and share my life, then you know you are doing the right thing. If not, then..." He raised both hands in the air as if to say, "Then you will have made your choice and there will be nothing I can do to save you. You will disappear."

True to his Germanic nature, his demands and their consequences were precise; everything must go strictly according to his sick plan or there would be a horrifying end for me and mine. His demand that I initiate and enjoy sex with him created a difficult situation psychologically, more so than if I were to be raped and abused by him. Forcing me to take the lead in our sexual relationship compromised my mental protection as an unwilling victim. It confused my mind and my body and it led to unintended consequences.

The German added a new and frightening fact to their pre-Occupation connection with my life. "Nazi agents were watching your Artist boyfriend even before you met. His file was passed to us by the Italian Fascists and he was identified as an enemy of the Third Reich. Most of the Artist's Bohemian friends who stayed in Italy were exterminated. He was not a French citizen and the Italian government classified him as a criminal, so no one would have protected him. The Artist was a marked man; if he had still been in Paris when we arrived, he would have been one of the first that we arrested and killed. He was fortunate to flee. He would have met a terrible end if he had stayed.

"You first appeared in our files when you and the Artist became lovers. We tracked all of his friends and associates, and you were given your own file. When you wrote those articles criticizing the Allies for appeasing Hitler and warning of the military buildup in Germany, you came too close to the truth. You were subsequently classified at a higher threat level than the Artist."

The First Time: The German

In consideration for what had been done to me, I was allowed to sleep one floor below the German's room in the guest room alone for two nights. On the third day, the German decided to claim his bounty; he wanted the sexual pleasures he expected of me. In a calm voice, laced with authority, the German concluded our breakfast by stating, "Tonight you will sleep in my bed. I will have your bedroom attire laid out for you. Please prepare properly for the night by bathing and wearing scents. We will dine alone on the patio and then we will retire early. Is there a special meal you would like to have prepared for tonight? I will order the champagne and wines early and allow the wine to breathe properly during the late afternoon."

I did not care what we ate and I shook my head to indicate my answer. The remainder of my day was spent taming my anxieties and imagination. I hadn't healed mentally or physically from the rape and the beating, and now I was faced with a new sexual challenge with the German. I struggled to grasp what the coming night would bring.

I mulled the upcoming night over and over. My mind attempting to rationalize away my fears: a man is a man; he is just a man. All men have the same body parts, the same intimate places for stimulation, and are ultimately satisfied by the same release. I knew how to have sex with a man; it was now a matter of accepting with whom and for what reason. It was essential that I succeed, and I locked my mind into those thoughts to create the right attitude in my mind.

Dinner would have been exquisite under normal circumstances. The hotel staff and chefs went to every effort to create a meal for a king and his queen. It was a warm night so we dined outdoors with a full panoramic, breathtaking 360 degree view of Paris. A stunning full moon over the Louvre, complimented the twinkling stars and lights of the city. The table setting was classic; vases with rose buds, white candles burning brightly with hotel china and silverware.

The German came to dinner wearing expensive, stylish civilian clothes. He appeared as handsome as ever though I did everything I could to ignore it.

Appetizers, side dishes, entrees, desserts and the proper accompaniments were lavished upon us. I ate dutifully. The champagne and wine were perfect choices: a 1921, Dom Pérignon, the first vintage of this champagne produced by Moet et Chandon, and an exquisite 1929 Chateau Lafite-Rothschild. The wine had been opened to reveal its secret tastes through the exquisite qualities nurtured from the grapes only by the finest vineyards. I indulged fully and willingly. Part of my plan was to drink enough alcohol to buffer the reality of the actions I knew I was about to take.

Strangely, dining seemed almost normal. The service was impeccable yet predictable. It was a formal French meal done to perfection. Nothing was said about the coming sex. We engaged in limited small talk until the time came for us to go to bed. I rose from the table to go to the toilet and prepare myself by freshening up and changing into the negligee he had put out for me to wear. I was a little dizzy from the alcohol and felt as though I was stepping outside of myself, becoming detached, like watching myself through the window of a passing bus.

If I turned to my good side, the side without the gash in my mouth, I could see my beauty in the mirror. My breasts were firm and perfectly formed and they were visible through the sheer material. My stomach was flat and my backside formed in just the way men like them to be: each side of my buttocks round and firm. I wore the negligee with nothing underneath, no bra and no panties. I dashed myself lightly with French perfume from the *House of Silence*. I knew he would approve. There was nothing more I could do to prepare for him.

When I entered the Master Suite, I was involuntarily impressed with the magnificence of the room. There was a large bed with a midnight-blue canopy. A bathroom done in Italian marble adjoined the bedroom, with circular mirrors. It had a large tub with views of Montmartre and Sacre Coeur on one side and the d'Orsay train station and the golden dome of the Invalides on the other. It was a suite for royalty, but for me it was a place of danger and deceit. I climbed into the pale blue satin sheets next to the German's naked body and took the next step into hell.

The German stayed true to his preference to be sexually passive, with the exception of unbuttoning my negligee to reveal my naked breasts. I told him to lie on his stomach and he obeyed. I touched his shoulders, back, legs, feet and butt gently, and then I returned to each area for a more vigorous massage. I ran my hands over the entire backside of his body, gently rubbing him. My fake-loving was imperceptible in my touch, but my heart was full of hate. I remember thinking I could kill him, slit his throat in the midst of sexual foreplay.

I let my hair touch his skin as I moved my hands from his head to his feet. I sat on him, butt to butt, and massaged his shoulders. I pressed my bare breasts to his back. He was trim and fit and I could feel his muscles relax under my touch. As I stroked his body, I thought, this is how it is to smell, taste, feel, see, hear, and touch evil, to lie with Satan.

I told him to turn over and he obeyed. He was not yet fully aroused. I touched and rubbed the front of his body from his forehead to his feet, letting my hair and occasionally my breasts touch him. Unlike the other men I had known, he had no chest hair. Fortunately he didn't speak, he was there to take and I was there to give.

As I worked around his body, my hands, hair and breasts would "accidentally" brush his penis, and he became fully aroused. I knew what I had to do.

As I brought my focus to his full erection, he became *any man* to me. The cherished bonds between sex and love, the intimacy of the body and the soul, the preciousness of sexual sharing with a loved one, were broken. My body parts falsely mimicked lovemaking, as they were replaced by mechanical sex. It was beyond the negatives of loveless-sex; these were acts of love performed on a man I hated. Nonetheless, I used all the techniques I knew; using both hands to squeeze and stroke, my tongue to lick, my broken mouth to painfully suck. I eventually climbed on top of him and brought him into me to complete the sexual cycle with rapid pelvic thrusts. After he finished, it appeared that he was pleased and satisfied. He then turned away from me and passed into the world of sleep.

I was heartbroken. He was unaware of my suppressed weeping and indifferent to my prayers for God's help and forgiveness as I lay naked beside him. During my sleepless, emotion-filled night, the German slept as if he were a child. At one point, I quietly got up and went into the bathroom, where I used a towel to muffle my sobs.

When he awoke in the morning he gave little acknowledgment to me, just a nod and a half-smile, as I hid from the harsh reality gradually exposed by the rising sun. He had business to attend to and left me alone in the lavishness of the Bell Etoile suite. During the day that followed, I wept repeatedly. I fought the bitterness that was grasping at my heart, and the pain of the cut in my face. I washed my body in hot water to take away the residue of the sexual acts still hidden in the hours of darkness but no matter how hard I tried, I couldn't clean him off my body.

The first night and the first time with the German had ended. I had crossed another line, lived another experience that I had never dreamt would happen to me; I had fucked the devil.

Café Talk: The German

1945. *"I didn't want to tell the story of the first time the German and I had sex. I planned to leave out the difficult reality of having sex with the Nazi General as a captive. I thought it too harsh, too raw for you and for the readers of my Journal. But I thought carefully about including it and decided it was one of those truths that are almost always hidden, denied and therefore unknown. So I told you, and doing so has relieved me of the burden of keeping this an intimate, lonely secret. I thank you for listening to me."*

In the progression of story of Christine's captivity, only two days had passed. The American went to the bar in his hotel and started drinking. Three hours passed and a bottle of French wine was emptied before he slept alone in his small bed.

When Christine and the American were reunited, she began gravely but her energy rose as she told the next part of her story. She wanted to talk, to release herself from this part of her story. She wanted to "confess" her "sins."

"I must go deeper into the truth of my situation with the German so you know why I carry so much guilt in my heart. I will make no excuses and I will tell you the absolute truth.

"You may have guessed the rest, or maybe not. You American men are so innocent, like your cowboys out on the range; you may not want to hear or believe this part of my story but it is true, very true."

The American ordered a Pastis and sat back. "In the beginning, every thought was focused on my Husband and my family. Whatever the German and I did sexually or publicly, I remained insulated from reality. If I could not be faithful physically, I maintained my commitment to my Husband mentally, but soon things changed, and changed for the next three years of my captivity."

Sex with the German

As I had first noticed when I met him at the Casino de Paris the year before, the German was an incredibly handsome man: square-jawed, muscular, tall and a perfectly proportioned man. Hitler would have described him as a perfect example of his Master Race. His good looks, high intelligence and heroic performances in the battlefield earned him the coveted position as commander of the Gestapo and SS forces in Paris. His authority gave him control over the people of Paris and many Nazi forces as well. Almost everyone, French and German alike, feared him and his SS troops and Gestapo police. He was a man who possessed a great deal of power, with the looks to match. It was a combination that made him highly desirable to women but, in the context of the Nazi perversion of life, he used his skills and good looks to serve the most evil man in the world.

I did as the German told me to do; I became the initiator of sex. I created a sensuous and exciting sexual world and used every sexual technique I could devise to make him happy. I also gave every impression that I was enjoying sex with him. I closed my eyes and pretended I was not his slave but his lover; it was what I was forced to do to stay alive.

We had sex almost every night. Sex was his drug; sex kept him from going insane. Sex was his method for falling asleep after implementing the most horrible cruelties of the Nazi Occupation. I faked climaxes to deceive him, screaming loudly to make him believe I was experiencing pleasure. The troops stationed outside his door could hear our trysts, and I was sure there were many jokes about our frequent encounters.

After having sex with the German for some time, it was impossible to avoid becoming sexually aroused. He was a strong and hearty man, highly sexual in every way, well endowed, with a remarkable body and incredible endurance. He was like a Viking; his arms were so strong he could literally pick me up, lower me onto him and we would have sex while he was standing up. His attractive, natural smell enhanced our elongated embraces. The German was fastidiously clean. He was unlike many European men because he bathed daily and wore at least one clean shirt every day. His physical and personal attractiveness and sexual potency produced involuntary changes in me. My sexual pleasure rose naturally; it was unavoidable, automatic, and I couldn't stop it. I was in a hate-and-desire paradox and sex became my way of fighting back.

Soon I didn't want to stop. I was screaming in true ecstasy as we had sex in every room of his suite. I would climb on top of him and have a hundred little climaxes as I rode him like a horse. He called them "machine gun orgasms," something only a professional soldier might say.

I had first learned the pleasures of giving and receiving oral sex during lovemaking with the Artist. My Husband and I had also enjoyed reaching frequent orgasms this way. However, the German and I took oral sex deeper. He could not get enough of it and neither could I.

I fulfilled the fantasy many men of the world have about French women, that we are experts at making love with our mouths. It has to do with the way we speak and how our lips form words and sounds. Whenever I spoke French, it drove the German crazy; he told me that every time I spoke French it made him want the pleasures of oral sex from me.

I continued to take the lead sexually and do sexual things I hadn't done before. My experience had been on the receiving end of my lovers' aggression. Now I was the initiator. I was in sexual control and I loved it. My sexuality burst over him and, as a sexual pacifist, the German was in heaven.

We went on like this, day after day, night after night, month after month. I lived a decadent life of sex, food, wine and socializing. It was the strangest and most conflicted situation I could have imagined. I hated him as the Nazi monster but lusted for him as a man more each day. Instead of inhibiting me, fornicating for my continued existence gave me a mental license to embrace each sexual performance as an act of survival. I seduced him and gave myself without sexual inhibition. As soon as we were near each other, we became aroused, ready for the next encounter that always came. We started to have an ongoing contest to see who would climax first, and I nearly always won. I was not faking anything.

We didn't make love, we fornicated like animals; we indulged in lustful sex fueled by hate and fear, living on the razor's edge of a momentary death sentence. My body embraced his passion with my full sexual self. He needed relief and I needed life. My animalistic lust and eagerness to participate in our sexual adventures grew far beyond survival. It was not the least bit forced; I wanted every bit of it. *My terror became my pleasure; my disgrace the source of life.*

Café Talk: Sex and Opportunity

1945. *"As a wife, a woman, a Parisian and a human, there is nothing I feel worse about than my intense sexual enjoyment with the German. My sexual desire for him is a source of overwhelming guilt and angst. All I wanted was to be faithful to my Husband for the rest of my life, but there I was, deeply involved with a Nazi general.*

"However, fate bestowed a special opportunity on me. My illicit escapades as the German's enthusiastic whore yielded an unexpected and important opportunity. It is one of the important reasons to write my Journal. A strange turn of events provided my life with meaning, value and purpose and they inverted our negative relationship into a positive. The consequences of my capture went far beyond the German's original intentions when he took me from my life, from my Husband, and forced me to become his public mistress and his private sex slave.

"My greatest insight into my new destiny came during sex with the German, particularly when I was on top of him, riding him as hard as I could. In the midst of this sexual exertion, my mind revealed the possibilities of using the German's power to benefit Paris instead of contributing to her destruction. The prospect of positively manipulating the German became more distinct with each step in becoming his eager sex partner; the more intense our sex, the clearer my vision."

The American fought his strong feelings about Christine's sexual activities with the German. His interest was high and he wanted to hear more, but he suffered from passing judgment coupled with his feelings of jealousy and rage. The American was not accustomed to a beautiful woman describing her sexual activities with none of her attention directed at him, especially a woman for whom he was feeling increasingly strong attraction and who was describing her enjoyment of having sex with a Nazi general.

The semi-normalizing of their relationship put him on edge. The German epitomized the most evil of evil in humans. Christine's enjoyment of the most intimate pleasures with the German was inconsistent with *his brutal acts against her, her Husband and the French people. The American knew her behavior was a matter of survival but, within his inconsistent morals, her sexual passion for the German bothered him intensely. It was not the fact that she was forced to have sex with the German; it was that she enjoyed it so much. He didn't understand how Christine could hate the Nazi general so vehemently, miss her Husband so intently and feel such intense sexual passion for the German so wholly. It was a paradox he could not comprehend. After all, he was American and a man, while she was French and a woman.*

The American was sensitive enough to know not to verbalize his judgments, and he knew if he did Christine would expose his hypocrisy. What were her choices anyway? The American let his judgment sit dormant. He was being taught how to forgive and how to not judge. He was learning how his condemnation was partially about his own guilt and jealousy, but these lessons were hard to learn.

He was not a smoker before Paris. But here, with cigarette smoke filling every establishment, the American began to smoke. He decided to have a smoke outside, to leave the table for a pause to collect his thoughts out of sight of Christine's face, her scar and her sexual past. Smoking on the street, he thought of reasons why Christine could have become so involved with the German sexually, including the German's insistence on sexual passivity, the German's physical attractiveness, and female magnetism to illicit sex with a monster. He hated the thought that Christine became so highly aroused from mechanical, sexual stimulation, and his objection stuck in his craw like a jagged fish bone. He acknowledged that there was a feminine component to her embracing of the German sexually that he may never understand.

He took a deep breath and said to himself, "She is not a hypocrite like me. I chose to commit adultery many times only for my selfish pleasure. I didn't have Christine's burden of survival. She did what she had to do and she reacted as many people would have reacted to the situation. There was no choice for Christine as there was for me."

*Half in jest, the American asked himself a question: What if I,
as a man, were captured by a beautiful Nazi woman and forced to
have sex with her to save my family and myself? How would one judge
Christine's behavior if the roles were reversed and it was a man who was
the captive, the one who was forced to have sex with a beautiful and sexy
German woman every night?*

*When he returned from having his smoke, Christine was as impatient
as a teacher waiting for her pupils to settle down at the start of class. She
began almost before the American's pants hit the chair. She wanted her
story out and over with. Write! She seemed to command.*

*"Before I tell you the rest of the story, I have to make an important
admission. My intense sexual enjoyment with the German preceded
my plan to use sex or his love as tools for a positive end; I lost my
"innocent victim" excuse to cover my guilt long before I conceived plans
to manipulate his power for altruistic purposes. I know I made a huge
and incredibly difficult leap when I stopped having sex with him because
I was forced to and began, as a woman, to intensely lust for the sexual
acts with him as a man. At that point, I know I stopped being true to
my Husband and as a result of my betrayal to him, my guilt is often
insurmountable."*

*As she spoke, the American kept his pen busy and his lustful
imagination and condemnatory mind in check. He was fulfilling his task
as an author and had to stop judging her as a woman.*

Transformations

While I found myself involuntarily enjoying the pleasure of the sex with the German, he found himself unexpectedly falling in love with me. The German's life was focused on military training and military conquest. He killed and ordered others to kill. He captured and tortured his enemies, but he had never fallen in love. I wanted to use the German's power. If I had to use sex to develop love in his heart so I could tame and redirect him, then that is what I would do.

The German experienced deep, unfamiliar emotions and I watched him look at me with love in his eyes. I peeked at him while he sat on the edge of the bed pondering his rising feelings in a boyish manner as I pretended to be asleep.

During the years of captivity, I wore my hair in a French twist. It both reflected my mood at the time and helped me to look more sophisticated when we socialized with top Nazi brass and Collaborators. The German's admiration for my hair inspired one of his first clear expressions of love and tenderness. After one elongated sex session on the big bed of his suite, I watched him staring at me. I was sitting on a stool, naked but for a towel covering my lap, brushing my hair and looking in the mirror. I could still the feel tiny beads of sweat on my back from the exertion of bringing us to multiple orgasms.

As I looked at his reflection in the mirror, he was unaware I was watching him. There he was, the big Nazi general standing there, half limp, fully spent, looking more like a boy who just lost his virginity than a big, mighty Nazi warrior. He was not the Vicar of Hitler and not the Nazi SS officer feared by everyone; he was just a loving man staring at the beautiful woman he loved. He gently took the brush out of my hand and, with long, slow strokes, began caressing me with the brush. I looked at his face in the mirror and watched a moonstruck man.

He said he was trying to understand what was happening; new feelings were coming alive inside of him; emotions were growing in his heart not related to killing, capturing or fighting. He experienced sudden, unexpected bursts of childhood memories of his father, mother, brother and sister. He remembered friends and times of innocent, youthful joys not thought about for twenty years or more; repressed memories he had denied since he'd become a member of the German youth groups where he learned how to detest people because they were different. He also remembered, as an innocent boy, the abuse and severity of the environment of the Nazi youth camps, which partially explained his brutality to others.

The German revealed his new feelings to me openly but not to anyone else. That wasn't his way. Emotionally he was a private man. He wasn't ashamed of his feelings because they brought him much pleasure, but he was confused and a little embarrassed by them. He asked me how he could change so much and so quickly. His need to be in control as the perfect Nazi soldier became almost unimportant to him. His pledge of undying loyalty to the Third Reich and the Führer became small in comparison with his feelings for the "sleeping beauty" lying on his bed.

As his heart changed, so did his behavior toward me. He stopped abusing me mentally and started to show respect. He became interested in me as a person and viewed me less as an object.

I called his major shift "the transformation." He spent time kissing and holding me before expecting delivery of his pleasure through my acts of sex that he loved so much. Instead of having sex and then turning away, as he had done in the beginning, he would touch me afterward. He would hold me and stroke my legs and my back. He wanted our bodies to touch as we slept. He brought me champagne for no reason other than to celebrate his growing feelings. I was no longer just his whore.

However, even as the German began to act more like a lover and less like a captor, I knew I would not be freed. He was like a man who loves his favorite dog but would never consider freeing it.

His changes occurred elsewhere; his Teutonic rage was softened. He no longer enjoyed the brutality of enforcing the Nazi Occupation. His orders for torture and reprisals were less draconian, less brutal. He pointed out how, other than members of the Résistance and the Jews, many Parisians benefited from his feelings for me and the decreased need for brutality which they produced.

He didn't become an entirely different person all at once; he changed in shades, one step at a time. He started bringing gifts: the finest jewelry, books and clothing Paris offered. Unfortunately, these things had often been stolen from Jews who had been deported or killed. Jewish shops were raided and closed. Jewish homes were ransacked and left bare of valuables. Jewish bank safety deposit boxes were broken open and the contents confiscated. The best of the bounty was brought to the German to take what he wanted before it was shipped to Germany. He didn't see the poison of these goods; he saw them as his possessions and as legitimate presents for me. I refused nothing. There was no need to provoke him and it would not have helped anyone anyway; for most of the previous owners of the property, it was already too late.

His focus on his job became diffused. He made up a number of little love poems like the Cyclops Polyphemus wrote for Galatea until he found she loved another and then killed the object of her love in a jealous rage. The German reminded me of the Cyclops in frightening ways.

One night, we had an excellent dinner matched with the perfect wine at Maxim's. The Nazis had brought in their own chef; Berlin restaurateur Otto Horcher who ran Maxim's like a German restaurant. We returned home to experience as much "happiness" as I could enjoy as a captive in Nazi-occupied Paris while having a sexual relationship with an SS general who held my Husband in prison. When we were preparing to go to sleep, he asked me to sit next to him on the bed. He touched my damaged face with his forefinger. He stroked my scar softly and gently as one might pet a loving dog. He didn't verbally apologize for the wound he had caused, but he demonstrated his change of heart with his small actions. I didn't sense that he experienced guilt; his capability to feel guilt seemed nonexistent. I do think he recognized my pain and he wasn't happy that I had suffered. His love was as innocent of a love as he, the Nazi general, could experience.

An important sign of the German's changing feelings was a decision he made about my Husband. He moved my Husband from the concentration camp to the safer environment of an airline production facility. The factory was located in a converted American car factory and was making Nazi engines for the airplanes to bomb the Allies. As a factory worker, my Husband was allowed to live, eat and sleep as long as I continued to take care of the German.

In a decision that may have saved my Husband's life, he moved him again, this time twenty miles from the French coast to help build the Nazi defenses of France. The German boasted how he made my Husband's life better with these changes, though I silently objected to my Husband's captivity at all.

By the second year of living with the German, our relationship took on some qualities of a long-term, man/woman affair. If I was too tired or too cold to attend a social event, I would complain almost like a wife. He didn't mind at all. If I was uncomfortable or not feeling well, he would change plans if I wanted him to do so. He was happy to stay at home with me.

There was a synergy to these changes. As he became comfortable in our relationship, the center of control changed. He enjoyed a certain dependence on me to help with personal things like his attire and grooming decisions. As his expressions of love grew, he would ask me what I wanted to do or where I would like to go. He loved to ask my opinion of people, of French Collaborators and Nazis alike. I gained a significant amount of control in our day-to-day lives as he responded to my female seduction. I was moving into the German's heart like a Trojan horse towed into the center of the enemy's fortress, lying still until it was the perfect time to emerge and change the battle from defeat into victory. These changes in our relationship were to directly impact how our story would end and how we drastically changed the history of Paris.

Café Talk: A Woman's Surprise

1945. "*I want to reveal something important to you, something you have not heard and something that is a large part of my story. I want you to understand the full context in which the German and I lived.*

"*The German and I bore a child together, a daughter; her name is Gabriella. She continues to be one of the most complex aspects of my life. I know you will want to discuss her, but I want to wait for Gabriella. We can address her later, when we have covered the rest of my story. Will you please be gracious and let her rest for now?*"

The American was stunned by the news that there was a child. He was frustrated by Christine's request to leave Gabriella out of the story until later. He responded as best as he could. "*Christine, I am shocked you had a child with the German. Yes, I have many questions. A child changes things dramatically. You have an heir; a vital part of you will remain after you are gone. I am so glad for you! Gabriella is such a beautiful name. She must be gorgeous. Can I meet her? Where does she live?*"

Christine stuck to her position of deferral. "*We will cover this later. I will mention two things to put her birth in context of the rest of the story; she was born on September 8, 1942, and she lives in Versailles with her nannies. Now I want to continue with the German. There is much more ahead.*"

War Games

A second part of the transformation took place when the German began discussing the details of the war with me. Nazi officers were obliged to support Hitler's policies and decisions without question; they were precluded from expressing doubts or criticisms of Hitler's self-proclaimed manifest destiny to conquer Europe or any of his military decisions. The German was too intelligent and knew too much to be absolute in his support of everything Hitler did. He was full of doubts and questions about the direction of the war and about Hitler's leadership, but the German could not trust his fellow Nazi generals. Each general was ordered to report any suspicious, disloyal behavior to the Nazi supreme headquarters. Even suspicion of disloyalty would lead to demotion or death.

In contrast, the German came to trust me completely. He needed to honestly discuss his opinions about the war with someone and he chose me; there was no one else.

He spoke of his opposition to Germany breaking the Soviet-Nazi Non-Aggression Pact and the invasion of Russia in June 1941. He studied other battles with Russia in the war college and watched the toll on the Nazi fighters grow as Germany repeated this historic mistake. He knew it would take a huge commitment of Nazi military resources to win on the Eastern Front, resources in limited supply which would be taken from other battles and occupied territories.

Because of Hitler's unprovoked attack on Mother Russia, the French Communists and the unions they controlled turned violently against the Nazi occupiers. The Communists became the base of the French Résistance with whom the German and his troops continuously fought. "Hitler should have waited until we conquered Malta and North Africa, he should have waited until we conquered Egypt and England before he attacked Russia. Hitler's premature attack on Russia will weaken our ability to defend Paris. Both our defensive and offensive capabilities have been compromised by redirecting our forces to fight in Russia.

"General Rommel knew we must take Malta to conquer North Africa and we needed North Africa to control Europe. Once Rommel said, '"Without Malta, the Axis will end by losing control of North Africa."' Hitler didn't conquer Malta and he didn't invade England because he just couldn't wait to attack Russia. That was a huge blunder. Russia is the Achilles heel of the Nazi empire."

The German went to the war room to observe the troop movements and the projected thrusts of the armies on both sides. Each day the maps changed; each day an advance by one army was matched by the retreat by another. He showed me maps with the immense stretch of land the Germans would have to take from Russia to truly dominate her. The magnitude of the Russian Front dwarfed the combined battles for Holland, Belgium, France, North Africa and the Mediterranean. His concern was evident in his tight facial muscles as he spoke of Russia and her extraordinary ability to bleed and endure even against the vastly superior Nazi fighting force.

We discussed military tactics, the weaknesses and strengths of various positions and the probable outcomes of battles, victories and defeats. I found myself strongly attracted to the logistics of war and we had intense discussions about various battles. I surprised him again. The German said my comments and arguments were sound and often better than those he heard in the official Nazi briefings. It was another way of engaging him. It was another game to play and I became an expert at playing it.

Sometimes I was wrong. A defensive position would hold when I thought it would fail or an army would make progress when I thought it would fall back. We played this game almost every night. Sometimes we bet, usually something sexual between us, and we always paid our debts.

To prevent cheating, I insisted on writing down our predictions so neither of us could change them after the fact. We used the Hotel Meurice stationery to make our notes, which I secretly kept. On the top of each sheet we wrote the name of a battle or a place where the fighting was to occur. We argued and debated the possible next moves of the Allies and the Nazis. We wrote down the outcomes we predicted. On the top of the page we wrote Malta, Stalingrad, Greece, Sicily, Normandy or wherever the battles were hot at the time.

Under the heading, we wrote points such as the estimated length of time for the battle and the ultimate outcome. The war room contained detailed data compiled by the Nazi reconnaissance from throughout Europe, North Africa and Russia, including troop strength, armor, aircraft and ships committed to a given battle. Eventually, we wrote Paris on the top of a sheet, but we didn't debate the outcome. At that point, we knew who was going to win. We stopped playing the game all together and switched our efforts to surviving the coming Allied attack.

Café Talk: An Embedded Journalist

1945. *It was misty and cold the next time Christine and the American met. Though it was warm inside the café, Christine carried a persistent chill. She pulled her jacket tight as if she were searching for a level of comfort that could not and would not exist for her again. She became like a trusted mistress of a man who was wrapped in terror and death. She knew he would never fully leave her; she would always have the mark the Nazis seared on her face; like the seared symbol of a branding iron or the permanent mark of Cain.*

The American put down his pen and took off his glasses. He fiddled with the worn glasses case as he gathered his thoughts, flipping it from side to side a couple of times as he contemplated what he was going to say. "I continue to be amazed and stunned as your story grows. I imagine you standing in the Nazi war room, looking at the maps and listening to the German speak of the war as a huge puzzle with many moving parts. The two of you had a unique and complex relationship. You earned his love and his trust. He was a lonely man who didn't understand his emerging emotions. I don't blame him for falling in love with you. I don't think any man could experience you so intimately and remain detached or indifferent. Receiving your affection, real or not, would make the heart of the hardest man soften.

"It is strange that you could make a game out of the war and give each other 'prizes.' How were you able to separate yourself from the reality of the real horror your game represented?"

Christine responded with a quick, understated smile and said, "I saw history unfolding on those maps, which were rarely observed by anyone but top military commanders. I knew the red and black pins showing the attacks and counterattacks were boys being pushed to kill and people trying to survive in the midst of human-created hell. I knew innocent people were being crushed under those moving arrows. I knew their terror was absolute and many Guernicas with their death and dismemberment were occurring every time the arrows moved, but my revulsion and sadness remained hidden and compartmentalized. Initially I listened and offered limited responses when asked. This was his world, his war of tanks and death."

Christine told of watching the maps change as the war machines of strong armies fought for dominance, violently trying to take or to hold territories that weren't even theirs.

"After I played at the German's war, I would retreat to the bathroom or wait until he was out on an assignment to record what I learned. I remained a journalist, playing and recording these war games. As the Allies advanced hedgerow by hedgerow toward us, fate pulled me closer and closer to the core of the evil force occupying Paris.

The American became curious, "Why didn't you find a way to turn over the information to the French or to the Allies? It might have helped win the war."

"I lived in an isolated Nazi-bubble. I trusted no one. The consequences of such an act were too threatening. I could never trust the Communists in the Resistance and they would not trust me, for they believed only evil things about me. I knew I could not violate the confidence of the German, he was my lifeline. At the same time I was learning the military information, Father Jean had left France. I decided I would do it on my own. I needed no help in making the German love me or Paris.

"I will not turn my notes over to the Allied interrogators; they are the ones who honor my rapist. There is no evidence that the goals of these French and American bureaucrats correspond with mine in any way.

"My war was elsewhere: in his bed, in our socializing and in the monuments and buildings of Paris herself. My arsenal was not tanks or airplanes, not rifles or knives that defeated troops and captured territory. My weapons were my mind, my body and even our daughter. My goal was not death but life. My victory would be the saving of my Husband, daughter, family and myself and, in the end, the writing of my Journal."

My Aunt, Dresden Destroyed

My Aunt was forced to leave Paris because of her German citizenship. The crosscurrents of hate drove her back to Nazi Germany. She did not leave Paris in good graces with my family, for they hated all things and all people who were German, even in-laws. Later, she was killed in the massive British-American bombing of the Nazi controlled city of Dresden on February 13th, 1945. It was an immense bombing raid, a British-American massive Guernica-like attack meant to warn the German people to surrender or die. She was my other-mother; I loved her profoundly and her death was exceedingly painful. I lost another important person to the war, this time killed by British and American airplanes.

Malta, Sicily, Italy

July 10, 1943. The Nazi and Italian air forces tried everything to turn the island of Malta into dust, to take this irritating player out of the war, but they failed. Malta lived after enduring three years of bombing with intensity many times greater than London at the height of that brutal bombing campaign. The siege of Malta was finally over. The Maltese citizens and the British soldiers assigned there proved again that human willpower can change history even when it is against all odds. Two times in their history the Maltese fought off the strongest militaries in the world, and both times Malta survived through her pure, stubborn will.

As a result of Malta's unlikely survival, she remained a British military base. Malta was next used to assemble the largest amphibious assault force in modern history for the Sicily invasion. Hundreds of ships loaded with thousands of men and tons of equipment departed Malta and successfully landed on Sicily at three points: the British at Syracuse led by General Montgomery, the Canadians at Piachino under Montgomery's command, and the Americans on the Gela beachhead led by General Patton. In the war room we watched the black arrows move off the beaches piercing the heart of Sicily as the Nazis were driven back.

The Allies fought against heavy Nazi and light Italian resistance as they moved through the island. Five weeks after the invasion, the Allies controlled Sicily—that is, if anyone could ever "control" Sicily. They drove the Nazis off the island. However, due to Allied command errors and Nazi cunning, most of the Nazi army successfully retreated to mainland Italy before they could be captured or killed. Complete Allied victory in Sicily was stymied by competition and conflict at the highest and most personal level between the American and British generals, Patton and Montgomery, which allowed the Nazis to evacuate 100,000 troops right under their noses. It was a large military force they would have to fight again, further north, deeper into Italy's heart.

The Allied deployment didn't seem to bother the German; he was suspiciously casual about the Allied invasion of Sicily. He said he wouldn't bet with me on the outcome of the Italian Campaign and commented it wouldn't be a fair bet. What did he know that he wasn't telling me? Regardless of his odd behavior, I was elated. Malta survived and the Allies opened a new front against the Third Reich. The Allied victory in Sicily was a rare piece of good news in 1943.

September, 1943. The British and Canadian troops crossed the straits at Messina and landed on the Italian mainland unmolested. The Italians saw the writing on the wall, as it was obvious the Allies were going to conquer all of Italy. As a result, the Italian government voted to make the King of Italy commander of all Italian forces. He removed Mussolini from power. In an abrupt change of alliances, Italy declared war on Germany and Italy's allegiance was pledged to the Allies. The Nazis lost an ally and the Ring of Steel was broken.

As newly converted friends, the Italian leaders shocked the Allied command with precise information on the immense, grossly underestimated Nazi defenses and troop strength in Italy. The German then told me why he had been so cavalier about losing Sicily. Conquering Sicily was not the victory the British and the Americans had thought it was; it was a well-designed Nazi tactic, a calculated delay and retreat which gave the Nazis time to fortify their defensive positions in central Italy. They built massive defensive lines across the Italian peninsula south of Rome with names like the Volturo Line, the Barbara Line, the Gustav Line and the Caesar C Line—defensive fortifications that crossed the peninsula of Italy like walls of death.

Each successive line was constructed to stop the Allied soldiers and prevent the Allies from reaching the soft underbelly of Nazi-controlled southern Europe. The proximity of the Nazi defensive positions would assure massive destruction in the Italian towns of Ortona, Pescara, Casino and Anzio Beach, which happened to be located where the Nazis chose to make their stand. The Allied commitment to drive the Nazis out of their defensive positions guaranteed large civilian casualties as men and machines clashed in heated battle in and near populated villages.

Most of the Italian fleet escaped the wrath of their Nazi friends-turned-enemies by successfully fleeing to Malta and surrendering to the Allies. However, the Nazis sank the Italian battleship *Roma* as she attempted to escape the nest of the angry Huns.

Because Mussolini was allied with the Nazis, the Italian King Victor Emmanuel III had him arrested and imprisoned in the Gran Sasso in Abruzzo on Italy's Adriatic side. He was held in Campo Imperatore, a mountain town just two hours from Pescara, the birthplace of his deceased friend and the idol of the Artist, Gabriele D'Annunzio. Mussolini escaped with help from Nazi paratroopers who, in a daring raid, flew gliders into the mountaintop prison and rescued him. He was first taken to Nazi-occupied Austria and then to Salo on Lake Garda in Nazi-controlled Northern Italy to re-establish fascism. Again, the fates and spirits of Mussolini and D'Annunzio continued to interact; Lake Garda was also the location of the estate named *Vittoriale* that D'Annunzio had built in honor of himself, which became the poet's final resting place.

In Mussolini's second escape attempt, he tried to reach Switzerland. He and his mistress were caught and killed near Lake Como by Communist partisans. Their naked bodies were hung upside down in a gas station for viewing and defilement in Milan, where they were spat upon by their fellow Italians. Mussolini was decapitated and his head was marched around Italy to remove any doubt of his demise.

The German was not particularly discouraged by Italy's switching sides. As noted in the world's press, the Allies' movement up the Italian peninsula progressed at a snail's pace. The Allies were yet to encounter the most difficult defenses and the Nazis remained in control of most of Italy.

Although Italy was one of the greatest countries in the world, Italian armies were not the best allies for the Nazis; many of their soldiers did not want to fight and gave up easily. The Italian people's hearts were not in this war. The Italian positions were points where the Axis defense lines often broke, the weakest links in the Axis' defensive chain. The Italian pilots were known for dropping their bombs and heading home as soon as the antiaircraft guns started shooting at them and, in doing so, widely missed their intended targets. Many Italians, who were fighting side by side with the Nazis before the Italians switched allegiances, were taken captive. Many died under the same Nazi boot that had goose-stepped with them just a brief time before.

Despite the German's smug attitude, I saw hope. I saw a glimmer of the light not seen since my capture. Maybe the Americans, the British and the Canadians could defeat the monolithic Nazis at their own game: attack, attack, attack.

November 28, 1943. The Big Three, American President Franklin D. Roosevelt, British Premier Winston Churchill and General Secretary of the Communist Party Joseph Stalin, met in Tehran, Iran. The purpose of their meeting was to jointly plan the destruction of the Nazi military and the defeat Nazi Germany. The German showed far more concern about this meeting than he had about the Italians' betrayal. He feared the

Big Three would formally and effectively coordinate their forces to wage total war on Nazi Germany, and he was right.

Immediately after the Tehran meeting, the Nazi generals in Paris were visited by high-level officials from the Nazi command in Berlin. They discussed their strategies in light of the increasing Allied threat. After the Nazis' failure to conquer Malta, the loss of Sicily, the toll of the Russian Front and the coordinated efforts by the Big Three, the German began to worry about the long-term success of the Third Reich. He kept an optimistic front for the troops and generals; to discuss his honest thoughts, he had only me, and I was a very willing listener.

Café Talk: No Longer A Victim

1945. *Christine paused to explain the shift in her mind and heart. "I was no longer willing to be a victim, no longer willing to wait for the next particle of cruel fate to crash on my head and no longer willing to accept life as others defined it. I was waking up from self-pity and becoming more like the people of Malta. Instead of giving up, I was standing up. I paid every price I could pay except for my death, and I was angry, very angry. I refused to accept defeat. I was becoming stronger from the growing fire burning inside of me. My mind reached an incredible level of clarity. Instead of lamenting, I started planning. I was determined to make a contribution to the defeat of the Nazis. The next step was to convert the German from a Paris-hater to a Paris-lover. Then the possibilities of using the German's power for purposes of good could be explored."*

The American asked, "How could you change someone like the German, a man born and bred into evil?" Her storytelling continued as she gave a slight smile. "I knew Paris could melt the heart of any man. All I had to do was take him to my favorite places and he would be hers."

French Compagnons and "My Paris"

I proposed to the German that I show him the special places in Paris that I loved. I called them *"My Paris."* He enthusiastically agreed. I was about to change his attitude forever. I knew the spirit of Paris would become like a lover and a friend to him so I designed a methodical plan to make each of her "body parts", her beautiful sites and creations, intimately known to the German.

Much of what I learned about Paris monuments and buildings, I learned from my father. Before the Occupation, my father was a master builder. He was a member of the French *Compagnon*, a secret society of builders with roots in the Middle Ages which originated during the building of King Solomon's Temple a thousand years before Christ. During that historical time, the Compagnons were the builders and the Knights Templar were their protectors.

In modern France, Compagnons are certified in a specific profession, such as a mason or a carpenter. The Compagnons were men who loved their work and produced works of love. My father became a joiner and cabinetmaker after he followed a rigorous training program, served an apprenticeship, and completed the Compagnon *Tour de France*, where aspiring Compagnons travel and work in five French villages over five years. After completing his courses and the extensive apprenticeship, he became a *Compagnons Finis*, a Master Craftsman. He was given a secret name and sworn into the guild. We didn't know my father's secret name but his training was integrated into every aspect of his disciplined life.

Our family, without my mother, would spend Sunday afternoons visiting the great Parisian buildings. My father would explain various challenges and techniques involved in constructing these buildings and the purpose they were intended to fulfill.

During Occupation, my father was part of the Compagnons who opposed the Nazis and the Vichy French. Other members of the Compagnons were turncoats who gave Compagnon secrets to the Nazis and, because they violated their oaths, they earned the deepest scorn from my father.

My father's steadfast refusal to join the Nazi sympathizers put him in constant danger. The German knew of my father's refusal to cooperate, but as long as I took care of him, he kept his Gestapo from harassing my father and protected him from persecution.

I spoke to the German about Paris' beautiful buildings and parks. I tried to make the visits similar to the outings with my father and to give the German a positive view of the famous and not-so-famous sights of Paris. Because he had only approached her as an aggressive conqueror, the German had aroused Paris' defensive and protective side as he touched her soiled back alleys and entered her putrid sewers to chase his enemies. He did not know Paris' grand sites of elegant beauty and stunning brilliance, which stood, unseen, all around him.

I showed the German *My Paris* as if he were a foreign tourist visiting Paris for the first time, not the Nazi SS general responsible for repressing and killing her citizens. I gave her to a man—and I knew Paris was a master at handling men. But to know Paris openly and deeply, he would have to learn how to be her patient seducer, luring out her best features through love and tenderness, not through his excessive dominance and abuse.

I repeated my father's descriptions of the construction techniques used to build the Paris monuments, parks and buildings. Coincidently, the German had begun studies in architecture as a young man, so he understood my father's comments about construction and design. Without the war, the

German might have become a successful architect instead of a professional soldier, but that was not his fate. Under Hitler's control he became a destroyer, not a builder.

Before the tours of *My Paris* began, I decided there was nothing I wouldn't do to convert the German from a Paris-hating Nazi to a Paris-loving human being. I wanted him to love her as I loved her. I would use my love of Paris and his love for me to create a link: learning to love Paris through his love for me. Her survival would depend on it.

I committed to give all of her to him; her Tuileries, her neighboring Versailles, her Palais de Luxembourg and Gardens, her Notre Dame, her Place les Vosges, her islands, her bridges, her Champs Elysées, her St. Julien le Pauvre and more. I would fully give him the Paris I truly loved as I had wholly given him my body, my life and my passion. Only by fully revealing my deepest feelings and showing my genuine love of Paris could I hope to convert the German. I needed the force of unbridled love on my side or I would lose this battle to evil ambition, weakness and hate.

For our first visit in the *My Paris* tour, I "gave" the German the *Tuileries*. Even as an occupied city, the streets, parks and cafes of Paris were open and busy with Parisians and German soldiers. We walked over the site where the massive Tuileries Palace once stood. It was burnt and destroyed by radicals of the Commune in 1871. There was no trace of this once-magnificent palace. He said, "Yes, the Commune is an example of French chaos, a 'cult of multiple sensations,' which we have ended for you. We have rid Paris of these Bohemian anarchists. There will be no revolution by the unwashed, degenerate, false intellectuals while the Nazis are in control of Paris."

Ignoring his comment, I explained how the building of the Tuileries Palace was begun in 1564 by another French queen who was from Italy: Catherine de Medici from Florence. She was Henry II's queen consort and mother of Henry III, to whom she was also an important advisor. She was related to Queen Marie de Medici, the second wife of King Henry IV, who rebuilt the Palais de Luxembourg and Gardens fifty years later. They were both part of the wealthy Italian Medici clan who brought huge dowries and wealth to support the lavish living of French royalty.

I pointed to the two open ends of the Louvre. The Tuileries Palace connected the Louvre on both ends after it was expanded in the nineteenth century by Napoleon, also a resident of the Tuileries Palace. This final construction created a massive Louvre-Tuileries complex, which squarely surrounded extensive gardens. I tried to list the kings and queens who lived there but I forgot some of them. I explained how extreme jealousy and anger directed toward the Royal Family, aggravated by the Royals' indifference to the common peoples' needs, led to violence and their obliteration. The German was fascinated by the stories of the ongoing turmoil in French society and lamented the "meaningless destruction of what must have been a grand palace by a bunch of immature, misdirected idealists who knew only how to destroy, but not how to create." I didn't mention the parallel with the Nazis' tendencies to do the same destructive things and it did not occur to him in his Nazi mindset.

We walked up to the Place de la Concorde and then back to the Louvre. The trees in the Tuileries had only a few leaves remaining on the branches but there were many leaves on the ground and they were colored red, yellow and orange. Small circling winds picked up the leaves and swirled them into mini-tornadoes, only to let them go, leaving them to settle back to earth. It was cool but sunny. The sky was light blue with pink, cotton-like clouds slowly drifting to the east; fall was holding the approaching winter at bay for just a bit longer. It was another perfect Paris day.

In contrast to the tranquility of the Tuileries, we passed a formation of Nazi Panzer tanks on our left which reeked of destructive might. We encountered heavily armed Nazi troops at the Louvre and along the Rue de Rivoli. As we walked arm in arm, the German smoked a cigar, something he rarely did. It smelled sweet as the smoke vanished into the cool air. I held on to him as we walked past the sailing ponds. I almost smiled in memory of my childish attempt to paint the boats and my foolish hope to instantly become a great artist. That time of seeking seemed so long ago as I walked with the Nazi general in his full uniform.

At the end of the park, the German and I looked up the massive avenue of the Champs Elysées leading to the Arc de Triomphe. It was here where the Nazi conquerors had marched into Paris unopposed, and where they had marched incessantly and played their irritating music since the beginning of Occupation.

On our second Sunday visit, we took a car to *Versailles*, a massive chateau filled with beauty and history. The German wanted to visit the palace where the German Empire was created and housed from 1870 to 1871, after France lost to Germany in the Franco-Prussian War.

He smugly wanted to gaze into the room where the signing of the 1919 Treaty of Versailles ended World War One, the *War to End All Wars* that didn't. Amazingly, both historic events occurred in the same room, *La Gallerie des Glaces, the Hall of Mirrors.*

According to the German, the Treaty of Versailles required Germany to pay impossible World War One reparations and placed unrealistically tight restrictions on German development of military equipment and armies. He credited the restrictions of that unfair World War One treaty for creating World War

Two. I silently agreed that the terms of the treaty were too harsh for Germany, but that clearly did not justify the Nazis' murderous attacks on other countries or their brutal occupation of most of Europe. I knew the treaty problems were another Nazi rationalization for their imperialistic goals, but I said nothing as he went on. "These events eventually led me to Paris as a victor and allowed me to be your conqueror."

I pointed out how King Louis XIV, *the Sun King,* moved into the Chateau de Versailles in 1682. This grandson of Marie de Medici took fifty years to build the most magnificent chateau in the world. He filled it with extraordinary art and furnishings. The king's bedroom was in the center of the chateau and the sun's path crossed directly over his bed. King Louis XIV moved the French court to Versailles to fully integrate his personal and professional life in this spectacular setting.

The chateau gardens were created by Andre Le Notre and were the largest gardens in the world. The king's engineers developed a unique pumping system called *La Machine de Marly* to bring water from local lakes and streams. There were ponds and streams everywhere. The earth exploded with a million flowers and trees.

The German appreciated our visit to the village of Versailles. It was such a pleasant village that the German commented how it was the kind of place he would like to settle in after the war, and a great place to raise a family.

One Sunday our walk began again at the *Jardin des Tuileries,* through the gate across the street from the Hotel Meurice, but this time we turned left and crossed the Pont Royal Bridge over the Seine. We walked up the Rue du Bac and turned right on the Boulevard St. Germain toward the *Palais de Luxembourg* and the gardens.

I couldn't help thinking of the innocent day when I had walked toward the Artist's show and what had happened in my life since. I revealed nothing of my thoughts to the German. I didn't want to distract him from the presentation of *My Paris.* I remained careful to avoid speaking of men in my life to keep alive the illusion that there had been no others. It was part of our complex man-woman, captor-captive, fanaticized German-Parisian dance.

Regardless of my facade, my mind was free to think of whatever or of whomever I chose. I privately enjoyed thoughts of my Husband whenever the need to escape mentally arose. I thought of each day of our love affair and marriage as my mind walked through our times as student and professor, our meeting over spilt tea, our passion, our wonderful marriage and our short lives together as husband and wife. I tried to remember each moment, each laugh and each kiss. My sanity depended upon thoughts of simpler, happier and freer times. I hid my smile from the German as I recalled these wonderful moments of life and love.

I focused only on good memories of my lovers. I ignored the problems with the Boy and the Artist; I needed positive memories to overcome the harshness of my reality. I remembered the day I met the Artist and how quickly it had progressed into open-eyed lovemaking between two strangers on the dining table of his studio. That was an amazing day!

Outside the garden gates and across the Rue Compte, the German and I sat on a bench for an hour and talked. I spoke of the reasons why I loved Paris and why people from everywhere in the world loved Paris, as he listened intently.

On another Sunday visit, we visited the Roman *Arena at Les Arenes de Lutetia*, the favorite refuge for the homesick Artist. Built in the first century, the arena could hold fifteen thousand people, with spectacular views of two rivers before the city grew up around it. As we sat in the stands, a boy kicked a soccer ball on the arena floor where gladiators once fought Christians and lions to the death.

I discussed ancient Paris with the German, with an emphasis toward military conquest, because I knew war was his passion. The people of Gaul lived in ancient Paris beginning in the third century B.C. They were conquered by the Romans four hundred years later, in 52 B.C., when Emperor Julius Caesar is credited for founding the Roman colony of *Lutetia*. Lutetia was established on the Left Bank and on the Île de la Cité. Lutetia became a thriving Roman town. The name was changed to Paris in 212 A.D. after the original tribe of Gallic people called "Parisi" who lived before the Romans.

The German knew nothing of ancient Paris, but he respected the Roman armies and their society, especially how they achieved and maintained world dominance for so many centuries. It was a level of conquest he envied and desired.

As we discussed the Roman Empire, the German drifted off into a vision he often described to me, to a dream of world dominance by the Nazis. In the dream behind his Nazi eyes was a Third Reich much greater than the Roman Empire where he and other Nazi generals would reap immeasurable bounties, a dream very close to becoming reality. I again wondered to myself, *who or what can possibly stop them?* The German was lost in dreams of castles and chateaus spread over the vastly expanded Nazi Empire. "All of this is ours," he seemed to say in his faraway eyes.

When he returned from daydreaming, we discussed the cruel games played in this arena almost two thousand years ago, and how the Romans relished public violence and death for sport. The arena reminded him of the spectacular 1936 Berlin Olympics he'd attended, where Hitler created early films in an attempt to document Nazi superiority. I did not remind him of the performances of American Negroes like Jesse Owens, who outperformed the German "Master Race" in many of the competitive events staged in the heart of the Third Reich.

From the Roman Arena, we visited the Roman baths at Cluny. We continued to speak of Lutetia and of the ancient people who fought, played and loved on these grounds. The emphasis on baths and massages lead the German to comment on Roman excesses. He was critical of Roman debauchery, indulgences and their lack of discipline. He claimed it led to the decline of their society and ultimate defeat. He stated that such indulgences were not necessary for Germans, as he contrasted the Third Reich with the rise and the fall of the Roman Empire. "The Germans will not do that," he said flatly. I began to gently protest his logic, but he dismissed me with a wave of his hand.

As we explored the old Roman baths, there were many wild cats living in the ruins. I wondered how they survived in a city of starving people. Afterward, the German relaxed a bit. I knew he was enjoying himself. He even laughed at one point when I told him I would have liked to take a Roman bath with him. He pointed out that men and the women bathed separately in ancient Rome. I countered with my expectation that generals in Rome or Germany could probably take a bath with whomever they pleased! A broad smile and a look of desire were his only responses.

On our next visit, I decided to take him to the most visible building in Paris, a hallowed place for all French; the *Cathedrale Notre-Dame de Paris* on the Île de la Cité. It was one of my favorite places and one of the most sacred. We stood outside the cathedral and I explained that the Île de la Cité was the original heart of Lutetia. "This is the center of Paris, a protected island located in the middle of the Seine. It has housed the city government since the beginning of the civilization of what is now called Paris, even before the Romans, even before Christ. It was to this sacred island, under the protection of Saint Genevieve, that the Romans retreated after Lutetia was attacked by Attila the Hun in 451 A.D. The Germans have been trying to occupy Paris for fifteen hundred years," I said as gently as I could. "Yes, and now we have her and will keep her for a thousand more," he replied calmly. I went on.

In Parisian lore, the Île de la Cité is referred to as a ship with Notre Dame positioned at the stern. The building of this Gothic cathedral began in 1163 under the guidance of Maurice de Sully. It was built upon the ruins of an ancient Roman Temple to Jupiter. Notre Dame took two centuries to complete. For six hundred years, it has been the scene of thousands of baptisms, weddings and church services. Notre Dame Cathedral has suffered war, attacks and neglect, but she has continued to survive in magnificent beauty and grace.

We walked around the cathedral on the outside and gazed at the flying buttresses used to hold the tall cathedral walls in place. I explained how my father told me the original design for Notre Dame did not include buttresses but, due to the thinness and height of the walls, they were added to prevent cracking or collapse. We were amused by the gargoyles protruding from the roof top, their mouths wide open in silent screams. This magnificent Notre Dame Cathedral was first built and later restored by the Compagnons, the ancient building guilds to which my father belonged.

The German focused on the statues to the right of the Portal of the Last Judgment. It was the statue of *Synagoga*. Her head was bowed in shame and she was holding a broken staff. She violated the Tablet of the Ten Commandments by standing on it. He innocently asked why they had created an image of a beautiful woman with a serpent wrapped over her eyes and the snake's fanged, open mouth poised upon her head. "What does the statue mean?" he asked. I explained how *Synagoga* represented the spiritually blind Jews, reflecting the negative perception of Jews held in French society for many generations, particularly at the time of the remodeling of Notre Dame.

ECCLESIA   SYNAGOGA

He looked at the statue on the left side of the door, toward another beautiful woman. "And who is the other woman?" the German asked. It was *Ecclesia*, the wide-eyed representative of Christianity. The two women represented the contrast between good (acceptance of Christ) and evil (rejection of Christ) represented by Christianity and Judaism. The German appreciated the use of Jews as scapegoats, and how this evil perception coincided with the Nazi message, and he asked an interesting question: "Have you ever noticed how close the spelling is between Judas and Judaism?" He also commented that our two countries might be more similar than I thought.

I didn't want to enter into a defense of the Jews with him or discuss the stupidity of these long-held prejudices. Given what the Nazis had done to my Husband and many Jews, this was a subject I avoided discussing with the German. I was glad to move on to other things.

We examined the Zero Milestone marker in front of the Cathedral, the point from which all distances are measured in France. He wondered aloud, "Do you think the French are so self-absorbed they believe every point in the world should be measured from this point in Paris?" I ignored his comment and restated how Notre Dame Cathedral is the center of France. "Notre Dame is the *piece de resistance* of Paris and the nation."

We entered through the huge center doors of the massive Cathedral, leaving the daylight behind. We turned our gaze upward to the grand ceiling fifty meters above. In doing so, we followed the intentions of the designers of the cathedral: to look heavenward and experience the cathedral's beauty and grandeur. We lowered our eyes, looked straight ahead and focused on the altar and the cross ahead of us. It was breathtaking.

Sometimes my family attended church at Notre Dame as an alternate to St. Julien across the river. I fondly recalled the huge bells ringing and ringing to awaken our souls. I felt a pang of sadness hit my heart, but I ignored it and pushed forward, breathing in the hallowed air and lifting my head for courage.

The German was clear about what he wanted and liked. He knew he wanted me and he did everything he could to have me in exactly the ways he wanted. He knew he wanted to lead a world dominated by him and his Nazi friends. They would do anything to achieve their imperialist dreams. But in Notre Dame that day, he also knew he was in a special place, a place to be protected, honored and loved.

Joan d'Arc

The German paused as we walked to the statue of Joan d'Arc close to the center altar. She had died five hundred years before, yet she was still deeply revered and worshipped by the French as a saint. The German pondered out loud, "How does one become a saint?"

It was not a question I could sufficiently answer, but I gave him one concept to think about. *"When faced with choices, the saints made the right decisions regardless of the consequences to them personally—even if their choices resulted in their certain deaths, which they often did."*

I translated Notre Dame for him: "Our Lady." I hoped he was beginning to evaluate the negative impact he and his Nazis were having on the world.

I pondered the Nazis' ability to perpetuate stark evil while also claiming to be Christians who followed the greatest peacemaker of all time, Jesus Christ. It was a dichotomy that left me in perpetual confusion; their ability to maintain good and evil in such close proximity without conflict made me leery. I was unsure if I saw the full German or, if after all our time and sex together, some mysterious evil lurked too far behind his blue eyes for me to see.

Even with my doubts, I believed the German was becoming a greater man than the one who had captured my Husband and me years before. His love and the magnificence of Paris were bringing out a different man from deep inside him. Slowly, I was shifting control of the German from Hitler to Paris and me. The majesty of Notre Dame helped. I believed there was a good human being inside of him and *we* were going to pull him out.

We paused under the soaring vaults above and the German looked at the boarded-up windows. "Where are the windows?" I answered that they had been taken down for repairs. I didn't mention how, in 1939, they were removed in anticipation of the Nazis bombing Paris and were hidden from the Nazis and their insatiable desire to steal beautiful and precious things that belonged to other people. I quickly changed the subject by telling him how the wheelbarrow was invented during the building of Notre Dame. That little detail surprised him and diverted his questioning from the windows.

We climbed the 422 stairs to the top of the North Tower and touched the massive bell, *Emmanuel*. It weighed thirteen tons and, like the other church bells in Paris, it ceased ringing at the start of the Nazi Occupation. He commented how he would like to hear the bells ring, and one day his wish would be granted. Unbeknownst to us, the bells of Paris would not ring again until the moment the German was to fulfill his fate and complete his mission on earth.

The German spoke of the story of *The Hunchback of Notre Dame* and how the clever plot had stayed with him throughout his life. Standing high above Paris, he loved the vantage point from the tower, where we surveyed every point in the city: the Seine, the Pantheon, Montmartre, smaller cathedrals, the hills and the sky above. The German began to understand what a precious city he occupied as his appreciation of her value, beauty and magic grew.

After our climb down the stairs of the tower of Notre Dame, we walked to the back side of the cathedral to view her majesty. Then we crossed over the narrowest bridge in Paris, Pont de l'Archeveche, which linked the 4th Arrondissement to the 5th Arrondissement on the Left Bank. We looked back to Notre Dame as it began to rain while the sun was still shining. The façade of the church was bathed in soft Provencal sunlight. An enormous full rainbow framed the cathedral like an inspired French Master's painting. I took a mental photograph of the image. It was beautiful and gave me a rare sign of hope.

Our next visit was to the *Place des Vosges*. I explained that these apartments were built as residences for members of the

Royal Family. Place des Vosges was where I lived with my parents as a child. It was an especially personal place, and my return under these circumstances was painful. I overcame my difficulties and focused on showing the German the splendor and magic of the Place des Vosges.

Built by King Henry IV, the Place des Vosges was constructed as a city within the city. He named it in honor of the people from the Vosges Mountains, who were the first to pay their taxes to the king.

The buildings surrounding the large park were a favorite residence for families seeking a quiet respite from the busy streets of Paris. Fashionable houses were lined up in neat rows in a large rectangle with gray slate roofs. The facade of the entire square consisted of red bricks and large stones set in a consistent pattern. Victor Hugo's home nestled in one corner. It was one of Paris' most desirable places to live. Even during Occupation, artists, politicians and writers continued to live in the elegant and stylish residences of the square. Only the Jews were gone.

In pre-Occupation times, the square was perpetually full of children having fun while proud parents watched. Days in the square were a constant din of laughter and parental instructions. The covered shops and cafes were full and musicians played under the convex ceilings of the hallways, which provided excellent acoustics for their songs.

The day the German and I visited, the square was mostly quiet; the loud play and squeals of childish joy were gone. Only one family strolled about the park. The husband and wife looked comfortable and their little girl dressed as I dressed in my childhood: a red coat, gray dress and tights. The only thing missing from her traditional Parisian ensemble were black patent leather shoes. Apparently, even her father could not find those shoes during Occupation.

The father was throwing the little girl up in the air and catching her in his strong arms again and again. I watched this wonderful moment and thought how most children knew not fate or pain, though unfortunately some did. What would become of this little girl in a world gone mad? Would she grow up as a French woman or as a grotesque Nazi protégé? I wondered how her father was prospering in Nazi-occupied Paris, what services he was providing the Nazi occupiers. He may have been wondering the same thing about me.

The German and I sat under the arches in the only restaurant serving dinner. I was pleased that two musicians played under the passageway, which gave their music an extra vibrancy. A few couples strolled by, and it was almost as if the war was not ripping the heart out of Europe and Asia. The momentary sense of normalcy died when I refocused on the man sitting across the table from me and I saw a Nazi general in full uniform.

Afterward, we strolled under the covered arcades and stopped to look in at the various artists' works creatively displayed in the store windows. The German strongly desired possession of objects that he liked. He joked about sending his SS troops to take the art for himself. If he did this, it was kept from me.

On one cold Sunday morning, the German and I walked down the Rue de Rivoli to visit *Île St. Louis*. On our way, we walked past the restaurant Chez Julien where my Husband and I had dined so many times, including the night of our first wedding anniversary. I turned my head away to avoid looking directly into the restaurant to keep away the memories of days of love and peace that were long gone.

We crossed over the Pont Louis-Philippe Bridge and walked past the home where my Husband and I had once lived. It showed no signs of wear, but being there made me sad as my memories of our loving times poured into my mind. Thoughts of my Husband were of simple things, of times when he was especially considerate and arranged little acts of caring to show his love. One day it might be a surprise breakfast in bed, another time it was a small gift like a record or a flower. Sometimes I would just see him quietly sitting in his favorite chair, reading the paper and sipping tea. I kept my thoughts of him in the past. I refused to speculate on the horrible reality of his present. I needed all my strength to push forward, free of the mental clutter of fear and hate.

The German and I walked the full length of the island, past the many closed shops with empty windows and past mostly empty hotels where visitors from around the world had once slept. We went into the old Eglise Saint-Louis-en Île church where Parisians were gathered. No one looked directly at or spoke to us, but there was a rustle of whispers. We were treated as if we were forbidden, the untouchables. A group of children gathered near the altar were softly singing a familiar French hymn. It was not the vibrant, open-hearted singing of pre-Occupation Paris churches, but it was touching in its purity. French music of any kind was a welcome treat, since all I heard was depressing German music, and it was so rough and crass. Outside the church, we turned back and retraced our steps down the center of the island. This change of course avoided the pain of looking at the entrance to my house again and prevented contact with our traitorous neighbors.

The German briefly mentioned my home on our walk through the Île St. Louis. He was in an exceptionally good mood and promised that he had ordered full protection of my home. The Nazis would not harm it. The German loved Île St. Louis. Before we left the island, we sat on a bench on the northernmost point and gazed at the water below. It was a special place, a place where I paused many times in my life. The German put his arm around me to help with the cold. I fought off my fears and persevered toward the goal to save my family.

Pont Alexandre III

Paris is a city of *bridges* and I showed the most beautiful and interesting ones to the German. I described how people hustled across Parisian bridges from one place to another, from one chip of their lives to the next. I had crossed each of them often and, while doing so, left one part of my life on the one bank to discover new elements of life on the other.

I noted how Paris is cut in half by forceful water rushing from the mountains to the sea. One side is connected with the other by thirty-seven bridges. Each bridge in Paris has its own personality; each bridge serves a different part of this complex city. Often, these bridges are more than a practical means to cross the river from one side to the other. They become destinations in and of themselves, as Parisians and visitors linger above the moving water below.

We visited the *Passerelle des Arts or Pont des Arts,* one of my favorite bridges in all of Paris. It was built in 1804 of cast iron instead of the traditional stone used for the other permanent bridges. Its nine arches were for support and beauty. The Passerelle des Arts is only for pedestrians and was full of life even in the midst of Occupation; lovers, artists, performers and tourists were putting on a show of just being alive on the day of our visit. It was a spectacular place to pause any time of day or night. The *Passerelle des Arts* connects the Institut de France and the Ecole des Beaux-Arts on the Left Bank with the Louvre on the Right Bank. We sat and watched the river flow around the Île de la Cité as we contemplated our lives without much talking. It seemed, even during the Occupation, that most people were happy while walking over or sitting on the Passerelle des Arts.

Next, we visited the *Pont Neuf or New Bridge.* I explained how Le Pont Neuf was called the new bridge because it was the first permanent bridge in Paris. It was built three hundred fifty years ago by King Henry IV, the husband of Marie de Medici. The queen commissioned a statue of the king to honor him for building this bridge. His statue proudly stood on the bridge for hundreds of years until the Nazis removed it and melted it down for its brass and copper, which they used to make bullets and weapons to kill Frenchmen.

The wide sidewalks and curved seating of the Pont Nuef were for those wanting a comfortable place to rest. The German and I stopped there for some time. He was intent on taking it all in, focusing on the many sites of *My Paris.* He asked, "How could a city be more than its architecture and history, more than stones and trees? How could one have feelings for a city?" The German's questions indicated a growing awareness, which encouraged me to continue the *My Paris* tours.

Before we left the Pont Neuf and the water flowing strongly below us, the German stopped, pulled me toward him and gave me a long, passionate kiss. He knew how he felt about me and he decided to show it at that precise moment. His enthusiasm came as a bit of a surprise, but I leaned into him and kissed him back. Something good was coming alive in him as he pulled me tight, and I was in no position to turn it away. It was strange; kissing was more difficult than having sex with him because kissing was somehow more personal and intimate.

Zouave soldier - Pont Alexandre III

Another day, we walked across the *Pont Alexandre III* to the shore near the Pont de l'Alma. We looked at the statue of the Zouave soldier, a member of the French Army of Africa, embedded in the supporting pillar to see how high the water mark was that day. The water was only at his feet, not nearly as high as it was during the flood of 1910 when it went up to the Zouave soldier's nose.

Quite often we simply strolled up and down the *Champs Elysées*, looking in the shop windows and watching the people of Paris. The shops were almost empty but they continued to dress their windows with stylish designs and fashions. Stores sold no leather shoes but had a few pairs to show off for the Parisian strollers or sell to the highly privileged Nazis and Collaborators with special authority to buy luxury goods. There were no cows for leather or food; they were consumed to feed and clothe the soldiers on both sides of the invasion and the ongoing war.

Our walks up and down the Champs Elysées would begin by turning right out of the Hotel Meurice, crossing the Place de la Concorde with its Egyptian obelisk, passing the long parks filled with trees, benches and lovers, and then onto the upper areas of the grand avenue. Sometimes, the German would stop and buy me a gift. Other times, he was too focused on his responsibilities to be concerned about romantic things. We would often walk in silence for some time before he would speak of his concerns and responsibilities. We walked arm in arm along the Champs Elysées until we reached Napoleon's Arc de Triomphe, where the noon march of the Nazi military band began each day. We stood on the curb as they passed. The soldiers saluted the German in respect for his rank and in fear of his power.

Arc de Triomphe

At the *Arc de Triomphe*, the German would stop for a moment to honor the fallen warriors from the many battles recorded on the ceilings and walls of the monument. He would sometimes comment on individual battles whose names are engraved on the ceiling of the vault. He knew many of the battles and their outcomes from his studies at the Nazi war college. Often he would speak of the bravery of soldiers and the sadness of the death of so many good, young men. He included enemy soldiers in his sympathies for the warriors who suffered and died. The German possessed no similar feelings of regret or sympathy when it came to the extermination of Jews and Résistance fighters. In their case, he was cold and unfeeling, as if he were slaughtering animals and nothing more. His life was broken into distinguishable chips of hate, love, or indifference which were mentally organized to justify his actions. This was another point of the psychological paradox of the German's mind, into which

I could not see or understand. A disappointment at the Arc de Triomphe was that the "perpetual flame" at the tomb of the Unknown Soldier had been extinguished by the Nazi occupiers.

There was little auto or truck traffic on the Champs Elysées, since only the Nazi military had fuel. Nazi soldiers and their French girlfriends could be seen riding in *velo-taxis*, small carts pulled by a French woman or man, similar in function, if not design, to a rickshaw one might find in China. Many people rode bicycles up and down the wide avenue in picture-perfect, quiet movements. The silence created by the lack of motor vehicles gave the center of Paris an eerie and unusual feeling of peace and quiet in the midst of war and Occupation.

Each time we strolled up and down the Champs Elysées, we would stop and sit quietly on the same benches. We always stopped once on our way up the avenue and once on our way back. The German locked us into this routine and didn't deviate. We sat and spoke little. It was a time of quiet reflection and adjusting to living in a conflicted world. I always enjoyed these stops, as they gave a peaceful break from the insanity of the rest of our lives.

We walked through the *Cimetiere du Pere-Lachaise* where poets, singers, lovers, politicians, artists and authors permanently slept in view of the City of Lights. We looked for graves of the famous people who were buried there. Much to my delight, we found the tomb of Pierre Abelard and his Heloise, the lovers from the story taught by my Professor/Husband. Seeing their tomb, my mind returned to the classroom where my Professor paced back and forth, beaming in all his glory and doing what he loved to do, to teach.

I kneeled for a moment at Abelard and Heloise's single grave and stared at their concrete images. Abelard and Heloise were lying there dead but they were somehow still in love, even if it was only in the minds of those who came to honor them. They seemed Christ-like to me, crucified for endless love. I wished I could have discussed this with Father Jean, but I suspected he would not have seen the Church's Christ in this story of lust, an illegitimate child and revenge—though more gruesome stories were found in many passages of the Old Testament.

In my momentary thoughts, I asked questions of no one and received no answers in reply: *Does one's suffering in life not matter, since each of us will ultimately find peace in the finality of death? Does only the end of one's story have meaning, not the various struggles or missteps one encounters along the way? Does the end of one's life ultimately nullify the difficulties one must suffer to arrive there?*

We finished our visit to Lachaise cemetery with a coffee and a walk home in the rain. Time was marching on and life was about to change, though we didn't know how and where fate would take us after this day of visiting the dead.

On our last Sunday visit to *My Paris*, I took the German to *Saint Julien le Pauvre*. It was more than a year since we had begun our outings. St. Julien remained a very private and personal place, where my individual history lived in the stones, the walls, the icons and the pews. I knew my commitment to win his heart had escalated to an extraordinary level when I decided to take him to St. Julien. Visiting my church with the German was more painful than visiting Place des Vosges or Île St. Louis. I fought for control over my emotions as we approached.

Before we arrived, I gave the German similar historic information as I gave my Husband on our first visit to St. Julien. I explained that St. Julien was, to me, the most holy Church in Paris and the most holy place in the world.

As we entered, images of my First Holy Communion and marriage flashed through my mind. I glanced down the stairs to the basement where the Artist, Father Jean and I had met on that life-changing day seemingly so long ago. Inside the church, I was no longer able to continue my running commentary; I was simply too distraught. My Husband's presence was overwhelming as I visualized him standing before me strong and handsome on the day we were married. I started to reach out my hand to his image but returned it to my empty lap. My heart ached for him but, beyond my vivid reminiscences of our time together, he was not there.

Fortunately, the German remained reverent, respectful and introspective during our visit, and I appreciated his consideration. As we sat silently in a pew, I remembered the regular message from Father Jean that touched my heart: "Forgiveness is the best." I silently responded, Yes, I know, but it is so hard to do!

Father Jean wasn't at St. Julien, or even in Paris. He had converted hundreds of Jews to Catholicism. He gave Christian names and Christian baptismal records to them for protection. It was the largest rush to join the Catholic Church in ten centuries. I learned of his pending arrest through the German and I sent a secret message to him that his life was in danger. He was smuggled out of Paris immediately and remained in exile in California for the remainder of the Occupation. If he had stayed, he would have been arrested and possibly killed for saving Jews. He escaped just before the SS agents located him. Father Jean had a great deal to forgive the Nazis for—as did I.

The ironies and paradoxes within which I lived with were becoming overwhelming, the complexities and conflicts intolerable. As a Sartre character once said, "I felt as though my fate was being worked out three feet above my head." But when life began to break me, I reached inside myself and pulled out the strength I needed to take action on my plans. I would not let the German's torture and killing of my countrymen deter me from my ambition. I damned the pain; nothing could be worse than what I had already been through. I was proceeding straight ahead, undeterred by obstacles or self-pity. I knew what I had to do and I was going to do it!

Saint Julien's loving spirit was so strong that, even as a captive sitting quietly next to my captor, I felt his nearness and strength. I also knew Father Jean was supporting me, though he was far away, out of touch, living in exile in the magical state of California.

With the love of Saint Julien and Father Jean in my heart, I touched the *cosmic soul*. I let it all go—being a captive, the rape, the thousands of lives destroyed and my Husband's imprisonment in a concentration camp. I pushed these thoughts out of my mind and opened myself to draw on the strength of love and forgiveness.

Before we left St. Julien le Pauvre, I told the German, "If I am lost, this is where I can be found." I knew I took a chance with my words, knowing this truly was the place I would go if I had no other place to turn, where I could sink into the stones and become part of my family's living and dead ghosts.

Our *My Paris* tours ended. In those ever-changing times, no routines could last. The German had changed, and I was ready to use his power to protect Paris and stay alive.

As we walked forward, it was unclear where our paths would take us. We were walking into the future, slowly pacing ourselves to hold onto the moments one by one. A cool breeze blew in; we tightened our coats and picked up our pace, forgetting that we were rushing to cross bridges toward predetermined fates as we headed back to the Hotel Meurice.

Café Talk: Paris, the Woman

1945. Christine sat tall in her seat; her posture was erect and her head was held higher than it had been for some time. She was in her faraway mind when she continued to speak of Paris to the wide-eyed American. "I always speak of Paris as a woman, as a lover. Paris is a place where one's heart opens to love like nowhere else in the world. Look at her; she has a deep, wet river running between her gently curving banks, where her secrets of passion are hidden in the deep core of her womb. Her hills are like full breasts, places where her people are cared for and nurtured. Her trees are like hair, neatly parted to accent her beauty and her femininity. Her avenues are like long, curvy legs reaching from here to there, to where nobody knows. Her parks are like a woman's back, smooth, luscious and containing only traces of the finest hairs, just enough to make one wonder what mystery they lead to. Her mind is cunning and explosive. She can endure, absorb and survive; she is a woman. She is a lover. No other city in the world evokes such feminine feelings of love and passion as Paris.

"Each time we explored Paris, the German understood a little bit more of her and developed more feelings for her. Each time, he understood more how Paris was a woman-city, a lover. Each time, he discovered something about the Paris he had missed while knowing her only as his captive, and each time she seduced him and brought him tighter to her bosom and nearer to becoming a lover under her spell.

"After our visit to St. Julien, the German assigned one of the Nazi curators, a man who was helping the Nazis steal French art, to research the history of St. Julien le Pauvre. He uncovered another new fact about my old family church. St. Julien was thoroughly restored in 1825. The man who remodeled St. Julien was a German named Franz Christian Gau from Cologne, Germany. The fact that he became a naturalized French citizen was offered as an unimportant afterthought. Once a

German, always a German, especially when they want to take credit for something.

"The German general's point, like the Italian Artist's point and like my Jewish Husband's point, was that St. Julien belonged to everyone; many cultures worshipped here and people of many backgrounds appreciated the holiness of this precious terra and blessed structures. Its environs had been settled by Jewish, pagan Roman, Roman Catholic, Merovingian, Clunaic and Eastern Catholic Melkites – a full range of human societies."

The American said nothing but contemplated his own growing love for this City of Lights. His thoughts were like nomads drifting through the streets of Paris, Bohemian feelings wanting to sensuously embrace the amazing beauty of her sights. The American wondered why Christine didn't take the German to the Eiffel Tower, a seemingly obvious place to take a man who was being seduced by this marvelous city. Later he found out it was mined and scheduled to be dropped across the Seine.

Christine had said enough. She rose up and, with two cheek kisses to the American, left the café. She entered the waiting cab, a vehicle that would return her to her Husband and to their home on the Ile Saint Louis. She needed a rest before she could finish with the German, the man who was turning away from Hitler to love a woman and a city.

CHAPTER FIVE
THE "CHRISTINE" GERMAN

A woman who loves to love,
has the energy and the will to love,
can powerfully impact a man
upon whom she focuses her womanly talents

It is an error to underestimate the power of a woman
especially if she is a woman who has been violated

Café Talk: The New German

1945. Christine and the American were able to meet again after two days apart. After waving to the waiters across the room, she greeted the American warmly. She seemed energized as she sat down and began to speak.

The American continued to be amazed at Christine's willpower and the convergence of the fascinating historical events surrounding her life. He was particularly impressed with her plan to seduce the German with her sensuality and reinforce it by using the charms of Paris.

Christine was ready to present the American with the most significant event in her life story. History was changed because Christine wrestled the German away from Hitler and took control of him using sex and love.

One Man, Two Loves

My plan worked; two loves grew in the German's heart. He fell for Paris like he had fallen for me, all the way. He could see that Paris and I were one. The line of separation between us was very thin; I was Paris in human form and Paris reflected my being. By getting to know Paris intimately, he traveled deeper into my heart and soul and vice versa.

The German's respect for the genius of the French architects, engineers and builders grew with each visit. He understood how Frenchmen, not Germans, designed, built and created these majestic structures, and how they uniquely reflected French culture and skill. These experiences softened the German's desire to conquer, destroy and loot. He evolved beyond viewing Paris simply as one more of the spoils of war. He came to understand that it was better for French masterpieces to remain French. The German gained an understanding that there were things of value which were French, not German.

The German's plan to control me on the most intimate physical and psychological levels was very effective for a while, but not forever. Eventually it backfired. What the German did not know, and what most men do not know, is that a woman has a variety of feminine weapons at her disposal, against which a man has little or no defense, and I was an expert at using these sophisticated, feminine methods. My strength was further increased because I was a woman on a mission. I was angry and motivated enough to do anything to succeed. Giving frequent sexual pleasure and performing any sexual act for him was just one tool in my arsenal. I could also be weak when I needed to be, emotionally and physically cold when it fitted the situation, supportive or not as I determined which mood fit best. I made the decision to use every one of my weapons to reverse our roles; *I was to capture he who had once captured me.*

My power became great enough to change the German's heart from hate to love. Unbeknownst to the German, the Nazi occupiers, the Parisians and the commanders of both sides of the war, the German's love was to become powerful enough to thwart the horrific plans and direct orders from the most powerful man on earth—the absolute dictator of the Third Reich, the Führer himself, Adolf Hitler.

The German's unexpected love for me and his new love for Paris eventually created a new man in him. He didn't acknowledge that he had given up control at all; things changed in shades as parts of his life gradually slid away and his will to resist abated as he fell deeper in love. While it is often said people never change, it was clear to me that he had. I was sure of it.

I realized I had an opportunity to help Paris by using the German's power and I became obsessed with taking advantage of my position in every way possible. Short of murder, I committed myself to use whatever means necessary. My life became a plot which went beyond the survival of my family—it was a plot to help an entire city and millions of people.

I was able to answer the question I had asked myself during our first lunch: what force could offset Hitler's evil? Evil could be defeated by the strength of the individual and collective goodness and a willingness to act. I drew upon this force in myself and I used it to change the German's mind. The soldiers and countries that carried the strength of good into battle were eventually victorious. The eternal struggle between good and evil played out in the grand mystery of World War II. The fact that good defeated evil is amazing proof that good can prevail in the end, though there were so many days, months and years where it appeared evil was going to win.

After I was held as his captive for two years, my feelings for the German had also changed. He was no longer just the frightening Nazi officer who'd taken me from my Husband and held my family hostage. I still hated him for what he had caused in my life, but I softened as he softened. I viewed him more as a man and less as a monster. Most importantly, I cared deeply that he responded when I gave myself to him and how, as a result, he was becoming a more decent human being. I observed how his life, his upbringing, his position in history and his fate brought him to Paris, to me and to our shared destiny. I didn't accept these things as justification of evil but more as an explanation.

I dispensed with my personal pain and saw issues much bigger than me and mine. I rose from the whimpering rape victim, sucking my thumb on the floor of the Gestapo headquarters, to become the aggressor, methodically plotting to help Paris, my family and myself. I became ecstatic as my hope and power returned. We had reached a marker in our relationship. Not only was I able to sway his feelings and influence his actions as a man, but *I could use the power of his position as the commanding general of the Nazi SS and Gestapo forces to help Paris instead of hurting her.* I became exhilarated that fate had placed me in this important and historical position; the survival of Paris would depend on how effective I was at influencing a man to whom I gave my body every night, and whose heart was increasingly becoming mine.

Café Talk: Female Weapons

1945. *The American was unable to simply sit and listen as Christine's story unfolded through to his pen onto the paper. He needed to express his wonderment at her recovery from abject victimhood to a Venus rising from the ashes.*

"*What specific female weapons?*" *he asked for himself as a man as well as the author of Christine's Journal. "I have known many women; I have participated in the man-woman dance many times. I thought I understood but when I listen to you, I think men are operating under a grand illusion and we have little or no control at all. Do sex and a man's need for a woman's respect blind us from everything else that's going on? Are we that simple?"*

Christine looked at him with understanding and gave her explanation of how she was able to get what she wanted from the German. "I figured out how high-class prostitutes work, using techniques to entice men who pay large sums of money for sex over and over again. A woman's focused attention on a man can be a force so strong and so controlling that he will give up command, fortune, family and reputation: everything and anything for her. I tapped into the force of sensuality with respect and my influence increased rapidly until I controlled the man inside the Nazi uniform.

"The power of a woman is somewhat of a witch's brew, a combination of explicit sexual acts designed to elicit the greatest possible pleasure, feminine dances of seduction using smells and special attire and sensuous behavior to create mystery, and promises of sexual surprises to excite a man.

"To a degree, it is acting; giving such a level of complete attentiveness and effort to a man may not come naturally, especially in circumstances such as mine. But, when sufficiently motivated, a woman can emphasize her positive, supportive side and suppress her less-pleasant traits, such as excessive complaining and over-criticizing. It is more like a job where one has to maintain herself with a certain level of decorum, and less like a

marriage where a wife may act out her personality deficiencies on her husband with predictably negative results.

"The German was more complex than most men because he only wanted sex that I initiated. I think he set up our relationship that way to abdicate his responsibility and diffuse his guilt. As long as I was the one making sex happen, there was no way he could resist. How could he or any man say no to a beautiful, sensuous woman committed to seducing him at every turn?

"To my surprise, I found I was perfectly designed for this 'game.' It was as if I were created for sensual play. On the physically intimate level, I loved sex. I loved every dimension of giving and receiving sexual pleasure, from the first flirtations to kissing and more and more. Until I grew up and learned that many women enjoy sex, I used to think I was sexually more like a man than a woman. Given my motivation to save our lives and my preexisting proclivity for sexual pleasure, I enthusiastically took the German to levels of ecstasy few men are blessed to enjoy.

"The ingredients in my brew included more than sex; it included support and respect. Succeeding in the world of Nazi public relations, the other requirement for my survival required me to give the German everything he wanted in that arena too. I was prepared for any situation. I exceeded the role he expected and demanded of me every time. I knew how to make him look good in front of others and to lead them into believing he was man enough to have me not as a captive but as his lover. I became the supportive woman every man needs. There was no chance to be anything less; the stakes were too high, my undertaking too grand.

"Even with our passionate sex, my plan would have failed had I not shown him admiration as a man and a human being. He didn't question whether my behavior was real or not; it didn't matter to him.

"I was able to achieve this connection with him because I first took control of myself and then decided how to use my fate. With one choice after another, my life led to a magical moment in time, delivering me to the exact point where my destiny could be played out. My fate was conditio sine qua non, *it was the "but for" of my choices; my hand was dealt and I played it out with every resource I could bring to the game.*

"Historical events continued to feed my fate like a zookeeper feeding the lions. The next raw meat of the story was to be the largest military assault in the history of the human race, and I sat in a center, front-row seat in the enemy's theater watching it unfold."

The American was ready to continue, ready for another vignette, another electrifying event, but he wanted to comment on Christine's description of her female tools and weapons before the next story began.

"You gave the German what every man wants from the woman he loves. You gave the German what men seek and expect when they fall in love and marry, but what they seldom find for long. You were like the perfect 'wife'; you gave him everything I love about women. No man could have resisted you.

"What I don't understand is why women don't continue with this magnificent, feminine behavior in marriage. Is it just an act, part of a plan to get something from a man and then revert to the other side of their womanhood, the side without mystery or joy, the side that works more against her husband than in support of him?"

Christine couldn't answer the unanswerable. Without even a smile in acknowledgment of his disappointments in love and his broken relationships with women, Christine returned to her story in a world in severe conflict, with stories of persons with unheard-of human courage.

D-Day (disambiguation)

June 6, 1944. The Allies' massive attack on the Nazi defenses on the coast of occupied France was called *D-Day* to mark the point in time when the invasion began. The Nazi weathermen mistakenly determined that there could be no attack because a major storm was sweeping across the English Channel. The German weathermen convinced their Nazi commanders that the Allied invasion forces would be unable to cross for at least another month, when conditions would again be right for an invasion with a full moon and high tides.

Based on their weathermen's misinformation, General Rommel, one of the three top Nazi generals in charge of defending the French coast, left the front to go home to Germany and celebrate his wife's birthday. He and the German were old comrades, so he stopped in Paris to have lunch with us and purchase real French shoes for his wife's birthday present, an exquisite gift only top Nazi military officers and a few senior Collaborators were able to buy during Occupation.

Rommel was a charming man but full of himself and overconfident. He was sure the Nazi military could hold off the Allies whenever they came. He initially bragged about his defenses and the might of the Nazi army, and noted the difficulties the Allies would have in landing massive troops and equipment on the rugged, heavily defended French coast.

After we had consumed two bottles of wine and a tremendous amount of food, Rommel made an ominous and revealing complaint about conflicts within the Nazi military command structure: Hitler was personally controlling a number of Panzer tank divisions. Hitler would personally decide when and where these tanks would be used when the invasion came. These Panzers were concentrated at Calais, waiting for the "real" invasion. The command of the remaining Panzers and the armies supporting them was divided between the three commanding generals who disagreed on tactics and priorities. At this extremely critical moment in history, the legendary, monolithic Nazi command structure was anything but.

Rommel was home with his wife in Germany celebrating her birth on June sixth. He was not at his post to lead the opposition against the massive Allied assault thrown at the Nazi defenses. The German cursed Rommel and called him a Dummkopt in private. "Who cares about his wife's stupid birthday? The Americans are coming to France soon and we must be prepared to stop them on the beaches!" I was silently excited that Hitler's best field general, the "Desert Fox," was out of action, and thanked his wife for being born on the exact day when France and the free world needed him to be out of the battle.

Unlike their Nazi counterparts, the Allied weathermen saw the potential of a short break in the storm. After receiving strongly conflicting advice on the go, no-go decision for the invasion, General Eisenhower decided to take the enormous risk of launching his armada of ships, weapons and soldiers. They were coming to liberate France and to open a second front against the Nazis, and their success was dependent on good weather for crossing the channel. The weather held and the Allies' invasion plans proceeded. If the Nazi-predicted bad weather would have hit the English Channel, it could have resulted in such a massive disaster for the Allies that the end of the war would have been postponed and the victor would have remained undecided. Paris would surely have remained occupied for much longer and she would have met a fate of indescribable horror. Instead, the Nazis let their weathermen's predictions change the outcome of the battle and possibly the war. I thought to myself, everyone knows weathermen can't predict the weather. Why would these powerful and intelligent men accept such a weak reason to let down their guard?

Before we knew that D-Day had commenced, the German and I left the hotel to have lunch at the oldest Alsatian restaurant in Paris, Brasserie Bofinger's near the Place de la Bastille. It was a surprisingly calm, cool June day and the German noted how this directly contradicted the Nazi weathermen's predictions of a giant storm.

The excellent dining experience at Bofinger's began as soon as we entered the door. Two young French women graciously took our coats as the maitre d' bowed and indicated with a sweep of his arm that we should precede to the best seats in the restaurant. The aromas of the kitchen greeted us at the front door and stimulated my appetite as we walked through the entranceway. I looked forward to this time away from the events of the war, which dominated our every waking moment at the Hotel Meurice. Our booth was in the far corner of the room where we could experience maximum privacy while enjoying the spectacular décor of the cut glass, art deco, leaded-glass dome ceiling, leather seats and three tree-sized branches of lilac bushes in the center of the room. Every image was duplicated multiple times in the mirrored walls that surrounded the room, which gave the pleasant sensation of dining in a grand garden of colored light.

The professional waiters at Bofinger's were known around the world for their arrogant and stuffy attitudes. However, for the German, they were deferential and highly respectful. Everyone knew the force he represented. The staff treated me as royalty, though I suspected there was deep resentment hidden behind their pleasant, superficial smiles. Surely they saw me as a Nazi Collaborator/whore and nothing more.

We began lunch with excellent *gros escargots à la bouguingone,* snails in garlic sauce accompanied by a smooth German Riesling wine. We moved on to our entrée, the specialty of the maison; *tartare de boeuf charolais,* steak tartar. Unlike the usual way this dish is served, the chef premixed the ingredients with the highest quality meat. Perfect! During the meat course, we drank a proper French wine, a 1932 Clos des Papes from Chateauneuf-du-Pape. Dessert was a *concerto au chocolat croustillant,* chocolate flowers in the shape of Edelweiss. This wonderful concoction was served with a luscious, semi-sweet 1932 Alsace Gewürztraminer produced on the family farm of the restaurant's owner.

We sat in opulence surrounded by servitude and ate with decadence while, unbeknownst to us, the Allies were charging forth to change the world's destiny—and the Nazis didn't even know they were coming!

We had not yet finished with the delicious chocolates and scrumptious wine when the German's attaché burst into the restaurant and came to our table, inappropriately wearing his coat and hat. He interrupted us in a panic. He brought urgent, top-secret news and said the general must come at once. We rushed back to the Hotel Meurice in the general's command car, leaving the bottle of Gewürztraminer half full and the chocolate morsels partially eaten. On the way, the sergeant briefed the German on the Allied invasion. The attack had begun, but where and when was unsure.

When we returned to the Meurice, we passed through the command area where reports from the Nazi front lines were pouring in from many different outposts. I stood unnoticed on the side of the room, barely outside the expanding chaos and growing panic of men bracing for a siege.

The information they were receiving was strange, confusing and startling. Nazi officers were screaming hysterically into phones and at each other. Phones rang unanswered as generals on other phones loudly demanded unavailable answers. Nazi military order disintegrated into disorganized human fear and chaos.

The Nazi air of superiority disappeared into the ugliness of self-preservation and fear of the heavily armed and highly motivated enemy armies heading toward them.

One officer claimed the Allies under American General Patton were coming across from Dover to Calais, the narrowest point in the channel between England and France. The Nazis had planned for Calais to be the primary point of attack in the Allied invasion. They had closely monitored General Patton's activities in Dover. According to Nazi spies in England, Patton and his army were actively preparing for an attack on Calais. He was considered the best American general by the Nazis, so his leadership of the invasion made sense to them. The Nazis asked each other, "Why else would Patton, with all those troops and equipment, be in Dover unless he was heading to Calais?"

There were also reports of massive paratroop drops, with a tremendous amount of radio traffic coming from paratroopers dropping behind the Nazi lines at Calais. The initial information indicated an invasion at Calais; it looked like Hitler's Panzer tanks were in the right place, waiting to kill the invaders. But there were also vague and unbelievable reports of a huge naval assault on the beaches of Normandy and massive bombardment of the Nazi shore defenses there.

The citizens of Occupied France hid in secret places to listen to war reports on forbidden radios. Word of the Allied invasion spread throughout Paris like wildfire. There was finally hope for the Parisians, for France and for Europe. The American, British, Australian, Canadian and French soldiers were coming to purge the Nazi plague, and they would not be stopped.

The Allies Are Coming

D-Plus-One. I ate breakfast alone the morning after D-Day. After a night of little sleep, the German was in the war room before I rose from bed. When he returned, he brought news from the French coast that seriously disturbed him. The Allies were successfully pushing the Nazis off the beaches of Normandy, and it looked like the Nazi coastal defenses would fail. Three thousand Allied soldiers and thousands of Nazi defenders lay dead on the beaches or buried in their concrete defensive positions after just one day of fighting.

There was no invasion at Calais. Hitler was wrong. In information provided too late for the Nazi command to react, Nazi intelligence revealed the chatter of paratroopers and the threats of Patton's Army in Calais were well-planned Allied diversions and illusions. The paratroopers were actually small dummies dropped behind Nazi lines with radios broadcasting false radio messages, as if they were real soldiers attacking. There was no Patton army; it was a ruse using fake blow-ups painted with images of tanks and trucks and a small number of real soldiers changing uniforms and marching in circles to appear to be a very large force. The Allies sent out thousands of phony radio transmissions to phantom divisions as if they were moving out and landing on the beaches appropriate to an invasion at Calais. It was a hoax, a successful deception. There would be no landing at Calais and there was never going to be a landing there.

The real Allied military assets were sent to Normandy in an assault of unprecedented magnitude on the French coastline; everything was committed to Normandy. The German expressed deep frustration with the Nazi command: Hitler's interference with the military, the gullibility of believing little dummies were actual paratroopers, the stupidity of relying on the weathermen, the incompetence of generals leaving their posts and standing down because of an alleged storm which didn't come.

D-Day, the term for the first day of *Operation Overlord,* was one of the most welcome events in French, English and Russian history. The Allies were coming to destroy the Nazis. As D-Day rolled into D-plus-one, D-plus-two, D-plus-three, the Allies breeched the coastal defenses and conquered the Nazi defenders. The Second Front was open. The Allied armies established numerous beachheads, which would acquire new names like Omaha, Utah, Juno, Sword and Gold. The Free French armies arrived shortly after D-Day to join the Americans, British, Canadians and Australians in the fight to take back France and defeat Nazi Germany.

The Allies moved inland, struggling their way off the Normandy beaches under heavy fire. Fighting went from bunker to bunker, hedgerow to hedgerow, man to man and bullet by bullet. Allied planes gained air supremacy over the Nazi Luftwaffe, and their contribution to the success of the invasion was invaluable. With the beaches clear, tens of thousands of Allied troops, millions of pieces of equipment and tons of supplies streamed ashore on a multitude of different landing craft. The Allies' massive military machine was positioning itself to defeat the Third Reich by forcing them to fight on three fronts: Russia, France and Italy.

The Nazi defenses broke again and again. After the Allies penetrated the coastal line of defense, the German and I did a tactical analysis of the Nazi defensive forces of Paris and the incoming Allied military strength; a more sophisticated and frightening version of our war games. The size and power of the Allied armies attacking was too great, and it was clear the Nazis could not stop the Allies without immediate, massive reinforcements. Without them, the Allies would be in Paris soon and there was nothing the Nazis could do to stop them.

We went to the war room to look at the maps and the data. There was no need to debate or have a contest over the outcome. We monitored the movement of promised Nazi reinforcements coming from Germany and it looked like a dead heat, an even bet on which would arrive first. We grasped the enormity of the circumstances but said little.

We were told of a dramatic attack on Pointe-du-Hoc. U.S. Rangers stormed up hundred-foot cliffs to knock out the suspected huge Nazi guns pointed out to sea, set to pound the arriving Allied forces. Led by James Earl Rudder, the Rangers came under precise fire from Nazi defenders. The Rangers lost 60 percent of their men but took the point and prevented the Nazis from using it as an observation point for directing defensive fire. It was the best of the Nazi defense against the best of the American offense and the Americans prevailed, though at great cost.

The German began to lose confidence in his ambitious dreams. I had learned his ways while sharing his bed for three years and I saw a tensing in him, an edge and a doubt not present before D-Day. Our social life screeched to a halt. The German spent all of his time at military headquarters and pursuing the Résistance. He was receiving a constant stream of commands from Germany, some directly from the Führer and many from other commanding officers in Hitler's military headquarters.

He showed his loss of self-assurance through his actions and moods. He also lost his incessant interest in sex. He needed more of my effort to help him perform sexually, to take his mind off the threat of the Allies and the shattering of his visions of world conquest. He began to drink heavily. He paced the room at all hours of the day and night, obsessing over maps documenting the Allied troops' progress toward Paris and vociferously condemning Hitler and his commanders for their foolishness. Soon the Nazis in Paris would be on the receiving end of an Allied equivalent of the Blitzkrieg. The pressure on the Nazi command became debilitating as the map's black arrows representing Allied advances closed in on Paris, replacing arrogance with fear.

The German's physical and mental degradation became more pronounced with each Allied step toward Paris. His condition reminded me of the Artist and his destructive behavior after he was accused of appropriation. Again I witnessed the fall of a strong man succumbing to unexpected weakness; his demise strangely not anticipated by me, the woman who had shared his bed for so long.

August 1, 1944, D+25. The German and I sat for another eye-to-eye discussion. This time, he was pleading. We knew the Nazi Occupation of Paris and the entire Third Reich were endangered by the advancing Allied armies. He had attached himself to the rising Nazi star, but as that star fell from the sky, he was being pulled toward his ruin in its wake.

The German presented a completely different image of the future than he had during our "Thousand-Year Occupation" lunch long before. His vision of the Nazis controlling France had vanished. Instead, he told me he would be finished in Paris soon and I would be in grave danger from my own people as the Nazis lost control and the Allied armies and the Résistance took over.

The German was pensive. He spoke softly, not barking out his words as a general but speaking as a man whose illusion of control was imploding. He began to speak of Mexico! I didn't know where this conversation was coming from. In our three years together, he had never mentioned Mexico in any context.

"Mexico is a place where one could become lost, where one could rid themselves of their present and their past—especially with enough money. Mexico has a perfect climate, particularly their beach towns, and the Mexicans are gracious people." He became more enthusiastic; I could see hope rise in his eyes and his posture. "Christine, we could leave Paris and live in Mexico together! We could escape now with Gabriella, before it is too late. I could arrange it."

I was shocked but hid my thoughts. I gently reminded him of his position and his duty. I told him it was already too late to leave. The Allies were coming to Paris and I couldn't leave Paris. I was afraid to point out that I was married and his captive, not a voluntary lover who would run off to a foreign country to start a new life with him. I didn't speak of my Husband because I was afraid the German would eliminate him as an obstacle. I deferred my reaction as much as I could. I wondered how he could believe *we* could be together anywhere but here, in any time but this, and under any circumstances other than these. He didn't understand that there was no "we" and there never would be a "we," but I revealed nothing.

The German changed as rapidly as the war situation changed. His abject control over me was dramatically reduced and I became increasingly more in control of him than he was of me. Our relationship evolved as I had planned. The shift in power further motivated me.

As the French and American tanks rolled closer to Paris, the German looked like he might break down mentally. A broken German would jeopardize my plans to use his power to help Paris; I needed a fully functioning Nazi general to keep my family alive. I'd paid for it with my body and my soul and I wasn't going to let it go. We spent time alone and I calmed him down. He didn't bring up his Mexico fantasy again. We were staying in Paris and heading toward our destinies, no matter what lay ahead of us. Mexico was his last grasp at the fantasy of survival; he knew the Nazis could not retreat, they could not achieve victory in Paris, and it was not going to end well for him.

Café Talk: Loss of Control

1945. "*Before D-Day, the strength of the Nazi armies defending the French coastline and Paris had been reduced and redeployed to fight the epic battle with Russia. The Allies were successful on D-Day because of other reasons as well: the effective Allied deceptions, the confused Nazi command structure, luck with the weather and the determination of the Allied armed forces.*

"*On the Eastern Front, the Russian soldiers and the Russian people died in massive numbers as they engaged and absorbed the Nazi attacks with their blood and bones. Russia's ability to grind down their enemies crippled the Nazi war machine which, together with the Russian winter, saved Western Europe from defeat. The Russians bled for us.*"

Christine experienced an insider perspective on events of the war, but soon she would do more than record history; she would be more than just the lightning rod...she would become the lightning itself and help change history in an unfathomable way.

Christine continued to "battle" Hitler's attempts to control the German and Paris. She refused to accept defeat. The time for which she had prepared was coming upon her and she was not about to let the mad dictator win. But another appalling event was about to occur: evil was trying to work itself back into center stage, and the next move was Hitler's.

General Choltitz

August 9, 1944. D+64. Hitler responded to the Allies'
progress by changing the commander of all Nazi forces in Paris.
The Nazi general in charge, General Hans von Boineburg-
Lengsfeld, was a lover of Paris and fully enjoyed himself in
the Parisian society and the city's high living. He frequently
socialized with Parisians. The German and I dined with him and
his wife on numerous occasions. He loved good food, fine wine
and interesting company.

General von Boineburg-Lengsfeld was abruptly removed
from his position and sent packing. He was replaced by the man
known as the "City Destroyer," General Dietrich von Choltitz.
General Choltitz was given broader authority and the higher rank
of Military Governor of Paris, with full command over all Nazi
forces and personnel.

General Choltitz's realm of authority included the German's
SS troops and the Gestapo. However, in Hitler's world of paranoia
and fear of his own generals, the SS still operated with some
degree of independence from the standard military organization.
Hitler could use the SS to remove a commanding general if he
sought to do so. The SS and the Gestapo were Hitler's enforcers;
dedicated, fanatical troops who could be used to enforce his will
if the standard chain of command failed. Therefore, the German's
control of these special forces put him in a position to enforce the
Nazi command structure...or not.

A few days after the arrival of General Choltitz, Allied
gunfire was heard from the outskirts of Paris. General
Choltitz was given little time to settle into his new job. He
ordered the burning of military papers and correspondence
and evacuated nonessential personnel as he carried out his
military duties.

The German returned from a long meeting with General Choltitz and senior Nazi officers. He told me something no Nazi general would be expected to reveal to any French woman. Since the Nazis could not hold Paris for themselves, then no one would have her. Hitler had commanded the German, General Choltitz and all Nazi forces in the Paris area to conduct a campaign of total destruction and leave nothing of Paris for the Allies except ashes and death. "A field of ruins" were Hitler's exact words.

Choltitz and the German were ordered to set charges in every major building and monument and to blow Paris into rubble. The Nazi combat engineers found the kingpins in each bridge, the point where the bridges were designed to be quickly dropped with little force in the case of a retreat. Explosive charges were placed at these points on all bridges. Specially trained military engineers, specialists in explosives called sappers, or sapeurs, of the 813th Pionier Kompanie set massive charges in the Eiffel Tower, the Palace Luxembourg, the Opera, the electric power stations, the telephone exchanges; everything was to be destroyed. Hitler commanded the Luftwaffe to immediately bomb the city with "all forces" available. Hitler intended to kill most Parisian residents and physically destroy the city. The German quoted Hitler: "The Allies are bombing German cities, aren't they? Destroy Paris!"

Choltitz was sent to Paris by the Führer not to defend but to obliterate her! According to his conversations with the German, this was not fully known by General Choltitz before his arrival in Paris. It was another deviant plan conceived by the insane supreme ruler of Nazi Germany.

Hitler chose Choltitz because he was a man with a history of destroying cities. He appeared to be the perfect choice. Choltitz had actively participated in and led the Nazi destruction of Rotterdam and Sevastopol, in brutal attacks that left nothing of these cities but smoldering wreckage and death. In the siege of

Sevastopol, Choltitz's command numbered 4,800 troops going into the battle, and only 347 of them lived to the end. Choltitz was wounded but survived to lead more attacks on more cities. Because of Choltitz's ability to destroy cities for him, Hitler had handpicked Choltitz to annihilate the world's most beautiful city and the 3.5 million people who lived there. He knew Choltitz would, without question, do exactly what he was told to do, just as he had always done.

When the German explained Hitler's orders to destroy Paris, I was jolted into action. I envisioned the aftermath of Paris burning. I saw her monuments, buildings and bridges fallen into twisted wreckage throughout the city and her people dead and dying in a gigantic, horrific Guernica. Hitler's orders were the epitome of evil. It was a gruesome picture; not a military undertaking but mass murder. The German said, "You will die, Christine. Those you are protecting will die. Paris will die too."

The horrifying vision created a sudden epiphany in my mind, body and soul. My focus coalesced like a finely sharpened knife point. All that had happened, everything I had been through with the German and the Nazis fueled my strength. I was prepared to defy Hitler and defy fate herself. "We can stop this. We can save Paris. Paris will not be murdered!" I shouted at the German.

My moment had arrived; I saw in front of me the purpose for which I was given life. The German was mine and I would use him to save Paris. My carefully laid plans, the *My Paris* tours, my suffering and giving of myself were about to pay off. It was time to act.

My first challenge was to convince these two Nazi career military officers to disobey Hitler's direct orders. I questioned my ability to accomplish this task for just a moment. Was I being naïve to think I could stop Hitler's plans for the total destruction of Paris? I pushed doubt away and pressed forward. No hesitation entered my mind again until it was over.

I indentified a number of essentials. Paris must survive, the German loved me, and now he loved my city too. The Allies were close, and they could free Paris with just a little more time; we just needed a delay of two days. If we failed, there would be nothing left of her; the complete destruction of Paris would occur and we would die a horrific death. An incredible opportunity was given to me. I only needed to be wise enough and strong enough to take it.

One of the lessons I had learned from captivity was that those in control could change fate and alter life. I could not rely on the two fearful men who were in a position to save Paris. They lacked my determined passion and they were under incredible pressure and dire threats to kill her. They would be hindered into inaction by the same characteristics that had brought the Nazis into Paris in the first place: overly masculine concepts of honor, duty and following orders without question. It was up to me to lead them away from hate and destruction. The path to survival was becoming clearer and clearer. I had to take control of Choltitz through the German.

"Don't kill her," I told the German. "Paris is now your city too; you love her as you love me. Paris belongs not just to France and the Parisians but to the world. She has to live. Germany cannot be her murderer. Save her! If you kill Paris, you, Choltitz and Germany will be forever known as her murderers. You will be loathed by people from all over the world for this despicable atrocity. They will abhor you personally for now and for generations beyond. You will become marked men, *The Two Judases of Germany*, linked forever in the mass murder of Paris. If you kill her, your beloved Germany will not be forgiven and there will never be reconciliation between France and Germany. The hatred of the Germans will be all that remains for the thousand years of which you used to speak. Germans will be despised as barbarians. When you lose this war, you and Germany will be punished for this mass murder far beyond the misery Germany suffered after her defeat in World War One."

Then I played my last card. "Versailles is the home of our daughter, Gabriella. She will be killed from the massive destruction and chaos you and your Nazis are about to create. Don't take away Gabriella's home and don't risk her life. You have to stop it. You have to stop Hitler and Choltitz from killing Paris!"

I held the German. I kissed him. I showered him with all the tenderness and affection I could give. I asked for his unwavering commitment to prevent this madness. With fear in his eyes, he said they were planning to blow up the four aqueducts that held the city's water supply to flood the entire city, bring down every bridge, and bomb the roads, eliminating escape routes for millions of Parisians. Simultaneously, the Luftwaffe and the new Nazi weapon, the V-2 liquid-propulsion rockets, were to rain explosive hell down on Paris' residential and commercial areas to create a firestorm from which there would be no place to hide. The explosives were in place throughout the city and the Luftwaffe's bombers were armed and ready to deploy. The preparations for Paris' destruction were complete. The executioners only waited for the command to kill.

I sat on the overstuffed chair containing my notes of the last three years as the German and I evaluated the multiple forces of destruction heading toward Paris and those within. It was a race between Nazi bombs and the Allied armies. The only chance for Paris' salvation was to delay the bombings and bring quick liberation by the Allies.

The German was gravely conflicted. He faced the most difficult decision of his life. It was his turn to sweat in fear. Wet beads of terror ran down the sides of his face and dripped onto his shirt. He slipped into a downward spiral of panic as he realized life as he knew it was ending. His dreams were disappearing into new visions of treason, defeat and death.

At first, he reluctantly agreed. Then his love of Paris, Gabriella and me opened his mind to the truth. He finally saw through Hitler's fanatical evil and how he had been blinded by ambition and nationalism. He realized how meaningless his ambitions were if the price to be paid was the destruction of everything and everyone he loved. The tug-of-war for the German's heart and mind was over, and I had won.

He stood up, gathered himself in a gesture of determination and stated emphatically, "Christine, I agree, Paris cannot be destroyed. For the love of Paris we must stop this madness; this murderous insanity has gone too far. One way or another, I will convince General Choltitz to save Paris' life. No one should destroy Paris; there is no military reason to do so, and I will not be known as her murderer throughout time. Choltitz will hold off exploding the city's vital facilities because I will give him no choice. Choltitz can defy Hitler only with the support of my troops and I will commit them only after he agrees to force the delay and surrender." He immediately called Choltitz and arranged for an emergency meeting.

The German had grown into a bigger man. He switched sides in the ageless war between good and evil. The change strengthened him as he began his willful attempt to alter a horrific fate and save our precious city.

The German's courage came from a greater love than self-love and a higher duty than commanding a military organization. His demand to save Paris' life would be simultaneously an act of treason and an act of love; he knew the price for his bravery was death, but he chose to pay it. He would be convicted in both camps—killed by the Allies for what he had done or by the

Nazis for what he was about to do—he was a man condemned to death by whoever captured him first.

My mind was racing; my ideas were exploding. I became highly organized and focused; there was no room for distraction or hesitancy. If we wanted to challenge Hitler and change Paris' fate, there was no time to waste. "You must take Choltitz a plan for the liberation of Paris. It has to be a plan he can implement immediately and one that will keep the Nazi forces under control long enough to allow the Allies to arrive. It has to minimize the destruction in the city during Allied Liberation."

The German's conflicted thinking remained partially unclear and disorganized but mine crystallized into precise actions. I told the German to find four sheets of hotel stationery and mark each with a heading: *1. STABILIZE PARIS, 2. DELAY HITLER, 3. INFORM THE ALLIES, 4. SURRENDER.* Under each heading, I told the German to write down the salient points.

Two problems had to be solved immediately: growing violence in the streets stirred up by the Communist Resistance, and the planned bombings by the Luftwaffe. The fighting between the Nazi occupiers and the Résistance was exploding into massive street fighting. In retaliation for the killing of Nazi soldiers, Choltitz had ordered the killing of Résistance fighters. The turmoil was destabilizing Paris and would interfere with the Allied liberation if it continued to grow. To de-escalate the conflict on the barricades, Choltitz needed an abrupt ceasefire with the Résistance, and to issue orders to restrain his tanks and troops from overreacting to the attacks. He must cancel the Luftwaffe bombings without delay. He could claim that bombing Paris would kill the Nazi soldiers who were spread throughout the city, so they must be delayed until the troops could be repositioned. He could claim anything but he must ground those airplanes. The German wrote the most important points of Step One as I dictated them:

1. STABILIZE PARIS:

Authorize negotiations with the Résistance

Offer a cease-fire to the Résistance leaders

Pull troops and tanks back from street fighting

Cancel the Luftwaffe bombings

Choltitz was to give Hitler and the Nazi High Command every impression that he was preparing the city for destruction for as long as possible. We had to be careful; Hitler could push Choltitz to carry out his sadistic plan or, if he lost faith in Choltitz, he would remove him and assign someone else to pull the Paris trigger. We needed a delaying tactic. It would be difficult for Hitler to know the exact status of the preparations from his distant bunker, so Choltitz would feed him reports saying the destruction was to be carried out imminently. Then Choltitz would cease all communications just before the Allied troops arrived. Hitler would become frustrated but he would have to wait. Step two was written on the hotel stationery:

2. DELAY HITLER:

Give Hitler and High Command the false assurance that Paris will be destroyed immediately

Put the sappers on high alert and issue direct orders to hold off lighting the fuses until Choltitz personally gives the command

End all communications with High Command and Hitler just prior to the arrival of the Allies, to confuse Nazi command and maintain Choltitz's authority.

Next, Choltitz must agree to formally surrender Paris and his seventeen thousand Nazi troops to the Allies as soon as the Allied military arrives at the Hotel Meurice. This would end the fighting and save the city from prolonged, door-to-door combat. If the Allies didn't know Choltitz was committed to surrender, they would be coming into Paris prepared to fight in the streets, from house to house until every Nazi soldier was killed or captured. Paris would be pulverized in the crossfire. With the assurance that Choltitz would surrender his troops, the Allies could come into Paris using minimum firepower and cause the least amount of death and destruction. The Allies must be informed by a trusted party of how critical the situation was inside Paris and the magnitude of the planned obliteration of the city.

The German stated forcefully, "The plan must assure Choltitz will live. His surrender must be to an Allied military command, not to the Résistance or street fighters who, in their hatred and vengeance, might not recognize the importance of his role after surrender. General Choltitz must continue to be the authority figure for all Nazi forces in Paris during and after surrender. Most of the troops will lay down their arms if he commands it, particularly with support from my Gestapo and SS troops. To save the lives of the soldiers on both sides and the citizens of Paris, the Allies need Choltitz as much as Choltitz needs them. I know the French will not allow me to live, I have been here too long and I have done too much to forgive. We will only negotiate for Choltitz's survival." Step Three of the plan was written on the hotel stationery:

3. SEND AN ENVOY TO THE ALLIES:

Communicate the urgency of liberating Paris before the Nazis destroy her

Inform them of Choltitz's commitment to surrender all Nazi forces in Paris to the Allies once they arrive at the Hotel Meurice

Make clear the threat of a Communist takeover of Paris and the escalation of fighting between the Résistance and the Nazi army

Communicate the magnitude of the planted explosives and aerial bombings and the dire consequences of any delay by the Allied high command

Obtain the Allied commitment to guarantee Choltitz his personal safety once he surrenders

Surrender was the "linchpin" of the plan, but surrender of the Nazi forces to the Allies presented a number of challenges. Some of the Nazi troops had personally pledged to Hitler to never lay down their arms under any circumstances; they had taken an oath to fight until death. However, most of the fanatical troops remaining in Paris were under the command of the German, so he would have to take control of them to prevent ongoing fighting. The German recorded the final points of our plan on the last sheet of stationery:

4. SURRENDER:

Prepare a message to the Nazi officers and troops, ordering them to surrender.

Select a group of loyal officers to implement and enforce the order for troop surrender.

Set up a process to direct all Nazi soldiers to stop fighting when Choltitz surrenders Paris, and to surrender their weapons.

Create a safe holding place for the disarmed Nazi soldiers to minimize post-surrender killings by both sides.

We finished writing the plans and it was time to implement them. When the German was leaving for his crucial meeting with Choltitz, I kissed him and reiterated the importance of the message he was carrying. He said, "I understand the enormity of our situation. We are about to change history and save millions of lives. You are an incredibly special woman, and together we will save Paris. I will not fail you, I will not fail Paris and I will not fail our daughter. I am not afraid to use my power." The German fearlessly set out to propose high treason to General Choltitz, a meeting of two professional soldiers who had never disobeyed an order in their lives. Afterward, the German gave me a detailed description of Choltitz's reaction to his demand to save Paris, which was recorded in my notes shortly afterward.

"I walked into the commanding general's office. He was sitting at his desk studying a detailed street map of Paris marked with codes showing German and French Résistance strong points. He was not pleased to see me and he did not stand up to salute or shake hands, though it was his custom to do so. He looked up and asked why I had requested an emergency meeting with him, as he was extremely busy. I remained standing and didn't waste any time in telling him we must not destroy Paris. We had to prevent Hitler from making this historic mistake; we must turn Paris over to the Allies unharmed. Slamming his fist loudly on his desk, Choltitz screamed at me."

"'Damn you! You come into my office on the pretext you have emergency business and you propose treason! You bastard, you will pay for this. I am required to arrest you immediately or I will also be guilty of treason. You and your Gestapo troops are supposed to be the enforcers of Hitler's orders and now you propose defiance.

"'I have sworn my loyalty and support to Hitler and the Third Reich. My father and my grandfather were Prussian army officers; we don't challenge orders from our commander-in-chief. I have fought hard for the Nazis and I will be rewarded for the destruction of Paris as I was for destroying other cities in Hitler's way. You have threatened my career and my life with your talk of mutiny!

"'You are the head of the SS. You know what your bloodthirsty troops will do to us for disobeying orders from the Führer. Even this conversation is treason. The new Sippenhaft law dictates families of Nazi officers to be held hostage to assure our loyalty to Hitler. If I don't burn Paris to the ground as ordered, I will be tried for treason and hung with my wife, my precious little girls and my new baby boy. You son of a bitch!

"'Why are you protecting Paris? The Allies are bombing German cities and killing thousands of our civilians. What is the difference if we destroy Paris and kill some of theirs?

"'Who else knows of this plot to commit treason? Is this coming from your French whore? You sound like that Collaborator-Chairman Taittinger who tried to convince me to save Paris yesterday. He was standing right there on my balcony, pointing to some girl riding a bicycle as if she should be the reason to defy Hitler, save Paris, be convicted of treason and killed with my family. You and he are insane! Your words have started something bigger than both of us, something we will not be able to control. There is nothing we can do. If I don't burn Paris to the ground, Hitler will send someone else do it. I will be arrested and sentenced to death and so will you. What were you thinking?'"

The German described his response to Choltitz's diatribe. "I didn't come here because I want to commit treason or defy Hitler any more than you do. I do not want to save Paris out of disrespect for you, our military or our country. However, we have to stop Germany from destroying Paris. So hear me out and consider my plan carefully.

"First, do not call for my arrest. Remember, I have been in Paris for many years and you have just arrived. You are viewed as an outsider by our troops and any support from the Nazi command in Berlin is a long way from here. My SS troops are the strongest soldiers in Paris and my heavily armed personal guards are waiting outside your door. They will follow my orders, not yours. It is impossible to arrest me. If accused, I will deny this conversation ever took place. Unless you intend to shoot me yourself, right now, my troops will not allow my arrest. They will easily handle any of your noncombatant soldiers who might be foolish enough to challenge them.

"Second, we cannot allow Germany to be responsible for destroying Paris. Such an act would not be forgiven. You and I would be known as the butchers of Paris for eternity. Why should we be her assassins? You are a soldier; you do not want to be the exterminator of millions of unarmed French civilians and the murderer of the most beautiful city in the world. There has been enough senseless killing. We need to save Paris for the long-term honor and survival of Germany, not destroy her and have the world condemn our country and our people long after we die. We are losing the war and we must think of Germany's survival in the peace to come, in a time when Hitler no longer rules our country.

"Paris is not a military objective. It is an open city that did not resist our occupation. Paris is not full of enemy troops; it is full of women and children. Our own troops will also perish if you pull the pin and drop the bombs. There are no enemy military objectives in Paris; the only military equipment and factories belong to us. Paris is not like those other cities in the way of our troops as we conquered enemy territory. There is no reason to destroy her other than vengeance and madness.

"We can stop this insanity, but we need to work with each other to create a short delay to allow the Allies to arrive. You have control over the *sappers* and the planes of the Luftwaffe; I have the SS and the Gestapo. I will keep my troops under control and use them to support you. You must stop your *sappers* from setting off their charges. Paris must remain the free and beautiful world capital she has been for two thousand years. Her magnificence cannot become a pile of rubble and death by our hands. It all depends on our decisions, on our choices."

Choltitz did not attempt to arrest the German. He knew he could not make such a move, he knew the German held the power of the moment. Hitler wouldn't care if Choltitz participated voluntarily or involuntarily, he would be considered guilty of treason in either case. Choltitz became part of the plot to save Paris from Hitler, like it or not.

Choltitz began to break under the pressure. He revealed his own doubts about the orders to destroy Paris and acknowledged his uncertainty about Hitler's sanity. "'When I met with Hitler on my way to Paris three weeks ago, he was acting like a madman. He was ranting and raving about everything, including the disloyalties of his generals, the failure of the Nazi defenses on the French coast and the problems at the Russian front. Hitler was particularly critical of and insulting to his Prussian generals, a core of professional soldiers of which I am a proud member. I had to sit there as he insulted my fellow officers and me; the same officers who had given him so many victories.

"'On the train from Berlin to Paris, I met another German general and we discussed the barbarian law which held our families hostage to guarantee our performance and loyalty. I know Hitler has made serious tactical errors, like holding back the Panzer divisions at Calais and invading Russia prematurely. I have learned today that the reinforcements and weapons promised for the defense of Paris have been diverted elsewhere. The Allied troops are coming directly at us and we have no time or resources to organize an effective, defensive course of action. There is nowhere to escape and there will be no victory, at least not for us. You are right about one thing, we have only two choices: to blow up Paris or surrender. Our occupation of Paris has ended.'"

Neither Choltitz nor the German fully understood their internal conflicts resulting from disobeying a direct order; they lacked the framework to comprehend such an act. They were bred to follow orders, to maintain the integrity of the command structure no matter what. To disobey the order to destroy Paris would result in the collapse of everything Choltitz and the German had accomplished in their lifetimes. The German had personally shot and killed a Nazi soldier who refused his orders on the battlefield. How could they defy a direct order from the Führer himself—impossible!

Regardless of his conflicts, he knew I supported him as he continued to press the commanding general of Paris to implement our plans. The German became bolder and more adamant in his argument. He had gone too far to turn back. He pointed out another dire fact to Choltitz that we had discussed.

If the Nazi forces were unleashed on Paris as Hitler had ordered, there would be no opportunity for either of them or their troops to escape. They would be killed along with the Parisians and everyone else. Killing Paris would also be suicide.

The German said, "Choltitz began to speak in an almost pleading way. I could sense him soften, though he continued to argue as he spoke."

He quoted Choltitz, "'I cannot surrender Paris; I have no authority to do this. Do you know what the French will do to our troops once we lay down our guns? The Parisians hate us. We have thousands of troops, personnel and many friends in Paris. If I surrender, it will be Germans and our allies who will be butchered. We will have no way to protect ourselves. Blowing up Paris is the only *safe* thing to do.'"

The German summarized Choltitz's fear, "With these words, Choltitz put his face into his hands and closed his eyes and tried to hide from the fate he must face and the choice he was doomed to make. General Choltitz finally realized I was right and there was only one choice, a choice that would dramatically change his life and the lives of many others.'"

The German and General Choltitz completed their pact for life: Paris would not be burned! Choltitz, the commander of all Nazi forces in Paris, agreed to commit treason and surrender Paris and his forces to the Allied troops. The die was cast. Hitler's orders to burn Paris would lay silently unanswered on Choltitz's desk. They would defy Hitler together. With a less than enthusiastic handshake, the two men cast their fate and the fate of millions of Parisians in a new direction, toward survival instead of death. There were no routine Sieg Heils to Nazi victory or salutes to the Führer as the two men grappled with the enormity of their decision.

Choltitz retreated from his office and left the German sitting alone for a few minutes. His mind was in disarray; he knew the implications of his acts and was terrified of the consequences—he envisioned the murder of his wife and children as the fate that would befall him as a traitor. Behind the closed doors of his bedroom, Choltitz took a large gulp of cognac. After a short while, he rejoined the German to discuss implementing their fateful decision.

The German presented our plans as written on the four pages of hotel stationery and reviewed each point. As the German spoke, Choltitz's awareness of what he was about to do grew, as did his fear. Choltitz went into his bedroom and fetched the bottle of cognac. He poured the German and himself a substantial amount of the golden brown liquor, which they each consumed in one quick gulp.

Once General Choltitz and the German had completed their treasonous pact, they immediately began to implement the plans we had designed. Everything began happening simultaneously; the French and American troops were arriving in the Paris suburbs and the street fighting was escalating.

In a private meeting the week before, the German had introduced General Choltitz to a special man who could be trusted to carry out special, unofficial assignments. That man was Swedish Ambassador Raoul Nordling, a close friend of the German's and mine for some time. He was a gracious and intelligent man and was always willing to help stop the killing in any way he could. The Ambassador kept close contact with all sides of the conflicts within Paris and with those fighting the greater war all around her.

I had asked the German to call Ambassador Nordling just before his meeting with Choltitz and have him come to the Hotel Meurice for an urgent request. The German asked Nordling to offer Choltitz his services to arrange a cease-fire between the

Nazis and the Résistance. Choltitz gave Nordling the authority to negotiate for the Nazi command, and he set off to arrange an immediate cease-fire. Next, Choltitz summoned his attaché and issued orders to his troops throughout Paris to stand down immediately.

The members of the Résistance who supported Charles de Gaulle agreed to the cease-fire, but after a brief pause, the Communist members would not adhere to it. They did not want de Gaulle to take control of Paris and they saw this as the last opportunity to take control before he did. The Communists wanted to be the Liberators of Paris and they were willing to sacrifice the death of "two hundred thousand or more Parisians" to accomplish their takeover.

The brief cease-fire did give each side the opportunity to evacuate their wounded and remove their dead from the streets. It deescalated the fighting for just enough time to allow the next steps of our plan to unfold. Step One of our plan was imperfectly implemented but it was enough.

Choltitz cancelled the scheduled Luftwaffe air raids on Paris. The Luftwaffe command accepted Choltitz's order to cease and desist for one day but, in defiance of Choltitz's weakening authority, they carried out air raids on the next. Hundreds of Parisians were killed or wounded in the attack, which was just a preview of the destruction ordered by the Führer.

Choltitz called the German a number of times to report the continuing activities. I listened in on the conversations as things quickly progressed. What upset Choltitz the most were the constant phone interrogations from Hitler, whose questioning escalated into a tirade. *"Is Paris burning?"* the Führer demanded to know. "Why isn't Paris burning?" He wanted answers and he wanted action—"I want Paris destroyed, now!" Hitler commanded Choltitz. "Burn it!" Hitler screamed. Choltitz gave our preplanned reasons for the delay, excuses for why he hadn't carried out the Führer's orders. Then Choltitz stopped taking calls from anyone in the Nazi High Command, leaving them in the dark as he permanently severed his connection with Hitler.

In frustration, the High Command turned to the German to determine the cause of Choltitz's non-response. The German lied to the High Command, saying Choltitz was doing everything he could to implement their orders, and that Choltitz was in the field assisting demolition crews to set up the explosives and was out of communication as he diligently worked to prepare for Paris' destruction. They believed the German, and a little more precious time was gained.

Choltitz gave his demolition crews strict instructions to stand by for his directive, but to do nothing until they received personal orders from him. Step Two of our plan was in place. The destruction of Paris was paused but not yet avoided.

The next step was to bring the Allies into the plan. When Ambassador Raoul Nordling returned from meeting with the Résistance, Choltitz asked him to take a party of men to the Allies with the vital message. It was a daring undertaking. The Allied command was stationed only sixty miles outside of Paris, but reaching it required passage through two warring fronts. While organizing the Nordling Mission, the severely stressed Ambassador suffered a heart attack and became bedridden. Choltitz's official pass authorizing the group to travel through Nazi lines indicated the name "R. Nordling." The only other person who could use the pass was the Ambassador's brother, whose first name also began with an "R." Brother Rolf Nordling took over the operation and led it through the Nazi defensive lines to the Allies.

The purpose of the Nordling Mission was to bring an urgent warning to the Allies that Paris would cease to exist if she were not liberated within forty-eight hours and to commit General Choltitz to surrendering his Nazi forces. They were to warn the

Allies that Hitler had issued orders to his Luftwaffe and rocket base commanders to bombard Paris with everything they had before retreating to Germany.

Coincidently, a man I mentioned before, Alexandre de Saint-Phalle, a secret member of the Gaullist Résistance and my Husband's family banker, drove the black Citroën full of the Nordling conspirators. They passed through the hostile Nazi defense lines and encountered extensive examination by suspicious Nazi field officers. Only after a personal telephone conversation with an agitated General Choltitz were they given passage to cross into "no man's land" toward the Allied Command headquarters. It was as dangerous a drive as one could take, straight through the middle of a war.

At one point, a Nazi soldier jumped on the hood to stop the car, severely startling the group. It was a warning: there were land mines three feet ahead of the Citroën! The soldier walked in front of their car reading his map of planted explosives. Saint-Phalle zigzagged his car through the minefield and then drove down a familiar road which happened to lead to his grandmother's house and also to the American front lines. With the help of that Nazi soldier, the lives of this group were saved and the messages were successfully delivered to the commanders of the American and French liberation armies. We were later told that Nordling spoke personally to General Patton about the conditions in Paris and the terms Choltitz would accept. The Allies agreed to guarantee Choltitz's safety and alter their tactical plans; the Allies would immediately save Paris instead of bypassing her. Step Three was in place.

August 23, 1944. In one curious aspect of these final days of Occupation, Choltitz showed a partial willingness to carry out Hitler's orders by burning down the Grand Palais in retribution for Résistance killings of Nazi soldiers. Seven days before he had lined up a group of captured Résistance fighters and ordered a firing squad to shoot them. Because of this conflicted behavior, the German and I concluded that Choltitz was playing both sides against each other. His final choice would depend on fate and the will of others. By secretly asking the Allies to come to Paris, offering to surrender, and warning them of the consequences if they did not make it in time, the Nordling Mission gave Choltitz cover with the French and the Americans.

After he made his offer to the Allies, Choltitz was no longer responsible for what happened. He was prepared to embrace the Allies and passively surrender Paris or, if they failed to arrive in time, he would oversee Paris' demise. His ultimate place in history and this critical chapter in the story of Paris were not yet written, and neither he nor anyone else knew exactly what the final pages would say.

Events were moving very fast. French General Leclerc began to move his troops toward Paris without the authorization of Allied command. Based on the information brought by the Nordling Mission and others, General Bradley ordered the battle-hardened American 4th Division to accompany French General Leclerc as they charged toward Paris.

The German and I read the intelligence reports on the approaching Allied armies and the fighting on the city outskirts. The French forces were slowed by the Nazi defenses just outside Paris that fiercely fought the attacking Allied troops. They had stopped taking orders from Choltitz.

Without the American 4th Division, it was clear Paris would not have survived. The French army would not have made it in time if they had been fighting alone. Even the shortest delay could have forced General Choltitz to destroy Paris.

The Communist elements of the French Résistance escalated their inter-city fighting with the Nazi occupiers. The call went out from the Communist Résistance leaders throughout Paris: "Man the barricades!"

Barricades were built and manned throughout the city; weapons and ammo were distributed and the street battles escalated. The Nazis under Choltitz's command tried a number of tactics to defuse it. They used threats, retaliation, the cease-fire and accommodation to try to keep the Résistance from pushing the delicate situation into the full-scale inner-city war the Communists sought. As the Allied armies came closer, the fighting with the Résistance intensified. The French fighters attacked Nazi troops and trucks, causing considerable death and destruction. Choltitz lifted the restraints on his troops and the Nazis pursued the Résistance fighters with a vengeance. They retaliated multifold for the killing of Nazi soldiers by killing many innocent Parisians who were picked up for simple curfew violations.

The Police Prefecture (police headquarters) across from Notre Dame on the Île de la Cité became the central gathering area for the retreating, almost ammo-less Résistance fighters. Despite Choltitz's previous disarming of the police in fear of such a move, police throughout Paris joined the fight against the Nazis with whatever weapons and ammo they could find. As the Résistance and police retreated into the large Prefecture building, Nazi Panzer tanks and their support troops closed in and started shooting. A deadly battle began, killing numerous Nazis and Résistance fighters. The Parisians knocked out Nazi tanks with "Molotov Cocktails"—wine bottles filled with gasoline and other explosives, which were thrown onto the tank turrets. The French fought bravely but the Nazis were gaining the upper hand as the Résistance forces' ammunition ran out and more Nazi forces encircled the Prefecture. The end of the Résistance appeared near.

August 24, 1944. It was a day that was lived at an intense minute-by-minute pace. In the middle of the violent street fighting, a single-engine French military plane flew over Paris dropping thousands of leaflets which said, *"Tenez bon, nous arrivons!"*—we are coming! While the Résistance fighters wanted guns and ammo instead of leaflets or Allied troops, most of Paris was elated to receive the news that friendly military was close. Even as the leaflets fell, the Nazis maintained their threatening control over Parisians; anyone caught picking up the leaflets would be shot on the spot.

First French troops and then the Americans entered Paris and forced the Nazis to turn away from their attack on the Résistance and retreat into defensive positions. As the Nazis pulled back, the Résistance fighters emerged from the Police Prefecture and were joined by Résistance fighters throughout Paris to engage in brutal attacks against the retreating Nazis.

An advanced group of the French Army, under the command of red-bearded Captain Dronne, led the first French forces into the city of Paris and arrived at the Hotel de Ville at 9:23 p.m. At that moment, General Choltitz's solemn staff dinner at the Meurice was suddenly interrupted by the incessant ringing of thousands of church bells throughout Paris. After fifty months of the Occupation, Paris was, though a bit prematurely, celebrating her Liberation. There were fruitless street battles yet to be fought, but Occupation was essentially over. The race between Paris' survival and her demise was finished. The French and Americans had won. It was time for General Choltitz to prepare for surrender and for General Charles de Gaulle to prepare for victory. "Paris lives!"

Café Talk: Choltitz

1945. "Choltitz! *I can't believe you and the German were able to force Choltitz to disobey Hitler's orders and surrender Paris! But the German held the real power and Choltitz had no choice but to join the mutiny once that became clear."*

The American was sitting wide-eyed, occasionally forgetting to write as he listened, mesmerized by Christine's story of good overpowering the will of the Führer, the evil dictator who wanted to own Paris for a thousand years but ordered her obliteration when he couldn't possess her any longer. Amazed at her relationship with the German, he wrote down the words, "She controlled him who once controlled her."

The American was impressed with the brilliant plan Christine had developed for Choltitz. "What magnificent insight! There were so many potential pitfalls in those last few hours. What if..." *His mind trailed off into the world of imagination, into Christine's vision of burning flesh, mass murder and Paris broken into millions of pieces. The potential for such horror was incomprehensible; but for a few extremely small changes in fate and human behavior, Paris and most of her citizens would have disappeared in an inferno.*

"The events which began with your capture and ended with the liberation of Paris unfolded like a master plan, with each piece connected to the other, and the sum of events building up until they reached this world-changing event.

"From what you have told me of your Professor-Husband, he would have loved this story, but for the fact that you and he paid such a high price for it. If the players in this story of the Occupation and Liberation had been strangers, your Husband would have made it a central lecture after the war. But then, the story would have been different if the German had captured anyone else but you for sex and propaganda. Only you could have created this extraordinary victory out of such an impossible situation.

"You are absolutely right about the long-term impact of the Nazis leveling Paris. It would have expanded the endless sea of hate for

Germany which was already extensive due to Hitler's atrocities in Poland, Russia and the Ukraine and the holocaust he had created for the Jews. Destroying Paris would have soaked Europe so deep in Parisian blood that it would have taken the thousand years to wash it away. European peace would not have come. The need for reprisals would have controlled Europe for decades and centuries, long after the current participants were gone. It was your breakdown of the German's hate and replacing it with love that served as the linchpin in the rescue. Thank God you were there, Christine!"

Christine did not respond to his compliments, they didn't matter to her. However, she did expand on what her Husband's reaction would have been. "My Husband would have loved the story of the Nordling Mission, how it succeeded despite a high potential for failure, and how such an extraordinary event helped change human history. It is an unbelievable coincidence that my Husband's banker, Alexandre de Saint-Phalle, drove the Nordling Mission through Nazi and Allied lines on the same road that he had driven many times to reach his grandmother's house. He so fittingly appeared to be a part of the Occupation establishment that after the Nazis were driven out, he was tried for collaboration. He was found innocent after testimony on his behalf by the Résistance leaders, and after they found three dead Nazi soldiers in his basement.

"Fate made a U–turn and a magnificent miracle happened. I thanked God for giving General Choltitz, the German and me the strength to prevent a Paris Armageddon. However, I was still living in the world of the Nazis and I was not yet free. I remained a captive woman waiting to face my own countrymen. But there have been few times in my life more joyful than the moment the Paris church bells started ringing again. It was like heaven opened up and joyful, free Parisians poured out. There was no stopping the force of the Liberation. What a sound!"

Christine, not the American, knew what was next. Her next dreadful experience pierced the core of her being and deeply impacted the rest of her life. Christine took a few deep breaths and continued with her story. "The hatred and violence did not end with Liberation. Frenchmen were angry and their repressed hate exploded when freed from the Nazi boot."

The German's End

August 25, 1944. There were to be numerous battles between the Allied military and remnants of the Nazi armies in the streets of Paris before she was liberated. When the French and Americans broke through the defensive ring around Paris, both sides suffered considerable losses. American tanks shot and killed Nazi tanks in the heart of Paris. Committed Nazi soldiers held strong points where they fought against attacks by the French and American soldiers. However, the occupying Nazi forces that had not been in recent combat were no match for the highly motivated, battle-hardened Allied forces, who would not be stopped until the occupiers were driven out of Paris, captured or killed. The military advantage switched sides and the Nazis were on the run.

The German and I stayed in his suite on top of the Hotel Meurice as the Free French and American troops swept into Paris. Some Nazis attempted to fight. When fighting failed, they attempted to retreat, but the Résistance slew them without pity; often there would be no surrender.

As the Nazis fought a losing battle with the Résistance and the Allied armies, we could hear the shooting and grenades exploding from our bedroom. The automatic gunfire didn't drown out the bloodthirsty screams of French killing or Nazis begging for mercy. Many of the remaining Nazi soldiers were office workers who had never fired a shot or hurt anybody during the entire war but met their deaths while trying to surrender. Many young boys died like the hardest of men and paid the ultimate price for the evil of others.

As chaos spread throughout Paris and the Allied armies began their sweep toward the Hotel Meurice, the German and I made love. We changed sexual roles and he took me as a dominant man.

For the first time in three years, he didn't leave the initiation of sex to me. He began by loving me tenderly but became aggressive, almost violent, as he completed what he knew was his last sexual act. He gave everything to me and I matched him by giving all of myself back. He lit my fires of passion instead of burning Paris to the ground. In my climax, I screamed "God!" as a way of connecting my many emotions in one word. For just a few minutes, we experienced the feelings of triumph, of victory over evil in the joining together of our minds and bodies. We knew we had taken Paris to a turning point and loved her over the bridge of salvation.

All escape routes out of Paris were cut off. Shots were ringing out in the Tuileries across the street from the suite in the Meurice. Bullets were hitting the hotel as fighting progressed up the Rue de Rivoli, coming closer and closer.

The German rose from the bed and quickly dressed in his general's uniform. He loaded and strapped his Walther PP Polizeipistole to his hip and I put on a dress. We could smell the explosions of tank and gunfire, even with the windows tightly closed. During firefights, the noise of the guns was deafening, though it could not silence the Paris church bells, which kept ringing and ringing.

The German and I had one last, brief conversation over the approaching gunfire, screams and attacks. He thanked me for changing him and showing him how to love me and teaching him to love Paris. He could not allow the destruction of something he loved so much, even if the Führer had ordered him to do so. He asked forgiveness for the horrific things he had created in my life, for the disrespect that he had shown me as a human being. He apologized for the scar. He touched it with his right hand as I gently held his wrist. He then told me how he felt sorrow and guilt every time he looked at it after he fell in love with me. He said, "Your injury was a dark beacon in the life we shared together, an unmistakable reminder of why certain events cannot be forgiven. It is a mark of evil I put upon you, the only woman I love and the only woman I have ever loved."

He told me he loved our daughter and his spirit would live on in her. "Please love her," he pleaded, "she is innocent and she needs her mother." I stared at him and said nothing. At that moment, it was impossible to explain it was he who had kept me from being a mother to our child; it was because of him that I had to push her away.

A lifetime of institutionalized acts of cruelty over other humans was being purged from him. He cried uncontrollably. I held him to my breasts as waves of sorrow and guilt came out in his sobs and tears.

As I embraced this Nazi general for the last time, I thought I finally understood how the German-Nazi mind worked, how they could live within the juxtaposition between the cruelty of their Holocaust and the humaneness of their "proper" society of sophisticated art, music, philosophy and literature. I honored his vital sacrifice and courage in saving Paris. He had done horrible things to other human beings, yet he had found love and acted for good when he faced his final test. I thought to myself, *if a Nazi general could change for the good, couldn't any man?*

The surrender of Paris began on the second floor of the Hotel Meurice, in a small area near Room 213 where General Choltitz lived. He was captured by the Allied Army and the Résistance and taken outside, where unruly crowds of Frenchmen waited. He was taunted, spat upon and his valise was snatched from him. The contents were strewn over the ground, torn up or taken as souvenirs by the crowd, but Choltitz survived and entered Allied military protection.

The gunfire and the chaos of killing continued floor by floor until it reached the fifth story, where we waited in the German's rooftop Belle Etoile Suite. The shooting and screams came closer to us as Résistance fighters mowed down the few Nazi soldiers remaining in the German's entourage and the church bells continued to ring their thunderous toll of liberation. Parisians were playing radios and singing as death and joy ricocheted off each other and roles of the conquered and the conquerors were dramatically reversed.

In thirty-six months, I hadn't uttered his name. I wouldn't personalize what we were doing regardless of the sexual pleasure I experienced, but I said his name for the first time that day. Moments before the end, the German said, "A last sip of cognac before I die and a final kiss to say good-bye." We drank quickly, we kissed briefly. *"Pass auf Dich auf Christine es war wunderbar mit Dir"* ("Take care of yourself, Christine, it was wonderful to have known you") were the German's last words as he looked deep into my eyes, deep into my heart, and the words "Au revoir, Rolf" were mine.

The doors of our suite were blown open with a grenade and I dove behind the bed to avoid the shrapnel. Smoke and fire engulfed the entrance of the suite and a group of four heavily armed French Résistance fighters, three men and one woman, burst ferociously into our bedroom. The German reached for his gun. He had no intention of being taken prisoner. He pointed his PP pistol and fired but hit no one.

There was no hesitation. The Résistance fighters shot him four times at point-blank range. His blood spattered over the lush carpet and onto the linen-covered walls, as his body hit the wall and slid to the floor. The sounds of gunfire were so loud I couldn't hear the church bells for almost a minute, a very intense minute.

The German's only remaining path was death. Too much hate encompassed him in the hearts of the French and he was a traitor to his Nazi master. There was no place left to live and nowhere to hide. He had to die.

When they shot him, they did not ask about his final act of mercy and love. They were ignorant of his critical role in saving Paris in an act of bravery which probably saved these very Résistance fighters' lives and everyone and everything they loved from a horrendous death. They were blinded by vengeance. He had performed one of the most giving acts of love anyone could give: he knowingly gave his life so others could live, so Paris and I could live, so Gabriella could live.

They threw the German's body out the fifth-floor window. It flew through the air and crashed below on the mosaic-decorated sidewalk of the Rue de Rivoli in a pile of blood and bones. On the street there were cheers for the Résistance and celebration for the death of the German. Members of the crowd tore off his medals and his clothes as trophies of their victory. They kicked and spat on his dead corpse in the ultimate degradation of this man. Now, after everything Paris and I had been through under his control, the German, my captor, the father of my child, was dead.

Paris church bells continued ringing and the people of Paris were in the streets loudly singing "La Marseillaise," the French National Anthem:

* * *

Sacred love of France,
Lead, support our avenging arms!
Liberty, beloved Liberty,
Fight with your defenders!
Fight with your defenders!
Under our flags, let victory
Hasten to your manly tones!
May your enemies
See your triumph and our glory!
* * *

General Choltitz was taken to the Gare Montparnasse. Without authority to do so, he formally surrendered Paris to the French Army and the Résistance on August 25, 1944. He gave up the remaining seventeen thousand men under his command to French General Philippe Leclerc and Communist Résistance leader Henri Rol-Tanguy, General Charles de Gaulle's archenemy.

If history could ignore Choltitz's previous roles as a Nazi mass murderer, destroyer of cities and killer of Parisians, then it could be claimed that he was a disinclined hero, for he was the man who did *not* pull the pin on the bomb Paris had become.

Eiffel Tower

The Nazi Occupation of Paris was officially over. Only days before, the Nazi SS engineers had been setting charges on the Eiffel Tower in their preparation to destroy this prominent symbol of Paris by dropping it across the Seine to block river traffic, to emblematically kill Paris through the death of her most

Café Talk: Surrender and Death

1945. Christine stood up and stretched. Her demeanor was calm, almost too calm. The American tried to grasp her mood, looked for hints of what she was thinking and feeling, but she was elusive and aloof. She had exposed nothing as she coolly reported the end of Nazi Occupation and the death of the German.

Christine and the American ended their day and her story at the point that Paris was saved. They were exhausted, so they went their separate ways to live their separate lives until they were to meet again. In doing so, Christine postponed telling of what was to unfold next until another day.

That night, the American took a broad look at Christine's behavior and thought processes during her journey. As the author of Christine's Journal, he searched for patterns, explanations and lessons from Christine's life. He worked to link together the events from the time she and her Husband had been captured until the death of the German and the liberation of Paris. He contemplated her crossing long bridges over the dark depths of mental and physical despair to become a powerful instrument in saving the greatest city in the world.

The American also made a note about the German and Christine "making love" just before he died. It was a term she hadn't used to describe their sexual relationship, and those words hurt him. He didn't want Christine to love the German and he couldn't fully understand their relationship. In a slightly tainted way, he became deeply curious about her true feelings for the German. He wrote in large, bold block letters on his work sheet: DID SHE LOVE HIM? Later that night, he sat alone in a café and stared at those four words, and repeated the thought over again: Did she, damn it, did she love him?

Whatever she had felt for him, Christine was free from the German. The Nazi forces were driven out of Paris, captured or killed. The American thoughtfully celebrated Christine's liberty and her relief from *suffering, though he couldn't fully anticipate the tragedy ahead. Christine would sink further before her freedom came, and even when it did, her freedom would not be free. For Christine, one level of suffering was preparation for the next, more difficult experience yet to come. They were to meet again after a day apart when Christine would begin in a direct and serious tone.*

Liberation for Paris, Not for Christine

Though the Occupation and my captivity were over, this was not the end of my troubles, not by a long way. While two Résistance fighters were disposing of the German's body, one young fighter held me at gunpoint and pinned me against the wall. I screamed repeatedly, "I am French, I am French, don't kill me!" He stared blankly, his tense finger on the trigger while he waited for the leader and his comrades to finish with the German. Fear was exploding in my mind; the only witness to my captivity and good deeds was lying dead on the street below.

The fighters knew me only too well. I had dined while they starved. They saw me in the newspapers with the German, the commander of the hated and feared SS who killed their comrades. I was the German's beautiful French mistress and I lived in his elegant hotel room. I bore a child with him and our daughter was indisputable evidence of my collaboration. Many Parisians hated me, just as the German predicted. I was about to face my new enemy and they were my own countrymen.

The leader turned from the window to deal with me. He slapped me brutally across the face, drawing blood from my weakened scar tissue and loosening two of my teeth. Blood trickled down my face and filled my mouth. They threw me on the bed; the same bed the German and I had shared for most of thirty-six months, the bed where we were passionate sexual partners, the bed where our daughter was conceived, and the bed where the German and I had *made love* only a short time before.

They ripped open my dress and tore off my undergarments. "No, please, I saved Paris," I pleaded. "I saved Paris!" Blood from my mouth stained the sheets in red blotches. The leader looked at me with total and utter loathing. He screamed in my face, "You didn't save Paris, you fucked her, and now I am going to fuck you back!" His hatred spewed forth as screams and blood gushed from my mouth.

Two of the Résistance fighters pinned me down with my arms stretched straight out to the side while the leader violently raped me. It was another deed of an angry animal, a brutal and vicious act of retribution for my "privileged life," a crucifixion for their suffering and the price for my life of Nazi opulence. I tried to shut out the reality of the rape, but I would not forget his smell: his offensive, unwashed body odor mixed with the smells of gunpowder and French cigarettes. I screamed the deepest and loudest scream I could possibly scream, but with the gunshots, the bells and violent death occurring all around us, no one heard me. I was just one more person screaming among many. I resisted in every way I could, kicking and wrenching my body away, but he would not stop; he was indifferent to physical pain. He used his penis instead of his gun to extract vengeance against the repugnant person he thought I was. I hated him and again I wanted to kill.

Regardless of what I had been through, including the saving of Paris, I could not escape becoming a repeat victim of war and hate; it was a horrific reminder that I could not control all of my fate. I was again raped by a monster, only this time he was French. I was raped by a man who professed the high ideals of Marx but a man whose subhuman morals were those of an animal.

The Résistance fighters spat on me, kicked me and yelled more obscenities at me: "You are the Nazi general's woman, a whore! A Collaborator! We detest you even more than the Nazis! We would kill you now and throw you out the window with your swine lover if we didn't have strict orders to bring you to prison for questioning." As I lay on the floor, the woman fighter pulled out a long knife and cut off my hair. She took out a pen and drew a crude swastika on my forehead. My long, detached, once-loved hair was thrown on the floor in hatred and disrespect. The rapist screamed at me, "Now stand up and come with us. You will meet your fate soon enough!"

Only God understood the reason for this brutal act; no human logic could explain why I was pushed further into the depths of hell after all I had been through. I sobbed as the burning between my legs and the degradation became unbearable. They barely let me put on my torn clothes as they dragged me out of the room and down the stairs. In my partial nakedness and near baldness, I was conscious of the rapist's body fluids mixed with my own blood running down my legs. I hated him with every part of my being: my body, my mind, my heart and soul. As they pushed and pulled me down the street, I struggled to cover my breasts and my private parts. Fellow Parisians taunted and spat on me as I walked. Their cries of "Collaborator!" and "German whore!" were as hate-filled as those from the rapist and his comrades. They wanted me exterminated.

Panic began to exceed humiliation as I saw death's finality coming toward me. A great fear gripped my heart, a fear that I would still not survive this war, even as Paris was being freed. As I walked toward the next endless abyss of death, one of the teeth loosened by the rapist's blow came out. I spat blood and the tooth into the gutter and stumbled on.

I was taken to the Drancy Prison, where I stayed a week with hundreds of other Collaborators who had been rounded up after Liberation. Drancy was the same prison where my Husband and thousands of other Jews were taken prior to their deportation to Auschwitz. The conditions of the prison were deplorable; we lived like pigs in a concentration camp. There were many French women with shaven heads and ripped clothes who had been paraded down the public streets half-naked as violent men continued to use war as an excuse and rape as a weapon of revenge and retribution.

My face wound did not heal properly. I felt constant burning between my legs. Human waste piled up at the corners of the prison and the stench was atrocious.

Deep in hate, mobs of French citizens attacked the prison. Some Collaborators were pulled into the streets to be hung or shot. Our guards and interrogators were as brutal to us, their fellow French countrymen and women, as the Germans had been to the imprisoned Jews before. It was terrifying to see the similarity between the behavior of the French and the Germans when their hatred became institutionalized. We were reduced to living like frightened animals in our own land, held by our own people, in the heart of *My Paris*.

Brasillach, the editor who had exposed my Husband and me to the French police and the Nazis, was also imprisoned at Drancy. On the morning that I arrived, accused Collaborators were lined up in the courtyard. Brasillach stood not ten feet from me, the third time in my life that I was near this reprobate. Standing directly across from me were our two neighbors who had so eagerly volunteered us to the Nazis and the police, their fate sealed by their collaboration.

Brasillach had been beaten, his left eye was swollen shut and he wore no shoes. Blood trickled down the inside crotch of his left leg and his lips were smashed. For a split second, with one open eye, he looked straight into my eyes. It was the only time we had anything in common; we shared an all-encompassing fear and overwhelming terror as we were marched toward death by our fellow Frenchmen.

Brasillach was the first prisoner to be taken out of the line. Moments later, we heard the gunfire as he was shot to death outside the prison. For two days his body was not removed from the street. It lay there for Parisians to see what happens to Nazi Collaborators. Each of us feared we would be next.

I was taken to the torture rooms of the prison to be questioned before my sentence was to be carried out. My inquisition began as it did for all accused Collaborators—with an assumption of guilt and an indifference to the truth. I was interrogated by high level officials in the French and American military commands. But one thing ultimately separated me from my fellow inmates and saved my life. The Allies knew the Führer had repeatedly ordered Choltitz to burn Paris and obviously these orders had not been carried out. They knew a great deal about Choltitz and his brutal path of destroying cities. They also knew I had lived with the German for three years and I would have insight into what happened, to why Choltitz had cracked, why he had committed treason.

They asked me many questions, "Do you know why Paris wasn't destroyed? What convinced Choltitz to disobey the Führer's direct orders? What was your connection to the German and Choltitz?"

The interrogators said Choltitz was being questioned in a secret bunker and his story didn't completely make sense. Choltitz took all the credit for saving Paris. He was obviously negotiating for better terms of surrender for himself. However, the interrogators could not understand how Choltitz had been protected from the SS and Gestapo and why the German didn't take charge and implement Hitler's orders when Choltitz refused to execute them. Why did the redundancy built into the Nazi command structure fail?

The men questioned me further. "Why was Choltitz so committed to saving Paris that he would sacrifice the lives of his wife, his children and himself for her?" They said Choltitz cited Hitler's erratic behavior, a spontaneous conversation with a Nazi general on the train, and pleas from Pierre Taittinger, the Collaborator-Chairman of the municipal council of Paris, as the reasons why he saved Paris. He didn't say anything about the German or my roles in his vital decision. As professional interrogators, they knew they didn't have all the information; it wasn't logical or possible that one man stood alone in defiance of Hitler and all the forces of the Third Reich to save a city he hardly knew and clearly did not love.

"Since the German is dead and you were his mistress, we need you to tell us what happened in the end. Why didn't the German's SS troops simply arrest Choltitz and destroy Paris as Hitler ordered?"

I was desperate to get out of prison, so I told my story in great detail. I filled in the missing pieces for the interrogators. I gave them the German and described how I influenced him through sex, love and by the *My Paris* visits. I didn't brag or claim credit; I told them why I cooperated and the consequences for my family if I had refused. I spoke in detail of the role I had played in preventing Choltitz from destroying Paris. I told them everything.

When they returned for a second day of interrogation, they had confronted Choltitz with my information and he had confessed that he would have destroyed Paris if the German hadn't stopped him. He also verified the reasons why I was captured, how I was used by the Nazis, and my eventual influence over the German.

Once I gave the interrogators the missing pieces of the puzzle, Choltitz's refusal to destroy Paris and his surrender made sense; Choltitz had no choice, the German gave him no option. They found what they sought: a logical and complete account of the events that saved Paris from Hitler's psychopathic commands to kill her.

As a result of the information I gave them, the interrogators changed their attitude toward me and I began to believe they would not kill me. However, I would not be free from the public shame and rejection by my family and my fellow Parisians.

The roles the German and I had played in saving Paris were to be kept as a military secret. My pardon would be granted only if I agreed to meet their unconditional demand: I could not tell my story to anyone. To divulge the truth would be considered treason and I would immediately be arrested and sent back to the Drancy Prison, a virtual death sentence.

The Allies' propagandists did not want the German, the hated SS Nazi general, to become a hero. They had repeatedly portrayed him as a top Nazi villain in the international press. The Allies had used the German as a centerpiece of their anti-Nazi propaganda campaign; his brutal techniques were well publicized. His murder of hundreds of French citizens was frequently presented as a prime example of Nazi brutality. The French and the Americans took great pride in the death of this symbol of Nazi evil. Photos of his body lying on the pavement below the suite were often shown in Allied propaganda films. Each time his atrocities and death were recalled in newsreels and print, more passionate acts of hate were directed toward the Nazis and more political and financial support was generated for the Allies. It was a carefully formed image, and they were not about to change in midstream; they would not give us the status of heroes when they had published so much propaganda damning us. A false account was given to explain the events of August 1944: Choltitz was given sole credit for refusing Hitler's orders and for saving Paris, something impossible in reality, but a story somehow believed by almost everyone.

To make matters worse, the French press and government publicly honored the bravery of the Résistance fighter who had raped me. According to their trumped up version of the truth, he bravely killed the wicked German in "battle" and was a national "hero."

The war in Europe and Asia continued to rage and there was much hatred and killing ahead. The German remained the evil vicar of Hitler, the symbol of the heartless, godless, purely evil Nazi devil, and I remained the German's French whore/ Collaborator. Changing these carefully crafted images would not fit their black-and-white definition of world politics, where there was no such thing as a good Nazi or a bad member of the Résistance.

After seven of the longest days of my life, I was released from Drancy and given my "freedom." I was given permission to return to the Hotel Meurice to retrieve my personal belongings with a U.S. army private to help load and transport my things home.

The Belle Etoile Suite was cordoned off and had not been cleaned because the military were not finished with their investigations of the battles that had raged in the hotel. I was shocked to see that almost everything was in the same place as on the day of death and rape. The bed was unmade. The sheets and duvet cover were thrown back on the bed in a haphazard manner. There were splats of the German's blood on the wall and floor and spots of my blood on the sheets. I was relieved that someone had picked up my hair. I would have been horrified to see my hair still lying there in a decoupled mess.

To see our bed in the once-luscious suite suspended at the moment of death and rape filled me with mixed emotions. My memories were covered with sadness and anger under a blanket of relief. I wanted to leave as quickly as possible. I took only clothes and personal things that were mine at the time I was captured, nothing the German had given me. I made one exception: I took the haute couture dress made for the party celebrating the attack on Pearl Harbor, a very significant night of my life. It was too beautiful to leave, and I had earned it. I took the pages of notes from the two Queen Victoria chairs. The private looked amazed when I opened the bottom of the cushions and took out folded toilet paper and stationery, but he said nothing. He was a U.S. Army private whose job was to escort me, not to question my behavior.

Once my interrogators understood I had helped their cause and contributed to the saving of Paris, they were willing to answer questions for me. I wanted to know what had happened to my family members and my Husband. They reported that most of my family was alive but my mother had died toward the end of Occupation. My father had aged so much from the many tragedies that he didn't recognize his surroundings or those who visited him. My surviving brother was in a hospital with permanent injuries after parachuting into France and landing in a tree. Many other family members and friends were alive, but the Nazi Occupation had cost them dearly.

I asked about my Husband. "Is he alive? Where is he? What happened to him?" My interrogators were specialists on Paris activities. They called an American who knew the details about Jewish prisoners. I was relieved when he told me my Husband was alive and under American protection. He did not provide details of his condition but, at that moment, I only cared that he was alive.

Café Talk: "Freedom"

1945. The American sat in shock. "That dirty French Communist Résistance fighter who raped me on the German's bed gave me syphilis. I am dying because of a stupid, violent act taken by a Frenchman against me, a Frenchwoman. I am dying because there were no drugs in Paris to help me; they were consumed by diseased troops while my condition progressed unabated to the incurable stage.

"In a tragic irony, I contracted syphilis while being raped on the day of Liberation, while the church bells rang and Parisians sang. Ultimately, my life has come down to this one act of hate. In that bed, on that day, my blood was branded with the mark of premature death. Paris was freed from her yoke of war, but I was not, and would never be.

"My mind became confused as I mixed both rapes into one emotion of abject fear and pain; the two rapists became one evil man, half Nazi and half French. My night terror returned. I did not want to be touched. I felt detached from my body. I feared other men wanted to rape me.

"Today I feel nothing; I am numb and unfeeling about these violations. Death's imminent arrival changes one's focus. It is as if the rapes happened to someone else. I am over the night terrors, the anxieties, the fears of men. I just don't feel anything at all."

The American had cringed in anger during the description of her rape. It made him ashamed to be a man. He wanted revenge; he wanted to hunt the rapist down and kill him. He was shocked at the behavior of the French toward their own people, who should not have suffered more. What chaos and tragedy war brought. What a waste.

"My mother died," Christine said sorrowfully. "Yes, we did not have a good relationship, but she was my mother and her death hurt me deeply.

"I tried to tell my story to a small number of people. Not a friend or a family member wanted to hear a word I said. They thought I was

trying to justify my opulent life with the German. Only the faithful and loving Father Jean listened and believed. However, his advice was strong and direct: do not tell my story to anyone else. Paris was free from the Nazis, but no one is completely free. Powerful interests did not want my story told. He cautioned me that I could again suffer greatly if I ignored their command.

"I could not reenter the Parisian society I had loved before the war. I was a marked woman of scorn, out of the Parisian limelight for the rest of my life. It was at this point of my life I decided to write the story of my life and that decision brought me to you.

My Husband's Hell

During my captivity, the German committed to keeping my Husband alive as long as I satisfied him sexually and supported him politically, and I believed him—but I did not know that my Husband would be crippled mentally and physically for the rest of his life. I did not know my Husband would never be a man again.

My Husband was deported from France in a "voluntary" program where the French government, the Parisian police and the French people turned Parisian Jews over to the Nazis. The Deportation that took my Husband from me was the most dishonorable event in France's long history of murder, violence and war.

Once the Nazis captured him, my Husband was processed with Germanic precision. He was sent in an overcrowded cattle car to the dreaded concentration camp at Auschwitz, located in Nazi-occupied Poland. He was numbered and assigned to slave labor according to the Nazi plan for Jewish captives. My Husband, along with millions of Jews, gypsies, homosexuals and Communists, was tortured and deprived of every human need for physical and mental survival.

The Nazi processing of Jews and "undesirables" followed a set pattern. First, they were stripped of their human pride and hope by taking their possessions, extracting their gold teeth and shaving off their hair from every part of their body. Second, they were starved and abused in the most horrific ways their creative captors could devise. Third, they were used as forced labor to support the Nazis devastating war machine being built to conquer the world. Fourth, they were methodically exterminated by firing squads and in gas chambers. *Eins, zwie, drie, vier*—one, two, three and four, the murder of six million Jews progressed with chilling expedience and without mercy.

My Husband completed the first three steps; everything they could do to destroy him was done except his murder. His body hair was gone, he lost his teeth, he was beaten, tortured and forced to work in the deplorable labor camps. The fourth step, his execution, was held in abeyance by the German so he could dangle my Husband's shallow breaths before me in order to guarantee my full and complete cooperation. My Husband was kept within a drop or two of losing life's essence; just this side of death. Most Jews were not so lucky and were pushed over the line separating life from death.

In the concentration camp, my Husband was also ordered to become a Capo, a Jew in charge of implementing the Nazis actions to torture and kill other Jews. As a Capo, my Husband was given special privileges. He ate a faintly healthier diet and lived under slightly better conditions. He was "saved" to do the Nazis' dirty work for them. As a result, he maintained some of his physical strength. Capos also experienced a psychological advantage that helped them survive: they controlled a small part of their lives and the lives of others. The other prisoners lacked control over any aspect of their lives except for one choice: to continue their struggle to live or die by their own hand.

Survival as a Capo came with a tough price; Capos were the *point men* in the Nazi operation; they were the enforcers of the SS rules, traitors to the other prisoners and crucifiers of fellow Jews—they were *Judases for the Nazis*. For many, nothing was worse than becoming a traitor to one's own people and helping the Nazis achieve their sick and hateful goal of cleansing every Jew from the earth. For others, becoming a Capo fulfilled their needs to dominate and take advantage of those less fortunate than they; these Capos embraced their "jobs" with enthusiasm.

My Husband was given a similar choice to the one given to me: to become a Capo and survive or refuse this order and die. They increased the severity of the consequences beyond death. If he refused to become a Capo or committed suicide, I would be tortured and killed in the manner described to me if I chose not to cooperate. My Husband and I saved one another from death by making a harder choice, the choice to live.

Without the other to live for, both of us would have died. Real love made us more humane than we thought we could ever be but *love also left us susceptible to human evil and the turns of fate, vulnerable to the pain of our loved ones and our helplessness to take away their suffering.*

The Nazis didn't love anyone but themselves and their dominance over others. They perceived love as a weakness and a tool they could use to control the minds and behavior of others. A love like my Husband's and mine was viewed as an opportunity. They knew a lover would do almost anything to avoid the suffering or death of their loved one, and we did.

My Husband found one source of temporary relief from the mental cruelty and physical anguish from his incarceration. An experienced Jewish psychiatrist, Dr. Viktor Frankl, was imprisoned with my Husband at Auschwitz for a brief period of time. When he was allowed to do so, Dr. Frankl organized some of the prisoners into groups to discuss survival under their circumstances of absolute human degradation.

My Husband spent time in Dr. Frankl's group. He also met clandestinely with him in private. Dr. Frankl said each individual has the choice to determine how and why they continue to live in any situation, at any moment. Each prisoner faces their difficulties and makes the choice to live with the circumstances or die through suicide.

Dr. Frankl gave the prisoners techniques to determine what was truly meaningful to them and how to hold onto the precious components of their lives in the midst of dire suffering. He helped the men find the precious jewels of their lives by forming a mental lifeline, a connection with a loved one or with God, to give them a reason to hold on to life no matter what happened in the concentration camp. He also helped them to see humor in the grotesque. His examples were difficult to accept: looking at the shapes of frozen human bodies in the snow, or watching a prisoner smoke his cigarettes, a sure indicator he was about to commit suicide. A man committed to living always saved his cigarettes to trade for food, clothing or other tiny favors. A man about to die, smoked.

Frankl quoted Nietzsche to them. *"He who has a why to live can bear with almost any how."* He used another unorthodox technique to help prisoners determine what was of value to them. He asked "Why don't you commit suicide? What is stopping you?" Frankl spent many hours helping the prisoners define their reasons to live. He saved some fellow prisoners from death. For those who were killed or took their own lives, he gave them the gift of clarifying who and what they truly loved in life, something they could take to the very end.

September 25, 1944. On orders from the German, my Husband was transferred to the French coast to help build Nazi defenses. Before D-Day, this area was safer and his chances of survival improved. This move also brought him home earlier than if he had remained in the concentration camp or the factory, because this area was liberated first by the Allies as they moved inland from the beaches. I viewed this act as a special gift from the German, who was becoming a caring man.

The advancing Americans freed my Husband and they gave him the medical attention he needed for some time. He eventually came home to Paris and home to me. He arrived in Paris three years after he was captured, one month after the Liberation of

Paris and eight months before the war ended in Europe. He had
been one of the first Jews deported from Paris, and one of the first
and few to return. The unfortunate others did not have a wife
who was having sex with a Nazi general to keep them alive.

My Husband returned a hero. He was paraded through the
streets of Paris and applauded in a burst of guilt-ridden, French
celebration. He was barely alive physically and weighed about
the same as a twelve year-old child. He was also mostly dead
mentally, but he could hold his head up enough to ride in the
parade car. I wondered if the same Paris police who had arrested
us on the behalf of Nazis were monitoring the crowds on the day
of the parade, if they were still working as Parisian police now
that their Nazi masters were gone.

His pathetic appearance, and the fact few other prisoners
returned to Paris, inflamed the French hatred of the Nazis and
the Collaborators. It gave me unspeakable pain to look at my
destroyed Husband, the love of my life, and there was more.

When my Husband returned to Paris I was shocked to the
core of my being to learn of a new horrific vindictiveness which
enraged me as much as anything I had faced. The German had
ordered my Husband to be castrated in the concentration camp,
thus guaranteeing that our suffering would continue regardless of
which side "won" the war. Learning of this barbaric act reignited
my original hatred for the dead German. He had betrayed me. It
was like being raped again, another filthy violation of the most
intimate and personal parts of our lives. I raged in silence. I hated
with a vengeance, but there was nothing I could do, no action I
could take. My mind closed to forgiveness or understanding of
the Nazi monster. All good I had associated with the German
evaporated from my heart.

I began to understand my circumstances on a higher level.
Once my Husband was castrated, the German was willing to

assure his survival. In a brutal act of jealousy and control, he made sure my Husband and I could never continue as sexual lovers, as Husband and wife, no matter what.

I could not understand how the German could love me while also ordering my Husband's castration. I realized his evil went so deep that he could not be truly rehabilitated into a loving human. In his cowardly act, he permanently and severely damaged the man he knew I loved best. The German held onto his sinister, perverted, controlling side even after death, with devastating consequences for my Husband and me.

I looked back and wondered if it was more in my imagination and naïve hope that I transformed the German into a different man after all. Maybe he didn't really love me; maybe it was like my love-fantasy with the Artist, another man who really only loved himself and whose love for me existed mostly in my mind. I became full of self-doubt and bitterness. The German's brutal act was more evidence of the disconnected duality in the German-Nazi character, how love and cruelty could exist side by side without any apparent internal conflict. It made me sick.

I didn't know what I would have done if I had known about my Husband's castration before the German was killed. How could I have changed anything even if I knew? Given this one more burden, this additional revulsion, I might have killed myself in pain, guilt, anger and hopelessness. My family would have died and Paris would have died with me. It was better that I didn't know of this atrocity until after the German was dead and my Husband was "free" and Paris' fate had been changed.

My castrated Husband and I, his scarred and diseased wife, returned to our home on Île St. Louis after three years away. We returned to the "other side," crossing the bridge from near-death back to abbreviated lives on the island. We had endured more pain than anyone should ever endure. We were wounded and could not recover. I was dying and my Husband didn't even realize it. I struggled to live each hour, each day, living with one suffering at a time—to try and hold onto the things that were truly meaningful for as long as I could.

As the German had promised, our Paris home remained under his protection, and it remained as we left it. It had been used as a residence by a mid-level Nazi bureaucrat, and even our books remained in the same order on the shelves. My painting, *Le Finestre Desolate e Sconsacrate*, still hung over the mantle in the stunning beauty of human loneliness depicted in paint.

The chair stitching remained intact where I hid my pre-Occupation secrets. I thought the man who lived in our home was probably a "good German," someone who also was caught up in the war and the Occupation involuntarily. I wondered if he was still living, was murdered by the Résistance, returned to Germany, or which of the many possible fates was bestowed upon him.

Our families and friends stayed away from us. They read the papers, saw the photos and felt profound jealousy and hatred toward me. They continued to view me as the Collaborator, an image first created by the Nazis and then reinforced by the Allies. Only blessed Father Jean continued to believe in me and in my role in saving the City of Light.

Finally, No Nazis

November 15, 1944. The Nazis were gone, and it was my 29th birthday. The German's vision of the Nazi-occupied Paris he had detailed in 1940 had not come to pass. There were no swastika flags, no German-speaking French children and no Nazi boots stomping on every aspect of our French lives. But Paris was not yet the Paris she had been: she lacked joy and lived in the settling ashes of sadness.

The recovery of many would occur over time. The recovery of some would not happen; we will die with nothing left to give and nothing left to take. There were tragic women in Paris hiding their shaven heads under French scarves, trying to find a way to take care of new, fatherless, half-German babies. There were more women who wore black armbands for the men they'd lost: their fathers, lovers, husbands, sons and brothers. There were many who grieved for the loss of future generations of French people who would not be born, and for lovers who would not love again.

I continued to love Paris, though, like any we fully love, she exposed glaring flaws which hurt deeply. I forgave her for her trespasses as one must do when one loves, and she forgave mine. She was me and I was her; we were one and the same and we carried each other's imperfections deep in our souls.

She was not a fully functioning city, just as I was not a fully functioning woman. There were no tourists; the ongoing war was too close. The damage to the Paris economy by the Nazi Occupation and the war around her continued; we lived on little food and almost no fuel and rationed electricity. Women continued to walk on wooden shoes, their steps on the cobblestoned streets still sounding like animal hoofs clomping by. Those who obtained a few potatoes to eat continued to use the skins for heating fuel.

Divisive and violent groups wanted to restore Paris in their own images, with their own brands of government and their own self-serving priorities. Each desired to impose their way of life onto others. Outside influences from Russia and America struggled for the dominance of Paris and France. Some Frenchmen wanted a Second Commune. They sought a repeat of *la republique democratique et sociale*, a socialist revolution like the one of seventy-five years before when thousands of Parisians died and more of Paris was destroyed than at any time in history, including the Nazi Occupation.

The Communists were angry because they felt betrayed by de Gaulle and the Americans. They still controlled many Paris unions and their sympathizers lived throughout Paris society, but they had been outflanked in their pursuit of power on the highest levels of government. It was unclear if they would become part of the efforts to rebuild Paris or work to destroy her from within. Life was better than during Occupation, but it was not good enough. Most of the buildings in Paris had been saved. However, the living hearts and souls of the Parisians were scarred and, like my face, would never be the same. There were few men left in the city. Many who remained were unpunished Collaborators, Nazi sympathizers, or cowards. Would they be the lovers, husbands, fathers and grandfathers of the post-Nazi Occupation generations to come; their children standing next to the half-German children building the new Paris?

In the near-chaos, one man stood tall to lead Paris to recovery. Charles de Gaulle rose to find the power he needed to put Paris back on her feet and keep the various factions at bay. Paris was his and, as a grown man, he knew what to do with her.

Café Talk: Dr. Frankl and The Final Days

1945. *The sunlight waned, hidden by a dark cloud cover, and the café lights came on as Christine described a visit from Dr. Frankl. "Shortly after the war ended, Dr. Frankl came to Paris after reading about my Husband's liberation. Since few prisoners had returned home, Dr. Frankl sought out my Husband to learn of his postwar condition and to see how he had adjusted to his return to society. He was sad at seeing my Husband's condition, but he understood completely. Dr. Frankl told me becoming a Capo did more damage to my Husband's mind and soul than all the other degrading, humiliating, dehumanizing acts he had suffered, but it saved his life.*

"During his visit, he provided me with descriptions of the conditions of the concentration camp and my Husband's life as a prisoner. He explained how my Husband found his reason to live."

"It was his love for you and his fear of the harm they would do to you that gave him the reason to keep going each moment, every hour, all the days and years. You led him away from death time and time again."

Dr. Frankl pointed out that her Husband had been castrated during his initial internment in the concentration camp, prior to the German's "transformation." Christine could not rationally address the atrocity; she could not think in terms of forgiveness and she didn't care when this evil had been perpetuated. Dr. Frankl and Christine discussed her renewed hate and he made it clear to her: it was Christine's choice to forgive the past or not.

Immediately after the war, Dr. Frankl wrote a book about his experiences in the concentration camps called Man's Search for Meaning. Christine read it over and over again in her effort to understand. No matter how many times she read it and how much she cried, she never could fully comprehend her Husband's suffering; she could never fully face the comparison between her life of opulence and sexuality and his life of horror.

*T*he American and Christine had met and talked for months. Christine believed there were only a few things left to say. Although most of her story had been told, there were missing essentials that were highly significant and extremely sensitive; there were questions about her love of the German and much more about her daughter, the secret, hidden Gabriella.

It began raining heavily outside the mostly empty café, but the temperature was moderate. It was the in-between time, after the workers stopped in for their morning café and before the lunch service would begin. The American watched Christine's every move, carefully listening to each word. He continued to be as captivated by her as he had been during each moment since they'd met. He looked at her scar and was revolted by the times when she was beaten and raped. He thought the German's tenderness was too little, too late, and much of his good was erased by castrating her Husband. However, the timing did make a difference to the American, as it occurred when he was still Hitler's German, before Christine transformed him. The German acted in an honorable way when he sacrificed himself to save Paris, and that indicated he had changed.

The American's hatred for the rapist Résistance fighter was deep; it was hate without forgiveness. He wanted to protect Christine, but it was too late; he'd arrived in her life after she was scarred and he could not defend her against her past, he could not undo her suffering.

Christine's hands shook as she reached inside herself for the energy to give what she intended to be her concluding remarks, the end of her Journal. "Paris will become even greater than it was before. Over time, Parisians will forgive and forget the brutalities, but recovery will take more time than I have left to live. Very few people know my real story and few will be concerned when I have gone. Paris will recover without me, and despite all that happened, my early departure won't matter much. I am thankful for the chance I had to help save her. As I look back, I am amazed at the twists and turns of my fate.

"Besides exposing my secret life in support of saving Paris, I want you to write my Journal as a love story. I have experienced many different types of love. From each, I have learned a great deal. Each time I thought, yes, this is love, this is real love. Now, at the end, I see love differently. Love was true in each case, but each time love was different. Love is underestimated—our thoughts of love are too limited. Love is grandiose, multifaceted, and should not be constrained by the experiences of any given relationship, or by cowardly authors who are afraid to let love grow over time.

"The only desire I have is to end my life with dignity and closure. In the end, Le Journal Parisien de Christine will survive; the Journal will be my legacy. It will be your writing skills that will deliver my truth. You are under no obligation to keep my story secret; you are an American and they cannot punish me in my grave!

"The burden of telling the truth is yours. I will depart to an indefinite place before Le Journal Parisien is fully written. You will stay; you will be in charge of presenting the truth of who I was, and you will determine who I will continue to be in the minds of the living. You have the remains of my earthly life in your hands, in your mind and flowing through your pen.

"I know you love me. I know the look of love. You know why I can't love you the way you want me to love you, and I will die without loving that way ever again. I want you to accept this and honor it. Don't be disappointed. In many ways, you have had the best of me. You knew me after I learned many lessons of life and became a woman. I have been open and honest with you, so you know me as I truly am, not as someone living a pretense created to comply with social norms. Accept me; hold my hand and hug me, for soon you will have to let me go. This is how my story ends: crossing over another bridge, over the last, one-way overpass that we must all finally cross. My brief life has been a series of Paris crossings. One day we may meet on a higher plane and I look forward to such a time and such a place with great pleasure and comfort."

Surprisingly, the American did not reach for her as she had invited. He was waiting to ask a question and it was the time to act. "Before you go today, I have to ask about the German. I am over my naiveté about your sexual relationship as much as I can be. Most of your experiences made sense, though I admit I struggle on a personal level to embrace everything you have told me, particularly your intense sexual enjoyment with the German. I will always be an American and a man.

"At the start of our writing together, you challenged me to search out the truth of your life, to push you to find and write only pure truth in your Journal. I recall how you even quoted Nietzsche about finding the 'courage of the forbidden' and how we must tell the truths that are the hardest to tell. I believed you then and I believe it now. I want to know the truth about your feelings for the German, something you have not revealed other than saying, at the end, you 'made love' with him and you uttered his name. I may be asking you things you cannot or will not answer, but I sincerely want to know, did you fall in love with the German? Tell me, Christine, did you love him on the day he died?"

Christine didn't answer. She stared out the window at the pouring rain. Deep in her thoughts, she was quiet and her breaths were shallow. She wandered off as she was prone to do, leaving the American and the café behind. Her face showed the stress of her memories and for the moment she was disconnected from the real world. Her coffee cup remained half full. Her left foot tapped lightly on the floor.

The American pulled back and waited. He was being careful. She was frail and he could sense answering this question would begin to break down the protective walls of her compartmentalized mind. She had reached the end of her openness, the edge of her psychological safety zone. She couldn't endure facing the duality of what she had lived for three years, especially her complex feelings for the German. How could she love the man who castrated her Husband mentally and physically? The unbearable guilt hidden in the secret places of her mind was becoming exposed like jagged rocks jutting out during low tide. She was able to address her feelings for the German but on only a superficial, indecisive level.

"This is all I will tell you. Not everything was difficult or horrific during my captivity. The German and I settled into a routine and we found common ground in our daily lives. He changed in positive ways and I encouraged him with my passion and my support. Spending so much time with each other, having so much sex and living so high in the Paris social life, it was hard to remain totally hostile and hateful in my heart."

Christine didn't answer the question of her love for the German. Given the limited definition of love contained within it and the confusion and guilt she carried in her soul, she couldn't. The act against her Husband had returned the German to the dominion of evil and brought her to dauntingly high levels of mental anguish. Even Christine's most expanded definition of love was too narrow to include forgiveness for this barbaric act. She knew no one else could possibly understand, because she didn't fully understand her feelings for the man who captured her, shared her world of passion, fathered her only child and kept her Husband alive only after he destroyed him as a man. It was the end of a long day and she was exhausted and not feeling well. She only said, "The German and I did what we did for the love of Paris. I cannot see you again this week. Call me next week, please."

Christine quickly left the café and was gone. The American decided to leave the question of her love for the German unanswered. He had a more important issue and little time. Gabriella was Christine's living legacy and documenting her life was essential to the Journal. The American pushed to prepare for the last chapter to be written before death—the story of Christine's daughter, the innocent Gabriella.

CHAPTER SIX
THE INNOCENT GABRIELLA

As a lone spark might start a massive fire,
a solitary drop may begin a devastating flood,
a single step can begin the longest journey,
an imaginary idea could lead to a written masterpiece,
and
a passionate act may produce a child—
so can a single individual change the world

The innocent always pay,
the innocent are always hurt—
but why,
why always the innocent?

Café Talk: Christine's German Daughter

1945. *Gabriella was missing from Christine's Journal. Christine avoided giving Gabriella's story to the American for as long as she could. Whenever they touched on the subject, Christine hesitated and deferred discussions to a "later time." The American was kept at a distance, on the outside of Christine's true feelings and experiences in motherhood. He had not been allowed to know Gabriella, and therefore Christine's Journal was incomplete.*

The time had come for Gabriella's story, for there was not much time left. The American was determined to learn about Gabriella and discover who Christine was as a mother. This time, he would not compromise.

The American knew a little about Gabriella. He knew the German was Gabriella's father, she lived in Versailles with her nannies, and she was visited infrequently by her mother and father. He knew Gabriella's short life occurred during incredibly tumultuous times, and she came into the world under highly unusual and complex parental circumstances. He knew no one in Christine's family would acknowledge Gabriella's existence, because her father was the head of the brutal Nazi Gestapo, and because they believed her mother was a Nazi Collaborator and a whore. He knew Gabriella would soon be completely alone in the world; she would be without family before she turned four years old.

The American sought to capture how and why Christine mentally compartmentalized Gabriella and to gain an understanding of why Christine could not face motherhood.

Christine and the American returned to their regular café in the late morning. It was raining lightly but the rain was warmer than usual. Again, there were few patrons in the café. When they walked in, the waiters were enthusiastic about seeing them, and they made their usual fuss over Christine. Their standing order was an espresso for Christine and a cappuccino for the American. They said, "The usual" to the waiter and sat at their favorite window table.

A man sat near them; he concentrated on reading every line in his French newspaper as he smoked his Gauloises cigarettes and drank his coffee. The American had become accustomed to the strong smell of French cigarettes; the aroma became a permanent memory in his mind, a sensory reminder that would stay with him for the rest of his life.

The American began by making a statement about Gabriella and the Journal. Christine was weak and less able to control conversations. She sat quietly and listened to the American speak.

"I need to know about Gabriella to finish your Journal. We made a mutual commitment to honesty and openness. Gabriella is the most important living person in your story. She is the continuation of your life and one of the most important reasons for writing your Journal—she must know the truth about her parents and your role in saving Paris. We cannot shortchange the Journal or the truth by denying Gabriella any further. It won't be complete without her!"

Christine met his insistence with a blank stare. She was not happy. She looked uncomfortable. To create a pause in the conversation, she sipped her espresso and chewed her croissant slowly and carefully. A small crumb remained on the corner of her lip, giving her a childlike look.

Christine protested one last time. She pleaded. "This is too difficult; there is too much at stake. Why not leave her alone? I don't have the strength or time to change anything now, so close to the end. What good will it do to pull Gabriella out into the open?"

The American would not capitulate and Christine finally gave in. "I will give Gabriella to you and to the Journal. I will open the most painful place in my heart, but I don't want to do it. I don't want to relive everything that happened or decisions I made that were not best for my daughter, but you leave me no choice. Do you know that giving Gabriella to you will take all the strength I have left? Do you know that facing the realities of my daughter and my failings as a mother will be my end? When I give you Gabriella, you will lose me—forever. Do you *understand?" She waited but the American did not respond. There was nothing left to say. The sadness sitting in his heart and the pain twisting in hers was enough.*

"This story may take you deeper into the intimacy of my life with the German than you want to go, but you asked for it. Let's get this over with. I will take you back to the beginning, to where this all started.

"As fate would have it, Gabriella's conception is connected to American history. It occurred on the night of a special dinner party held to celebrate the huge Japanese victory over the Americans at Pearl Harbor on December 7, 1941.

"First we must have lunch. I must eat or my medications will make me sick. Afterward, I will tell you everything about Gabriella. I promise!"

It was an uneventful lunch, but it gave Christine the opportunity to build up her strength mentally and physically before starting on Gabriella. They filled the break with small talk about Paris and life, any subject but Christine's daughter. The American spoke of his youth and how it was a time of economic hardship in America. He smiled as he recalled how the Depression did not prevent him from having a great deal of fun as a boy. It was the era of the late twenties and thirties when the American economic model faltered and many individuals switched from economic independence to dependence on the government for their livelihood. Then lunch and the time for avoidance ran out.

True to her word, Christine began her story of Gabriella as they lingered over the last sips of coffee and the final forkfuls of dessert. After she had eaten, she started on a more upbeat tone.

Gabriella

My first awareness that an unusual night was ahead occurred when the German told me we would be attending a special event in a few weeks, probably on the evening of December eighth. He did not tell me where we were going, with whom we would be socializing or what occasion we would be celebrating. He only said it would be an extremely important evening and I was to be at my very best in every way. His secrecy was curious, as he liked to talk about upcoming social events and gossip about the Nazi officers, diplomats and high-level French Collaborators we would be seeing.

He told me to have an *haute couture* dress created for the occasion, whatever I wanted as long as it was elegant. I was ecstatic at the chance to have a dress created for me. I picked the house of the famous dressmaker Lucien Lelong. Mr. Lelong had recently employed a new designer named Christian Dior, who would design my dress. I was thrilled when I saw Mr. Dior's work and the sketches he developed. While I didn't interact with Mr. Lelong about costs, I knew he was one of the most expensive dress designers in all of Paris, probably in the world. This was going to be a special night; I would be wearing a Lelong/Dior one-of-a-kind work of art, something every woman in Paris dreamt of doing.

Mr. Lelong was accustomed to taking months to create a dress so his client could walk into Paris high society flaunting her wealth in one of his dream designs. My dress was needed in three weeks. Creating a dress on such short notice would be done for only the most important people in Paris, and the German was one of them. Mr. Dior was taken off a project to design a dress for a minor countess and immediately went to work for me. "You have the complete attention of Mr. Dior and anyone else you need from my studio," said Mr. Lelong. An entire team was assigned to design and fabricate my creation. Each detail was planned carefully; even their best pin girl was selected to support the production. My dress took four hundred worker-hours to complete, and they finished it just in time.

My *haute couture* gown was a unique and spectacular creation of champagne-colored, cloud-soft chiffon. From the waist up, it was a series of cross pleats, which began below my waistline and rose up to my shoulders to reveal a great deal of my breasts. One vertical pleat pulled the dress toward the center to assure a perfect fit. From the waist down, it flowed smoothly to the ground. It was long in the back, leaving a small train flowing behind when I walked. Falling from my shoulders to behind my knees was a shoulder wrap of the same soft chiffon. The dress was form-fitting, extremely sexy and elegant. Every stitch and each cut reflected the fine workmanship that was part of the impeccable reputation of Mr. Lelong and his designers. I adored my dress and I was ready for the upcoming surprise celebration.

There was another reason to choose Lucien Lelong besides the quality of his work. The Nazis tried to steal *haute couture* from Paris and transfer it to Germany; the Nazis were again trying to obtain the class and creativity which were lacking in their Teutonic world, for the same reasons they were plundering French paintings and sculptures.

As president of the *Chambre Syndicale de la Couture*, Mr. Lelong successfully negotiated with the Nazis to prevent transporting *haute couture* to Germany. He declared that *haute couture* would be in Paris, or it would cease to exist! I encouraged the German to help Lelong keep *haute couture* in Paris and he spoke with his fellow Nazi officers. Contrary to their typical response to anyone refusing their orders, the Nazis backed down and agreed to *not* steal Paris' *haute couture* industry. Lelong was even more stubborn than the Nazis, and they respected him for his tenacity. Support from the German, the SS/Gestapo Nazi general, didn't hurt Mr. Lelong's cause either.

December 7, 1941. News blanketed the world with detailed accounts of the destruction of much of the American Pacific Fleet in Pearl Harbor by the Japanese. In his anger and resolve, President Roosevelt claimed December 7, 1941, to be "a day that will live in infamy," as he and the U.S. Congress prepared to declare war on Japan. Now I knew what we would be celebrating on December eighth, and why such a high level of secrecy was maintained. The German later told me that none of the other senior Nazi officers in Paris knew of the attack. It was because of the German's close association with the Japanese Ambassador to France that Hitler made him the Nazis' liaison with Japan on the Pearl Harbor attack.

On the day of the Japanese victory at Pearl Harbor, the German was very chatty. He was overjoyed that the Japanese had successfully attacked Pearl Harbor. The Japanese Ambassador to the United States had been falsely negotiating for peace with the Americans at the very same time the fleet of heavily armed Japanese aircraft carriers secretly steamed toward Hawaiian waters. Peace was the last thing on their minds. "What a spectacular political and military maneuver," he shouted. "Most of the American Pacific Fleet was sunk. They were asleep!"

The Nazi and Japanese reoccurring strategy to first appease with claims of peace and then launch surprise attacks had worked. The German asked out loud, "Why were the Allies so stupid to fall for that old trick again?"

The Japanese attack on Pearl Harbor altered the world's military balance dramatically; it would bring a crippled America into the war. Now the Nazis believed they could go forward without too much worry about American interference in their plans to finish conquering Europe and beyond. The

German added with glee, "The Americans will have to divert their military production away from Europe and their damned European Lend Lease program to defend herself against the Japanese, the real and present threat to America."

December 8, 1941. The party was an intimate, exclusive event in a private room in one of the best restaurants in Paris: La Tour d'Argent, located on the Left Bank overlooking the Seine. We were escorted into the private elevator and entered into an elegant private dining room where we were greeted by waiters wearing tuxedos and white gloves. Immediately, they offered luscious plates of hors d'oeuvres and flutes of Taittinger champagne. We dined on a clear night with a glorious moon floating in the blackness of endless space. Across the shimmering water to the left was Notre Dame. Nearer to us and just across the water was my once warm and secure Île St. Louis home where I had lived and loved with my Husband before we were captured.

There were six couples in attendance at the dinner: the Japanese Ambassador to France and his wife; the Collaborator and Chairman of the Municipal Council of Paris (mayor) Pierre Taittinger and his wife; the Italian Ambassador to France and his wife; General Hans von Boineburg-Lengsfeld, the Nazi commander of all Nazi forces in Paris, his low-class French girlfriend, and the German and me. After we were seated, the waiter explained that duck was the specialty of the house and each duck was given its own number. I ordered the duck as my entrée; it was number 765,700 and they gave me a postcard documenting the count.

During the dinner conversation we learned that once-proud American warships had become coffins for hundreds of sailors who could not escape, many of whom died a prolonged death from suffocation as their ships turned upside down and slowly sank into the mud right where they were docked. The group's frivolous response to this massive loss of life made me sick, but

I had a role to play and I was not going to lose my focus. My support of the German in this exclusive setting was as critical as having sex with him in the many ways he enjoyed the most.

The Japanese Ambassador explained how the Japanese admirals carefully studied the British attack on the Italian port of Taranto, Italy, in 1940. The British had used torpedo-carrying airplanes off their carrier HMS *Illustrious* to similarly destroy Italian battleships docked in port. Everyone else at the table loved how the Japanese used this British technique to cripple their friends, the Americans. The Japanese Ambassador beamed with pride.

During the evening I heard three comments which detracted from the many toasts to Japan's success, to the defeat of the Americans and to world domination by the Axis powers. I listened carefully to each concern and kept mental notes, which I would later secretly record in the bathroom and stuff into my special chair when we returned to the Hotel Meurice.

In a difficult translation into French and German, the Japanese Ambassador himself acknowledged the danger of awakening a "sleeping giant," as he called America. It was the same concern shared by the Harvard-educated Japanese admiral who led the attack on Pearl Harbor, Admiral Yamamoto.

A short time later, the Italian Ambassador slowed the celebration down for a moment with his questions and comments. "Where were the American aircraft carriers on December seventh? How did the Japanese miss them? Nothing is more dangerous than the American aircraft carriers and the destructive power of their airplanes," he flatly stated. The group gave the Ambassador looks of frustration and amazement. They were not interested in the full truth; it was a time for blind self-congratulation.

As the German finished his second course, a seared *pâté de foie gras* served with an excellent German icewine, Paris Chairman

Taittinger questioned the group's confidence in the weakness of America. He pointed out that the American Lend-Lease program was providing American military aid to the Russians and British, which had begun to put America on a war footing. They had already switched to building tanks, planes and guns instead of refrigerators and civilian cars. The German frowned at him from across the table with a look which said, "That is enough!" and the Nazi Collaborator-Chairman immediately shut up.

These few negative comments did not flatten the group's enthusiasm as they enjoyed the Japanese victory and relished the American defeat. They behaved as if there were no American carriers hidden in the vast Pacific Ocean, as if the war were over, as if America had given up without a fight and they were the indisputable victors. There were many toasts to the Axis Alliance of Germany, Japan and Italy—to the "Steel Ring of Power," as they liked to call themselves. To me, it was a night of excessive male self-congratulation and self-important arrogance, but I again stayed the course of providing the German with my unrelenting support and charm.

The Japanese Ambassador, usually humble in his outwardly demeanor, was uncharacteristically exuberant. The German arranged to have an excellent bottle of proper sake for him and his wife. The Ambassador drank most of it himself and was drunk with celebration and wine. "Their entire defense was asleep!" he suddenly exclaimed loudly.

Late into the night a messenger brought more astonishing news to the Ambassador. He spoke to our group in a hushed, reverent tone. "Today we have also successfully invaded Malaya and we will soon be in Singapore!" The international scope of the Axis Powers' military victories was daunting.

I wore my new *haute couture* Lelong/Dior dress with pride and beamed as everyone appreciated its beauty. I received compliments from both husbands and wives. The low-cut front of the dress generously revealed my décolletage. The German looked at me as if he wanted to have me right there, right then, right in the middle of the party. The other men tried to look at my breasts discreetly, but their stares lingered too long to be missed. Anyway, I didn't care if they looked. So what!

The only man I did not dance with was Chairman Taittinger. He was a Collaborator who traded his fascist soul and the soul of Paris to the Nazis for a handful of gold coins…or less. As a young man, Pierre Taittinger had founded *Jeunesses Partriotes*, Patriotic Youths, a fascistic, anti-Semitic group that imitated Mussolini's Blackshirts. During Occupation, he was connected to the Nazi *Aryanisation*, the stealing of Jewish businesses and property for personal profit and gain. With him I could not dance nor speak to directly. I ignored his attempts at communication, but I was sure he knew why I would not respond.

The Pearl Harbor bombings were also quietly celebrated by America's "friends" in London, Moscow, Singapore and Paris, because America would finally enter the war in support of their fledging efforts to survive. They knew America would become a fierce partner in their fight against the Nazis, Japanese Imperialists and Italian Fascists. America was finally awake. There would be a chance for victory over defeat just when it appeared there was none.

Our ride home was short and the German was quieter than usual. There was no sexual play in the car as his mind floated into his daydreams of world domination. For the German and the Nazis, everything was falling into place. He looked particularly handsome, confident and powerful. Much of the discussion during the evening had been deferential to him. His opinions and analysis of the world situation were well-respected. Even though he outranked the German, the Nazi commander von Boineburg-Lengsfeld yielded most of the lead in the conversations to him.

These visions increased the German's air of invincibility. He believed he could command the world similar to the way he controlled Paris and me. As we sped through the empty streets, I waited quietly for his focus to return from his dreams of world conquest, power and wealth. I patiently let him return from ambitions far beyond the realm of possibilities for ordinary men but close enough that he could almost touch them.

Though they were not yet at war on December 8th, the German shared a thought about the anticipated war with the Americans that amused him—it would be disconcerting for the Americans to know that the factories they had so profitably built to supply the Nazis would continue to efficiently produce planes, trucks and tanks under German management. The Americans would have to fight against their own Ford and GM equipment as soon as they came to fight in Europe.

When we returned to the suite, the German remained pensive. He poured himself a generous portion of 1915 Louis XII de Remy Martin Grande Champagne Cognac to top off the night. I stepped into the bathroom and added some perfume, brushed my hair and lowered my gown. I decided not to put on one of the many sexy French negligees the German had bought for me. Instead, I dropped the front of my dress just enough to reveal the dark skin surrounding my nipples, revealing most of my full breasts for his eyes and his touch. I showed him what the other men had desperately wanted to see. I made my enticement very clear. I was sure my message would be enough to pull him away from his dreams of world domination to the assurance of immediate pleasure, and I was right. A little tease was all the German needed to snap him back to the present. He complimented my beauty and continued his accolades on how well I had handled the important people during the night's celebration. "They loved you," he said with open eyes.

He slowly pulled down the front of my dress to release my full breasts for his caresses and kisses. After he had removed my clothing except for my panties, I began to undress him. Soon he was naked, and I pushed him backward onto the bed. The German was ready for every pleasure I could give him; he knew exactly what was coming and, he was right.

My passion covered him as I pulled him deeper inside and squeezed tightly. In the most intimate connection between a man and woman's bodies, he let go an overwhelming burst and filled me with the liqueur of manhood. When I felt him exploding, I let go too. We completed nature's mating dance and laid back, panting and content. He fell into peaceful after-sex sleep, confident of his glorious future as my conqueror and the ruler of continents. What the German and I did not know as we fell asleep was what else we had created that night.

Gabriella was conceived on the same day America declared war against Japan—a strange connection between catastrophe, celebration and conception; each event changing fate in its own significant way.

During Occupation, many French women had affairs, marriages and children with Nazi soldiers, so in many ways my situation was not unusual. These relationships developed because there were few remaining Frenchmen in Paris. The Nazi soldiers came to France as warriors, without women or families, and were the most eligible young men available for Parisian women. These young, handsome, often charming German men were constantly searching for French girlfriends, and they came with money, food and protection. The situation was ripe for French-Nazi romantic encounters. More than one hundred thousand babies were born of French-Nazi liaisons during Occupation. Nazi-fathered babies would make France partially German forever, regardless of who won the war. Nazi men had relationships with French women through seduction, payment or by force. The German race was here to stay, one way or another. It was a modern-day *Rape of the Sabine Women*. However, the fact that so many others shared a similar fate gave me no comfort and did nothing to relieve my anguish.

The German was thrilled that we were having a baby. He lacked any concerns whatsoever. On the contrary, he viewed our coming child as a highly positive connection between the two of us and between Nazi Germany and conquered France. To him, our child would be the next generation to lead the march toward the Nazi Thousand-Year Occupation of France. Our child was his personal contribution to the Nazi future, toward their dominance over all.

As the German became an expectant father for the first time in his life, his tenderness increased. Fatherhood was a new source of pride and awakening. He sang German songs to our baby in my womb, as I feared life after birth.

He looked at me in an increasingly pleasurable way, as he felt the many strange and enjoyable emotions of becoming a parent. Approaching fatherhood increased his appreciation of life—having a child became one of the humanizing factors that helped change his attitude toward Paris. A different kind of man was growing within him as our baby was growing in me.

I failed to share his enthusiasm about the birth of our child. As an expectant mother under these dire circumstances, I felt confusion and anxiety. I had rationalized sex with the German on a number of levels, including the survival of my Husband, my family and myself. It was the sacrifice I made; the price I chose to pay to live. I did enjoy making the payment, but my sexual pleasure was compartmentalized outside of my consciousness and covered with denial and rationalizations. I accepted and then embraced the need to give my body in payment for life itself.

A child produced a much deeper level of concern. A child involved a permanent bond with the German. It brought a precious new and innocent baby into my already complex, confusing life. My child was condemned from conception as a Nazi, regardless if Paris were freed or not. I was appalled at the direction life was taking me in.

After five months of pregnancy, I grew a little pouch and larger breasts. Overall I didn't gain much weight. My body was as it always was: trim and properly curvy with a tight backside. I experienced only one month of morning sickness; mine was an easy pregnancy. However, as much as I tried, I could not ignore the fact that I was having a Nazi general's child, not my Husband's.

I moved to Versailles at the end of the sixth month of my pregnancy. The German purchased an apartment not far from King Louis XIV's Versailles Palace, a town he loved from our *My Paris* visit. He hired a housekeeper and a nurse to care for me. It was a comfortable situation, one most any expectant mother would have appreciated. The German visited me weekly. I survived by refusing to think about my predicament as I stared out the window looking into nothingness, my daze only interrupted by the child kicking my womb from the inside.

I might have enjoyed being pregnant, as many women do. I admired mothers-to-be with their glow and earthiness; it seemed to be such a special time in a woman's life. But fate had taken me around a different corner, and I would have to live within my reality as best as I could. It was definitely not a pleasant time for me.

The German and I continued to have sex together, as my pregnancy did not diminish our lust. He said he found me especially desirable and feminine even as my stomach grew larger. To my surprise, I needed the German's continued affection as I struggled with the reality of having his child. I felt dependent on him for the first time. I was about to have an infant to care for and, like any new mother, I needed the father's support even if he was my capturer, a Nazi general, and I was married to another man.

September 8, 1942. It was the traditional birthday of Mary, Mother of Jesus and the day our daughter came into this world. We had a girl.

My body was made for childbirth. Our daughter entered our complex world easily and quickly. In a world without the war, I might have become the matriarch of a family of many healthy children with my loving and happy Professor-Husband.

Our daughter was healthy and hungry from birth. The German named her Gabriella. "Like the angel Gabriel," he said. He wanted her to become more than any of us, to be more than he himself and his Nazi Fatherland and more than the old France and me. He wanted a super-child and a super-woman. He wanted her to live in luxury on top of the world he was conquering. Without mentioning it, he wanted her to be an uber-human, about whom his Führer often spoke.

Gabriella was, in fact, the perfect child, albeit the perfect *German* child. She lived inside of me for nine months and entered the world through my womb—but as soon as she was born, I felt she was only his and no longer mine.

Gabriella didn't look anything like me; she was the spitting image of the German. Her facial mimicry of the German was the final step that pushed me to the very edge. Gabriella was another product of the Nazi military conquest of Paris and even as a newborn she was another victim of their Occupation.

When I looked at Gabriella, I could no longer deny what was going on with the German and me, and I could no longer bear the suffering of my Husband and the French people at the hands of the Nazi animals with whom I shared my daily life. Gabriella was the confirmation that everything had gone wrong. I could not deny the sexual passion and pleasure I had with the German, because every time I looked at her German beauty I thought of the night of our sexual bliss and her conception. My soul was riddled with guilt.

From the time of Gabriella's birth, I fretted constantly. I didn't like her name; it reminded me of Gabriele D'Annunzio's repressive philosophy of artistic superiority under which I struggled with the Artist.

I tried not to show it but I was becoming severely despondent. I lived with a constant feeling of irritability foreign to me. The German noticed my edginess and commented that it must be the natural impact of becoming a new mother, and he thought I would recover from it. He innocently asked me questions reflecting his concerns. "Is there anything wrong? Could I bring you anything to make you happy?"

My child and I didn't fit in anywhere. Our circumstances could not be fixed. Even if we escaped the Nazis, with a child my freedom could not be free; the past could not be undone; my baby would always be the daughter of a Nazi general and me, his French whore. She would always be the product of the hated Nazis and their brutal Occupation. Unwittingly I was an adulterer and I had betrayed my marriage vows to my Husband. I stared out the window and nursed my child unenthusiastically while Gabriella fed like there was no end to her hunger.

My fragile hold on my sanity cracked. When my daughter sucked on my breast, I thought of the German who so often sucked on them too. When I looked into the mirror of her blue eyes, I saw the German's blue eyes staring back at me. When I slept at night, I dreamt of my Husband and the German in mortal combat. My Husband always lost, falling to the ground with his arms reaching out in desperation, his power gone, his intellect erased, a broken man.

One night, I saw my Husband's face in a different dream. He was watching me nurse Gabriella from across the room. My full breasts were exposed and they were bursting with milk. He was puzzled and asked, "Who is that child? Whose baby are you feeding with your precious breast milk? Who is the father of that blue-eyed baby?"

My reaction to childbirth went beyond postpartum depression. It might have been better described as postpartum psychosis. I often considered suicide, but always came face-to-face with the German-created-fact that my death would kill everyone I loved. The German was emerging from an emotional desert, but it would have been too easy to have revenge on my Husband and my family if I ended our relationship by killing myself. I couldn't risk it, so I had to find a way to live with the situation; I had to go—to separate from Gabriella.

Two months after her birth, I pushed Gabriella away. We hired a wet nurse and a night nanny. I stopped going to her room except for occasional visits when she was sound asleep. When the German visited us in Versailles, the nanny brought her out and the three of us sat together for short periods of time. We pretended we were a normal family, but I couldn't stand the pretense even in small doses. We were anything but normal.

After three months of suffering in motherhood, I asked the German if I could move back to Paris, back to the suite at the Hotel Meurice and back to his bed. The German was happy to have me return. As I left my daughter, my heart was stilled and hardened in a way I had not known. *When I faced the choice to stay with my daughter* in Versailles *or return to a life full of superficial pleasures in Paris, I chose Paris.*

Gabriella stayed in Versailles with her wet nurse and nannies. We visited her seldom. Gabriella was comfortable and well-taken care of. On two occasions, she came to Paris to pose with the German and me for Nazi propaganda pictures.

One of Gabriella's nannies was French and one was German. Each followed a strict routine of speaking only their native language with Gabriella. She was also tutored in English and spoke baby-talk in all three languages, depending on which nanny or instructor was present. Her grasp of languages was uncanny, even as a baby. She lived a perfect life, albeit with no parents.

Because he was a man, the German felt no guilt from being an absentee parent; he was content with visiting Gabriella infrequently with no impact on his love for her. The German's life was full; he loved his German-French daughter, he was a respected Nazi general, and he had me to give him pleasure, passion and support. He told me this time was the happiest of his adult life.

The German's strong love for our daughter did affect him in positive ways. Gabriella became the third pillar in my plan to convert the German into a caring human being. I was his first love, the second was Paris and third the daughter he loved. It was a three-front assault on his Nazi roots, his uber-masculinity and his destructive approach toward all things French.

In an act that demonstrated his love for her, the German established a financial trust for Gabriella in Switzerland. The funds were converted to Swiss francs and were therefore protected from the unstable currencies of Germany and France. They were invested in a perpetual trust which would continue to produce income for Gabriella for the rest of her life. Gabriella's basic needs would be taken care of, no matter what happened to the German, our respective countries or to me. He went further: he made me a co-signer on the trust in case something happened to him. He had become a responsible father.

Though I could not live with Gabriella or care for her, I loved her in a passive way. Her existence inspired me to a new, higher level of motivation to use the German's power for purposes of protecting Paris, my family and now my baby girl.

October 1944. **E**ven after Occupation ended, the German was dead, my castrated Husband returned home and, I was released from charges of collaboration, I seldom saw Gabriella. There were many obstacles.

I spent considerable time in the hospital as they tried to control the advancing syphilis devastating my body. My Husband and I were trying to create a small amount of normalcy in our lives. He was a bone-thin, frightened and defeated man. He was mentally and physically incapacitated, childlike and dependent. Fortunately, a guilt-based assistance program of the French government provided full-time nursing care. Even so, it took all my energy to care for him and help him perform the simplest of tasks.

Gabriella turned two without me. I could not bring her into my life at home with my Husband. Neither my Husband nor I could have coped with a two year-old in our home, especially a half-German child fathered by a Nazi general.

Life was difficult. Much of the infrastructure of Paris was broken. There was almost no food, no heat, no fuel, minimum electricity, little transportation and no money.

My sins of collaboration with the Nazis were unforgivable to our family and friends. They would have nothing to do with us. It was as if I were dead. Some of them continued to live at such a low level of existence that their ongoing survival was not guaranteed. All were ashamed of their connection to me. Their loyalties were with those who resisted, and they believed I had helped the Nazis. Their abhorrence for Collaborators was overwhelming. None forgot the press releases showing my "glamorous" life with the German while they starved and died. No one forgot that I had conceived a child with the Nazi SS general. They could not forgive me, and I often joined them in self-condemnation, for I could not forgive myself either.

Because of the tremendous amount of guilt in my heart, I lived one breath, one day, one struggle at a time. The last thing I could endure during this post-Occupation struggle would have been to look into Gabriella's face and see the dead German looking back at me. I avoided contact with her for as long as I could and went about survival activities in the aftermath of the Occupation.

Before the war in Europe ended, I visited Gabriella in Versailles. I hadn't seen her for eleven months. My maternal pull became too great to stay away any longer. Motherhood temporarily overcame the guilt her face produced in me. I knew I must see her.

Gabriella was a healthy two-and-a-half year-old and she resembled the German even more than during my previous visit. She looked like a miniature, female version of him. She was precocious. The German would have been proud of her. He would have been a proud father.

While Gabriella was enjoying the playthings I had brought her, she asked questions and made cute comments. At one point, she looked up and pointed to my scar. "Mommy has an owie. How did Mommy get an owie? Tell me, Mama!"

How could I tell her that her father had caused this to happen? Your father had me captured, raped, beaten, and because of him, my own people cut, beat and raped me again." I wanted her to know the truth, but how could I tell her such things? I smiled a fake smile and prepared to leave. I couldn't take anymore.

My reaction to Gabriella was the same as always, only more so. I ended the visit early and returned to Paris and my Husband, hurrying away from the innocent Gabriella, full of blame, shame and pain.

Café Talk: Abandonment

1945. *Christine looked up at the American with sorrow in her eyes. "Do you understand? I abandoned my child for the life of Paris parties and the torrid sexual relationship with the German. I continued to ignore her after Liberation. Imagine the mental conflicts and the angst I faced knowing I provided the Nazi general with everything he needed and wanted while I gave her nothing.*

"The war in Europe continued for nine-and-a-half months after the liberation of Paris and eight months after my Husband returned home. In France, all available resources were directed to defeating the Nazis; civilian needs were a low priority. The quality of life in Paris was much the same as during Occupation, but fortunately without the Nazis harassing and murdering Parisian citizens. Relative to other active war zones, Parisians lived easier, without much direct combat in their city. However, Parisians suffered incalculable losses of their loved ones who were dying in battle elsewhere in Europe or being imprisoned by the Nazis as war raged on."

Christine closed the day's meeting by saying, "That visit was the last time I have seen Gabriella. She is healthy and safe, she is well-cared for and she receives proper language instruction and upbringing. She doesn't have a mother because I have chosen to stay away, which is no fault of hers. Do you have enough of me now?"

The American didn't answer her question, but he did want more. He insisted that Christine see Gabriella soon and told her he would accept no excuses. "You owe it to Gabriella. She has to see her mother before you die! She must have a last living memory of you."

Christine resisted. "What could possibly be achieved by connecting a dying mother with a little girl who hardly knows her? I can't look at her as I die—please! I have suffered enough; I want to die in peace."

"That is not enough. You are her mother, her sole surviving parent, she has no family to accept her and she is about to lose you. You cannot repeat your mother's rejection of you. That is not a life lesson to teach your daughter. You must put her first. She must see you soon!"

CHAPTER SEVEN
THE YANKEES IN PARIS

Some have thought me less than I am
Fewer have thought me more
No one has known me as I am
None have known my core

Café Talk: The American's Daughter

1945. The American had something important to tell Christine and Christine was ready to listen. She was weak and she had already said so much. "I want to tell you a very personal story about my family that will help explain why I am pushing you to see Gabriella before it is too late. This time it is my painful and important story to tell."

"My Wife's greatest passion in life was to have a daughter. She was obsessed with this since she herself was a little girl, playing with dolls in their tiny dollhouse. She wanted to dress her daughter in girl's clothes, take her shopping, discuss girl things and help her grow into a woman. She loved femininity and lace.

"Everything she wanted from a daughter was missing with our two sons. She didn't care about sports and my boys and I were avid sport fans. We especially liked American football, which made no sense to her. She didn't like our rough-and-tumble exchanges or the dirt and noise that we males naturally emit. When each of the boys was born, she wished for a girl. Each time the doctor told her the sex of our newborn, she was profoundly disappointed, while I was elated. Both times it was if I won and she lost.

"After the boys grew up a bit, my Wife became pregnant again. She glowed in this pregnancy, unlike either of her pregnancies with the boys. She knew it was a girl. She spent months preparing the baby's room; it was magnificent, with feminine wallpaper, baby girl clothes and pillows. She was very happy during this pregnancy. Her anxieties and frustrations had disappeared. She didn't complain about the difficulties of pregnancy and she made everyone's life easier with her positive attitude. I hoped this child would help overcome the difficulties in our marriage.

"About six months into her pregnancy, my Wife started having physical problems. She was bleeding and having cramps and was in so much pain she would often have to lie down for the entire day. After she was seven and a half months pregnant, she started having contractions and was hospitalized. The doctors told us she was going to have a premature baby and to prepare for significant difficulties.

"Our daughter, Isabella, was born two months early. She weighed only five pounds and was the tiniest baby you could imagine. My Wife would carry her around on a pillow singing and talking to her for hours and pouring out her love to our baby girl. Isabella's internal organs were not fully developed. She struggled to eat, breathe and digest her mother's milk.

"The saddest day of our lives was the day we lost our tiny two-month-old baby girl. My Wife was not the same after that; the core of her being was taken away, and it appeared nothing and no one could bring it back.

"Each day, my Wife would go to the cemetery with a bouquet of flowers to place at Isabella's grave. She would fall to her knees in the grass and weep. Each visit tore out another piece of her heart; each moment of mourning left another part of her soul at the gravesite of little Isabella. She became sadder and sadder in her downward spiral of grief.

"Isabella's death changed how she looked at the boys and me. I returned to a normal work schedule and our boys returned to school and playing with their friends. Our ache was deep but our recovery was much faster than hers. She hated that. She despised the return of our laughter and rambunctious behavior around the house. Feelings of happiness or joy were met with "How could you" stares of coldness and pain. My return to my usual life patterns drove us farther apart as a man and a woman, farther away from our union as a husband and wife. The slow passing of our passion fled rapidly toward nothingness.

"I suggested we try again. Maybe we would have another daughter. She refused. It would be impossible for her to survive this heart-wrenching wound again. It was over for her. Her dream had vanished; her heart departed with little Isabella. Even her face changed; her expression locked into a hollow-eyed look of despair. She preserved everything in Isabella's room exactly as it was the day she died. No one else was allowed to go inside. Some days, I would hear my Wife in Isabella's room, crying and crying without end.

"I worried a great deal about my Wife during this time. I didn't know how to love her, how to help her or even how to join her in sorrow. I was shut out. I could do nothing right. Her deep ache created an insurmountable wall between us, an obstacle that could not be overcome by fading connections as husband and wife. It was an incredibly sad time.

"My Wife developed another reaction that worried me. She became obsessed with other people's baby daughters. She would fawn over baby girls while ignoring boys of all ages. She became overly focused on them, which sometimes made the parents nervous.

"She was finished with males at this point. Fortunately, our sons were old enough not to suffer from her inattention. I would see smirks on their faces when my Wife slipped into her baby-girl obsession. They knew losing Isabella was a big deal, but they were young and couldn't fully understand how important it was. Maybe I didn't either.

"We passed two years in this state. My Wife lost some of her grief but none of her sadness. She stared less at other people's daughters but she continued to longingly watch whenever little girls and their mothers were going through their 'mother-daughter dance.'

"She didn't let me into her thoughts or her world. Her life became mechanical, dealing with the chores and going through the motions of family life without enthusiasm, without heart. She lost hope and saw nothing in life worth living for. Our intimacy ended. On days when her depression was most severe, I worried that she might consider suicide. I couldn't find a way into the heart of whatever remained of my Wife.

"Now you know one of the core reasons why I am in Paris; I am here because I could no longer live with the impact of the loss of Isabella and the overwhelming loneliness of my marriage that resulted from my Wife's grieving."

The American had revealed the most painful event of his life to Christine. He exposed this tender place in his heart to let her know that he also suffered greatly over a child. He could tell her everything about his life; he trusted Christine completely. The last thing he said about his daughter was, "Isabella would be the same age as Gabriella."

He told his story, and then they needed a break. It was lunchtime, so he and Christine quietly walked the short distance from the Café Editor to Le Procope on Rue de l'Ancienne Comedie. Christine asked in rapid French for a table on the ground floor, just above the room decorated as an ancient library. They sat silently as they absorbed the losses of each of their daughters, albeit losses of a different nature.

The bistro was busy and the waiters were occupied with other tables. A variety of splendid odors floated to them, only to be replaced by others and others again. The restaurant noise was high but it did not fill the silence that Isabella's short life brought into their hearts.

The American's mind wandered as he tried to turn his thoughts from their deep conversation to the perfection of this Parisian restaurant. Le Procope had existed for more than two hundred fifty years and claimed to be the oldest restaurant in the world, though it began as a café which served lemonade. He remembered a previous lunch he and Christine had enjoyed here. She told him it was opened by a Sicilian man named Francesco Procopio dei Coltelli in 1686, who also claimed to have invented gelato. She listed the famous people who frequented the café, including Napoleon Bonaparte. She pointed to the portrait of Benjamin Franklin and noted how he penned much of the U.S. Constitution while eating and drinking in Le Procope's dining salons. She further explained Franklin's compatriots, the True Friends of Liberty, as they called themselves, gathered here to mourn Franklin's death with ample food and drink.

These thoughts gave the American some respite from the deep, live child-dead child, parent-daughter discussion. After all, at Procope, they were dining with the ghosts of Voltaire, George Sand, Victor Hugo, Honore de Balzac and the Paris revolutionaries of the nineteenth century.

When the waiter came, the American ordered a Pastis. He added only a small amount of water since he wanted the full flavor and the strong jolt of alcohol to ease the stress. Christine would usually laugh at him for being such an American, for not knowing how to drink properly. This day she said nothing.

They ordered lunch: a civet of duck with pasta for the American and the plateau de fruits de mer for Christine. He considered having the grille accompagne de riz pilaff ou en homage à Benjamin Franklin l'Americain as his entrée but thought it would be gauche to order a dish named after a fellow countryman, even if it was named in honor of a wholly continental and exceedingly great American.

Their conversation had yet to restart. It was stuck in an awkwardness that sometimes occurs when people of different cultures and different native languages reach a point where they cannot communicate any further. They had encountered very few of these cultural disconnects during their many days together, but they hit one at lunch this day. It was a void sitting between them like an unwanted guest for lunch.

They were unsure of how or where to restart their intimate conversation. The American studied the décor of the restaurant. Their booth was separated from the main areas of the restaurant by an encirclement of glass display cases. This provided a feeling of privacy and openness at the same time. On the shelves of the cabinets rested artifacts of cooking, writing and revolution. Nineteenth-century pistols and books of philosophy shared a common space, while decanters and engraved wine glasses shared another. When the passing waiters and patrons were viewed through the thick glass, they looked as if they were embedded in a living Impressionist painting, their images altered by the thick, curvy glass. On the walls and the ceiling, everything was red. Rich red material hung as a backdrop to portraits of the authors and patriots who had dined here over hundreds of years. In spaces where there was no material, the interior walls were painted in the same shade of red. The vibrant color, the shimmering glass, the ancient books and the Renaissance paintings gave Le Procope a warmth and elegance which implied that interesting conversations were occurring throughout the restaurant.

Trying to deal with the continuing silent gap in their conversation, the American turned to reading the history of the restaurant written on the front of the menu. It told of columns of sugar which once hung from the ceiling for sweetening the "new" sour drink served there. Procope was the first café in Paris to serve recently imported Turkish coffee.

Christine finally spoke. "You and your Wife lost a daughter whom you loved and cherished with all your hearts and souls. Your loss has brought deep pain, unhappiness and confusion into your lives and marriage. I understand why you told me about Isabella—it is an important story for me, since I have a perfectly healthy daughter of the same age and I can't look at her.

"Through no fault of your own, you lost what you and your Wife wanted most, a baby girl. I have the daughter you want but I choose not to accept her. I see that your life has not been easy and this tragedy has caused you and your Wife to grow apart and separate. There is no rational sense in this. The separate paths you and your Wife are choosing will only lead to more pain for you, your Wife, your boys, friends and family. Why should one misfortune lead you to choose to create more tragedies?"

The American noted to himself how Christine was unaware that she had done exactly the same thing in her denial of Gabriella; she had made a sad story much sadder. He chose not to point out this paradox to her. He knew they were on highly sensitive ground and she was too unsteady for criticisms, so he simply recorded a note of the paradox for her journal.

Their meals were excellent and the service perfect. However, they were emotionally drained and lost some enthusiasm for the entrée but not for the dolce, the dessert. Christine ordered mousse glacée à l'amaretto et au caramel fine liqueur d'amandes and the American ordered glaces et sorbets "maison." They finished their lunches with espressos. But even with the sweets and coffee, there were no smiles and none of Christine's words of positive redemption. Sadly, this was the last time that just Christine and the American would have a proper Parisian lunch together; life was marching toward its inevitable conclusion.

Afterward, they took a slow walk and visited St. Julien. They both rubbed the Lucky Tree just outside of the church, the one Christine and her Husband had forgotten to touch. The American turned his head away and tried to cover his weeping; he wept for Christine, for Gabriella, for Isabella, for his Wife, for his boys and for himself.

In that little park, across the river from the majestic Notre Dame, on the grounds where Jews and Romans once lived and worshipped, on the holy land of St. Julien le Pauvre, the American and Christine shared the one and only intimate, physical act of their profound relationship; the American lovingly kissed Christine's scar. It wasn't a forever kiss, but it was much more than a peck on the cheek. He held his lips there for as long as he could without creating too much awkwardness. His left hand held the back of her head and his fingers were entwined in her prematurely graying hair. Christine remained motionless and did not react. The American pointlessly tried to take away Christine's suffering with his tender kiss. He yearned to show her how deeply he cared, that he loved her but this was all he could do, all he could give her and all she could possibly receive.

Two days later, Christine and the American met in the café and ordered as they had done many times before. However, this meeting took on a more ominous tone. Christine reported the prognosis of doctors who said she must be hospitalized soon. Her disease was progressing rapidly. The end was approaching quickly.

Despite the doctor's ill-omened opinion, Christine was experiencing a temporary improvement in her mental clarity, so the American decided to expand on his expressions of love for her before it was too late, before she was gone. It was something had he wanted to do for a long time and, according to their honesty pact, there was to be no holding back. The American spoke and Christine listened passively as she had done when he spoke of Isabella.

"I have written detailed descriptions of your sex acts and lovemaking, which was often more than I wanted to know. You wanted me to write the truth and I did. I understand how your sexuality was a critical component in becoming a woman and how it was vital to saving Paris.

"As I was writing your Journal and knowing you better and better, I was also falling in love with you. I learned graphically of the pleasures we could not share. Your descriptions made me believe that we have the same level of sexual intensity. If we had met earlier in our lives, I believe you would have been the One for me.

"I wanted to be all of your lovers—the Boy, coupling our bodies in our first consummated sexual experiences; the Artist, arousing your lust as a woman with my eyes and my mouth; your Husband, enhancing true love with tender, giving sex; and the German, living with you in lustful fervor. I would have loved to have a child with you, a child like Gabriella.

"Every day I contemplate the possibilities of what might have been. What if we had met as a boy and a girl and lived out the Romeo and Juliet bonds of young passion and virginal sex? If we had shared our first times with each other, would we have been able to hold on to our unique intimacy for our lifetimes? Could we have found pure love amid the chaos of reality, or would we have cycled out of childlike love and lost our blind passion for one another as you did with the Boy and the Artist and I did with my wife?

"What if we had met as young adults, after university, ready to commit to a lifetime relationship and ready for a family, as you did with your Husband? Could we have avoided hurting each other in selfish acts of immaturity? Would we have been enough for each other, or would day-to-day living, birthing and raising children, meeting pressures of a family and careers have spoiled our love? Would I have overcome my sexual addiction and been faithful if I'd married you?

"Or, is this end-of-life, sexless love the perfect love? Is it only achievable when one is free from life's attachments and responsibilities, or only when one faces death? I wasn't immune to my passion for you. I wasn't listening to some impersonal story written by a stranger to stimulate my sexual desires. As I listened to you describe your experiences and I captured them in writing, I held on tightly to the only thing I was able to have, my sexless love for you. How strange this has been!

"I have loved your presence, your mind, your actions, your surprises. You have kept my interest peaked every minute that we spoke. The pleasure continued long after we met, as I contemplated, laughed, cried and wrote about your life. There are no bad parts to you, only parts I couldn't have. In the Pyramid of Love, I loved you in the best way of all, in the most complete way one human being can love another: all of me loves all of you!

"It surprised me that I could love you as intensely as I do without being sexually intimate with you; I have often confused love with sex. No one who knows me would believe I could be deeply in love without sex, especially because you are so charming, beautiful and sexy. Yet, despite what others may think or what foolishness I am capable of, I do love you absolutely.

"Yes, there are clear reasons to assure that we could not have a sexual relationship, including your disease and your commitment of fidelity to your Husband. These barriers prevented our normal man-woman love cycle from progressing, which also upped the love-ante for me. I grew to find I could love deeper and greater by not consummating love with sex. You have taught me a purer love. You showed me love exists beyond sexual obsession, that I can love a woman without making her a conquest. I could have loved you as other men have loved you, but instead I love you more! I love you unlike any time I have loved before, and unlike I will love again.

"Amazingly, you have also taught me how to love my Wife better. I plan to return to my marriage with a changed heart and mind. My awareness of new dimensions of love and my expanded capability to love will transform our marriage and our lives. I think my Wife will love the changes. My thinking and acting like a sexual predator were a big reason for her unhappiness with me, even before we lost Isabella. I know I gave my Wife an incomplete, short-changed version of love. Sexual ghosts of my past, present and future haunted our marriage and dominated my mind. I was always thinking of my next conquest or my last, instead of thinking of her. The ghosts are gone now, swept away by you.

"But why should I hold back from expressing my genuine feelings for you? I am part of your Journal now, part of your story. I want you to know me and to know what I honestly think. That is our deal. There is no changing our commitment to honesty just because it becomes more complex!

"These are the thoughts I had each time we met and took with me each time you left at the end of the day. This is what I contemplated in the evenings when you were home caring for your broken Husband and I was sitting in a Paris bistro eating dinner alone."

Christine did not react or participate. There was to be no discussion; her mind was somewhere else. The American tried to capture the meaning of the look on her face when he spoke to her of his love and his impotent, "what if" dreams. He wasn't sure if she showed boredom, irritation or indifference, but clearly his love scenarios were not her top priority, she had known his feelings long before he expressed them.

Christine was left with only a small number of days to live. She was plotting to change reality again; preparing to exert her will one more time before her exit from the stage of life.

The American continued to speak of the lessons Christine had taught him. "I will give your 'damn the torpedoes' approach toward life to my children. I will tell them of your guts, from slide-tackling the Boy to your cunningness and courage in saving Paris from Nazi demolition. I will describe your amazing attitude by word and deed as an example of how one can meet life's challenges. Your influence will live on in my family.

"The lessons on love you have taught will become part of my marriage. I will tell my Wife everything, explain my special love for you and ask her to read your Journal. I will give my all to my Wife and then it will be her time to choose, her time to decide if she can love me, forgive me, remain married with me and share in a relationship bigger and better than before—or not.

"Don't think ill of me because I love you and also love my Wife. It is my male mind that allows me to love more than one woman at a time, though I love each of you differently. It is my male version of insatiability. I ask you to accept my truth as I have accepted yours. To me, loving you and loving my Wife are part of the grander possibilities of love about which you have spoken. Because of what I have learned from you, I will give my Wife the gift of honesty. Without honesty, love and marriage are just more lies, more hollow, imperfect connections that create more lonely people. These gifts you have given me. Thank you, Christine!"

When Christine met the American the next morning she didn't immediately respond to his talk of love the day before. Christine wasn't completely indifferent to his feelings and in her own ways; she agreed. She also knew this was not the time or the place for romantic love, and that the American, despite his claims of a new, higher love consciousness, maintained healthy but not wholly pure aspirations.

The American remained unsure of her reaction to his opened heart, but he was not concerned. He was satisfied he had accomplished his goal: he had revealed his feelings for her before it was too late, something exceedingly important to him.

After a short while, Christine did come back to the American's expressions of love and affection. However, her reaction wasn't exactly what the American expected. Like her reaction to the Artist when he spoke of D'Annunzio's philosophy of Artist-gods and the importance of sex-with-strangers, Christine broke through the American's philosophy with pointed comments.

"You can love me openly and completely because you know I cannot love you back. You know I won't try to possess you and I won't disappoint you. I am a 'safe lover' because you know our romantic relationship can only exist in your mind.

"Therefore, you are free to let your emotions and fantasies run wild, without restraint, because you have no fear of me as a woman, a lover or a wife. Your ability to love expands directly to the lack of responsibility you perceive to have from it. After all, aren't most of your fantasy women those you cannot have? Maybe they remain faithful to their husbands, maybe they are too young, or maybe they are just not interested in you. Aren't they the ones, like me, that you fantasize about and think could be the One for you, the women you can't catch?"

"I am puzzled by your question," the American answered. "Do you know me too well? I don't recall separating my feelings for women into categories of those I couldn't have and those I did. Your question strikes deep into my motives.

"If you are correct, what does that mean? Does your theory invalidate my primary excuse for chasing women—that I love them so much I can't help myself? If I love women, then why would I crave the ones I can't have and leave the ones I can? If I love women so much, why do I constantly lie to them and never want be faithful? How do lying and infidelity equal love?

"There is probably some truth to what you say, but I don't think the 'impossibility of love' determines entirely whom or why I love. I know that the only reason I love you is not just because I can't have you. That doesn't explain my respect, my attraction, my appreciation or my love for you. It is bigger than that.

"I won't deny I enjoy the lust of the chase. Many men are made for the chase, and we find it irresistible, a male aphrodisiac. I also won't deny that many men, including me, have difficulties with long-term marriage and remaining faithful to one woman. It is the Achilles' heel of our gender.

"But male wanderlust is also fueled by wives who stop using their wonderful, feminine love-tools and make their marriages hell on earth. Many wives have become unattractive physically, mentally, and dress in dowdy clothes. I know wives who view their husbands as a meal ticket or a personal servant and have stopped respecting them as men. Some have given up their sexuality and are no longer interesting to their husbands. Some wives undermine their husbands instead of supporting them. If a man like me is predisposed to sexual wanderlust, you can imagine what happens when his wife becomes matronly, hostile and sexually cold.

"That is enough about me. I fell in love with an angel, an angel returning to heaven. What issues I have are unimportant to your story. I wanted you to know about Isabella, my love for you and how you will live in my heart for eternity."

1946. Christine's mind was still capable of operating at lightning speed. She rose from the table, walked around and astonished the American by giving him a warm kiss on each cheek. Unexpectedly, he blushed. Any expression of Christine's affection in even the slightest form was powerful medicine for his lonely heart. Christine sat down and locked her eyes into his and spoke intimately to the American. A sudden spark came into her voice as she shared a peek of her vision with him. "You and your Wife have to reconcile, and it must happen here and now, in Paris. Call your Wife today and ask her to come to Paris at once. She will come. No woman can refuse a loving invitation to Paris; in fact, all invitations to Paris are loving invitations!

"I want to meet your Wife and spend time with the two of you before I die." The American was flabbergasted, but he obeyed Christine's command without debate. The background noise of the transatlantic cable did not block out his Wife's clear answer: "Yes," she said. "I would love to join you in Paris!"

The American reeled from the idea that his Wife was about to enter his new world; the world of Christine, the Journal and Paris. He had run away from everything at home, especially his Wife's negativity and the guilt over his own behavior. He had vacillated between anxiety and quiet pleasure and asked himself many questions. Would she bring the misery of her anxieties and sorrow with her as she crossed the Atlantic, or would she leave her dispiriting, gloomy self at home? Was there hope that Paris and Christine would cure her of her persistent unhappiness? How would he handle being with Christine and his Wife at the same time? After thinking about it, he concluded that he was excited to see his Wife and to share Christine and Paris with her. He felt a beat of hope pound in his heart.

Christine and the American spent the next two mornings discussing the final details of the Journal over coffee. She stayed on track, though she tired quickly and left by 11:00 a.m. each day. She had to push herself harder as her health deteriorated. He was losing her. She was giving the Journal the last of her life force. He had gathered all the information he needed to write her Journal except for the ending, and he knew, when the ending was written, Christine would exist in another domain, in the dimension of the spirit.

The day before the American's Wife arrived, Christine told the American that she agreed to see Gabriella but wouldn't tell him when the visit would occur. He was relieved and pleased with himself. It was the right thing to do. She had actually listened to him!

His Wife flew from San Francisco to New York and took the Pan Am Clipper across the Atlantic Ocean to Marseilles. From Marseilles, she took the train to Paris. She arrived in the most upbeat mood he had seen since they lost little Isabella. There was a glimpse of happiness on her face as she exited the train wearing a red patent leather jacket. The positive impact of her work with her psychologist, Dr. Adams, was evident in her long-absent smile. Clearly, from the start, coming to Paris was a good plan.

After they settled into his hotel and his Wife took a long, hot shower, the two of them sat down to lunch to become reacquainted. His Wife was impressed by how easily he negotiated the French menu. He thought she looked wonderful.

He had written letters to his Wife telling her about Christine, her pending death and the writing of the Journal. From his descriptions, his Wife knew quite a bit about his life in Paris. He expanded upon his relationship with Christine over their lunch at a local bistro. He spoke of his deep affection for Christine and clarified the limits of their relationship, a permanently sexless, though deeply felt, love. Directness and honesty had replaced coyness and lying. He no longer wanted to live any other place than in a world of honesty.

After lunch, the American arranged for his Wife to have a meeting with Father Jean. The American's Wife had known Father Jean after he had fled the Nazi Occupation and stayed with her husband's family in California. They had become close friends. Father Jean knew her grief over losing Isabella and the pain she suffered from her husband's behavior. She trusted Father Jean for she had often been blessed by his advice on forgiveness and love. Father Jean had been the only light during her time of deep darkness caused by the loss of baby Isabella.

Father Jean welcomed her to Paris with his loving and spiritual self. He asked the American to leave, to go out to a café or a walk, so he could speak with his Wife in private. Father Jean was pleased when she described her progress in relieving her anger toward her husband and dissipating the lingering pain over Isabella. He verbalized what she already knew: her husband had come to Paris at a crossing point, a place where he might not return to their family. Their marriage could only survive through an encompassing commitment to love, forgiveness and a great deal of work, for that is the nature of marriage.

Father Jean asked her directly, "Can you choose to forgive your husband, commit to your marriage and love him without driving a deeper wedge between you and your husband over the pain he has caused you?" She answered, "Yes, Father, yes I can. I have come to Paris to take him home and to renew the love we once had. I can do better than I have done; I can love him better despite the fact that I still carry some hurt and anger in my heart. I know I have to overcome this and show him through my actions that I love and forgive him. I am in Paris as a different woman than the one he left behind in America."

The day before, Father Jean and the American had spoken of similar concerns and solutions. The American had explained how he had also changed and how he realized the consequences of his behavior. Father Jean had made it clear, if his marriage were to be renewed, it must be with his unbroken fidelity and with his love focused only on his Wife.

The meetings with Father Jean were a positive tonic for the American and his Wife. They looked forward to their next Paris experience, a three-way meeting with Christine.

Midmorning the next day, they met at a quaint little tea salon in a small alley off Rue Saint-Andre des Arts, in the Cour du Commerce Saint Andre. Before Christine arrived, the American gave his Wife a little history of the area. It was from the back door of Le Procope and down this little alley that the revolutionists, edgy with overconfidence brought on by too much caffeine from Procope's strong coffee, stealthily fanned out into the city in their violent efforts to overthrow the Monarchy. The "Caffeine Revolt," as the French Revolution was called, was fueled by these over-caffeinated French revolutionists who dramatically altered the constitution and the government of France. His Wife was again impressed. She wondered how he had learned so much about Paris in such a short time.

Christine arrived and warm introductions ensued. Over a chatty pot of steaming tea and currant scones, the American watched the two most important women in his life become quickly acquainted. Theirs was an immediate and natural friendship, just like the American's meeting with Christine the first time they met.

His Wife was amazed by Christine's mind and the strength of her being, even as she carried the disease of her premature destruction. The American was proud as she matched Christine at each point of their conversation. Christine and his Wife sped through so many aspects of their lives that it made his head swim. Neither wasted a moment; it seemed like they hardly took breaths between their rapid-fire words. The growing link between the two women kept the tea warm and the scones fresh.

After Christine and his Wife discussed a multitude of subjects, they spoke of their children, one dead and one alive. This topic drew the American's close interest and attention. He wondered how his Wife would handle discussing Isabella with Christine and how Christine would present Gabriella. Children were a sensitive subject for both women and there was a great potential for misunderstanding and pain, for each bore their own child-cross.

Christine went directly to the heart of the matter and asked his Wife a number of questions; why didn't she want to have another child, did she think her marriage could be repaired, and what her boys were like. She was genuinely interested and asked in a loving way, so no offense was given and none was taken. His wife asked about Gabriella and Christine gave her a full report. She opened up about Gabriella's resemblance to the German and, because of the guilt, the pain and the difficult circumstances with her Husband, it was impossible for Christine to see her very often.

When they finished speaking about their children, they left their thoughts in a place of mutual understanding and empathy. His Wife asked Christine about her health. Christine responded in a cavalier manner. "Few have lived as much as I have lived in thirty years. I have seen life from the lowest level of human behavior to the highest and I have been disappointed by the worst and delighted by the best. Each year, I have become more dedicated to the truth. Each day, as I come nearer to the end, I forgive more. Love is at the heart of life, and I have loved and been loved in many ways. I hope you will think kindly of me after I am gone. I am so glad for this chance to meet you.

"Before I leave today, I want to speak with you about your husband, the man I call the American. I don't particularly want him to hear everything, so move a little closer. He will love us talking about him—when it comes to women, he is such a boy.

"Your husband is a good man, intelligent and unexpectedly intuitive. He understands a great deal about the complexities of a woman's feelings and many of our paradoxes as well. Sometimes, he has surprised me by seeing beyond my visions of myself; he has seen things that I thought I fully understood until he helped me to see more. This quality is rare. He understands women better than any man I have known, and he is an American!

"His ability to understand and relate to women is also a danger, and I am sure you know what I am talking about. An attractive man with his level of compassion is a magnet for women who, despite being married or single, are often desperate for an emotional and intellectual connection with a man. You know you have to be careful and so does he. It is not enough for him to stop his sexual aggression toward women. He must also be able to protect himself from wanton women on the prowl. Fortunately, he has come to understand something few men seem to know—it is acceptable for a man to decline an invitation from a woman, especially if she is asking for inappropriate sexual contact. Even a man can say no!"

His Wife replied, "Yes, I know. I fell in love with him because of his unusual level of understanding and sensitivity. To his credit, his compassion for and understanding of women is not a fake. He truly experiences life intensely, and he does live in a place beyond common male narcissism. He is a man who can cry, sing and listen and still behave in manly ways.

As the American watched, Christine put her hand on the Wife's arm, leaned forward and said, "He loves you very much. I think you and he can find a better way to live. It is worth it. It is largely under your control, you are the woman. He is ready for you. He has seen the error of his ways."

This is great, they both love me, the American thought, even though he couldn't hear Christine's comments or his Wife's answer. He was thrilled that they were talking about him; he was a sensitive and confident man, but he was still a man.

The American's Wife had arrived in Paris with trepidation about meeting the incredible Christine, but after a short time together, her concerns were gone. She wanted to have as much bonding with Christine as possible. She recognized the positive impact Christine could have on her and her family.

Suddenly, Christine made an announcement: "The three of us will visit Gabriella tomorrow." Her mind was operating on two levels: participating in the immediate conversation and, on another plane, thinking of the future in her post-mortal world.

The Americans were astounded by Christine's ability to make major adjustments to life on the spur of the moment. The American's Wife witnessed Christine's skill in creating a positive situation out of a negative one. No wonder she was able to save Paris!

Their visit with Gabriella was magnificent. They walked into a home of sun, order and cleanliness. The two nannies and the English tutor stood in the back of the living room waiting to be called. Gabriella sat in a small Queen Anne chair. She sat forward and upright, not touching the back of the chair. She wore a white-smocked bodice dress accented with pink rosebuds along the border of her empire waist. Her matching pink tights accompanied her precious black patent leather shoes, which were imported from Germany during Occupation. Her posture perfectly reflected her well-mannered upbringing and a respectful attitude.

There was a pleasant aroma in the air. The nannies, with Gabriella's help, had baked muffins, and the appetizing smells made the American hungry. It appeared everything was almost perfect; Gabriella lived in the well-disciplined world of professional child caretakers, missing only the presence of parental love.

The American's Wife and Gabriella warmed to each other immediately, but Gabriella was shy with the American. After all, he was a big boy, a man. However, it wasn't long before he detected her subtly flirting with him during breaks in the conversation.

Gabriella's multilingual upbringing was evident as she spoke with the Americans in English and her mother in French. Her tutor moved closer to assist if necessary, but Gabriella was not the least bit timid. She was a multilingual chatterbox.

The interaction between Christine and Gabriella was extraordinary. Gabriella called her "maman" in her sweet way, oblivious to her mother's pending death. The contrast between the light in Gabriella's life and darkness in her mother's melted the hearts of the Americans. They struggled to keep back the tears rising from their guts as they watched the mother and child connection interact, knowing that for them time had all but disappeared, and that only minutes remained of having life together.

It fascinated the Americans that Gabriella understood Christine was her mother after so little contact. Christine remained engaged, if not exuberant, as she and Gabriella spoke and played. Gabriella brought out two of her special things to show her guests, a small red ball and a raggedly old doll. She rolled the ball toward her mother who rolled it back. Then she held up the doll and said, "Gabby." She named her doll after herself, using the name her English tutor used for her. "Gabby tired, Gabby go to bed."

The French nanny withdrew to the kitchen and reappeared with warm muffins and hot tea. Pressed linen napkins were provided and the various condiments were placed on the table. The American chose honey and lemon for his tea. The women took only lemon. Each ate the muffins, which were perfectly made and tasty. The American ate two.

There was music coming through the window from the neighbor's home. It was a familiar American song left over from the war. Bing Crosby sang, "I'll be seeing you in all the old familiar places that this heart of mine embraces all day through. In that small café, the park across the way, the children's carousel, the chestnut trees, the wishin' well. . ." It was a tune reeking of war-induced loneliness, of troops fighting far away on foreign soil, and of women waiting at home with hope and memories in their anxious hearts.

Gabriella brought her doll to the American's Wife. She said the doll's name and handed over her best friend. "Gabby, hug Gabby."

Soon, the American's Wife was hugging Gabriella as well. Her timid self was gone; it was time for affection and love.

Inside the house, there were words of different languages laced with the universal languages of laughter, friendship and love. For Gabriella, it was a playdate. For the much too grown-up grownups, it was a tragic good-bye.

It was an extraordinary day that the living would always remember. When it was time to go, Gabriella gave cheek kisses to her mother and the American's Wife—she gave the American a quick hug but no kiss.

Gabriella became quiet when she saw they were leaving. She tightly held her ball and her doll and watched them depart with moist eyes as large as dew-dipped moons. Christine made a quick exit, which did not include looks back. The Americans followed her to a waiting car and they drove away.

This was to be the last time Christine and Gabriella would see each other until the very end, literally until Christine's last breath. This was the last time they would converse and the last time Gabriella would see her mother with discernible life in her body. The American was delighted that his Wife's arrival had prompted their visit with Gabriella. It left a memory to hold onto tightly as lives moved on and one precious life ended.

Paris, Father Jean, Christine and Gabriella continued to do wonders for the American's Wife. The increasingly upbeat rhythm of the city caused an undeniably positive shift in her mood and attitude. Paris was the tonic she needed to break her prolonged grief, to promote the healing started from her counseling with Dr. Adams.

The American had grown a great deal during his time in Paris. Seeing the impact of the war and the fortitude of the European people firsthand helped him expand his isolated American perspective of the world. His experience with Christine made him become a greater man than he would have been, more tolerant and less self-centered. Christine had changed him in ways he knew and in ways that he didn't. Her insight would transcend life and death. She would continue to live on in their lives as she changed destinies with her astonishing ability to see life's opportunities and act on her visions.

The American's Wife appreciated how Christine had helped her husband recognize the destructiveness of his insatiable lust and the loneliness brought by his infidelity. This pleased her immensely. She saw their future together again in a better marriage and she was delighted. His Wife was also aware that in a short time there would be life after Christine, which helped her manage her natural tendency toward jealousy. His Wife opened her heart wide enough to share her husband's love of Christine. It was a love triangle, a platonic ménage-a-trois.

The day after their visit with Gabriella, the American and his Wife sat down to discuss their marriage and family situation in detail. He spoke of his difficulty being separated from her and their boys. She confirmed that the boys were also suffering from the separation, and how a father and his sons belong together. She hesitantly told him she had missed him, too. She had learned a difficult lesson through counseling, that she shared in the responsibility for her husband's infidelity, how her emotional and physical rejection of him and her constant unhappiness had helped push him away not only to other women but to Paris as well. To understand this connection was a major jump in awareness unrecognized by most.

The American committed himself to change and to be an honest, faithful and supportive husband. He apologized for his immature behavior and told his Wife he was profoundly sorry for the pain he had caused her. He asked her to forgive him. He told her he understood how deeply Isabella's death had hurt her.

He wanted to help her overcome her grief and wanted the two of them to recover together.

He also made it clear that he would not accept the negative marriage they had before Paris, before Christine. He would not exist that way again. They must renew passion and respect in their relationship and he was willing to do whatever he could to bring this about, but he would not tiptoe around waiting for the next barrage of complaining and criticism to be thrown at him. That was not a life he was willing to live. She must let him back into her heart so they could share their victories and challenges. Her choices to criticize and reject him with her negative attitude had to stop. Otherwise, their marriage would come undone again, and this time it would be permanent; Christine would not be there to save it.

His Wife agreed. She also apologized for the agony she had caused him. She acknowledged her bitching and the destruction it brought to their marriage, and she vowed to end it. They cried a great deal in Paris. This time, he was holding her tightly as their tears came out. He did not want to be anywhere else or with anyone else.

It was a remarkable day.

CHAPTER EIGHT
THE ENDINGS; BEGINNINGS

Some days I see where I have been
Fewer days I see where I am
But seldom do I see
That which I need the most
Where I am going to be

Good-bye Forever

1946. **S**aying good-bye to Christine and the loss of Isabella were the two hardest things in the American's life. In both cases, there was so much more they could have been.

Though his and Christine's life experiences had been quite different, their relationship was so close that they often completed each other's thoughts and sentences or communicated without words at all.

Knowing she was going to die from the time they met did not help the American let go of Christine in the end. Christine became increasingly frail and less able to remember the events of her life. She suffered constantly and was given more drugs to sedate her, to relieve her pain. Each step downward, each step from life to death, was recorded on her taut face and in her waning memory.

In their last meeting, Christine was able to give the American her final instructions for the Journal. "We must protect Gabriella first and foremost. I do not want you to release my Journal until she is mature enough to understand the adult world we have documented. Then she will learn the truth about her father, about me, and about the circumstances under which her life was created. It will be her decision whether to release my Journal to family, the public, or to no one."

Christine was not concerned that it would be some time before Gabriella grew up and was ready to read her Journal. "Let the others—the public, my family and friends—think what they will" were her words. She had stopped feeling hate for them because they ceased to matter. "They will learn the truth in time...or maybe they won't." She added, "The truth stands by itself. The truth cannot be altered by wishes or lies or government agencies."

The purpose of writing Christine's Journal changed; it became a gift for Gabriella, written memories of parents who did not survive the holocaust of WWII.

She explained it: "My Journal was born in the depths of passion for righteousness and revenge. I was angry. I knew how Paris was saved and by whom. The government was lying to the people. I wanted to set the record straight and expose their lies, even if I did it posthumously. I sought to show my friends, my family and the public that I was not a Collaborator but a savior. I hoped recognition would replace scorn.

"But the process of writing my Journal became an end in and of itself—a journey that changed me and my goals like each turn of fate had done before. My pain from rejection and judgment lessened as my story unfolded through your pen. My healing came from hearing myself recap my life, and from your help in overcoming my resistance to telling my entire story. My anger at life has subsided as I travel closer and closer to death. I forgave life its imperfections; I accepted fate and found peace in my heart.

"My story is like most Parisian journeys, which rarely end up where they begin. It is the evocative power of Paris. I am deeply grateful for what you have done for Gabriella and me; you have far exceeded what I expected."

On an unusually dark day for September, the American received a call from Father Jean telling him the doctors had given Christine only one day more to live. Time had run out for Christine; her mission on earth was ending.

That night the American was tormented by grief and sorrow. When he finally found sleep, he woke after only a couple of hours to thoughts of his own death. He wondered how Christine was coping knowing she had such a short time to live. *How does one handle one's own death when it is lurking around the next corner?* He pondered the concept in his mind. *How will I feel on my last day?* Was it better to know death was coming or would it be easier if one were run down by a streetcar or killed by a fatal heart attack with only the last split second of life to see the onset of one's death?

He had asked Christine about her prolonged death march. She had said it was better that way. Without this knowledge she could not have written her Journal and she would not have met him. Knowing the flowing sands of her life were running out gave her the chance to tell her story before life ended, before she floated away with the clouds. "It is a blessing," she had said. Christine was completing a one-way trip to a mysterious destination, a graduation from life to the final stop on the lifelong journey from birth to death.

The American thought about her premature demise. But for a single act of ignorant violence, the one that infected her, she might have lived another forty years. What new miracles might she have performed if that vengeful man had found a greater level of civility than to violate her precious body? In a partially selfish way, he contemplated how they would not have met if this tragedy had not occurred. His fate would have dealt him a different set of cards and he would have crossed other bridges and landed on different shores.

Christine decided to die at home in her own bed, in her own apartment, overlooking the Seine with her Husband by her side. She requested three special people to be present at her death: her priest Father Jean, her daughter Gabriella, and, her friend the American who now held a position of honor in Christine's life and in her death.

During her last hours of consciousness, Christine intently watched the flowing river under the Point de Sully, the bridge that took the continuous traffic back and forth from the island to the Bastille on Boulevard Henri IV. Her gaze moved down the river to the left, to a row of blue-tinted trees standing above a laced wall of stones. The river curved smoothly like the back of a jaguar; an ever-present flow of life. Turning to her right, she looked upward to the rows of apartment buildings sprouting chimneys like they were posing for a Paris postcard; only in Paris were apartment roofs a work of art. Further along, she watched a road perched just above the water sending an endless stream of cars up and down the riverbank. A puffy cloud stood at watch above her and patches of blue sky backdropped it with color. The bridge offered travelers the opportunity to take a less traveled road to a different destiny; each driver making his choice of which road to follow, which bridge to cross and which life to lead.

The American's Wife did not go to Christine's deathbed. She fully understood and graciously supported her husband's presence there. His Wife was coming alive as a new woman. Her love elevated their marriage from the cooling ashes of near-divorce to the comforting, warm sunlight of support and a new life-journey together. After all they had been through, his Wife was genuinely on his side and he, her husband, was truly on hers.

The American arrived first and entered the room where Christine lay motionless in bed. She was propped up with pillows so she could see through the floor-to-ceiling windows to the world outside. Barges on their parallel voyages up and down the Seine were oblivious to the dying woman walking her final path nearby. Riverboat captains remained ignorant of a savior of Paris on her last voyage, slipping away so near to their watery passing. They motored along without knowing their individual versions of *"My Paris"* would not exist but for the woman who death-stared out the window above.

Christine's bedroom window

Christine's Husband sat blankly in one corner with his nurse close by. No one had loved Christine the way he loved her and Christine hadn't loved anyone the way she loved him. He appeared to be unable to comprehend Christine's death and did not move toward her. He gave no acknowledgment to the American, a man unfamiliar to him, as he walked to Christine's bedside.

Christine's eyes were closed and she breathed rapidly like the panting of an animal. She became distantly aware of the American's presence only when he came very near. The American gasped at the visual impact of death's approach. Her face had changed color; her porcelain beauty had become ghostly white. Not sure of what to do, he gently held her hand and whispered, "I love you, Christine." She responded with a faint squeeze of her hand, a minor acknowledgment of their momentous connection. Another faint squeeze and then he kissed her cheek. His tears began to flow as he stepped back from Death's open door, away from his darling, dying Christine.

The American lumbered to his chair in the corner of the room. He glanced at her stone-faced Husband. His blank eyes were staring into somewhere else, seeing places of horror no one should ever know. The American thought how great it would have been to have known this man before the world came apart and before the Nazis broke him. He was someone special; the American knew that from Christine. He imagined him as the star professor, inserting the events of time into the students' minds of those he awakened. Now he was a Nazi- produced, walking dead man.

Father Jean entered the room. The presence of the holy man soothed the American's spirits. He took a deep breath. The Father first touched the Husband's shoulders and then gave the American a tight hug. He smelled of prayer smoke and holiness. He carried the wisdom of a life spent worshipping God's existence and praying for the strength to accept God's will. He approached Christine to contact whatever was left on earth of her spirit and soul. He administered her last rites. His strong hands were on her head, then genuflecting to honor God's presence at her death. "God's will is strong, the depth of His love is limitless, His forgiveness is absolute and His indifference to our earthly desires complete. Go with God, my child."

Father Jean had birthed Christine into Christianity through baptism, performed Mass at her First Holy Communion, counseled her through the traumas of her youth, sanctified her marriage, introduced her to the American and administered her last rites; the full cycle of life, from birth to God, to death and unto heaven. The church bells rang often for Christine.

Father Jean finished his duties as her priest and took a pause from his role as a man of the cloth. For a few moments, he was just a man, someone losing a precious friend. His grief shook him and he succumbed deeply to it. He was not protected from sorrow by his robes or the cross, and he seemed to bend over further than before, almost to the point that it looked like he might fall forward onto the floor. Father Jean's human grief honored Christine; it acknowledged the great love she brought out in people. He sat near Christine and prayed silently to the only source of relief he knew, to the God to whom he had committed his life and his soul.

Gabriella was led into the room by her French nanny. She was holding her Gabby doll tightly in her arms. She hadn't seen her mother since the visit with the American and his Wife. Gabriella's presence radiated light into the room, her youthful energy drawing from the long future her elders would not know. In innocence, she remained closer to God, less earthly in desire than the adults who lived deep in worldly passions. Without trying, Gabriella brought hope into the midst of suffering.

Gabriella briefly acknowledged the American as she entered. Her eyes glanced at his, then immediately turned downward. She did not acknowledge Christine's Husband because she didn't know him. Father Jean rose and gave her a deep embrace. Holding her nanny's hand, Gabriella was led to her dying mother. Father Jean backed away and sat between the Husband and the American against the wall. He again bowed his head in prayer.

It was time for Gabriella and her mother to say good-bye. She held her mother's left hand with her own small, smooth hands.

At her age Gabriella didn't fully know death but she understood sadness and sorrow. "I love you, Maman." Gabriella and her mother were the *Pieta* in reverse, a virgin child saying good-bye to her dying mother who had given too much.

Gabriella kissed her mother and her small tears fell from her eyes onto Christine's face. Christine opened her cloudy eyes and looked up to her. They locked into the unique connection between mother and daughter, bound by a love like no other on earth. It transcended death itself, for Christine would live on in Gabriella and in all generations that might follow.

With her right hand shaking, Christine reached up to gently touch Gabriella's face with an intimacy they had missed in life. Christine's body temperature rose momentarily as the surge of death's energy sealed their souls together. Christine's hand dropped to the bed, her eyes closed and she breathed the final, deep sigh of death. From her throat came a gurgling sound as death smothered life. The worldly bond between Christine and the living was broken.

Gabriella's sobs began deep in her stomach, rose up and burst out of her mouth as she held dearly onto her mother's hand. Father Jean went to the bedside to comfort Gabriella. He separated their hands and made the sign of the cross over Christine. The American came to the deathbed and held little Gabriella in his arms. She hugged the American tightly and sobbed into his shirt. After a few minutes, Gabriella was led away from her mother's death bed and back to the world of the living; the torch of life had passed from generation to generation, from mother to daughter, though much too early in their life cycles.

Christine's Husband had not moved but, in a moment of unexpected clarity, he rose and walked to his wife's deathbed. He placed his fingers to his lips and then to hers. He covered her scar with his right hand so only her pure, unadulterated face could be seen. A single tear fell from his eye onto Christine's cheek as the force of her death fleetingly touched his near-dead heart. He sat back down and his face returned to the reaction-less expression he had learned as a means of survival in the concentration camp.

For a short time, no one moved. Then the nurse took the Husband back to his room. Father Jean, with another hug for the American, left to complete Christine's funeral arrangements. The American looked down at Christine for the last time and made a deathbed oath to keep her alive by completing her Journal.

He kissed Christine's still warm forehead and said his good-bye. Her face was that of an angel. Her scar, the tragic imperfection on her beautiful face in life, became a translucent mark of beauty in death. She had forgiven everyone and the scar of pain seemed to vanish; her beauty returned to goodness and innocence as she left for God's Heaven. The twenty-third psalm entered his mind and he softly prayed each word:

The Lord is my Shepherd; I shall not want. He maketh me to lie down in green pastures. He leadeth me beside the still waters. He restoreth my soul. He leadeth me in the paths of righteousness for His name's sake.

Yea, though I walk through the valley of the shadow of death, I will fear no evil, for thou art with me.
Thy rod and thy staff, they comfort me.
Thou preparest a table before me in the presence of mine enemies,
Thou annointest my head with oil; my cup runneth over.

Surely goodness and mercy shall follow me all the days of my life,
And I will dwell in the House of the Lord forever.

Death liberated Christine from her inhibitions, desires, and from the lies women have to live. Death reduced her scars from the hate, the guilt, the pain and the violence humans so readily and so irrationally deal out to one another.

Blindly, the American walked back to his hotel. He gave his Wife a complete description of Christine's death. Then he cried for a long time. His Wife's compassion and support remained unwavering as she wrapped him in her arms and rocked him back and forth as he sobbed out his grief. He treasured the newfound ways she had found to love him. He believed she truly cared. He fell asleep in her embrace and Christine's Death-Day ended.

Christine's thirty years of life were celebrated in a funeral Mass at her church, St. Julien le Pauvre, and was presided over by Father Jean. It had been over six years since Christine and her Husband had walked these same stones into marriage. Between their marriage vows and her funeral Mass so much had happened that it was unfathomable. The world had been ground down by hate and evil, but it was being reborn through love and commitment.

Long-stemmed white tulips filled the church; no other flowers were present, for Christine only loved white French tulips. Tall, pure-white prayer candles softly burned on their stands, flickering in perfect harmony with the curvaceous flowers.

As he waited for the mass to begin, the American's eyes focused on the holy images in the icons hanging on the church walls. He felt the strength of the sacred stones. He embraced the silent past of the thousands of parishioners who had walked upon them, each living within their own prayers and each communicating with God in their own way. He closed his eyes and rested his head on both hands.

Father Jean's sermon was about completing the circle of suffering, recovery and forgiveness. He spoke in the context of endings: the end of the brutal war, the end of the Nazi Occupation, the end of the murder of the Jews and the end of the punishment of the Collaborators. "While the war's major events are behind us, we are here to bury Christine, another of the war's endless stream of victims." The priest recognized that some, like Jesus, who was tortured on the cross, and Christine, whose body was destroyed by imposed disease, suffered greatly and died so others could live. He applauded the fact that, even in her greatest pain, Christine gave herself to others, even more than they knew.

Father Jean repeated his mantra about the unique gift Jesus gave us: "Forgiveness is our healing, it is our salvation. It is for ourselves we forgive, for our enemies and for God. Until you forgive, you cannot be truly free to love again. *You cannot hate in one part of your heart and love in another. Your hate will kill your love, but likewise, your love can kill your hate. Choose love.*"

Christine's family sat in the first two rows. They filled the front of the church as if they were there to pay honor and respect. Some ex-friends were there, too; they sat in a row behind the family as they met their obligatory mourning duties.

The priest gave recognition to the family members, although they continued to condemn Christine as a Collaborator, damn her as the German's mistress and deny her daughter in their war-torn, hate-filled, unforgiving hearts. Father Jean blessed Christine's Husband and followed with a blessing for Gabriella, which made some twitch in their seats.

The American wondered how many of the "mourners" lived as a result of Christine's courage, cunning and intelligence. They ignored her sacrifices and her love because they didn't know and they didn't want to know. In the midst of the American's own paradoxical disgust with the unforgiving, Father Jean's voice broke through with a strong message: "Forgive, heal, live, let go of your trespasses and those who trespass against you...hating and resenting others will cost you your life and your happiness. Let

them go, stop hating, stop seeking revenge, stop your jealousy. Love
thy neighbor. Christians, embrace the Jews. Turning our backs
on the Jewish people and the Jewish faith is one of Christianity's
greatest sins; redeem yourselves, love your Jewish brothers."

The American sat apart from the family and friends. His
Wife sat to his right. On his left, the American reserved an
empty chair in memory of Christine. It was where they had sat
during services at St. Julien. He told himself over and over again
that he must let Christine go, but he was as yet unable to do so.

Most people in attendance did not know who the Americans
were or why they were there. Father Jean understood the
American's importance in Christine's continued story; he knew
the American's pen and old typewriter would assure Christine
would live beyond death.

When the Mass ended, Gabriella rose up and walked to her
mother's casket and kneeled on the worn stones. She loudly cried
out, "Maman, Maman, don't leave me!" Her unfiltered, mournful
cry stunned the righteous mourners into frozen silence as
Gabriella's presence could no longer be ignored. The American's
Wife rose up to comfort her. No one else came to help; her nanny
was locked in a daze of inaction. The others continued to look
away from the illegitimate child as if she weren't there at all and
they couldn't hear her cries, as if she were invisible and mute.

After the Mass, many attendees accepted Communion
from Father Jean. He gave the mourners a Communion option:
"Any person who believes in the God of the Angel Gabriel and
Abraham is welcome at His Table." Rabbi Kaplan stood first
and then other Jews rose up and took Communion with their
spiritual brothers and sisters; with members of the tribe they call
Christians. For the first time in their lives, Jews ate the bread
of the Son's body and drank the wine of the Son's blood. In the
death and rebirth of the crucified Jewish Rabbi, these brothers
and sisters communed with The One God in the living water

of forgiveness. It was an unheard-of act of love which openly violated the dogmas of both faiths; a resurrection of an Interfaith Communion that, because of fear and misunderstanding, had not been included in Christine's wedding ceremony or any others since Jesus and His Disciples, all Jews, broke bread and drank wine during The Last Supper.

Following the feast of bread and wine, the somber procession of mourners walked one behind the other in a circle of grief around Christine's closed casket. Each mourner's consciousness of their own vulnerability grew as they touched the heavy lid hiding Christine's body, face and beauty in the endless darkness of death. The air was full of incense; hearts beat heavily with sorrow and pain. As they walked slowly, each one examined their own fates. Some contemplated how *God extracts a heavy toll from us; He gives us the knowledge of our deaths through indisputable evidence, but demands belief in an eternal afterlife based strictly on faith.*

The American returned to his chair and slowly chewed the Holy Bread of Communion and in each bite he tasted the Body, the Host. The tang of the Holy Wine, the Blood, lingered sweetly on his lips. He heard eternal music rising from ancient stones toward endless heavens above.

Gabriella stood up and bravely joined the choir of young women who sang on the left side of the church. When they began to sing "Ave Maria," tears fell down her face, though she never looked down or turned away. The youthful voices were the high-pitched music of angels: beautiful, powerful and haunting. Their harmony perfectly matched the ear to the heart; it was God's voice rejoicing.

Many women were in mourning clothes in honor of their lost fathers, husbands and sons. Postwar emotions were ready to burst. Some men sat passively with lost legs, severed arms or darkened eyes. Veterans bent forward in wheelchairs, forever unable to sit erectly. After all the suffering, it was a wake for everyone. Many were in tears—if not for Christine, then for themselves and their own personal suffering.

Far in the back, there were two men in military uniforms; one was French and one from the U.S. They appeared out of place but interested in Christine's funeral. The American surmised that they were from the debriefing agencies that had interrogated Christine about her role in saving Paris. The American stayed far away from them. He knew if Gabriella chose to release Christine's Journal to the public, he would ignore their attempt to control the truth and would release the information despite what they may wish. The American was glad he was a citizen of the U.S., where civil rights protected his freedom of speech beyond what might be practiced in Europe, though he also knew the American government had restricted citizens' civil rights dramatically in the name of war.

Father Jean finished with the Lord's Prayer and a universal *amen*, a word of prayer used by Christians, Jews, Muslims and many others the world over. The American listened and he tried to let go.

Rabbi Kaplan, who had performed the marriage ceremony for Christine and her Husband with Father Jean, sat directly in front of the American. The rabbi was permanently distraught. An endless stream of tears ran down his face. He appeared to have been crying for years. His small, chubby hands rubbed one another in constant worry about the souls of the living and the dead. He was unable to speak at Christine's funeral, his tongue paralyzed by the harm humans had done to other humans. In his personal goodness, the reality of life and death, the evil of the Deportation and Occupation overwhelmed him.

The American knew it was time for Christine's soul to rise unto heaven and for her to join his precious daughter. Isabella waited for them with the patience of the dead, waiting for each and every one to join her in their own time. He knew it would be soon enough for him as well, for life was short and, at the end, it is shorter than people think. His sobbing face was bent forward, resting in his hands. Father Jean appeared, placed his two large hands gently on his head and silently left them there. It was a gesture of pure love and empathy, and it relieved some of the American's pain, for the priest's God-force was strong and his compassion compelling.

Toward the end of Christine's funeral, the late afternoon sun momentarily broke through the clouds. A bolt of God's sunlight shot through a church window and softly hit the old floor below the casket, anointing the holy stones in heavenly light, but the American's eyes were tightly shut and he didn't see it. Instead, he pictured Christine's angelic face glowing as she endlessly rested in peace.

One by one, everyone left the church. Father Jean, Gabriella and his Wife were the last to go. His Wife understood his need to be alone. She left the church with a light touch to his arm as a sign of care and support. It was another time to keep her needs at bay; this day was not about her. She was growing out of selfishness into compassion and forgiveness. She wanted to do everything she could to support her husband in his time of need. Their relationship was finally in order.

The American sat alone in silence. Deep in his mind he could see Christine's image and hear her speak. He brought her back to him as he momentarily transcended the space between life and death. He could "see" Christine: her hands, her hair, her mouth, and her lips. He imagined her talking a million miles an hour about one thing or another, looking at him with her wide eyes and smiling while telling the stories of her life. The rest of the world evaporated and only her face and voice remained. He struggled to see every vision of Christine and hear every word from their first day together to the last. He feared he would forget a day, a minute, a word, or a look on her face. He begged her to stay, *but no one, not even one with the greatest possible love, can stop the unrelenting flow of life to death.*

He rose from his chair and walked to the Church exit. With a long glance backward toward Christine tightly sealed in her death box, he stepped through the worn wooden doors into the courtyard. The doors closed with finality behind him even before he reached the street. He left Christine's body lying alone in the empty church. He knew the church people waited patiently for him to leave so they could do their obligatory duties for the dead.

Day turned to night, light became darkness. He looked between the church steeple and the row-houses, up to a half moon which struggled desperately to shine. The weather had changed. Intermittent black ghost clouds rushed through the threatening night and extinguished the hope of the moon and the optimism of a slight scattering of still-visible stars. The clouds' death march increased in mass until only the darkest of darkness remained, until the stars' shine disappeared and the moon's light was eliminated by the omnipotent, unstoppable presence of the dark, passing void.

The American's face was hit by a primordial wind carrying death on its back and a poised sickle with bloodied blade in front; death was searching for its next victim. The American was overwhelmed with sorrow and sleeplessness. In a trance, he walked home in the rain and wind without a coat, but he noticed none of it. He felt nothing. Everything had ended for Christine except for her Journal and the daughter she left alone.

He woke in his hotel with no memory of his walk home or of his arrival, but with awareness that Christine was gone and his Wife was very near.

During the next two days, the American and his Wife toured Paris. They visited famous and infamous places and followed many paths of Christine's *My Paris*. They walked, sat, ate and drank, and walked some more. Their tour began as a mechanical process for him, even his descriptions of Paris' most exquisite jewels lacked passion. There was a void in *His Paris*. Her lights were dimmer, her colors faded, her doors were not as widely open or revealing. Her bridges were shorter and her cuisine lacked its vibrant flavors. Paris was Christine's town and Christine was gone.

His Wife's new Parisian outlook was the bright spot in the American's post-Christine world. She awakened from grief and overcame her emotional emptiness. She gave herself to him. When he was sad, she was tender; when he was tired, she soothed him; when he felt alone, she opened herself to him. The power of her love worked miracles for their marriage.

The American matched his Wife with openness and honesty as their love renewed. He gave himself to her willingly. He gave her honest compliments, was sensitive to her needs and spoke with her about her thoughts and feelings. He embraced her acceptance, attention, support and sensitivity by giving the same to her. He listened to her like she was his new love, which she was. He began to look at her differently, and she looked wonderful. Christine's influence was pulling them out of their thorny past and pushing them toward a better future.

On the afternoon of the second day of their Paris tour, they decided to follow the European tradition and take a nap after a large lunch. They joined many Europeans taking afternoon naps throughout the continent and they made love for the first time in years. Their union was exciting and full of passion and sexual exhilaration. Afterward, they held and kissed each other gently. He told her he loved her and she said the same to him.

His Wife decided to take the afternoon further and woke him from post-lovemaking through her tender caresses. They made love twice in one afternoon following hundreds of days without intimacy. His focus and his thoughts were on his Wife. They stayed in bed until it was time for dinner. As they crossed over the bridge toward Chez Julien, she laughed and held onto her husband's arm with both hands. They walked the Paris streets as one. *A marriage was reborn.*

Christine's lawyer requested the presence of the American and his Wife at the reading of Christine's will. It was scheduled at 10:00 a.m., three days after the funeral. It was attended by various Solicitors whose clients were apparently looking to inherit something from Christine. The American and his Wife were confused about the purpose of their presence; he was sure no assets would be left to him, confident there would be no passing of material goods requiring them to attend the proceedings. Despite their hesitancy, Christine's pull remained strong and they followed her posthumous request and attended the legal process for distributing the assets of the dead.

Christine's material goods were passed to her Husband and her daughter Gabriella. The Île St. Louis apartment was left to Gabriella with two provisions: her Husband could live there for as long as he wanted and Gabriella must keep the apartment for the rest of her life. Christine's gift guaranteed that Gabriella would always have a home in Paris.

Christine made one exception to the designation of her material possessions. She left one of her favorite material possessions to the American, the painting *Le Finestre Desolate e Sconsacrate, The Windows of Desolation and Sacrilege.* She wrote a note and it was taped to the back of the painting. She asked him to keep the painting and pass it on to Gabriella at the end of his life. "Please do this for me," she wrote above her signature. He looked into the painting and his mind drifted back to Christine's description of the first time she saw this painting at Marie de Medici's Palais de Luxembourg a lifetime or two ago.

As he fixed his stare on the godless windows, he wondered if, in death, Christine had found the answer to her questions. Was she finally relieved from her incessant loneliness? Did the wounds hidden behind the camouflage of her exterior beauty heal? Did death fill the void she felt from those empty, godforsaken windows?

After the will was read, the lawyer asked the American and his Wife to stay for a private meeting. As the others shuffled out the door making quiet small talk, the Americans sat and waited. Again, they were puzzled. What could he want? Was there something more Christine wanted to give? ·

At first, the lawyer spoke formally and his language was a bit confusing. His English was heavily accented and mixed with French. He handed a note to them and said, "Here, this says it all." It was a note from Christine to the American's Wife. The message was clear and it was enormous.

I give her to you,
A gift from death to life,
Mother to mother
Heart to heart.
She will take you over the bridge
From despair to ecstasy
She will be for you
What she could not be to me.
An American, a member of your family
You giving to her
And she to you
Together, your boys, your Husband
You and Gabriella I see
And a smile melts my dying heart
And brings love home to me
Au Revoir,
Christine

Christine gave them the greatest gift one person could give another, a gift even greater than the giving of one's own life. Christine gave the beautiful and innocent Gabriella to the American and his Wife to love and cherish as a member of their family.

Christine's lawyer presented Gabriella's adoption by the Americans as a question: Would they be willing to adopt Gabriella? Of course, they would be honored to adopt her! Gabriella would change everything for the better. They would have the only part of Christine's life that remained on earth and they would have her as their own little girl.

The American's Wife glowed from receiving this precious gift. She held her husband's hand tightly in anxious excitement as she realized the impact on their lives. She experienced an emotional transformation as the new, wonderful reality shattered the remnants of the protective shell she had built around her heart. Her skin flushed. Love's light shone brightly on her soul. It was the first time in years that she dreamt of a complete life. She said a silent prayer of thanksgiving to God and Isabella, who was not so far away in heaven. We have a daughter! Tears filled her eyes but did not fall.

They were amazed and shocked. The American took a deep breath and contemplated Christine's precious bequest. Then a wide smile grew on his face and his smile lasted for a long time.

It was a new day. There was much to do. The rain cleared as they left the lawyer's office and walked into their greatly expanded world. They had another airline ticket to buy—a one-way ticket to America for "Gabby."

Gabriella was to have a real family with a mother and a father, two older brothers and a new country to discover. She would have the boundless opportunity to grow up in a strong America and escape the struggles of postwar Europe.

Afterward, the American and his Wife had a long lunch at Le Procope. They were greeted with the friendly familiarity reserved for good customers and locals. The maitre d' and waiters expressed their condolences for Christine's death, which was deeply grieved by people who had been warmed by Christine's life-light.

Over another excellent meal, the American and his Wife talked and cried and talked and cried again. They hugged each other tightly like they hadn't done for years. They looked into each other's eyes and focused on each other's words with respect and without distraction. In the grief and joy that rejoined them, they followed the message of Father Jean and Jesus and forgave each other for what had passed. They vowed to make it work: their marriage, their complete family and everything Christine wanted. Toward the end of the meal, they laughed so hard tears flowed down their faces. The American's Wife kissed his tear-stained cheek. "I love you" was all she said, and she hugged him again.

The next day they went to Versailles to visit Gabriella. She was carefree and playful, not yet able to realize the finality of her mother's death. She was happy to see the American and his Wife again. She practiced her English with them as she spoke in properly constructed sentences. They explained to Gabriella that she was going to live with them and they would be going to America together. Gabriella tilted her head to one side, paused, then turned her head back the other way and said, "Can I have a puppy in America?"

"Of course!" they responded at once. There were hugs and kisses all around. They left her unsure of what Gabriella understood and what she did not. They were so excited about Gabriella joining their family that they could hardly contain their joy.

A week later, they returned home to America with their girl. The three of them held hands as the Boeing B-314 Pan

Am Clipper cut through the water with a roar and took off for America. As they flew from Marseilles to New York and then on a land-based plane to San Francisco, there was not a discouraging word said by anyone. Gabriella contently sat between her loving new parents and enjoyed every minute of the trip. As little Gabby slept between them, her parents discussed her future. They decided to use Gabriella's trust fund to pay for language tutors to build upon her multilingual gift and training. Their goal was to develop her fluency in French, German and Italian in addition to what would become her native tongue, American English.

During the last flight, the American put his old suede eyeglass case in the seat pouch in front of him. On their drive home, he realized he had inadvertently left his glass case aboard the plane and it was gone. He accepted his loss with just a moment of regret. Then he laughed as another piece of his worn-out personal history faded away.

They arrived home tired but at peace. The American could not have imagined the impact his trip to Paris would have on him and his family. The boys teased their new sister incessantly as Gabby giggled with glee. They were overjoyed with the return of their father and in awe of all that had happened since the last time they saw him. Within a month, Gabriella had her little tan and white cocker spaniel puppy to fulfill her one wish of America. She named her Penny, after the first American coin she saw and the color of the dog's copper-colored fur. The American, his Wife, Gabriella, Penny and the boys became a new family—the family that fulfilled Christine's last brilliant vision on earth.

November, 1946. Shortly after their return to America, the American took a long hike alone in the mountains near their home. He paused on a mountain peak overlooking a raging river.

He was home. As he breathed in the clean, crisp air, he gazed eastward toward Paris and toward Christine, forever asleep in the Pere-Lachaise Cemetery.

A cool, Paris-like breeze came up the canyon and caused him to shiver and grasp his coat in a familiar way. He looked down toward the wild river and to the bridge connecting the two shores. The opportunity to cross from one world to another spanned in front of him. He exclaimed out loud, "I welcome the new life ahead of me. I am excited to explore the other side, a world with my foolishness under control, my loving Wife holding me and my expanded family by my side."

The American paused with parting thoughts of Christine before he climbed down the mountain and crossed the bridge to his home. She had saved him in almost every manner one person can save another: as a man, a husband, a father and a lost soul. He realized that if he had not met Christine, he would have left his family permanently, and it would have been an enormous tragedy. He tossed a good-bye mountain-kiss to Christine with a glance in her direction. As his kiss blew away in the east wind, he said, *"Adieu mon amie Parisienne."*

"Au revoir, mon Americain," Christine answered silently in a swirl of whispering wind. He pulled his coat tighter and began the hike home, crossing over the bridge to the newfound joy in his marriage and the love of his blessed family. With Christine's memories etched on his heart and deeply in his mind, no one could ask for anything more. He knew he had been given many gifts and the best moments in his life were before him. He intended to savor and honor every one of them.

EPILOGUE

*Inside each man is a Boy, an Artist,
a Husband, a German, an American
and more…and less*

Paris in Glory and Mischief

1948. The American finished Christine's Journal with help from his Wife, who assisted with the editing. She also contributed a woman's perspective to help explain some of Christine's feelings that didn't make sense to him. He carefully kept intact the detail and the complexities of Christine's amazing life. He told the whole truth as he promised he would. Toward the end of the Journal he wrote, "Christine's life was a collision between her fate and her will, each force impacting on the other and each competing for dominance. Christine learned that fate is not fully predetermined; when fate was unraveling in a horribly wrong way, she fought it with every ounce of human will she could find in herself. Often she prevailed but sometimes she didn't, sometimes one's fate is unavoidable."

The Journal ended without answering the question of whether Christine loved the German or not. His Wife explained that only Christine knew if she ever loved the German, and maybe even Christine didn't know, because the answer changed over time. To the American, the answer should have been a simple yes or no, either she loved him or she did not. He looked skyward and shouted to the cosmos in frustration, "Is it because I am a man that I don't understand?"

For some time after Christine's death, her Husband was visited by friends, his previous students, professors and family who came to pay their respects. Victor Frankl visited him a second time after he published his book *Man's Search for Meaning,* which told the truth about surviving or dying in Nazi concentration camps. The Husband's life-force did not return and he remained wrapped in a cocoon of bare survival. Soon, the visitors stopped coming. They cared too much to witness his insipid demise. Three years after Christine died, the Husband stopped eating. Slowly, he returned to his concentration camp weight and then quietly slipped away without a fight.

He was buried with Christine in the Pere-Lachaise Cemetery to sleep with her for all time; it was an honor he deserved, a position he had earned. Christine's Husband was her true love but not her only love. Christine and her Husband's single burial place was close to the shrine for Abelard and Heloise, another pair of faithful and tragic lovers whose love was remade only in heaven.

September 8, 1963. On Gabriella's twenty-first birthday her father, the American, gave her the only physical object given to him by Christine: *Le Finestre Desolate e Sconsacrate.* He shared Christine's note which had asked him to give it to her after the American died, but he wanted her to have it now. Gabriella had grown up with the painting hung in the most prominent place in their California home, over the fireplace in the living room. She loved it; she loved the beauty, she loved the colors and she loved the story. She knew her mother's boyfriend had painted it. Gabriella moved *Le Finestre* to her Paris apartment on Île St. Louis; it crisscrossed the Atlantic to complete a full circle and hang in the same place Christine had hung it long ago, even before the war.

Gabriella's connection with the painting was strong, but it didn't match the deep emotional reaction it evoked in Christine. Gabriella didn't see the loneliness, she didn't see God's abandonment of the world and she didn't see her own emptiness in the vacant church windows. Gabriella had escaped the flaw in her mother's lonely heart: Christine's endless search for something to complete her inner self.

Gabriella's American father also gave her *Le Journal Parisien de Christine* on the same special birthday. He had waited until she was a woman, until he felt confident sharing the frank presentation of her mother's complex and passionate life. Gabriella immediately took the Journal to her room and read it cover-to-cover twice without a break. Then, with a smile and a tear or two, she put it aside.

Gabriella saw no need to share the intimate details of her mother and father's lives or her personal history with the public; she saw no reason to tell of her parents' role in saving Paris from Nazi death and destruction. She felt no desire to publicize that her father was a Nazi general who had captured her mother and turned her into his willing sex slave. These truths need not be revealed. The Journal became an avenue for Christine's healing and a vehicle to bridge back to the lost time between a mother and her daughter. That was enough.

After attending college and graduate school, where she studied international relations, Gabriella used her education, European heritage and extensive language skills to work in the international world of diplomacy and economics. She focused on connecting America's powerful economic engine to the needs of devastated, postwar Europe. She also worked on conceptualizing a long-term plan for the countries of Europe to form a common union, a "united states of Europe," as the idea was called by some.

Gabriella's second international interest was in support of efforts to repay the losses suffered by European Jews, and to assist in efforts to return their lost property to them. In her multicultured, international world, she rode airplanes the way others took taxis.

June 5, 1965. Father Jean lived for eighteen years after Christine's death. He and Rabbi Kaplan explored the ancient teachings of the *dual-covenant theology* originated by Rabbi Moshe Ben-Maimon in the 12th century. Under *dual-covenant theology*, Jews remained eternally bound by the Torah and were required to keep the Law of Moses. However, Jews were not required to convert to Christianity to be saved and to ascend to heaven, because they already believed in the One God and His commandments. Under this theory, Jewish Jesus' purpose for coming to earth was to convert Gentiles to the Seven Noahide Laws, and only Gentiles were required to make this conversion to be saved. The Father and the Rabbi found *dual-covenant theology* a good place to begin healing the wounds that had grown between Jews and their Christian brothers.

Father Jean was given honors for risking his life to save Jewish children during the Deportation and Occupation by converting them to Christianity. He had again violated the rules of the Church, just as Jesus the Rabbi, the Iconoclast, did when he healed and performed good deeds on the Sabbath in violation of Jewish law.

Father Jean connected Jews and Christians many times in his career. His commitment to reunite Christians with their Jewish roots was based on his many interfaith experiences, including the wedding of Christine and her Husband. In one sermon Father Jean exclaimed, "Jesus is the most famous Jew on earth, He is the Number-One Jew!" He often spoke of Jews and Christians as members of the same family, as believers in the same Book.

While Father Jean created controversy with his ideas, he also stimulated introspective thought in the Church hierarchy. He was well-connected to the Pope, who brought him to Rome as an advisor and a friend. Father Jean became the Pope's emissary to many multi-faith gatherings throughout the world. He was well-respected for his inclusive interpretations of Holy Scriptures and loved as a man of loyalty, integrity and caring.

Father Jean was given a state funeral by the Vatican. The Pope presided over the Mass and his accolades were presented by attendees from all over the world. The American and Gabrielle attended Father Jean's funeral. The rest of his family was too involved in their lives and responsibilities to go to Rome.

Gabrielle knew about Father Jean through the many stories told by her father and from her own meetings with the man who had guided her Mother and her American parents through many trials and tribulations. The American's connection remained deep with this man who had helped him bridge many of his life experiences. He would not have missed the privilege of saying his proper good-bye to Father Jean, regardless of momentary obstacles.

June, 1967. *The Summer of Love.* Twenty years had passed since Christine's death and Gabriella's move to America, and the family and friends who abandoned Christine were mostly gone. Paris' future arrived and she was fully alive. She had discarded the shadows and scars left by the Nazis and fully returned as "Belle Madame," the most beautiful of the beautiful cities in the world, and again the world's eyes were upon her.

With a tremendous amount of work and financing by the USA Marshall Plan, the world overcame the wreckage of what was to be the last world war of the century. Memories of the war faded as new generations took their place in postwar Paris and the older generations learned to forgive. Many French, like the Nazis, compartmentalized their sins against the Jews and indifferently waved away their contribution to the terror and deaths. The deportation and execution of Jews was pushed into denial and their guilt had not surfaced, not yet.

Gabriella became a magnificent young woman. She was the unbreakable link in the chain of relationships between the American's family members. She solved family conflicts and softened hurt feelings. Her new mother was reluctant to let her grow up too quickly, although Gabriella was always mature for her years. She brought joy to everyone with her positive attitude and brilliant mind.

Gabriella's passion for life, quick smile and charm were only matched by her beauty. She did not look like the epitome of a German, as Christine had feared; her appearance reflected the mixture of both of her parents' heritages. Her welcoming face was a delight to behold. Her long hair was an unusual color in Europe: silky light brown with strong red highlights, and it tumbled down past her shoulders. She was blessed with Christine's magnificent porcelain skin, and her eyes were an endlessly deep, dark sea of cobalt blue. Somehow, Gabriella retained French facial expressions. She conveyed her emotions with a pucker of her lips or a toss of her head in similar ways to what Christine used to do. The American would often do a double-take at the uncanny similarities between Gabriella and her mother.

Gabriella retained some distant memories of her birth mother, of the magnificent Christine. She remembered a few intense events in the Paris of her childhood; particularly her mother's last visit with the American and his Wife, and her mother's funeral.

In America, Gabriella and her dog Penny were inseparable for the twelve years her canine companion lived. They engaged in incessant one-way conversations about Gabriella's thoughts and concerns. Penny listened carefully and gave love-licks when needed. On the day Penny died, Gabriella saw her father, the American, cry for the first and only time in her life. After Penny, Gabriella didn't want another dog; she didn't want to ever forget her Penny.

The American returned to Paris for the last time during the special summer of 1967, a time when much of the world's youth momentarily tried universal love. He had become a successful playwright. When he had returned to America in 1946, he was inspired to create works he had only imagined before Paris. He wrote a two-act play, *God Is, God Is Not.* It was the highest level of his creativity. The cast included some of the most interesting characters one might encounter in a convergence of insightful minds. Each character presented a vastly divergent set of beliefs as they debated the existence, or lack of existence, of the spiritual world. He was well-recognized for the depth of his creative intellect.

The American went to his beloved Paris alone in 1967 to visit his memories. They were like old friends one could just drop in on without calling ahead. On his third day in Paris, he went out for a morning espresso. He had stopped drinking cappuccinos—too much milk. He ordered his regular brioche in the old café, though no one recognized him as they used to do. Then he went for a long Parisian walk. He revisited many of Christine's *My Paris* haunts and met up with many ghosts and memories. It filled him with joy to see that everything in Paris remained just as it was in his mind: the river Seine, the Palais de Luxembourg and Gardens, the Medici Fountain, Notre Dame, St. Julien, the bullet-scarred buildings of the Police Prefecture, the Eiffel Tower and the islands. Paris was his familiar lover by now and he treasured exploring her intimacies again and again.

He purchased special perfumes for his Wife and daughter. They were manufactured by Mr. Lucien Lelong's company; he was the dress designer and hero who saved Parisian *haute couture* from the Nazis. The perfume for his Wife was called INDISCRETE, and the one for his daughter was simply named "N." He also purchased a bottle of TAILSPIN, a perfumed dusting powder, for each of them. In addition to the exotic and intoxicating smell of the body powder, it was contained in a magnificent, collectable bottle, a work of art from Lucien Lelong's private collection.

The Bench - Ile St. Louis/Pont d'Arcole

Toward the end of the day he reached Île St. Louis. His feet hurt from walking, so he sat down to rest on a bench not far from the home that was now Gabriella's, on the northern tip of Île St. Louis. It was the same bench where Christine had paused many times. It was the bench where Christine and the German rested on their *"My Paris"* visit to Île St. Louis.

The American sat and thought of his kiss to Christine's scar long ago. The park at St. Julien le Pauvre was just two little bridges away from his Île St. Louis rest stop. If he could have been able to see through the massive Notre Dame Cathedral, he could have seen the spot where they stood near the oldest tree that special day. His kiss to her scar was the most intimate, physical touch between him and Christine. He laughed at himself for, as a young man, he had wanted so much more. By this time in life, he was deeply moved by the memory of the scar-kiss which he held in his heart, and that was enough.

He looked down the river to the Pont d' Arcole where the first tanks of General Leclerc's 2nd Armored Division had rolled into Paris on their way to the palace de l'Hotel de Ville during the Liberation of Paris in August 1944.

His thoughts turned to his family: his Wife, his boys and Gabriella. He loved them completely. A smile appeared on his face and he gave a little laugh as he visualized each of them. He was at peace with himself. He smelled the familiar odor of a Gauloises cigarette belonging to a woman sitting not far away. He inhaled the memories of that odd smell from long ago and smiled contently in his soul.

After sitting for a while and enjoying these pleasant and loving thoughts, the American suffered a massive heart attack. He fell off the bench, hit his head and rolled onto the bricks below; he died on the opposite end of the same tiny island where Christine also took her last breath. He clutched the bag holding his Wife and Gabriella's perfumes and didn't let go. The American was blessed by an incredible life and a full journey, but it was over, and he too was gone.

The American's body was not returned to America. Regardless of where he died, he had instructed his Wife to spread his ashes on the Seine in a quiet, nondescript manner. His death on the Île St. Louis made his desire simple to carry out.

The American's Wife and sons flew from California to Paris to pay their final farewells. His boys were fine men who loved their father dearly. Gabriella, already an accomplished woman of twenty-five, flew in from a business meeting in Berlin to Paris, to the city she loved as her mother had loved it. This time they flew on Boeing 707s, a jetliner with speed and technology far exceeding the flying boat Gabriella and her parents had flown to America twenty-one years before. She came to say good-bye to the only father she knew, to the person who loved her unconditionally, to the man who connected her to the past and continued to define much of her present self.

His Wife, the boys and Gabriella gently poured the American's ashes into the flowing water. His Wife smiled and cried all at once. She loved her husband. She loved him so much that she had fulfilled her promises to love, forgive and support him since Christine died and Paris lived.

With her father's ashes, Gabriella released a red balloon tied with a small weight to keep it bobbing on the water and said, "Good-bye, Papa." She watched the strong current take the balloon away. She glanced up to the people watching from the bridge above. From a nearby café, she heard the lingering, haunting voice of Edith Piaf, the little sparrow, who sang, *"Non, je ne regrette rien,"* *I will have no regrets*! The ashes and the balloon were swept down the river, under the waiting bridges, and the American ended his brief journey on earth. He would join little Isabella, Father Jean, Christine and the other characters in the amorphous domain of the living spirit of the physically dead. With the passing of the American, another chapter of Parisian history closed.

A California college student in Paris for the first time stood on the Pont Neuf Bridge. He looked down to the smoothly flowing river and watched with curiosity as a bobbing red balloon surrounded by gray ash passed under him. He was young and strong but not fully a man. He wore the American trademark: a white T-shirt showing under the collar of his shirt, and odd tennis shoes. But despite his fresh-off-the-boat appearance, his mind was open to Paris, to the European people and to their many different cultures. He came to Paris seeking the love of the greatest city in the world and occasionally she gave it to him, but only in small doses. He joined in the parade of Parisian Pilgrims, some of the world's greatest men and women, who had worshipped her splendor and beauty over the past two millennia.

As he traveled, walking the streets and crossing the bridges of Europe, he learned the European history he missed while spending his life in the California public school system. He would return to Europe over and over again during his lifetime to increase his understanding and love of the same European cultures his grandparents had left behind in their search for the American streets of gold.

Two days after they spread her father's ashes over the Seine and after her family returned home to America, Gabriella was alone in Paris. She arranged to meet a Parisian girlfriend in the Luxembourg Gardens and they strolled through the floral display together. Paris was even more beautiful than she was before the war, as she flourished from the lavish attention of new and old lovers. After they walked past the garden's ponds and statues, they paused at the Medici Fountain. It gurgled, provided shelter to the birds and gave wonder to the tourists. Gabriella explained how this was one of her mother's favorite places in all of Paris, but Gabriella shied away from describing her mother's afternoon with the Artist long ago.

They walked to Le Procope for lunch. Gabriella and her girlfriend shared an eight-person booth surrounded by cut glass shelves full of antique objects. She knew it was the same booth where her first mother, and her second father, the American, had lunched together, because it was described so well in the Journal and in the many stories her father had told her.

A young man was sitting across from Gabriella and her friend. He wore the identifying as-an-American white T-shirt and canvas shoes; he was the boy who had stood on the Pont Neuf watching the American's ashes and the red balloon pass under the

440

bridge just two days before. He struggled with the French menu. They softly smiled at one another and Gabriella offered to help him order lunch.

The war heroes and cowards of Paris were dead and gone and a new generation had arrived in the eternal City of Lights, but in her noble splendor, her stately grandeur and her epic history, Paris was up to her same old wonderful mischief.

THE END

Timeline Leading Up To The American Meeting Christine, September, 1945

1870

Paris Miracle Number One—Paris is saved by the prayers to St. Genevieve; the German-Prussian armies bypass her

1871

Founding of the German Reich at Versailles following France's loss of the Franco-Prussian War

1915

November 15—Christine is born in Paris

1918

Paris Miracle Number two—World War One—Paris is saved from the Germans due to German tactical errors and opportunities seized by the French army to drive the Germans away

Adolf Hitler is wounded fighting on the Western Front

1919

June 28—End of World War One; The Treaty of Versailles is signed

Mussolini founded the Fascist movement in Italy

1924

Pierre Taittinger founded fascistic *Jeunesses patriotes* - Patriotic Youths in France

1937

Christine meets the Boy—for soccer and much more
April 27—The Nazis and Italians bomb Guernica, Spain
The World's Fair opens in Paris
May Day—One million Parisians protest the slaughter at Guernica
Picasso paints *Guernica*

1938

Nazi Germany annexes Austria
March 1—Gabriele D'Annunzio dies
Christine meets the Italian Artist
Jean-Paul Sartre publishes *Nausea*

1939

Czechoslovakia ceases to exist; absorbed by the Nazi Third Reich
June 2—Christine and her Husband's wedding
A U.S. Gallop poll = 99% of Americans oppose U.S. involvement in another European war
Nazi Germany and Fascist Italy sign the Pact of Steele agreement
Nazi Germany and the Soviet Union sign a nonaggression pact
September 1—Nazi Germany invades Poland; France and England declare war on Germany
President Roosevelt signs the Neutrality Act of 1939, making U.S. support of both the invaders and the invaded illegal

1940

May 10—The Nazi armies invade Holland, Belgium and France in a massive Blitzkrieg
The Boy dies in combat
May 27—British and other Allied troops evacuate the Continent at Dunkirk
June —Christine's first wedding anniversary, age 24
June 10—Mussolini declares war on Britain and France; The French government flees Paris
June 11—The Italians bomb Malta, beginning an Italian/ German three-year siege
June 14— The third miracle to save Paris did not occur; Paris is declared an Open City, the government flees and the Nazi forces move in to occupy Paris
September 21—Parisian Jews are required to wear a yellow Star of David and register with police

1941

March—The Lend-Lease Act is passed by the USA, cancelling the Neutrality Act of 1939
April—Greece falls to the Nazi onslaught
June —Hitler invades the Soviet Union in violation of their peace pact
August—French police round up over 4,000 "Stateless" Jews in the 11th Arrondissement and imprison them
September—Christine, 25, and her Husband are arrested by French police and Gestapo agents
December 7—Japan bombs Pearl Harbor
December 8—America declares war on Japan; the day of Gabriella's conception
December 11—Nazi Germany and Italy declare war on America and America responds by declaring war on them

1942

February 15—Singapore falls to Japanese attack, the largest surrender of British forces in history
March—1,148 Parisian Jews are deported to Nazi concentration camps
August—Operation Rutter/Jubilee; an attempted Allied invasion to open a second front at Dieppe, France fails--3,623 Allied troops are killed, wounded or captured
Christine has spent one year in captivity

1943

June—King George V awards Malta the highest award for bravery
July 10—Patton and Montgomery invade Sicily, disembarking from Malta
September 3—Italy surrenders to the Allies
Christine has spent two years in captivity
October 11—Italy reverses her allegiances and declares war on Germany
November 28—The Big Three, President Roosevelt, Dictator Joseph Stalin and British Premier Winston Churchill meet in Tehran to plan the defeat of Nazi Germany

1944

June 6—D-Day, the Allies open the Second Front in France
August 9—General Choltitz arrives in Paris and takes control of the occupying German troops
August 19—Choltitz orders the murder of 35 members of the Resistance at the Bois de Boulogne waterfall
August 23—Choltitz burns the Grand Palace in retribution for Nazi soldier deaths
Christine has spent three years in captivity
August 25—Paris Miracle Number Three--Choltitz surrenders Paris to the Allies and the most beautiful city in the world is saved
August 25—The German is killed, Christine is imprisoned as a Collaborator by the French
September —Christine is released from Drancy prison after interrogation at age 28.
September 8—The first V-2 rocket to hit a German enemy hits Paris with 6 dead
September 30—Christine's Husband returns to Paris after spending three years in Nazi concentration and labor camps
December 16—The Nazis launch a counter-offensive in the Ardennes – "Operation Autumn Mist/The Battle of the Bulge--catching the Allies off guard

1945

February 13—Dresden is carpet-bombed by the British and American air forces
May 8—VE Day: war in Europe ends
September 6—VJ Day: Japan surrenders, WWII ends
September 8—Christine, 29, meets the American; the writing of Le Journal Parisien de Christine begins

Reference Books

Ten books helped me write *For the Love of Paris*. Without the knowledge these authors provided and their creative efforts to publish their works, *For the Love of Paris* would not exist and I would understand much less of the War, of Paris, and of life. I thank the authors. They are:

Becraft, Mel, *Picasso's Guernica, Images within Images*

Bradford, Ernle, *The Great Siege of Malta 1565*

Bradford, Ernle, *Siege Malta 1940-1943*

Collins, Larry and Lapierre, Dominique, *Is Paris Burning?*

D'Annunzio, Gabriele, *The Triumph of Death*

Frankl, Victor, *Man's Search for Meaning*

Harris, Mark and Banton, Simon, work regarding the secrets in Guernica

Horne, Alistair, *The Seven Ages of Paris*

Kamins, Toni, *The Complete Jewish Guide to France*

Woodhouse, John, *Gabriele D'Annunzio*

About The Author

For the Love of Paris is Tom Rutter's first novel, but he has been a writer all of his life. He was conceived in December, 1944 in Chicago, Illinois, during the Battle of the Bulge. He was born in 1945, just two days after the Japanese surrender on the battleship USS Missouri in Tokyo Bay which ended all of World War II. He is a Son of the Greatest Generation, so Tom grew up listening to the stories of WWII and their unambiguous definition of right and wrong. He became a young man during the Sixties in California, a nebulous world of searching and dreaming.

Tom's mother, Inez Pizzica (deceased), was a first generation Italian-American whose family is from Riano, Ripa Teatina and Pescara in the Abruzzo Province. His grandfather lived in Pescara when Gabriella D'Annunzio also lived there. His father, Harold Rutter, who passed away at 97 years-old as this second edition was being written, was from an English/German family with American connections back to the 17th century settlers in Baltimore, Maryland.

Tom first traveled to Paris as a college student in the summer of 1967, when he fell in love with the City of Lights where he learned the benefits of roving the Paris streets as a *Flaneur*. He has been drawn back to "her" many times and will live with her in 2015. He is eternally grateful to those who prevented Hitler from destroying Paris in August, 1944, though he doubts the official version of this event, particularly the impression that General Choltitz made his solely-independent decision to save her.

The professions which took Tom away from his creative side were many years as a student financial aid administrator (U.C. Davis, U.C. San Diego and San Francisco State University), Associate Vice President for Enrollment Planning and Management at San Francisco State University, and Chief Financial Officer (CFO) for a San Francisco law firm.

During the writing of *For the Love of Paris*, Tom visited Paris often and lived in Montalcino (SI), Italy, and Marin County, California, with his wife Donna Marie (Lumia) and their daughter Justine. Tom has two grown children, Matthew and Caroline; a daughter-in-law, Courtney Murren; and twin five-year-old grandchildren, John Solomon Rutter and Maria Sophia Rutter. In 2005, Donna and Tom renewed their marriage vows in St. Julien le Pauvre in a wedding ceremony conducted by Father Nicolas, a man of great wisdom and compassion.

For the Love of Paris initially emerged as Tom sat on a bench along the Champs-Elysées reading Alistair Horne's *Seven Ages of Paris* in March of 2007. The initial story was created and transmitted to his wife Donna via his BlackBerry in a series of e-mails, as he walked the streets, sat in cafes, and the city of Paris grew to become a major character of her own.

18417355R00253

Made in the USA
Charleston, SC
02 April 2013